# A Shadow of Gulls

# A Shadow of Gulls

## Patricia Finney

G. P. PUTNAM'S SONS

NEW YORK

First American Edition
© Patricia Finney, 1977
All rights reserved. This book, or parts thereof, may not be reproduced
without permission from the publisher.

SBN 399-11979-5

**Library of Congress Cataloging in Publication Data**

Finney, Patricia, 1958–
  A shadow of gulls.

  I. Title.
PZ4.F516Sh    [PS3556.I54]    813'.5'4    77-5733
PRINTED IN THE UNITED STATES OF AMERICA

# Author's Note

For the purposes of this book I have decided, quite arbitrarily, to set the events around 113 AD.

As background I have simply taken most of what is called the 'Ulster' cycle of Hero-tales and assumed that, barring the more magical incidents, it was all true. However, although I have tried to keep the events of the Cattle-Raid of Cooley as close as possible to the original account, I have had to modify the itinerary.

Similarly, the explanation for Conor's non-arrival is my own idea.

The character of Lugh Mac Romain is entirely invented, though he is mentioned once in the Raid itself, but most of the other main characters occur in the legends.

The Tuatha de Danaan are a compound of evidence, legend and my own guesswork and invention.

I have used the original names of all the characters who are mentioned in the legends and have only used Irish names for my own characters. Unfortunately, Irish spelling tends to seem difficult and the names are not spelt consistently in the different versions of the legends: since this might be a hindrance, I have anglicized spellings wherever possible and included a list of the names with their original spellings (and pronunciations where difficult) at the back of the book. I have also provided a glossary of the more obscure technical terms used.

While researching for this book I have consulted many sources, but for anyone wishing to read further, these are the books I have found most useful: *Cuchulain of Muirthemne* by Lady Gregory. (This is a composite account and my main source for all the events I have taken from the Raid); *Everyday Life of the Pagan Celts* by Anne Ross; *Ancient Europe* by Stuart Piggott.

I would like to thank my family and friends for their patience and helpful suggestions while I was writing this book. I would also like to thank the Golders Green Branch of the Barnet Public Library for their efficiency in getting me the sometimes obscure and rare reference books I needed.

P.F.

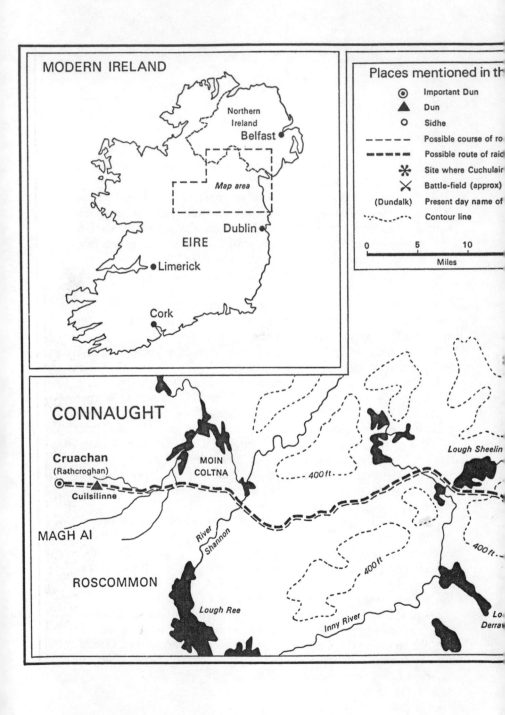

MODERN IRELAND

Northern
Ireland
Belfast •

Map area

Dublin •

EIRE

• Limerick

Cork

Places mentioned in th

⊙ Important Dun
▲ Dun
○ Sidhe
----- Possible course of ro
━━━ Possible route of raid
✳ Site where Cuchulair
✕ Battle-field (approx)
(Dundalk) Present day name of
······ Contour line

0      5      10
       Miles

CONNAUGHT

Cruachan
(Rathcroghan)
⊙━━▲━━
Cuilsilinne

MAGH AI

MOIN
COLTNA

400 ft

Lough Sheelin

ROSCOMMON

River
Shannon

400 ft

400 ft

Lough Ree

Inny River

Lo
Derraw

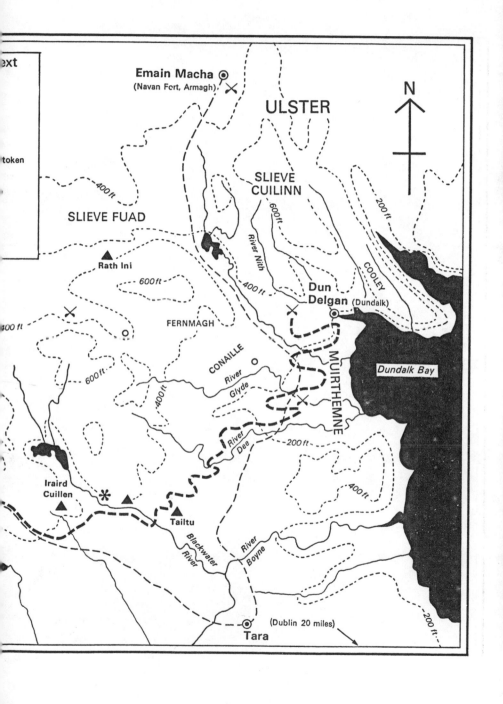

*To my parents, with love*

# A Shadow of Gulls

# Prologue

To my honoured friend, the Emperor Hadrian.

I am writing this history, Lord, in fulfilment of the promise I made you, to write of the Sedanta, Cuchulain Mac Sualtim, Champion of Ulster, whom I once knew. I sang you some of the songs I have made, but you said you wished to hear about him in a language and a mode which you could understand fully. You also asked about the Queen of Connaught, Maeve (which in Latin means: She Who Intoxicates), and how her life entwined with mine.

And so I have written this history. I have told only what I myself knew, or what I heard from the people who witnessed the events, and I have tried to explain in some measure how I came to be the man you know now.

I ask your patience with my Latin: it is a language I learnt after I was a grown man and although I can make poetry in it, Irish was my Mother-tongue. Fortunately, harpsong has no languages, but I cannot write that.

Here then is the first part of my history.

Lugh Mac Romain,
the Harper.

# *Cruachan*

## I

The night I left Connaught, the night I killed the King, was three days before Samhain when the King would have died anyway. Strange how one night can change so much. When I think back about it now, I can see all the things that happened after radiating from the night three nights before Samhain like the spokes from the hub of a chariot wheel. And, like the hub of a war-chariot, that night had a knife in it.

I had been at weapons-practice most of the afternoon with my spear-brother Dalaigh. We had thrown light holly-wood throw-spears at each other and warded them off with our shields; we had had a mock fight with our stabbing spears and then finished by fighting with our swords, as if we had been fighting a single combat. Dalaigh had learned a new trick while I had been away which was why he suggested the weapons-practice in the first place. I had hardly started to attack properly, before he casually knocked my blade away with a twist I had never seen before and stopped the thrust just short of my breastbone. I stood there, breathing fast and sweating a little with exertion and looked ruefully down at the blade as Dalaigh lowered it, grinning broadly.

'All right,' I said. 'Now how did you do that?'

'Ailell showed me while you were away.'

'Ailell? I should have known. How do you do it?'

He tried to show me, but I find it difficult to learn new tricks of swordsmanship, though I'm adequate enough as a swordsman. Dalaigh delighted in them, collected them and treasured them as the children of Cruachan did the wooden dolls and carts he made for them. He gave up in disgust when I got it wrong for the fifth time and announced that he was hungry. We wandered into the Queen's hall, routed out one of the slave-women and told her to find us some meat and make us a couple of oat-cakes. She started off with sighs and black looks, but by the time the oat-cakes were half-burned Dalaigh had his arm round her waist and was grinning down at her in a way she understood perfectly well.

She ran off to put the goats in the pen for the night and Dalaigh and I munched the meat and oat-cakes, washed them down with a dipperful of mead from the vat by the door and complained to each other that it had all gone sour.

We checked our weapons in case of rust and the leather in case of perishing, and to his fury Dalaigh found a rivet coming loose from his dagger-sheath. So we went to the armoury and left our weapons there and called in at the blacksmith's forge down by the main gate to ask him to mend the rivet. When we came out again the sun was setting and the clouds clearing away beyond the red and gold hills around Cruachan. Last year I had been out rounding up the cattle for Samhain, but this year I had nothing very much to do because I had only just returned from visiting a poet in Kerry to learn some songs from him.

Dalaigh wanted to check the hooves of one of his chariot-ponies which he thought might be splitting and so we went out through the gate of Cruachan and down the muddy path to the home-pasture, where the chariot-ponies and riding horses were standing black and brown and dun against the green, cropping the grass. They were all of them shaggy with their winter-coats and I could see Conin, my own horse, eating absent-mindedly in a corner: he had a white patch on his rump which was why I had called him Conin. It means 'Rabbit'.

We ducked under the poles around the field and went among the ponies, Dalaigh going ahead, laying a large square hand on the hindquarters of the horses which stood in our way.

I stood and watched while Dalaigh gave his pony a lick of salt from the palm of his hand and then carefully lifted the right forehoof. He was very gentle as he did that: Dalaigh had infinite patience with animals and small children, which was why the children loved him so much, apart from his carving of dolls. It wasn't something you could tell from looking at him. He was big, broad-shouldered: almost as tall as myself, though more muscular; he had pale blue eyes and a broad smiling face and a moustache which he trimmed with care every few days when he shaved. I prefer to remain clean-shaven when I can, though my beard is dark and difficult to get rid of.

Dalaigh checked the frog and the sole and trimmed the side of the hoof where it had grown uneven. As he reached for the other hoof, he pushed his pale brown hair back from his face and said,

'How was the poet?'

'Curoi's poet?' I turned my head and spat at a tuft of grass growing in the middle of a bare patch nearby. 'Him? He wasn't worth the journey.'

'No good? What's his name?'

'Fercertne. He's not bad – I got a couple of songs out of him I hadn't heard before – but he's not good. Think of any Ulster poet you care to and he'll be better. The south breeds better harpers than poets.'

Dalaigh made a grunting noise and looked at me oddly.

'Mind you,' I went on, 'even without the new songs the journey wasn't an entire waste of time.'

'No?' He turned his attention to the left back hoof.

'Curoi's wife is worth a journey from here to Rome and back. There's a beautiful woman for you. I didn't think they existed like that except in songs and much use they are there to anyone but a harper like myself. It's a pity her husband's a Druid.'

'If you go on talking like that you'll get yourself cursed, bard or no.'

13

'Never mind: I can always make a satire about him and raise a blemish on his face.'

'Hah!' said Dalaigh, and had to steady the horse. 'You can't make poems to order and you know it.'

'I'll bet you your new stabbing spear to my old one that I can,' I said.

'Done!' said Dalaigh, reaching for the last hoof. 'Curoi? That was the Druid King Conor of Ulster sent those three warriors to, wasn't it? The time they quarrelled about the Championship of Ulster.'

'It was. I asked him for the true tale when I was there and he said that he'd never had any doubt about the matter at all. He said that there would never have been any quarrel over it either if it hadn't been for that trouble-maker Bricru stirring it up at his feast. They were firm friends before and they are again now.'

'Who got the Championship?'

'Who do you think? The Chief of the Sedantii, Cuchulain Mac Sualtim, of course. Besides the fact that he's Conor's nephew, Curoi says he's a genius with any weapon whatsoever and he's been trained by experts – first Ferghus Mac Roich and then the woman-warrior Scatha on Skye. He has Druid-knowledge too – Cavath Chief-Druid is his great-uncle.'

Dalaigh looked thoughtful. 'Now there's a head I'd like to take.'

'Curoi said that the man's too brilliant for his or anyone else's good and that trouble is as natural to him as breathing.'

'Hmm.' He finished checking the hooves and patted the pony on the neck. 'I'd kill him and you'd make a song about it.' I smiled. 'And I'd bring his head back and give it to the Queen.'

A cold feeling descended on my stomach as it always did at mention of the Queen. I looked away and said, 'The Queen.'

'You can just see her, can't you? Sitting on her pile of cat-skins with her silver apple-branch on her lap and her crow on her shoulder. She'd like a gift like that.'

'Yes.'

Dalaigh looked at me puzzled under his untidy brown hair. He pushed it back absently.

'What does that mean?'

'What does what mean?' I knew what he meant, though. I could not speak of the Queen without my mouth going dry and that faint cold feeling in my belly. I had not thought it showed so badly.

'The way you sound when I talk of the Queen. You sound as if you don't want to think about her.'

'I don't.'

'What?' Dalaigh's mouth was open.

'I think about her as little as I can.'

'You . . .? But why?'

'I don't know,' I said. 'Yes, I do know.'

'Well?'

'I'm afraid of her,' I answered slowly. 'And I hate her. It's as simple as that.'

I wasn't looking at him, but I knew that Dalaigh was making the Horned Sign against the Evil Eye. I heard him swallow. To be truthful, I wasn't sure why I hated the Queen, and feared her. Perhaps because I had seen the King Ailell die, seven years ago, when Maelchon, who was Ailell now, had killed him and taken his place as the Queen's Consort; perhaps because my mother had told me how the Queen had had my father killed before I was born. Well, in three nights' time Ailell, who had been Maelchon, would be killed and a new Corn King would take his place and name. I wondered idly who it would be. There was no knowing who the Queen would send her finger-shaped bone token to, save that he would be young and strong and perfect in his body.

I looked up. The clouds were bruised on the dark hills in the west, the sky deepening blue.

'We'll be too late to get through the gate before Finn shuts it,' I said, breaking the unhappy silence between us. 'Come on, I'll race you to the gate.'

Dalaigh relaxed and smiled and we started off together,

running through the pasture and vaulting over the poles and running hard up the hill to the gate. I like running and I beat Dalaigh easily because I have longer legs than he has. I waited for him pointedly, standing by the heavy wooden gate with my arms folded.

'It's not fair,' Dalaigh complained, punching me lightly in the ribs. 'You with your great gawky heron's legs. And don't forget that satire you promised me. My new spear to your old one.'

'I haven't forgotten. When do you want it by?'

'Tomorrow. We'll get Iollan Hen to decide on it.'

'All right.'

Dalaigh was about to say something, but he saw the slave-girl from earlier on walking past him and he went over to her and took her arm. She had big flopping breasts and greasy yellow hair and her dress was old and stained, though it might have been green once. It clashed vilely with the dark red of Dalaigh's tunic, even in the dusk. The woman took Dalaigh's arm and put it around her shoulders so that his big cloak could keep her warm as well. He looked at me over her head and winked.

My mind was already turning over the idea for the satire. It would not be a very strong satire so I decided to make it about Fercertne and Blanad, Curoi's beautiful wife. The words started falling together and I quickened with the excitement of song-making, but the harp-work needed my harp to work out the music. I turned quickly towards the Queen's hall, large and sharp-pointed against the twilight. The stars were beginning to come out where they could be seen behind the muffling clouds. The wind was cool and damp, but I thought it wouldn't rain: it had veered round until it was northerly. Winter was well begun and the trees half bare of their finery.

I came to the door of the hall and stood for a moment beside the carved doorpost. It was later than I had thought: the light seeping through the cracks in the window-shutters and the walls was quite dim; light made by a banked up fire and torches mostly gone out.

16

The man supposed to open the door had gone to sleep and so I pushed it open gently and stepped over his legs. That door had a habit of banging when you shut it and I closed it quietly so as not to waken anyone. One of the dogs dozing by the hearth padded over and sniffed at me. Apparently satisfied, it went back to its place and went on snapping at a discarded bone.

The remains of the Queen's evening meal were still hanging on the spit and filling the hall with the greasy smell of cold pig-meat. All but one of the torches in their sockets on each of the house-pillars had been put out, and the fire banked up so it would smoulder until the sun rose. Most of the people in the hall had pulled their wicker screens across the front of their cubicles, making the hall seem smaller. Only two or three of the cubicles were still open: in one of them two of the Queen's sons were playing fidchell and one of the others was the one used by myself, Dalaigh, Dalaigh's girl and sometimes Maine Andoe, another of the Queen's sons. There was someone squatting just inside that one and at first I thought it was Maine.

The other cubicle not yet completely shut up for the night was the Queen's. The screen was pulled half across and the enamelled stags decorating the front of it glinted bloody-seeming. The one torch still alight was on the house-pillar to the right of the Queen's cubicle. There was a gap between the pillar and the red yew edge of the screen. I didn't like that. The cubicle inside was dark, with no light working through from the torch which gave life to the enamel stags. What was the Queen doing in there, in the dark? I could see her in my mind, kneeling in the soft hay with the deerskins around her, making magic with her fingers and her eyes. I made the Sign of Horns with my hand and looked away.

As I did the person squatting in my cubicle twisted round

to look at me, as though he didn't want to be seen there. He stood up as I crossed the middle of the hall.

It was Ailell, the King.

I stopped under the torch and watched him. Ailell coloured up and moved out of the cubicle. His eyes were odd as they looked at me: bright and hard and thinking. He had been smiling and very handsome seven years ago when he first took the name of Ailell. Now there was something hang-dog about him and something desperate. I felt sorry for him. In three days' time it would be Samhain: three nights from now it would be exactly seven years since the last King-making, when he killed the King and became the Queen's mate. Yes, I could understand the desperation hiding in his eyes.

But I could not understand why he had been searching in my sleeping-place and looking so guilty about it. Yet the song in my head was clamouring to be let out and there was no room for me to wonder much about Ailell.

I moved past him to pick up my harp-bag and stopped again. My harp was lying on its side on Dalaigh's wolf-fur from last winter, and the otterskin bag lying crumpled beside it. It looked as though someone had picked up the bag and simply emptied out what was inside.

I bent down and picked up the harp and rubbed the horse-hair strings to see if they had been damaged. I carefully put it back in its bag and scrabbled around in the hay for the spare strings I always keep in the bag as well. I only found three out of the full set and it would take a long while to find the others amongst the hay, which wanted changing anyway.

A movement behind me made me turn round. Ailell had walked to the fire. He toed a hound out of the way and casually, as though his mind was not really thinking about it very much, dropped what looked like a stick into the red embers. Little flames licked around it as it settled out of sight.

I tied the neck of the harp-bag and slung it on my left shoulder, much the same way I would a shield. Ailell watched me as I stood up.

'What were you doing with my harp?' I demanded.

'Nothing,' he said hurriedly.

'I don't believe you. What were you doing?'

'I told you. Nothing!'

I felt my mouth begin to smile. He looked very awkward, standing by the fire and lying in his teeth.

'Ailell,' I said, 'as a horse-trader you would starve in a month. You were looking for something and it wasn't fleas. What were you looking for?'

Like many men of fair colouring, that Ailell blushed easily.

'I *told* you. Nothing!'

'Did you find what you weren't looking for?'

'No . . . I mean . . .'

The screen in front of the Queen's cubicle was moved aside a little more, by a long, white, blue-veined hand. Gold gleamed in the dark: the bracelet round her wrist and the gold of her hair. The Queen's voice came: slow, deep, proud and sleepy – and old. In the cream, a hint of sourness; in the soft, a certain rasp of experience. The voice of a woman who is getting to the age when she can no longer bear children. But it was the Queen's voice and the Goddess is always young and so it was young as well. It made my hackles rise. There was never any way to forget that she was the Queen.

And yet, all she said was, 'Ailell, when will you come to bed?'

Ailell started to answer, but she interrupted him.

'Don't bother to hurry. But don't keep me awake with your talking.'

She pulled the screen shut with a slam.

Ailell stared at the floor and, with infinite care, brought his foot down on one of the rushes and squashed it flat. One of the dogs whined and twitched in his sleep.

'Ailell,' I said quietly, 'don't touch my harp again.'

I went past him and out of the door, almost tripping on the door-keeper's legs. As I walked away from the hall, through the thick night-smells, I heard Ailell tripping on the man and kicking him awake. The man's voice raised in whispering protest and Ailell's scarcely-controlled hiss followed me out. And the door banged.

## III

My mouth felt sour as I walked to the other side of the dun. A smell of goats greeted me and a silly bleating. I did not feel in the slightest bit sleepy, which often happens when I am thinking of a song.

I found a sheltered place and sat down upwind of the little goat-shed and arranged my legs so they wouldn't cramp. The damp of the ground soaked up through the wool of my tunic as I settled myself and drew out my harp.

For a wonder the strings were still in tune. I leaned the top of the soundbox against my shoulder and started running my fingers up and down the strings, doing finger-exercises to supple them up. I started to play a jiggy little tune and changed my mind, letting my fingers wander where they willed. Patterns rose and danced and lay down again, but there was no tune in it, no shape. It was like clay before a potter comes at it, or perhaps a wild colt from the hills, before it comes under the breaker's hand.

Then, all at once from a small beginning of three notes, there was a good tune to play against the words of a satire. I started to say words to myself, seeing how they lay together. Then just as the whole song came together in my head – a fine song, I knew, which would make a hall gust with laughter – one of the short strings broke. The end whipping up caught my hand and made it sting. I cursed and drew back, turning to reach for my harp-bag lying beside me and the strings I kept in it.

A streak of fire ran down my back, the tip of a stabbing knife meant to go in above the shoulder-blade and pierce the lung. I dropped the harp and rolled instinctively. Somebody crashed down on top of me, knocking the breath out of me and making sparks shower in my eyes. I caught a glimpse of the cold gleam of a knife, a knife tipped with dark, and the snarling teeth of the man. My hand went up to grab at his knife arm and the other to where he was trying to throttle me. I couldn't breathe. I tried to push his hand away, but he was stronger and the knife in his other hand was coming down slowly, slowly, closer to me. I could hear him panting like a hound. My eyes were going dark red.

We rolled against the side of the goat-hut and I dimly heard their panicky bleating. I crowed in some air and banged his head against the side of the hut. The wattle-and-daub was rotten and he broke it. He growled deep inside himself, like an old dog, but his grip was weaker. I knocked his hand from my throat and gasped for air. It rushed in like wine, but now he had both hands on the knife hilt.

Whisperings like bats went round my head . . . Think! How can you beat him? (Who is he anyway?) Why doesn't someone come and see what the noise is about?

I rolled again, frantically trying to catch him unawares. One of his legs flailed and crunched into something that sang and twanged. My harp! Fury burned me. In it I found strength. Out of the corner of my eye I saw a jagged-edged stone. I hit his hand against it and saw his fingers relax and drop the knife, but he swung his elbow round and knocked it out of reach. Then he went for my throat again. Somehow I brought my hands up between his arms and knocked them away. I heaved away from him, got my feet under me and came to a crouch. I saw the knife just a little way away and flung myself on to it. So did he, but I was that much faster. I felt the hilt between my fingers, smooth it was, of carved bone. It fell perfectly into my grip. He was trying to find my knife hand, so I changed it from left to right. I squirmed a little way out from under, put the point into his belly somewhere near the navel and ripped upwards. He gave a little soft sick sighing noise and collapsed. The full weight was very heavy.

I pushed him off me quickly and sat up and scraped off the worst of the blood and entrails. There was blood everywhere:

21

all over my clothes, my hands, in my hair as I wiped it away from my face and put the strands behind my ears. I sat in the mud beside the ruins of a man and a harp and shivered. I felt sick. How did it feel? A knife piercing the skin of your belly and pulling up, spilling you out on the ground, how did it feel . . .?

I reined my mind back from those thoughts, swallowed and caught my breath and tried to stop shaking, lashing myself with my scorn.

I turned for reassurance to the dead man who had tried to kill me. He had rolled so that his head was back, his face skywards, the little thread of blood trailing from his mouth, dark and shining in the starlight, blotting through his fair beard . . .

It was Ailell.

I think my heart stopped beating. I know that for a long time it was as though his hands were around my throat again. I could not breathe. I could not think. I could only kneel there, staring down at him: the thread of blood ran through his beard, as though someone had been sewing his mouth and left it unfinished. I had sewn his mouth.

Very slowly I started to breathe again, panic clawing my mind. I started to gasp. I wanted to shout and yell: it wasn't me that did it! Oh no, no. It wasn't me. Please not me. Light of the Sun, Lady of the Moon, please, it wasn't me. I didn't kill the King untimely. No . . . Let someone else have done the sacrilege, let someone else be Cursed . . .!

I stood up carefully, shuddering; some other part of me had taken over. A part that knew and accepted what I had done, but had no time to imagine what the Queen would do to me when she found what I had done (I knew. Once, long ago, a man killed the King untimely. The Queen of those days tortured him until he begged to die, and beyond that, but in the end he did die – blind, tongueless, handless, footless, castrated and mad). That part of me held my thoughts back. It stopped me from thinking of the curse that would follow me. Only the New King may kill the Old King. For anyone else the Curse of the Queen follows . . .

Working without thinking, I pulled off Ailell's cloak and wrapped him up in it, gathering together his innards and dropping them into the hole in his stomach and then tying up the cloak. Putting out all that was left of my strength, I carried Ailell's body stumbling over to the goat-hut and put him behind it, between its back wall and the turf bank of the rampart. The blood was already soaking through the cloak, making it feel clammy and sticky. Irrationally, I wiped my hands on my tunic and then looked round, already imagining the Morrigan standing, spear raised, behind me. But despite the row the goats were making, protesting at the smell of blood, there was no one near.

I saw the broken splintered remains of my harp, lying smashed by one of the poles of the goat-pen. I looked at it more closely in the vague hope that it might be repairable, but it was hopeless. Soundbox, forepost, strings – all broken. On top of it all, that was too much. I felt as though a part of me was torn away, but beyond that, nothing. I was cold, benumbed.

I crept behind a storehut and wiped myself down with some wisps of hay. Then I stood and made myself think. By now I had stopped shuddering, I had stopped picturing what would happen when . . . My thoughts ran clear as a meltwater stream.

I weighed up the men I knew: Maine Andoe? No, he was the Queen's son. Dalaigh? Perhaps, except that he revered the Queen, even loved her. I remembered what had happened earlier on. Besides, what I needed more than anything else was advice. I could get out of Cruachan, but where to go after that? Without a clan, without a tribe, without a friend because of the curses of the Queen, lonely to die in the wild forests or the boglands.

And then the answer came to me. Iollan Hen the Harper. The man who first let me use his harp, when he was already old and I was only seven years of age. Old Iollan, older than Sencha of Ulster; older, it was rumoured, even than Cavath, the Chief of all the Druids.

He had first guided my hands across the harp-strings, first

23

taught me of music or rather explained what I knew already, he had channelled my restless urges and taught me how to sing and speak and play the harp. If anyone could help me, he would.

## IV

After what seemed like a year of walking through the sleeping dun, walking through a camp of the dead, I came at last to Iollan's little hut, nestling in the protection of the rampart. He was old now, and preferred to live in his own bothy, by himself, except for a slave. All the hut was to me in the choppy starlight was a shadowy turf-roofed lump against the greater darkness that was the rampart. The gate was nearby: I could hear the gate-guard humming to himself.

I scratched softly on the door. Iollan slept lightly, as many old people do, and he heard well still. I don't think he could have borne to have gone deaf.

'What is it?' he demanded angrily the second time I scratched.

'It's me, Lugh.'

'*Which* Lugh?'

Despite my impatience and fear, I almost smiled. To a Roman perhaps it may seem strange that a man could carry the name of a god and not be struck down for hubris: my name is Lugh, but that is also the name of our Sun-God, our Apollo. But then our gods are not Roman.

This was not the first time Iollan had made a word-play on that, but I had no time for it. I knew I had to be out of the dun before sunrise, when the slave-women would go to milk the goats and find what I had done . . . Sweet gods, what had I done?

'Iollan Hen, let me in.'

I heard him getting up and grumbling at his aching joints. He unlatched and opened the door and stood peering up at me.

'Harp of the Dagda, what have you been doing, boy? Get inside.'

I nearly fell past him into the hut. He shut the door immediately and stood in front of it, wrinkling his eyes to see me in the dim light from the embers of his fire. I said nothing and looked at the lumpish shape of the slave-woman lying by the door. From the sound of her snores she was safe.

I bent to the fire, picked a piece of twig from the floor and stuck it into the centre of the red mass. The end of it mirrored the red and turned into flame; with the flame I lit the small bronze lamp of Roman make – bought, most likely, from Goll the One-Eyed Trader – which hung on the single house-pillar. As the light sprang up, I heard Iollan draw in his breath. I turned to face him, apprehensive.

'Who did you kill?' he asked.

I could not look at him. I watched the woman's breathing as though it mattered and finally said, 'Ailell.'

Silence. Strange how a silence can say more than any words. Like some hunted animal I felt what he felt, absorbed it through the tips of my nerves: first horror and disbelief; then fear and then . . . concern? pity?

I raised my eyes to his, but he looked down and, as a glimpse before he hid it, I saw him make the sign against bad luck, the Sign of Horns. That was the first time I felt betrayed, though it was only to be expected.

I think he too felt it. When I moved again, making to leave, he said in a tired voice, 'Strip off.'

He didn't wait to see if I obeyed him. He bent down to the woman and pinched her ungently on the arm, putting his knotty hand over her mouth to stop her exclamation. He spoke to her low-voiced as she heaved to her feet. She nodded and gave him a vacant gap-toothed grin. Her dress shrieked greenish-yellow and her pebble beads clattered. She shuffled through the door, picking at a louse in her hair.

Iollan turned back to me and I started stripping as he had told me. My body still moved mechanically; my mind was still numb. I noticed things very clearly, but I only registered them; I could no longer feel much. I let my torn and soiled

25

clothes drop on the floor as I stripped and, as I did, Iollan kicked them into a corner. Perhaps he would have them mended if they were mendable – I didn't know, not being a woman. Or perhaps he would burn them because of the magic blood on them . . .

Iollan looked me up and down and a shy little grin pushed its way through the greying bristles of his face.

'You're a sight,' he said. 'Did he try to throttle you?'

'Yes,' I said ruefully, feeling the bruises tenderly. Although it was sore I felt relieved to talk about it. Turning the thing into words made it seem more normal. After all, it wasn't as though this was the first man I had killed.

'Umph. Turn round.'

I did so and he looked at the long scratch that Ailell's dagger had made down my back. It was already scabbing over and was only sore and a little stiff.

The door opened and I started. It was only the woman coming back with her arms full of clothes. She went over to the pile of bracken covered with deerskins that Iollan slept on and opened her arms, letting them fall anyhow.

'You stupid woman, get some water,' said Iollan without heat.

She gave him a fish-like look, went out and reappeared with a large pot full of water from a nearby water-barrel. This she set on the ground and, at a nod from Iollan, went out again.

I washed the blood off me while I explained to Iollan what had happened. Iollan sat on the deerskins beside the clothes and listened without any words until I had finished.

'You say he smashed your harp?' he asked at last, as I rubbed myself dry with some hay from his bed and pulled on my other tunic which the woman had brought. It was a winter one with long sleeves and made of a heavier wool and better than my other one: it was dark blue and embroidered with many colours: white and yellow, red and gold, all around the hems. A girl I knew had made it for me.

'Yes, I heard his foot go through the soundbox and the strings part. The forepost has gone too, but even so it couldn't

26

be repaired.' I smiled shortly as I pulled on a pair of coarse-cloth riding breeches, tucked the ends into my boots and tied the bindings tight. 'It probably saved my life.'

'How?'

'When he broke it, that made me angry. I hadn't wanted to kill him properly before.'

'Ha!' Iollan seemed amused at that. 'Did you leave the harp there?'

'Yes.'

He sighed.

'A pity . . .'

'Why? The Queen is bound to find out anyway . . .' I stopped. 'Iollan, what am I going to do?'

Iollan gestured towards a small cauldron standing near the fire.

'Eat!'

I was about to protest that I wasn't hungry, but then I thought again. It would be just as well to fill my belly now, in case I couldn't get any more food for a while. Concentrate on practicalities, I told myself, even if they are useless against a curse . . .

I squatted down beside the cauldron and picked a piece of meat out of it. It was still warm and belonged to some description of bird. I chewed quickly.

'Where will you go?' asked Iollan at last.

'I don't know,' I answered, round a mouthful of meat. 'Curoi?'

'No. He'd send you straight back to the Queen. So would Finn Mac Ross of Leinster and Cairbre Naifer in Tara. They all revere her as Goddess on Earth and fear her more than they love her, for what she is and the power that is in her. I am too old to love her or fear her any more. But if you want to be truly safe, leave Erin completely. Go to the Island of the Mighty, that the Romans call Britain now they've conquered her. After all, aren't you half Roman yourself?'

I stared at him. Leave Erin? It didn't seem possible then.

'I may be half Roman, but I was born here. Are my father's people so strong in me, then?'

'No. The music of your mother is stronger, for all you have the nose of an Eagle. But you'll not be safe anywhere here in Erin, with the Curses of the Mother baying at your tail.' I flinched, but he went on. 'Overseas, they might be weaker. Perhaps they can't cross water at all. And besides, any king of the south will send you back to her so fast you won't know what's happening.'

'Any king of the south, yes,' I agreed slowly. There was a thought blossoming at last in my head. 'What about the King of the North?'

'*Conor?* You'd trust yourself to that . . . that fox in wolf's clothing?'

'Why not? From what I've heard and seen there's little love lost between himself and the Queen. And his people worship the Sun first, not the Moon.' I smiled. 'They might even take me for a good-luck thing – after all, I'm called Lugh, the same as Lugh of the Bright Spear.'

'You're mad!'

'Am I? I think not. And if he won't give me shelter, I would have to go to Ulster anyway to wait for a trading ship from Britain.' I fished another lump of meat from the cauldron. 'And then there's Cuchulain Mac Sualtim.'

'What about Cuchulain?'

'If King Conor won't take me in, then Cuchulain will as a matter of principle. From what I hear, he and the King haven't seen exactly eye to eye ever since the King exiled the Sons of Usnach because of that bitch, Deirdre. And he being the Champion of Ulster now has made things worse.'

Iollan's lips pursed in a silent whistle and his eyes went narrow, like two drops of blue water between wrinkled dead leaves.

'Oho,' he said. 'So you think Cuchulain's ambitious, then?'

I shrugged. 'From what I hear, he's mad enough to be anything.'

Iollan snorted amusedly. There was silence as I finished eating and drank a long draught of water from a fine pottery flagon beside Iollan's bed. I stood up to go, with an odd feeling of hurry. It felt as though the night was slipping greasily away from my grasp although it was only just reaching the end of what the Romans call the second watch.

Iollan understood what I felt. I was unnaturally calm now, able to talk coolly of what to do, but I wanted to be away. Later on, when I was safe, my mind would have time to understand fully what had happened.

Iollan went into a corner and dug out a leather pouch. Into it he put several strips of dried meat and a handful of dried fruit from the storage pots there. He took down a leather flask from a hook on the wall; the stopper was bronze and shaped like a man's head, asleep or dead. Everything was strangely clear to me and sharp-edged, as though seen through crystal.

He filled the flask from a barrel in the corner and gave the supplies to me to hang on my belt. I had already put on my cloak: thick and heavy it was, big enough to cover me well against the night; the kind of cloak the Romans tax very heavily because they are much in demand even in Rome herself. This one was chequered black and white, fastened with a gold enamelled brooch. I put on all my jewellery: my bracelets and the torc which showed I was a nobleman and two silver rings. Then at last I turned to leave.

'Wait a moment, Lugh,' Iollan called after me, just as my hand touched the latch. I turned back. He was standing by his bed with a strange expression on his face.

'There are two things that you've forgotten.'

'My sword and shield? I'll collect them from the armoury before I leave.'

He smiled softly.

'I told Mata to get your sword. She'll give it to you outside. No. Lugh, your harp was smashed – how will you live? By the sword?'

I had not thought of that. I suppose I had not yet quite realized, with the numbness of the other things, what it meant that my harp was smashed. It was true. What is any trained harper if he has no harp?

'I . . . I hadn't thought of that. I . . . suppose I could make one.'

Again that small, half-shy smile.

'It's not necessary, Lugh.' Abruptly his voice lengthened and deepened, so that it became again a voice that could hold a hall full of feasting warriors spellbound with its music. It was no longer the voice of an old man, it was the voice of a trained bard.

'I have known for some time that this moment would come. Now you have lost your harp, you must have another.'

I did not quite understand him. Or rather one part of me did and another part – not quite. He turned and pulled back the deerskins hanging over the end of his bed of bracken and hay. Under them was a shape covered by otterskin, glinting with bright threads. Iollan picked it up gently and held it between his two hands, looking over it straight into my eyes.

'I can no longer play this,' he said, his voice still deep. 'She is yours.'

I could not say anything. Two steps took me near enough to take it from him and my arms were outstretched to do so . . . but I let them fall.

'I cannot, Iollan Hen,' I said, hearing that my voice too had become richer, more measured, answering the music in his. 'She's . . . she is your harp.'

He smiled. 'No. I said I can no longer play her and no man should keep a harp he cannot play. My fingers have grown too knotted and thick, too stiff and painful and worn with playing. She hasn't been touched in two years now, except to keep her in tune. Take her Lugh, and play her.'

Then, as I still hesitated, 'Lugh, Lugh, if you're thinking of my sons, forget them. They can strum, yes, but none of them have the music running in their souls, none of them can hear the music of Lugh Bright-Spear's Birds and draw it from the sky through the strings and their fingers. You can do it, Lugh Mac Romain: you're the only man I've met who can raise the hairs on my neck. Yes, you're raw still, but when you reach your flowering, there'll be no poet or singer of songs or plucker of strings in the whole of Erin to match you; not Diarment of the Songs, not Gennan Bright-face in Ulster, nor yet Athairne Mac Eterscel that everyone thinks so great, for all his meanness.'

He snorted. 'That man's a bad lot and he'll come to a bad end . . . Take her, Lugh. I've never been able to make poetry, only music, but you've brought me as close to it as I've ever come, or ever will for that matter.'

He snorted again and shook his head. At last I took the harp from him, feeling her sweet weight in my arms. Her name was Fiorbhinn – Truesweet. The only time I had ever played her was at the age of seven, when Iollan had found the music in me. I had longed for her ever since without hope of ever playing her again.

I looked down at the otterskin bag, still not quite able to believe it: the glossy brown waterproof fur was embroidered with intricate curling patterns in gold and blue thread and the shoulder strap was stained blue with woad.

I began to try and stammer my thanks, the ready words deserting me for once. Iollan only coughed and growled.

'Go on, get out! Are you going to stand here blabbering all night like a drunken Greek? I thought you wanted to escape!'

He fairly pushed me out of the door and shut it firmly after me. I stopped a few heart-beats longer, before slinging the harp on my back. She was heavier than my old harp. I turned to stride off and almost bumped into the slave-woman, standing yellow, dumb and cow-like in the light of the fitful quarter-moon. She was waiting patiently, holding my sword and swordbelt in her left hand and my stabbing spear, horse-blanket and harness in her right. Seeing my stabbing spear I thought I would never keep that wager with Dalaigh now and I felt a sudden pang of regret at the thought. For a moment I considered going to say goodbye, but then I decided against it. It would waste time when I had already wasted too much and besides he was probably with the girl by now and would not want to be disturbed.

Wondering how best to get out of the dun after the gates had been closed, I took the sword-and-belt from the woman and buckled it round my waist, automatically shifting my weight to my right side as I did so, to balance the heaviness of the sword. I took the other things and thanked her. She seemed not to understand: she turned away and went back into Iollan's hut without another word. I looked after her for a moment, then shrugged and started to pick my way through the sleeping dun of Cruachan.


## V


I judged it to be the time of night when the guard on the horses in the home-pasture was changed – there was little likelihood of a cattle-raid so far into Connaught and close to Cruachan, but horses were quite another matter and Owen of Fermanagh might think it worth his while to reive them. As I walked quietly over to the gate, I thought to myself that I was bound to be recognized. You can hide a face, but you can't disguise my kind of length. I stepped over a small pig snoring across the path between two storehuts.

As I came within sight of the gate, I dropped to a crouch and went forward carefully, using the shadow of the ramparts and waiting for clouds before moving. The gate-guard was whistling in his teeth: I could see his silhouette up on the sentry-walk, leaning against the log fence, bored and half-asleep. I knew I couldn't get up there to overpower him – the steps up the side of the turf-bank creaked and he would know someone was coming. There was only one thing I could do.

I stood up straight and came up close to the turf-bank.

'Psst!'

He turned round, reaching for his spear.

'Who is it?' He was keeping his voice down, thank the gods, so as not to waken the sleeping dun.

'Donall!' I hissed. 'Come down and help me lift the gate bar.'

'Why? You know you're not supposed to . . .'

'There's a girl I'm meeting,' I said, snatching at the first excuse that came into my head.

'There would be! All right, I'm coming down.'

The steps creaked and Donall came up to me. To my relief he had left his spear leaning against the fence.

'You pick your times, don't you, Lugh?' he grumbled. 'Who is it this time?'

The moon came out. He saw I was holding my horse-blanket and bridle, saw the spear I had ready. He tensed and his hand moved towards his dagger.

'What are you . . .?' he began.

I hit him. He wasn't expecting it and staggered back, tripped on a stone and sat down. I put my spear-blade to his throat.

'What the . . .? What are you doing? Have you gone *mad*, Lugh?'

'No,' I said. 'Turn on your stomach.'

'Why?'

'Do it! And stay quiet.' I let him feel the coldness of the spear: I didn't want to kill him, but he didn't know that.

He turned slowly and lay flat. Keeping my spear at the nape of his neck I pulled his sling from his belt and tied his hands with it. He took breath to shout, but I put my hand over his mouth and half-strangled him. While he recovered I stuffed straw in his mouth and bound his legs with his belt. He started to struggle.

'I'm sorry, Donall,' I said. 'Nod if you can breathe.' I didn't want him to choke on the straw.

He nodded, his eyes popping with fury and made muffled noises. I toed him gently into a shadow thrown by one of the torches.

'I'm sorry, Donall,' I said again.

The bar across the gate was heavy to draw back, but at last it creaked grudgingly across. I slipped through the gap and hurried down the path to the home-pasture where once, long ago, I had watched Dalaigh checking his pony's shoes and we had talked of Cuchulain – and the Queen. The Queen who would curse me, no matter how far I fled . . .

Was it really only that same evening, or had I somehow slept for a thousand years in a faery-hill, a sidhe.

I found the man guarding the horses, standing by the fence. He was alert and I wondered if he had heard anything. He stood up straighter and grabbed his spear when he heard me coming. The moon went behind a cloud and I called out hastily.

'It's me, Lugh.'

'Oh. What are you doing here?' I knew him. His name was Lugaid and he was not over-blessed with intelligence.

'I've . . . er . . . I've come to relieve you,' I said.

Pause.

'Eh?'

There was something wrong there and my heart began to beat uncomfortably fast again.

'Yes.' I moved closer, in case.

'But I've just relieved Conall.' He sounded suspicious and I heard him shift, bringing his spear towards me.

'Shh! Listen!' I hissed. 'Over there!' I pointed away from the dun. It was an old trick, but I saw him turn his head; I shifted my grip on the spear-haft and cracked him over the head with the butt.

He grunted and collapsed. I bent over him and felt the pulse in his neck and round the back of his head where I had hit him. The pulse was still there and a lump beginning on his head.

I lifted the heavy pole barring the gate and dragged it to one side. I pulled Lugaid a little way off and laid him under a bush, because I had an idea for stopping pursuit. By men at any rate. Curses I could not stop . . .

Most of the horses were standing asleep or lying down. I walked through them and they awakened and moved uneasily. There were enquiring nickerings and sniffings. I whistled,

'Phhee*wit*!'

Hooves thudded over the grass at the third repetition and a velvet muzzle butted into my chest. I thanked whichever god had been looking after me that night that Conin had felt like coming to me when I called. I was prepared to take any of the riding horses there, but I was pleased that my own horse had come to me when I needed him. He knew me and I gentled him and wished I had some corn to give him.

I put the bridle over his head, feeling the warmth of his mouth and breath as I pushed the bit into the proper place; hearing the chink of the bronze ornaments as he shook his head and champed a little to get it comfortable. I hung the horse-blanket on his back and strapped it securely under his furry belly and then vaulted on my spear on to his back.

I had to grab for the reins as Conin started to buck. He always did, every time I rode him, which perhaps was why I liked him so – and another reason for his name. I fought him to a halt with difficulty because my spear got in the way – it is more a weapon for a chariot than horseback – and when at last he stopped bucking we were turned round facing the dun. There was just enough light to see some movement by the gate. The gate-guard must have got free quicker than I expected.

I reversed my spear so that the head was close to my hand and turned Conin around the little group of horses and chariot-ponies. I started to lay about me with the spear-butt and managed to drive them in a snorting bunch towards the gate. It was something I had done often enough in daylight, bringing in the wild colts from the hills and moors west of Magh Ai and Cruachan; in the night-time with only the uncertain deceptive light of the Moon-Lady to help me it was far harder, with an odd sense of unreality about it. But Conin entered into the spirit of the game and answered to me before he felt the pressure of my knees or hand on the rein. We got them unwillingly through the gap in the fence, with threats and whispered shouts, and then, when they were all out, I charged into the middle of them, scattering them in all directions.

Out of reach of the restraint of fences or bridles and chariots, they felt the call of their old homes in the hills; they reared and most of them started frisking away in transitory delight. They would come back later when they decided that the grass far away wasn't as wonderful as it looked, but for the moment, no one could give chase.

The movement by the gate was becoming more excited and men started running down the hill. I shouted at the ponies to make them move away faster. Some of them bolted and that set the others off. I took a last look round at Cruachan and Magh Ai: at the turf ramparts and the fence on their crown; at the top of the hall, just visible above the fence, with what might have been a whisp of smoke from the sleeping fire within hanging above its peak against a patch of stars; at the home-pasture, emptied . . . In the moonlight it was like a stronghold in a song, shadowy and insubstantial: at its centre the Queen, ageing and young; golden hair and long, used face; sitting like a she-spider at the centre of her web . . .

I shook myself, trying to rid my mind of its fancies, but they held me in thrall for just one moment more. Then the spell broke and it was only Cruachan where I had been born, though not begotten, the only place I had ever really known and truly dear to me. At that moment I thought I was losing it . . .

I swallowed, turned Conin's head roughly west and kicked with my heels. Three days before Samhain, in the noon of night was when I left Cruachan forever, leaving the Old King dead behind me.

# Part Two

# Emain Macha

## I

That was a long hard ride from Cruachan to Emain Macha beyond the Gap of the North. I would say that it would be more than six days' march for a legion and that along roads not straight. For there are roads in Erin, chariot roads for the meeting of the fairs, and they all go to Tara where the fair and the Tara King-making is held. I did not keep to the road, though I did when I could, because this was near to Samhain and Samhain is the beginning of winter: the road was often muddy and full of pot-holes so I dared not let Conin go on it. When I took to the flanks of the hills, and had to go through the trees I kept my spear ready and Conin on a tight rein. The land was empty and dripping like a drowned corpse and for most of the time I was soused by a cold mizzle that came from a sky merged into the crowns of the round hills. It was silent except when I met herdsmen bringing cows in to Cruachan and Tara for Samhain and the winter slaughter: there were few even of the herds about because of the time of year and no other riders: no man would willingly travel so close to Samhain.

I pressed on, slapping Conin's thick dew-covered shoulders in encouragement and ignoring the ache of my backside from his spine. I was not dry for the whole of that journey, for I did not dare go to any of the farmsteads I passed nor the blacksmith's forges by the fords of streams because of Samhain and because of the Queen's Curse. I was afraid that even if I had outrun it on Conin's back, they would know of it and drive me out with dogs and stones; also I did not want to bring the Curse down on any who gave me hospitality. I was not even so afraid of being robbed because they will not kill a bard for fear of bad luck and satires, and anyway the reivers were all hiding away because of Samhain. And I hoped and prayed to Lugh of the Long Spear, who was so hidden by the weeping clouds, that I would reach Emain before the fall of Samhain Eve: I was so afraid of it that I drove Conin on unmercifully, glad that he was of the tough hill-breed who will go on forever if they have to.

On the second day I forded the rising Boyne and passed the two duns of Tailtiu and Cuile and rode on a little way into the plain of Muirthemne, held by Cuchulain Mac Sualtim, the Sedanta. I camped there on the side of a hill and knew I had a long way to go to Emain, and Conin was close to collapse. I was too tired to eat the little food I had left.

The next day was the day before Samhain: I could feel the fear and the magic building up all the daylight hours as I cantered and trotted and walked north along the road of Midluachair. The road was a good one, for the Sedanta kept it in good repair and I was slowed more by having to ford the streams of Muirthemne than the road. It rained less that day, and was almost fine at times.

For all the speed with which I rode and the way I pressed on, evening was drawing near some time before I saw Emain, though I had long since passed into Ulster when I crossed into the hunting-runs of the Sedanta. I soon saw that there was no way that I could reach Emain before the last light fled the sky and the faery-hills, the sidhe and the barrows of Heroes opened and the goblins of the night swarmed out on the one night of the year when they are free to do as they like: the night when everything is turned around the wrong way and 'now' and 'then' become one and the same thing. The night when Dead and Living meet in the Feast for the Death of the Year.

I stopped Conin and dismounted to let him rest a little,

and watched the sun come out from behind the clouds before dipping below the wet hills into the western sea, beyond Tir-na-nOg, the Land of the Young. There was a strange kind of fear on me. Not fear of the Unknown, but fear of something that perhaps I knew and understood too well.

I could have turned aside to Dun Delgan, Cuchulain Mac Sualtim's house-place. But I remembered that like all the nobles of Ulster, or Connaught for that matter, Cuchulain and all his household would be in the King's dun, in Emain Macha for the Samhain feast. His house would be deserted – and there is nothing more eerie than an empty habitation of men.

I mounted up and rode on again, my spear held firm under my arm. The weight of my harp, Fiorbhinn, on my back between tunic and cloak was a comfort as she banged a little with the swing of Conin's canter.

We went on and on, along the road, now well into the Gap of the North, by great Slieve Fuad and Slieve Cuillen, between the guardian hills of Ulster. As night came on, the hills seemed to press us in; they bent down breathing the breath of giants and seemed unwilling to let us pass. I am used to the hill country, but these were different, more dour, more dark. Perhaps the difference in their quality came from the night, not from themselves. I know that as I rode my hands around the spear-haft and reins grew sticky and my heart thumped. I had not met and lived with the Sidhe-folk then, and when all that came between me and the stars was an owl, my eyes made a Bocanach of the Air out of it.

Conin was infected by the fear of the night and my fear, and he drove on harder and harder without need of urging from my heels. The trees of the gap became infused with their own life and the leaves whispered strange songs of the dead . . .

Samhain is not a sad feast, for death is not sad for the dead, but only for those left behind. We hold it, each state in its own chief dun, and a fine feast it is, the finest of the year, with harp-song and laughter, mead and food of all kinds from the harvest. A happy feast. But the laughter and song and mead and firelight are fences as well as pleasures in themselves: fences to keep out what men fear most at the joining of the year. As Conin's hooves drummed on the road I remembered another drum and the smell of another fear.

Now, on Samhain Eve, in the high place by the Cave of Cruachan, the Old King should be dying – but I had killed him three days ago. What would happen now there was no Seven-Year King to die at the end of his time, no Old King for the New King to kill? Would they play-act the death as the other peoples do, as they do in Ulster? Or would someone else be killed instead to slake the Mother-Earth's thirst, so that the New King could rule a fruitful land?

I remembered the Samhain of seven years ago, although only in little bright particles, as though the memory had been smashed into jagged-edged shining pieces by the mead and the ale and the special drink of the Queen. That drink with the smell of herbs and dreams locked in its fire, that is the Magic of the Queen and it is made by the Sidhe-folk themselves. But I remembered the Queen's long face and her golden hair swinging and her face leaned forward with lips parted, drinking in the dance as the young warriors stamped and pranced and flashed their knives before her. We were all first-year warriors with the tattooing still raised and sore on our skins; I remembered the strange look in her beautiful eyes and had no words to describe it with: even then, I remember, I hated the Queen more than I loved her, even then, though that was just before my mother died . . . And the King-Killing.

Most of the other younger ones were stretched out dead-drunk on the floor of the hall along with the dogs and the remains of wild feasting. But I was still dancing drunk: either my head was already stronger than most people's or else I had somehow contrived to drink less. At any rate, I remember what happened, vaguely, in glimpses.

It was outside. We had wound our dancing way with torches up to the Cave of Cruachan and the Queen dancing in the centre, with the Old King painted for death walking beside her, weighed down with the curses of Connaught.

Everyone was leaping and making patterns against the wet night with smoking flaming torches so that shoulders and knees and nipples of breasts would suddenly shine out red and then disappear into the Night. My mother was with the Priestesses, but I scarcely looked at her: my gaze was fixed on the Queen as she danced, but always stayed the same, promising all, denying all. Among the mature warriors strode Maelchon, tall and fair and somehow different and I knew, as everyone else did, that he was the New King, he would be Ailell next.

Then the Queen standing and the challenge being called thrice and Maelchon stepping forward and showing the Queen's token: a bone carved to look like a man's penis, but smaller and with secret letters written on it. It was a human bone, I knew.

We all shouted for the New King and cursed and hissed at the Old King, who stood, bowed down with our bad luck. Then the Queen shook her silver apple-branch and the fight began between them and we shouted and howled like dogs. Somehow I had fought my way to the front and so I saw the finish: saw the glazed drugged eyes of the King as he lay under Maelchon's grip and then went limp. How Maelchon took the stone knife from the Queen and, singing a strange triumph song, cut the King in the three ritual places and then cut his throat.

I looked up, straight into the face of the Queen and she was smiling, her lips curving up in ripe curves like her body, her eyes pleased and proud and thirsty.

Then the Night is confused and drunken and dark again except for one moment when I lay in the shelter of a bush with a woman. That was the first time I ever lay with a woman: I do not know who she was, though I know she was painted for I found the paint on me the next morning. I also know that she was not young, that she was a wise and experienced lover, that she knew who I was for she whispered what sounded like my name. I do not know who it was, but I can guess . . .

I shook my head and made the Sign of Horns with my fist

to try and rid my mind of the pictures that swirled through it. My body moved without thought to the rhythm of the horse, but my eyes flicked from side to side: I tried to stop, tried to look straight ahead for the light from Emain Macha, but my thoughts wove Things out of the dark, things made of thistledown and cloudy starlight, things of no substance. They spawned from the night and the smell of my own fear. I longed for light, any light: lamplight, firelight, sunlight – Oh yes, sunlight above all! I felt as though I had always been riding on the Road of Midluachair, Samhain pressing on all sides; always like this: an insubstantial spirit riding on and on, alone in a fog of fear, in a darkness coming wholly from my own mind and therefore wholly inescapable . . . The sour thick taste of panic rose in my throat. I think I caught in a breath to scream . . .

. . . And let it out again in a sigh of relief. There was light ahead. Not stars or moon, but red light, firelight, light that came from the torches hung all around the walls of Emain Macha. They made a crown of jewels, red jewels, garnets like the ones studding my harp. I sobbed with relief and then laughed at the noise I made. I thanked all the gods I had been praying to: Lugh Sun-Face, Manannan of the Sea, the Dagda. I think I babbled a little. And it was not really so late.

I rode up to the high gate set into the line of the turf walls. There was a flaring torch on each side of it and a branch of rowan on both of the doors.

I rode close to them, reversed my spear and hammered on the wood. I went on hammering until the gate-guard had climbed to his vantage point beside the gate whence he could see me in the light of the torches. I could not see his face because he was in the shadow above the light of a torch, but I knew he was there. I sat, my spine drooping a little with sudden tiredness, hearing Conin's laboured breathing, squinting up at him.

'Who is it wants to come into Emain Macha after the Sun has gone down?'

'Lugh,' I shouted back, without thinking.

'*Lugh?*' gasped the gate-guard. I heard the break of fear in his voice and understood what was in his mind. I had to laugh. I think I was light-headed with relief at being close to other men at last.

'No! Not that Lugh. I'm Lugh Mac Romain of Connaught.'

'Oh.' There was a pause. 'I can't let you in until I've spoken with the King. Wait there until I come back.'

'I'm hardly likely to leave,' I shouted back at him.

Conin stood with head hanging, and I wondered anxiously if I had broken his wind. It would hardly be surprising if I had. I let the reins fall loose along his neck. Although the Night pressed in, I felt protected by the walls and light. I looked down at the ruts left by the chariot wheels in the ground and noticed as something important the way their sharp shadows shifted in the torch-flame. I watched the shadows, tranced by the way they moved. I think I slept a little.

A cough from above made me look up again.

'Are you Lugh Mac Romain, the Harper, foster-son to Maeve of Connaught?'

I flinched at his casual use of the Queen's name. No man of the South would ever use it in that way, as though it were just the name of any woman to be thrown casually by men from ear to ear. It was shocking to me, then. More than shocking – it was sacrilegious and on that night of all nights, it was laden with ill-luck. And I had no need of it, on top of the Curse.

My fingers formed the Sign of Horns of their own accord – or maybe they had been clenched like that ever since the sun had gone down. It was difficult to remember.

I swallowed and answered, 'I am that man.'

'Ah. Then I'm to let you in.' Another pause.

'Well, why don't you open the gates then?' I asked, hungry and impatient to be in the warm.

'Ah, yes. Er . . . is there anything with you by any chance?' said the gate-guard with elaborate casualness.

After his common use of the Queen's name, that was a bit

43

much. I choked with laughter.

'No,' I got out at last, 'No, there's nothing with me. You can let me in quite safely.'

'Yes,' said the gate-guard doubtfully. 'Yes, all right.'

There was a clatter and scraping as he pulled back the big gate, just enough to let myself and the horse through the gap. Another man helped him to push the gate shut again and put the bar across the join. I slid from Conin's steaming back and slapped him on the side of the neck and let the second man lead him away to the stables where the other horses were kept for Samhain. I stood and stared around me.

## II

There was an astonishing amount of light in the place. There were torches everywhere, hanging from every available point; in their light I could see the shapes of many anonymous sheds and animal-pens, smelling the rank smell of dung and animals and people and smoke. I could see the shapes of the three great houses of Emain. I learned later what their names were: there was the Speckled House, the armoury, quite near the gate; there was the House of the Red Branch, the guest-house of Emain and, finally, the Royal Hall, even bigger than the Queen's hall at Cruachan. It was a hall with nine house-pillars and a shingled roof, going up to a point where the smoke escaped. Light was coming from it in all directions, seeping under the door and through little cracks in the painted walls, squeezing past the withy-shutters closing the small windows in each partition, spilling out from the place where the roof joined the walls.

The gate-guard left his post and came after me as I started towards the door of the Royal Hall.

'You must leave your spear and sword in the Speckled House,' he said. I was about to protest at being parted from my weapons, but he went on hurriedly, 'It's law. There's a geasa against bringing weapons into the Royal Hall. It's to stop them killing each other when they start fighting, you see.'

If it was geasa I had no choice. I went with the old gate-guard to the Speckled House and I left my spear and sword with all the others there. I saw why they called the place the Speckled House then. There was a single lamp hanging from the roof in its centre and the lamp swung as we entered. The reflections from the burnished weapons made dapplings across the walls like sunlight in a forest.

We left before I could notice the other weapons there clearly, the gate-guard shutting the door firmly behind us. We parted as he went back to his gate and I went towards the door of the Royal Hall.

I banged once on it and the door-keeper opened it to me. I stepped across the threshold and automatically hitched the folds of my cloak back across my shoulders, so as to leave my arms free.

The heat and light and noise slapped me in the face like a hot wave. Even the torches outside had not prepared me for this after the solitude and terrible silence of the night. It was friendly and human, but the noise, the smell of crowded people and mead and smoke, the dazzle from the lamps and the torches and the fire – it all hit me full between the eyes, overwhelming and confusing me.

I hesitated for a moment, two steps from the door and a silence fell as every head in the hall turned to me. The door-keeper shut the door quietly behind me: the click sounded loud as a thunderclap.

My eyes unblurred a little and I looked round at the faces all pitted with eyes, staring at me. For a moment it was as though my mind's eye had skipped away from my body and was looking at me with the eyes of someone in the hall. I saw myself with unnatural clearness. A tall thin man with long soft dark-brown hair; a long slightly spiky face with deep-set green-grey eyes and black straight eyebrows which quirked up oddly at the ends, and, as it were the most strik-ing achievement of the face, a big Roman nose leaping out from it.

45

This vision came and went in a flash of clarity. I looked round again, picking things out this time: especially the cubicle on the right of the door that beamed with precious metal, and the close-faced greying man who sat amid embroidered red deerskins holding a silver rod with three golden apples on it before him on his lap. I recognized it for what it was: the same as the Queen's apple-branch. And I saw the young man in the cubicle on that man's right, for he was one to stand out anywhere, in whatsoever company.

The silence still held, but somehow it quickened my blood like the silence which falls before you start to harp and sing. I breathed in as I would then, and walked slowly forward: through the gap between the two house-pillars with the central fire on its great stones directly before me; across the middle part of the floor which was littered with sleeping dogs and bones and crusts and rucked-up rushes and one or two men lying prone and breathing stertorously; and turned so that I was facing the magnificent cubicle and the man who sat in it with the apple-branch in his lap and no thoughts on his face.

He was wearing a tunic made of cloth with a warp of gold thread and a woof of white linen; it shimmered with shot gold. The torc around his neck was triple thickness with the ends shaped like horses' heads. He leaned forward as I stood before him, his elbow on his knee. His fingers began playing idly with his grey beard. His eyes were light brown and there was a wall behind them which let no thought spill from his thinking to his face.

I waited for him to speak, since clearly here was the King. King Conor, the man whom Iollan had called the 'fox in wolf's clothing'.

He nodded and a servant came up with some food – meat, wastel bread and mead. I sat down cross-legged on the herb-strewn rushes and ate some of it, but I was nervous and my hunger had disappeared. The hall buzzed curiously until I had finished and then fell silent again. I dropped what I didn't want in the rushes and stood up. Now I had eaten they could ask me questions. I waited.

46

The King said nothing, but looked first over my shoulder at the cubicle behind me. Then his eyes swivelled to me, and stayed there, his glance pressing against mine.

'You are Lugh Mac Romain, foster-son to Queen Maeve of Connaught?' he said. His voice was very non-committal, neither deep nor light, nor soft nor harsh, but carrying.

I hid my instinctive flinch at his naming of the Queen's name and answered, 'That is my name, King.'

'You ride on a strange night of the year.'

'It is not of my choice, King.'

'Indeed? Is there a reason?'

There was something in the way he asked that set my back up. I smiled at him and said, 'There is.'

'Will you tell us what it is, Lugh Mac Romain?'

This was another voice, the voice of a totally different man. It was old, but there was the unmistakable strength in it, the timbre of the trained speaker. I should know – my own voice bears the same mark, from the self-same training. But there was more than that to this voice.

I was too proud to turn round or let my eyes rest from the King's stare. I took a deep breath and had time to notice that my hands had turned into fists beneath my cloak. Now was the testing. What would they do when they knew?

'Here then is my reason,' I said, answering the voice behind me, not the King before me.

'I have ridden from Cruachan and the Queen of Connaught, because the Queen will surely kill me if she catches me. Three days ago I killed a man who attacked me when I was unawares, making a song. He was Ailell, the Queen's Consort, the Old King.'

There was a gasp from everyone present. Then it swelled into a roar: shouts and curses and fear of curses. A tall fair-haired man jumped up and said, 'He can't stay here! He'll bring the Curse of the Queen down on us.'

'Throw him out!' 'Yes, kick him out!' 'Before he brings it on us.' 'Out!'

I stood still, my tongue sticking to the roof of my mouth, my hands sticky with sweat. I stared straight in front of me,

47

hearing the shouts and the growls. I dared not move, in case I provoked them to kill me. Even Ulster was afraid of the Queen, even Ulster would not have me . . .

I saw that the man sitting on the King's right was saying nothing, but leaning back with his eyes narrowed. He spoke to his wife and nodded at what she said. The King sat still, waiting for the noise to die down. His eyes had opened wide, then hooded themselves half-shut. He could not give me shelter against the will of his entire household.

'Indeed?' he said, softly.

'Lugh Mac Romain!' said the voice I was too proud to look for behind me, and the noise instantly died. 'Face me.'

I turned on my heel and looked across at him. The fire that was between us settled suddenly, going down so I could see him before the flames leaped high again. I needed no second look, no telling to know who this was.

I walked round the firestones, picking my way carefully among the litter, feeling the hostile staring of the warriors. They shrank back as my shadow passed them.

At last I faced the man who had spoken in his cubicle, as I had faced Conor. But this time I bowed to him deeply, bringing both fists to my forehead in salute. Then I knelt, so that I was on a level with him.

'You know me then, Lugh Mac Romain?'

'I know you, lord.'

'Look at me.'

I looked at him. His face was old, his eyes dark, his hair white as bog-cotton. He was wrapped in a thick purple cloak: yes, purple, Imperial purple, the purple that comes from the shellfish in the Tyrrhenian sea and each yard of it costs the life of one of those who gather it. Rarer and more valuable it was than even the King's gold-shot tunic. And he sat on soft supple skins that I knew came from horses, for this was Cavath, the Chief Druid of the Three Lands and their Three Islands.

'You killed the King untimely?'

'I did, lord.' I did not bother to offer excuses. In this they had no meaning. Does the sea listen to the excuses of the

48

sailors who drown in him?

'And you are not dead.'

'My lord?'

'You know the power of the Queen of Connaught. Did you think you had outrun the Curse?'

'I don't know, lord. I . . . I ran. You can outrun wolves – perhaps you can outrun curses.'

'Some curses can be outrun. But not the Queen's Curse. That follows and kills within the day of its setting. Now you see why it is strange you are not dead?'

'Yes, lord.'

'Can you think of any reason why?'

I shook my head. I couldn't think and I didn't understand.

Cavath smiled a little.

'Perhaps,' he said gently, 'you have not been cursed.'

'But . . . But I killed the King.'

I had the strange feeling he had already known before I arrived, that he had been prepared. That he knew more than I did about the matter and was not going to tell me.

'I don't understand, lord,' I said. 'The Queen must know by now. She must know who did it. Why hasn't she cursed me, then?'

'Why indeed?' said Cavath. He raised his voice. 'I believe, King, chieftains, warriors, women, that Lugh Mac Romain has not been cursed by the Queen, nor will he be: that he is not outcast from men, but only from Connaught and that he will bring no curse on those who give him shelter.'

He nodded at me and made the sign of the Druid's Blessing. There was a sigh of pent-up breaths and a movement from the King's cubicle. He had come to his feet and so I rose to mine. The long sleeves of his tunic were red at the cuffs, embroidered, as though he had just that moment dabbled them carefully in blood. The effect of the gold was that he should have blazed with light, as a King should. But for some reason, he didn't.

'Do you wish to stay here, Lugh Mac Romain?'

'Yes, King.'

49

'As what? As a warrior, eating my food and receiving my generosity in return for the strength of your arm and the sharpness of your sword?'

'As that, and perhaps as a harper, a singer of songs, a teller of tales.'

'You are a bard.' It was a statement, not a question: he had seen the harp-bag on my back.

'I have trained the full eight years and have passed the tests. I know the seven fifties of songs and more and I am able to make my own, from Hero-tales and praises to satires that will raise a blemish on a woman's face.'

His hooded eyes flickered.

'Indeed?' he said. 'You are . . . very sure.'

I was not going to answer that. I watched him under my own eyelids and smiled faintly.

Behind, Cavath made a noise that might have been a dignified snort in a lesser man.

'I heard the opinions of the men who tested him at the end of his training,' he said. 'He has a right to be very sure.'

I was amazed. From the Chief Druid this was praise indeed! Conor smiled under his beard and somehow that smile lessened my pleasure, though how or why I cannot say.

'Swear your faith to me and you may stay in Emain as one of my men, to sing or fight for me and yet keep the freedom of a bard.'

This was against custom. No harper need ever swear fealty to any lord in order to stay in a place. It is his right to go wherever he pleases. But then, in my case, it was . . . different. I hesitated and then thought, what had I got to lose? I went back to where he stood and knelt before him.

I put my hands between his. The palms of his hands were dry, hard with sword-callouses. Then, looking straight at the buckle of his belt, I swore my faith to him.

'The sky is over my head, the earth is under my feet, the sea is round about me: unless the blue sea goes over the face of the earth, or the earth breaks open under my feet, or the high heaven and its shower of stars falls down upon the earth, I swear that I will keep faith and life and truth with you and do no harm or hurt or damage to your house or your women or yourself.'

And Conor the King answered my faith-swearing with his own in the self-same words that I had used.

When it was finished the silence endured a little longer. The King turned away and went and sat down again on his deerskins and began to talk with the woman who sat beside him. I came swiftly to my feet and for a moment felt as lonely as ever I had before, alone in the hall of people with not one man or woman there that I knew.

Then before the full weight of the solitude could hurt me, the man who sat on the King's right, in the Champion's Place, leaped to his feet. I found myself looking down at a very small-sized, wiry-built man with a dark, sad-looking face and wiry blue-black hair. He smiled up at me and when he did that his whole face was transformed to joy and sheer simple pleasure, like a boy's. But behind that a strange shadow hid something.

'Lugh's your name, is it?' he said, his harsh deep voice sounding well with its hard Ulster accent, but the hiding shadow was in his voice too. He smiled again and waved his hand at one of the servants who were beginning to move about again.

'Come and sit down with us,' he went on. 'Since you have no appointed place and your rank is outside all others, being a bard.'

I smiled at him in answer to his courtesy and undid my brooch, letting my cloak fall to the hay covering the ground in his cubicle. I swung my harp from my back and leaned it carefully against the partitioning wall. We sat down together. The servants he had beckoned brought over the joints of meat and the cheese and buttered loaves and honey-cakes fitting to a feast and replaced the empty flagon lying abandoned a little way away. I thanked the small nobleman and asked his name.

He grinned and tossed his head up in an odd gesture of

irrepressible pride.

'My name's Cuchulain Mac Sualtim, the Sedanta,' he
said. 'And I'm the Champion of Ulster.'

## III

I remember little more of that night. I don't think I drank
very much, although the mead flowed as freely as it should
on Samhain Eve and Cuchulain had brought two amphorae
of Roman wine which he shared with all. I remember being
merry, not with drink since I hadn't drunk enough, but with
relief at being in a safe place again and out of reach of the
Queen. I didn't think about the Curse: Cavath had said she
had not Cursed me, but perhaps she would do so later when
I thought I was safe. There was no telling what the Queen
would do next.

There was another reason for being merry: it was the relief
of walls and human warmth after the great wildness of the
forests and bogs, where the gods have strange faces and do
not care about men, where the Goddess is if you look for her.
I had been naked, like an ant on the hills – it is not a pleasant
feeling. I think no one quite realizes what it is to be outside
the protection of a clan, thrown out of the place where you
belong so that you have no anchor. Until it happens to you,
you cannot understand it. And there is no way of protecting
yourself against that feeling of nakedness without a clan,
though in time you grow used to it. In time you even prefer
it, to be without the restrictions of kinship and the family.
But even so, the world is a far colder place.

And so that evening's feasting passed in a bright haze of
relief: I talked and laughed and drank and danced a hunting
dance of Connaught for them, but I can only remember
flashes of clarity between the blurs.

Cuchulain introduced me to his wife, Emer. Her hair was
thick, rich brown, the colour of the skin of a chestnut and

her skin creamy with a faint tinge of tan. Her eyes were deep set and brown and her face long and strong-boned – there was strength there, in the slight unevenness of the features, in the slightly over-wide mouth, in the firm chin that would probably stick out when she grew older. Emer was never a beautiful woman but, like her husband, she was one you would notice in the middle of a crowd of fair-haired beauties. I don't even remember clearly what the rest of her looked like, I was so fascinated by her face. I know I stared at her for a long time, while her husband got himself drunker without showing a drop of it. I think I was thinking of the beginning of a song for her. She noticed my stare and instead of blushing as most women would, she smiled and said,

'Will you be singing for us, Lugh?'

I was very aware of voices that night. Hers was unusually deep for a woman. The same colour as her hair, I thought, slightly drunkenly.

'For you, Emer, I'll sing any time,' I answered. She smiled again and turned her head away.

Cuchulain was spending most of his time laying bets on the races and contests for the next day, when he wasn't dancing or breaking up fights between his tribesmen and others. Emer asked Gennan Bright-Face over and introduced us: he was Cavath's youngest son, a quiet smooth-faced man with eyes like his father's. He was pleasant and ambitious and high up in the Druid priesthood, and he was frighteningly intelligent. He did not question me about Connaught, but I knew he would later on, perhaps the next day or the day after. It is the Druid's way. Although he was still quite young his hair was already greying: it made him look strange, in his dull blue tunic and cloak.

Another time I remember craning my head up from where I was lying comfortably full length on the hay and watching Cuchulain deep in argument with an ageing warrior: the man had a fiercely scarred face that reminded me of one of Dalaigh's hunting-dogs especially as his eyes were so light a brown as to be almost yellow. I asked Emer who it was and she told me he was Laere the Victorious, one of the men with whom Cuchulain had quarrelled that spring.

They were deep in argument now, and Emer watched anxiously. Laere had his hands on his hips while Cuchulain leaned forward to tap him emphatically on the chest, his dark face vivid with argument.

'That's all very well, Cuchulain,' growled Laere, 'but he did run off with the King's woman, and his brothers helped him. What would you do if a man ran off with Emer?'

'I'd kill him, of course,' said Cuchulain. 'But it wouldn't happen. Anyway, I'm not talking about that.'

'Then you should be. It's a serious matter. When I was a young man the King's woman was the King's woman and no man even looked at her, let alone ran off with her. It's against all custom, doing a thing like that. It'll encourage these impetuous youngsters to snatch other men's wives if Conor lets the sons of Usnach get away with stealing Deirdre. It's against all custom.'

'That's not the *point*, man! I say we need them.'

'Need them? What for? What about yourself?' he laughed deep in his chest. 'That's the first time I've ever heard you modest, Cuchulain. Why do we need the sons of Usnach now? After all . . .'

'Listen!'

'I'm listening.'

'How many powerful men, high nobles, Warriors of the Red Branch did Conor have owing fealty to him before Naisi ran off with Deirdre?'

'Twelve. Why?'

'How many has he got now?'

'Nine. But he's got his sons and all the other nobles . . .'

'I'm talking of men who could hold off an army.'

'An army?'

'Yes. An army.'

'Why?'

'You could and so could Conall, my spear-brother, and Ferghus Mac Roich. Celthair Mac Uthecar, Cethern Mac

54

Fintan, Duvthach the Beetle, Munremar Mac Geirgind and Owen of Fermanagh. And myself of course. That's nine. Now . . .'

'Hold on, Cuchulain, wait! An army? Whose army are you talking about? Leinster's? Tara?'

'Laere, my lands border on Connaught and I have . . . contacts in Cruachan. Ferdia Mac Daire of Domnand – you know the man: he was with Scatha on Skye at the same time as myself and the sons of Usnach and we swore to be spear-brothers – well, he's one of Queen Maeve's chief warriors and he sent a message to me recently. He said the Queen was making alliances with Leinster and Munster and Tara itself and she had sent to Curoi of Kerry as well. But he said she has not consulted Conor of Ulster and nor will she.'

Laere was silent for a while.

'I see,' he said at last, heavily. 'Yes, I see. Well, I'll do my best.'

'If we can just get enough men to agree . . .'

'Have you ever seen Deirdre, Cuchulain?'

'No.'

'I have. And I think, if all Ulster were against him on this matter, Conor would want her back. And Naisi would not let her go.'

'Yes, but if we can get him to agree . . .'

'*If.* Hoy! You over there! Bring me some of that mead. Leave it for the moment, Cuchulain, that's my advice. Besides the seas are closed and Goll the Trader won't come till spring.'

'Yes, and when he does come I'll talk to him.'

Cuchulain intercepted a servant passing with a leather flagon and drank half the contents before handing the bottle to Laere. He wiped his mouth and looked thoughtful and then he sauntered over to me. I sat up straight to give him room to sit down. He plumped into the hay and crossed his legs, tapping with his fingers on his knees. He moved restlessly and finally said, 'Lugh, you're foster-son to Maeve, aren't you?'

'I was.'

'Do you know anything about her alliances?'

I shook my head. 'No. I haven't been in Cruachan much these last few years. First I was training to be a bard and then, most recently, I've been travelling around collecting songs. But she has always hated Ulster because you do not look to her as the Goddess. She'll humble you for that if she can.'

'What is Maeve like?'

I shrugged. I didn't want to talk about it. 'She's a woman. She doesn't think the way a man would.'

'Do you love her?'

I stared at him. He was watching me very closely, trying to judge which side I would support, Ulster or Connaught. Whether I would betray him. Whether the Queen was Goddess in my mind.

'She killed my father,' I said at last. 'In a way she killed my mother. Ever since I have been her foster-son she has tried to break my will, bend my thoughts to hers. If it hadn't been for Iollen Hen sending me away to train for a bard, she would have succeeded. I would have been her creature as completely as . . . as Ailell was.'

'And now?'

'I don't know.'

He left it at that.

That was early on in the feast: later things became more indistinct. I did wonder if I would be asked to sing and was glad that I wasn't. I listened to the King's Bard, Athairne, and thought he was good, but not as good as some I had heard. The food was plentiful and surprisingly well-cooked: it was Conor who provided it at Samhain as he did at Beltain, Bron Trograin and Oimell and I suppose it was a point of pride with him for it to be as good as possible. But really I was too tired to notice it. In the end I simply curled myself into a corner of the cubicle where people wouldn't trip over the length of my legs and went to sleep, with the feast roaring on heedlessly all around me. I don't know who it was put my cloak over me against the colder part of the night, when the feast would have drowned itself in its own drink, but I suspect that it was Emer. It was the sort of thing she would do.

# IV

The Ulstermen had started their feast of Samhain the night I killed the King and they had acted out the Killing of the King on the Eve of Samhain, before I arrived. There were three days more to go: they were spent in sports and alliance-making; in law-suits at which Cavath presided and gave his judgement according to the Brehon Laws and tried to decide which cows belonged to whom without starting yet another feud. I no longer regretted that I had not studied to become a Druid: the power may be greater, but I have never had a great interest in law. Conor's courts were interesting because they were the only courts in Erin where the Druid's Riddle-speech was not used for the arguing of cases, but plain ordin-ary Irish. It was very strange to hear the Druids defending and prosecuting quoting their laws in their special tongue and then translating into Irish for Conor's benefit. You could see they didn't like it, but Cavath must have given his approval or else not even Conor could have made the change.

Apart from the marriage-making and trading that went on, what interested most of the nobles, as at Cruachan, were the contests of skill and speed and their gambling on the result. Most of them took part but out of all of them the one I remember is Cuchulain – for needless to say, Cuchulain entered every one of the contests. To his great disgust he didn't win everything and on several occasions Cavath or Gennan had to intervene to stop him attacking the man who had beaten him. He bet enormous sums and frequently lost, but it didn't matter because he was the richest man in Ulster – some said he was richer than the King.

I did not take part in the big running race three times round the outside of Emain. I remember him at the starting place: it was spitting and he was squelching his bare toes in the mud and laughing at Munremar who was complaining that everyone would slip in it. Munremar was a fat man whose pleasures were fighting, feasting and women in that order, and there was more of him to be damaged if he fell. Cuchulain won the race and had a fight with Munremar who accused him of tripping him up. He won the fight too, but Cavath insisted that they make it up again afterwards.

A few moments later Cuchulain came over to where I was standing watching with Emer. A slave-girl brought him some ale to quench his thirst and when he had finished drinking he wiped his hands on his red tunic and grinned up at me.

'Why didn't you run in the race, Lugh? Afraid of being beaten?'

I smiled. 'No,' I said, 'but I don't have very much to gamble with and I'm not a man to run without some stake on it.'

'If that's the only reason . . . I'll wager you a song for a bracelet that I can beat you.'

'A song for a bracelet?'

'That's right.'

'Done!'

I took off my soft leather boots and hung my cloak over one of the poles of Emain's home-pasture, where the boys of Emain would fight a hurley match that afternoon. We walked up towards Emain and Cuchulain announced the contest and Gennan agreed to judge it. Ferghus put a bet of two cows on Cuchulain and Duvthach took it and then most of the nobles who had run in the race were placing bets and making jokes about the stake I had with Cuchulain.

At last we stood behind the log which was the starting line, Cuchulain jumping up and down and leaning forward as Gennan told us to get ready. He shouted and we were off, once round Emain on the cleared space around the walls. I ran at full speed all the way: I had thought I would win

easily because of the combination of my long legs and fresh-
ness, whereas Cuchulain was small and had already run in a
race.

My eyes watered from the wind and light rain and the
ground was soft underfoot: I could feel it going through the
gaps between my toes as I ran and it slowed me down
because I did not want to slip. For Cuchulain was much
faster than I had thought he would be and he was lighter
than I: he didn't seem to have noticed the other race he had
run and his breathing was hardly deeper. He kept me close
and though sometimes I would draw ahead and sometimes
he would there was no great difference between us.

We rounded a sharp curve in the cleared space and there I
slipped. It was only for a moment and I soon recovered my
balance but it gave Cuchulain an edge. I was not going to be
beaten for I would be remembered for it. I ran to burst my
lungs and still Cuchulain was just a little in front of me and
I could hear the shouts and the yelling from the group of
people round the finishing line and the screeching from the
women and Cuchulain was just a yard ahead of me now, just
a yard. I sprinted and I had not thought I could run any
faster, but I must have, for we crossed the line together, as we
had started.

We slowed down, panting and walking to ease the cramp,
while Gennan consulted with bystanders and found them
about equal on who had crossed first.

Cuchulain pushed back his hair.

'Whew!' he said happily. 'That was a race! Pity you
slipped.'

'Otherwise I would have beaten you.'

'Not at all.'

Gennan came up to us then and said that he would call it
a draw if we were agreeable.

'Now wait a moment,' protested Cuchulain. 'I wagered a
song with him. I still want that song.'

Gennan looked at me.

'He can have his song,' I said. 'But that would make everyone say that I lost.'

59

'What was your side of the bet?' Gennan asked Cuchulain.

'A bracelet, but . . .' Cuchulain was already beginning to look angry. Gennan thought quickly.

'Well, if he sings the song and you give him the bracelet as a present, will that settle it?'

I was agreeable and after some argument, so was Cuchulain. When I had rubbed most of the mud off my legs and fetched Fiorbhinn from the Royal Hall I went away alone to think of a song to sing for Cuchulain. It had to be praise-song to give him some reason for making me a present and I am not good at praise-song. But I remembered him in the chariot-race, earlier that morning, in his chariot at the start holding the reins in his teeth as he tied back his unruly hair. That too was three times round the dun and there were two chariots that crashed as they turned, half-killing one of the drivers. Cuchulain came charging in past the winning-post, well ahead of anyone else: he had run along the pole as he came into the home stretch and passed the post standing with one foot on each of the ponies' backs. In the end, sitting behind a storeshed, I made that into a praise-song – more interesting than the usual ones about battle-winning and overflowing generosity. It was the first song I ever made about Cuchulain.

And so, in the evening, when the nobles of Ulster were feasting again in the Royal Hall, I picked up my harp and stepped forward into the central area of the hall and sat by the fire, on the spread skin for the bards and harpers: it was a pale brown, spotted fawnskin, edged with black. I settled Fiorbhinn on my lap and waited for quiet, feeling the tension and the pleased thrill of anticipation. They soon settled down to listen, while I stroked the carving of the forepost and checked the tuning of the strings. Then I struck the first chord and began to sing.

> '. . . like the coming of storm, like a river in flood,
> the hooves thunder in the walls of Macha,
> a song to remember in the halls of Conor,
> earth spraying from the iron-shod wheels,

broken by the beating hooves,
     ahead of the crowd like the stag before the herd,
     like the Champion in forefront of battle . . .'

Cuchulain liked it immensely. Conor not so much, though he understood why I was praising Cuchulain and not him. It was quite good, but I have since made better songs, even praise-songs. I was pleased with it at the time and Cuchulain said he would give me the bracelet gladly. Athairne, Conor's bard, watched me shrewdly for most of the rest of the feasting, as though he saw in me possible competition. But he was a mean man, was Athairne, and in the end he went too far and Conor killed him. That was in the future and now his eyes narrowed angrily when I finished and went back to Cuchulain's cubicle and Cuchulain presented me with one of his plain gold bracelets. When I put it on it was still warm from his wrist.

That simple praise-song was the beginning of my reputation in Erin. I had sung my own works before, but never in front of a King and the Chief of the Druids. After that people started asking me to sing or make them songs and they paid me for them, mainly in jewellery. Later they began to call me 'the Harper' as though there was no other in Erin.

Cuchulain dominated Emain, through the three days of the feast: he argued with everyone, often about the sons of Usnach, and fought most people at least once; he made advances to every girl there who was under forty and didn't actually squint; feasting in the hall he managed to drink twice as much as anyone else – I have seen him so magnificently drunk he couldn't see straight and yet he never reached the stage where he could no longer stand up. And through all his wild career, Emer watched him: she never tried to hold him back from anything he wanted to do, no matter how dangerous or mad; but sometimes, when Cuchulain once again came to within a hairsbreadth of killing himself, I saw her bite her bottom lip until it welled red.

61

# V

After Samhain passed and winter bit deeply into Ulster, many of the nobles and tribesmen went home to their duns and homesteads to wait out the winter. They all streamed out for days after Samhain, churning the ground about the gate to deep mud until Conor ordered some men of his to put down logs and stones to try and stop the wagons bogging down to their axles. It helped, but not much. Only the Romans know how to build roads properly. Cuchulain hesitated as to whether or not he should stay in Emain Macha or go back to Muirthemne for the winter, in case the Queen attacked. In Erin winter is as much a campaigning season as summer, because it is easier to persuade men to leave their fields and herds to fight in the army, and disease doesn't grip so quickly.

In the end he decided to stay at Emain Macha, partly because he preferred it there, partly because he was the Champion of Ulster, partly because his steward, Rochad Mac Fingal, was entirely dependable and finally because if the Queen did attack then Cuchulain felt he could persuade Conor to bring help more easily if he was at Emain than if he was at Dun Delgan with all his enemies in Emain. Besides, winter at Emain was more bearable than anywhere else.

I stayed at Emain Macha because I had no choice.

As time passed I began to know the men of Ulster, their qualities and loyalties, who was client to whom. Emain was crowded even in winter, for all the greater nobles who stayed kept at least a few of their tribe with them and some slaves. There was a rota for who would provide the food each day according to his wealth and the number of men he had with him: it was the main form of tribute to Conor, apart from fighting for him. Naturally it led to arguments over who owed what: sometimes fights would develop between nobles,

62

and Cavath or Gennan would have to intervene again and arbitrate. Several times when no other Druids or bards were about I was called upon as a trained bard to decide between two quarrelling noblemen. Emain was like a badly-built haystack: outwardly calm and orderly, but inside fermenting and smoking and ready to burn.

In one matter the nobles of Emain were more or less split and it was a dangerous division which could get worse. I could not at first understand all the reasons or the depth of the split, but I soon saw that it centred on Conor and Cuchulain: those two led the two parties of chieftains and warriors and the gap between was widening.

On Cuchulain's side were Laere, Conall Cernach and some of the young men, Ferghus and Cormac Connlonges, King's-son. Conor had with him Owen of Fermanagh, Munremar and most of the older warriors. The two parties spent much of their time circling and watching each other, while Cuchulain thought about the Queen and quietly collected support for something he seemed to intend to do when Goll the Trader arrived in the spring, though what it was I could not find out. But it livened the dark months.

Winter anywhere is always dull. Food is rarely too much problem at first, after the autumn harvest and slaughter of the cattle and sheep and horses not likely to stand the winter. Just after Samhain any dun always smells of smoked meat. During the day there are horses to see to and exercise, weapons to clean and practise with, hunting for the pot, training the Boys' troop and watching them play hurley, women to chase. In the evenings there is little to do but listen to a bard or play fidchell and make eye-play or love with the woman you are chasing.

As winter deepened and widened and the roads from Emain became mud-bound and impassable I came to know Cuchulain and his friends better. I shall always be grateful to Cuchulain for that: he gave me the hospitality and warmth of his clan and the people he knew, quite simply because he saw that no one else would.

Cuchulain's spear-brother, Conall Cernach, one of the

nine remaining greatest chieftains, was spending part of the winter in his hunting-runs and part in Emain, because he was carrying on a feud with Daire Mac Fachtna of Cooley. Conall and Laere were Cuchulain's best friends and allies: apart from the previous spring, when Bricru Poison-Tongue had managed to make them quarrel over the Championship of Ulster and the matter had had to be resolved by Curoi of Kerry because Cavath would not arbitrate in a case which concerned his great-nephew, they had always stayed firm together. I saw Conall when he rode into Emain in late winter after a frost had made the roads passable for a few days: I remember him chiefly because of his extraordinary colouring. Apart from that he seemed a pleasant enough warrior, second only in skill to Cuchulain. In fact he was the stuff good Hero-tales are made of – strong, brave, honourable and something of a fool. He was very big and well-built with a mass of fair wavy hair. On his right cheek he had a great strawberry splash of a birthmark which seemed to have drained all the colour from the other side of his face, so that its left side was as white as a maiden's breast with the eye above it bright blue; the cheek with the birthmark was mostly dark red and the eye above was black as the back of a beetle. The Druid who had inspected him at birth when his father wanted to know if he should be exposed or not, said that it was a lucky sign: a sign he would survive.

I went hunting a great deal with Cuchulain and his charioteer, Laegh Mac Riangabra. The sons of Riangabra were generally accounted the best charioteers in Erin and it was typical of Cuchulain that he should have as his charioteer, the man accounted the best of the sons of Riangabra. All his brothers except the youngest, Gaiar, drove the chariots of the greatest men of Ulster. Gaiar was still training with Laegh in Dun Delgan. Laegh went well with Cuchulain: he was tall and very thin with orange hair he held back with the charioteer's yellow band. His face was a mass of freckles and generally grinning gap-toothedly. He had lost one of his dog-teeth when a rogue stallion kicked him a glancing blow on the face. He was a tremendous joker, considered horses pleasanter companions than men and was invariably exceedingly rude to Cuchulain. They were the best of friends.

In the evenings I played my harp to the hall, or just softly to Emer and Cormac Connlonges, one of Conor's many sons, though he was legitimate. I liked him best of all Cuchulain's friends. He was a man of average height and silky yellow hair and a face which a woman would, I think, consider handsome; he was strangely modest and utterly honourable and he loathed his father. He sometimes stammered slightly, but in matters where he felt his honour was involved he was immovable and even more unpredictable than Cuchulain. But he was not an easy man to remember – he didn't stand out in the crowd. In important matters he preferred to follow than to lead.

We played interminable games of fidchell, Cuchulain and I: he was a good player though usually too reckless. But the other great amusement of the winter-time, the reason why so many babies are born nine months later, held unusually little attraction for me. Although several of the girls of Emain made it quite clear that I was not unpleasing to them, I followed up none of the chances for one reason: I preferred to be with Emer.

I have never quite understood what happened between us. I think it was not love as I would sing it in a song set to music. There was love between her and Cuchulain: they would sit quite quietly together, playing fidchell or not doing anything, the black and the chestnut heads close together and nothing at all passing between them. They were happy just being together.

This was something I could not break and had no wish to. Yet there was an odd attraction between Emer and myself: it was that which had made me stare at Emer's strong, intelligent face when we first met on Samhain Eve, so that I still have no idea what she was wearing that night. And after a while I saw it was the same way with her.

Often in the long winter evenings, when it is not yet late enough to go to sleep and far too dark to do anything outside,

Emer would come and sit near me when I practised my harp-playing in the corner of Cuchulain's cubicle. She said very little – unlike most women she never said anything unnecessarily, though we would sometimes discuss the songs in Poet-speech, which she had learnt from her father who was a Druid – but she would more often simply put her chin on her drawn-up knees and stroke the soft wool of her russet-coloured dress or turn the bracelets on her wrists. Sometimes Cuchulain would be there too, but usually he was too restless to sit still as Emer did and listen to my music.

So I played songs for her and practised my fingering and the positioning of my hands to stop the strings which is just as important as the plucking of them, and far more difficult. She gave me intelligent criticism and gravely discussed the origin of this or that allusion in this or that poem or the history of this or that king. She was the daughter of Forgall Manach, Druid Forgall the Wily, whom Cuchulain killed when he fought to take possession of her. Their wedding has become a byword for a particularly bloody series of battles, for Forgall's sister, herself a Druidess, also tried and failed to take back Emer from the husband she had chosen. Cuchulain added Forgall's lands to his own afterwards, though, of course, they were still Emer's.

It was about a moon after Samhain or perhaps a little more. I had been practising as usual on Fiorbhinn, though the practising had degenerated into little wanderings of my fingers as I gazed through the wall of the Royal Hall.

'What are you thinking about, Lugh?' Emer asked. We were quite private since there were only the two of us in the cubicle and I generally pulled the yew screen across the front of the cubicle so that others would be less likely to listen to the mistakes I made. The screen was half-drawn across now and Emer was in her favourite position, seated on a wolfskin trophy of Cuchulain's, her knees drawn up to her chest, her arms folded across her knees and her chin rested on her arms. There was a smelly little lamp hanging on the pillar behind her and so the cubicle wasn't as dark as it would have been otherwise.

66

I pulled out three notes from the short strings by my head, looked at the way they fell together and let them die away.

'Nothing much.'

She smiled. 'That's what Cuchulain says when he's wondering what some man or other would be like to fight against.'

Another deeper note came, all by itself.

'Well then,' I said slowly, 'I'm thinking about Connaught.'

'Ah.'

The note seemed lonely and I played two more to keep it company. Something in the way she said nothing and yet waited drew me on to say more.

'I was thinking of the Queen, the Queen of Connaught. And wondering . . .'

'Wondering what?'

I smiled.

'Nothing,' I said, listening to the beginnings of a tune.

'What's she like, the Queen of Connaught?' Emer asked, after a pause.

I looked up in surprise. It was strange to me then that anyone should not know what she looked like. She was such an all-pervading part of my life, the hate and fear of her so filled my mind, especially at night, that it seemed strange she should not likewise fill everyone else.

'She was beautiful once,' I said. 'You can still see it. She's like a Queen in a song. Long-faced and golden-haired and she has the figure of a young woman, though she has grown men for sons. Beautiful. Yes, she was beautiful. Now . . .'

(Now? asked the harp).

'. . . Now she must put a paste of flour on her face to hide her wrinkles and paint her eyelids with green malachite and chew berries to make her lips red again. She's *old*, Emer, old! She's like a fruit that has become rotten, starting from the stone at her centre and spreading, until now it has reached her face. Old she is, for all that she is the Goddess-on-Earth. She's passed the three stages of women, from the Girl to the Woman, and the Crone is what she is now . . .'

I was silent and played a piece from some lament. It was

67

the ending and it went up in a wail where the Red Washer at the ford cries out the last 'Ochone!'

'I chew berries to make my lips red,' said Emer thoughtfully. I looked up at her, slightly surprised at the irrelevancy.

'But Emer, you're not *old*.'

'No.'

'Ach, and it's not just that. I remember when I was a little boy and she quite young, she was still the same. You couldn't see it in her face then, but if you dared to look into her eyes, you could see it there and her eyes have never changed. They're blue, dark blue and there are fine veins of white coming from the pupil like . . . like lace laid across velvet . . . like a foam on the surface of a summer sky . . .'

Emer smiled. 'You hate her and yet you make her sound very lovely.'

'She was lovely. My hating her can't change that.'

'Why do you hate her?'

'Why?' I had never really thought of that before. It had seemed as natural for me to hate the Queen as it was for me to love listening to any kind of music, from the harping of bards to the piping of shepherd boys. But it was a hate that had grown slowly from the awe of a small boy, always conscious of the Queen's eyes, to what I felt now.

'Why? I fear her. In a way I always did. And then, when my mother died a little after I became a man and she told me, the day before she died, who my father was and why they called me "Mac Romain" – the son of the Roman, I had a better reason to hate the Queen . . .'

Still Emer said nothing. I played something heartrendingly sad, a little snatch from the story of Suibhne the Wild Man of the Woods. But Emer was a woman who called your secrets out of you. I laid my hands along the strings and they ceased their singing:

There was a cattle-plague in Connaught: the cattle were dying, the harvest was poor and it looked as if there would be a great famine. And so the Queen of Connaught, who had been engaged in hunting down a merchant for whom

68

she had curses and hatred, sacrificed to the gods and went at last to consult the Old Mother of the Sidhe of Rath Cruachan, Fedelm the Seeress. The Seeress listened to her complaints and consulted the Earth-Goddess, and what she told the Queen as she stood in her chariot and Fedelm sat on a catskin in a glade near the sidhe, was this:

'One of the Queen's kin, a woman and a virgin, must go to Brugh na Boyne, the Hill of Angus. Mac ind Og, the Young Lad, and offer her virginity to the Goddess by lying with the first man who comes to her.'

So the Queen's youngest sister, Devorgill, who was still a virgin, went to Brugh na Boyne in the Queen's chariot, wearing the Queen's robes. She was a tall girl, dark-haired, with the Queen's long face and she was, in her way, beautiful, but she was young and afraid, though she was a Priestess and knew it must be done.

The Druid of Brugh na Boyne met her and she spent that day in purification and then in the evening, they opened the chamber of Brugh na Boyne, the long chamber where the shaft of light strikes on Midsummer Day when it rises from the Land of Silk in the East and so they know when to light the fires. And she stayed there, wrapped only in marten-fur, alone in the shadows for half of the night.

At last she heard angry noises outside and she went to the mouth of the chamber and looked out over the spiral-decorated kerbstone. There were torches on the ninefold ring of stones round the Brugh, marking the Inner Sanctuary. The Druid was standing there, protesting, in his many-coloured robe, but he had only a boy holding a torch with him. There was a man crouching by the decorated kerbstone, close to the mouth of the chamber where Devorgill stood, breathing fast and watching.

Just outside the circle of stones there were four of the Queen's men with their swords drawn.

'You may not come here,' said the Druid. 'This is Brugh na Boyne, the Holy Place of Angus Og.'

'We have orders from the Queen to capture that man and bring him to her in Cruachan. He's a Roman, a traitor.'

The Druid of the Brugh was an old man who preferred his calculations about the sun to speaking with warriors. He looked unhappily at the man the Queen's warriors were hunting.

'Is this true?' he asked.

The Roman stood up. Devorgill saw in the light of the flames that he was not tall, but he had a nose which reminded her of an eagle. He was wearing the ragged remnants of a tunic and fur cloak and he had only a knife in his hand, but he stood up straight.

'By the Unconquered Sun!' he said, 'I say that I came back to the Queen of my own will and although I am a Roman, I am no traitor.'

'The Queen wants him. She has cursed any who give him shelter.'

The Old Druid looked from the men to the Roman.

'Is this a sanctuary?' asked the Roman.

'You are standing by the Brugh of Angus Og, the God of Love.'

The Roman looked round swiftly and breathed in.

'Then I demand sanctuary,' he said.

'The Queen is the Goddess,' said her lieutenant. 'She is supreme. The Sanctuary has no protection.'

The Roman saw he could run no further and he dropped into a fighting-crouch, with his knife ready.

'Well then,' he said.

The warriors started forward.

In that moment Devorgill stepped out of the Brugh and shouted, 'Wait!'

The men stopped. Devorgill recognized the chief of them as Naiman of the Slaughter and as she came through the gap between the kerbstones, into the pools of torchlight, she said, 'I am Devorgill, sister to Maeve, the Queen of Connaught. I am Priestess to the Goddess and I am come here to offer my body to the Goddess and ask her to stop the plague that is killing our cattle. Will you intrude on the rites of the Goddess, Naiman of the Slaughter?'

Naiman stepped back a pace and brought his fist to his forehead.

'Leave us,' said Devorgill.

'But the Queen . . .'

'For this night and for this rite, I am the Queen, I am the vessel of the Goddess, I am the Goddess-in-flesh until this matter is completed. And this man is the first man who has come to the Brugh this night and so he must be the Man Chosen.'

'The curse . . .'

Devorgill had always been shy, in the shadow of her sister the Queen. But now she half-raised her hand and chanted, 'Naiman of the Slaughter, if you do not go immediately, leave this place for the rest of this night, then I will curse you and all your families and clans and cattle, to the very land that you hold, so that it shall be withered and barren and sterile from now until the gods die; so that you and yours shall be wiped from the face of the earth; so that the blue sea shall rise and cover you, the green earth open and swallow you and the blue heaven of stars fall down and crush you . . .'

Naiman and all his men turned tail and fled; even the Druid backed away. Only the Roman stood watching her, not knowing what to expect, but his eyes kindling with interest as the torches picked out the curves of her half-naked body. Devorgill came and took him by the arm and led him into the Brugh where a bed of soft skins was prepared for them. There they made love, and so Devorgill conceived a child.

Afterwards they lay side by side in the half-darkness: there was one torch so placed that it shone along the passage lined with high flat stones and into the chamber where they lay. They could see the way the stones of the Brugh's roof were laid together, so they fitted perfectly without need of support for the dome; the three chambers with their big stone bowls filled with ashes.

'I've never seen any place like this,' said the Roman in a whisper.

71

'It was made by the Fomor, the people who ruled Erin before the Tuatha de Danaan – they built the Sun-Rings in the Island of the Mighty, Britain, where you Romans rule now.'

'Tuatha de Danaan?'

'The People of Danu, the Great Goddess. They held this land before us, after they took it from the Fomor: they were a great people and their gods are our gods. They ruled Britain too, long ago.'

'You are the sister of Maeve?' asked the Roman after a pause.

When he said that, using the Queen's name which only women and her lovers are allowed to say, Devorgill knew why the Queen wanted him. She knew of a lover the Queen had had years before. He had been a young man, a merchant from Rome, people said. At that time the Queen had only lately come to her Queenship and she was not yet as she became later.

'Yes,' was all Devorgill said.

'And your name is Devorgill?'

'Yes.'

She asked him his name and he told her and then she asked him why he had come back to Erin when he knew the Queen would kill him. It took him a long time before he answered.

'When I first came to Hibernia – Erin – I was a scout, a spy for the Roman Governor of Britain, Agricola. He wanted information on the political strength of Erin and the likelihood of a pro-Roman faction or rebellion. So I volunteered because I knew some Irish and I had contacts with the Greek half of the Veneti traders to Erin. So I came and observed the situation in Erin and when I reached Cruachan, Maeve fell in love with me and I with her. We became lovers.'

He sighed. 'I was a fool. But she was beautiful and I loved her.' He went on, 'But then when I was going to leave, she asked me to be her King and I knew what that meant. I am a Roman. Romans are not ruled by their wives, or if they are then they lose their honour. And I could not betray Agricola.

So I refused and explained why. And she no longer loved me, she hated me, she tried to kill me and so I fled to Dun Delgan where Chief Sualtim, the Sedanta, sheltered me until the ship came for me.'

'I knew of that,' said Devorgill. 'The Queen was raging for a long time afterwards. She asked the Sidhe-folk to look out for you in case you ever came back and to tell her if you did.'

'So that's how she knew. I did wonder. I don't know why I came back. I was still in love with her; I thought perhaps I could see her again now, that after all these years her anger would have had time to die down.'

Devorgill shook her head.

'Maeve can either love or hate. When she loves, she absorbs. When she hates she destroys. She is the Goddess in the third aspect, she is She Who Intoxicates.'

'I know. Now,' said the Roman. After a moment he turned to her and said, 'Listen now, Devorgill, I have fulfilled what . . . I was supposed to, haven't I? The Goddess is satisfied?'

Devorgill smiled.

'You have fulfilled, yes, Chosen Man,' she said.

'Then I can go. Before that man – what's-his-name – Naiman of the Slaughter can come back with more men.'

'No.'

'Why not?'

'Because you must not leave the Inner Sanctuary before dawn.'

'But . . .'

'And besides, I know Naiman. He will already have surrounded the place.'

'I see,' said the Roman slowly. 'Yes. Devorgill, you know the Queen as she is now. Which should I choose? To be taken back to Cruachan a prisoner – or to fight . . .'

Devorgill wept then and the Roman comforted her. They made love again and talked of other things between small sleeps, until the night passed. Dawn came and the torches around the Brugh paled into wilted flowers in the grey light of an antumn day. It was raining outside.

Devorgill wrapped the marten-cloak around her and went along the passage to the opening of the Brugh. She saw beyond the ring of torches and stones fifty men, armed and waiting. The Druid was coming to take down the torches: he hesitated when he saw the men, but he could no longer stop them without a curse and now that the rite had been accomplished the Queen was all-powerful again.

He and his helpers took down the torches quickly and retired into their small rath on the Mound of the Druid, near to Brugh na Boyne. Devorgill went slowly back to where the Roman still lay, watching her. The daylight lit up the spirals carved on the walls. He sat up as she came to him; she picked up his dagger and put it silently into his hand.

He dressed himself and came out of the Brugh, leaping over the kerbstone and charging into the middle of the men, just as the sun came up through the clouds and the rain stopped.

Two men held Devorgill to stop her from killing herself. The Roman killed three of them with his dagger, before they bore him down and cut off his head. Naiman took the head back to the Queen at Cruachan, along with Devorgill in the chariot. The Queen put the head on a spear by the Cave of Cruachan and her pet crows fed on it, and used the Roman's black hair to line their nests.

'. . . And that was the manner of my begetting,' I said. 'Years later when I had become a man, the Queen commanded Devorgill my mother to marry one of her chief nobles. My mother died the next year, after giving birth to a still-born baby girl. She told me that tale as she lay dying of fever in her womb. So you see why I hate the Queen, my foster-mother.'

That was the first time I had told the full story to anyone, although most people knew I had been fathered by a Roman. I looked up at Emer and found that she was staring thoughtfully at my harp. The shadows of her face moved with the lampflame and my throat suddenly felt tight, my mouth dry.

'A strange tale,' she said softly after a while. 'It could be chanted by a bard to the sound of the harp and told of Ioruath or Lugh Long-Spear himself.'

'No,' I answered, making discordant noises by twanging the harp any old how. 'No, for Romans do not make good material for songs.'

I stopped the strings and bent closer, playing a soft little tune with my fingernails. It had a fine sound, but I played it on the long strings so that it had a warm brown feeling to it. My thoughts bubbled and I began to make the tune into a proper song which had been waiting for its release for a long time. It came out easily, seeming to put itself together and grow like a foxglove from the look of Emer's face under the lamp. I sang and I sang a song that I think was one of the best I have made. It was about Emer.

When I had finished I felt oddly embarrassed and my legs cramped. I put aside the harp and stood up. The lamp hanging above her head was guttering and sending out clouds of smoke and stink. I felt hot.

I went over to the lamp and leaned over her to trim the wick. When the flame was steady and clear again something made me look down at her.

I met her eyes, set deep in the hollows of her head and suddenly loved the way her face upturned to look at me, loved the curve of her neck to her collarbones and the way the tendons moved as she swallowed. I wanted her then, ached for her as I have rarely ached for a woman. For a moment I stood, looking at her. Her mouth moved, opening a little. I began to bend towards her, reaching for her to kiss her . . .

Her eyes flicked to the side, looking through the gap between the half-open screen and the pillar. She stiffened and came suddenly to her feet, gathering her legs under her and jumping up. The moment broke and I realized in a cold way that we would never come so close again. Then I too looked into the hall.

Cuchulain was standing by the fire with a strange expression on his face. He was standing as though he had

75

stopped in mid-stride, staring at us. Emer ran to him and kissed him and he relaxed from his rigidity and the expression left his face completely to be replaced by his joyful smile. But it had been there and I could not put a name to it. I followed Emer out of the cubicle, covering my harp.

'There you are, Lugh,' said Cuchulain. 'How about a song?' Was there any suspicion in his voice? Had he seen anything or did he only suspect? And yet I had done nothing. Nothing had passed between Emer and myself except a look and the still-born beginnings of a kiss. Did he suspect what would have happened if he hadn't come in at that moment?

I was about to say that I didn't mind playing for them, but I suddenly found that I did mind. I had no wish to sing any more that night and burn the flower, the little foxglove I had made out of the shadows on Emer's face. Emer was ignoring me completely and Cuchulain had his arm around her in a strangely possessive way.

'No,' I said.

'Why not, Lugh?' asked Emer in dangerously normal tones.

I made a gesture.

'My hands are tired.'

It was a lie since I can play for a whole evening without stopping and my fingers will only ache a little. Both Cuchulain and Emer knew it. Cuchulain's eyes narrowed, but he only went into his cubicle with Emer, not quite pushing past me.

I turned away, hearing their voices murmuring and then the over-loud slam of the screen. No, they would not want my presence tonight.

I went to the two vats by the door. The mead vat was only half-full and there was something floating in it. I went over to the other one and scooped up a beakerful of ale with one of the beakers lying beside it. I finished it quickly and decided it was not very good, being weak and sour, but that I might as well get myself a bit drunk. It was something to do after all.

In the rest of the hall everyone was either asleep with their cubicles closed or playing fidchell. Cormac was playing fidchell with his father the King, which was surprising since they usually avoided each other. Conall Cernach was not there and Ferghus was away doctoring a horse with colic.

I turned back to the ale-vat, wishing I felt sleepier. Someone came in through the door, opening it for himself as the door-keeper was asleep. I turned to see who it was and found myself facing a small fair-haired girl wrapped in a big blue cloak. I recognized her as being one of the ones who had looked on me with pleasure. I smiled at her now, thinking with sudden loneliness on Cuchulain and Emer behind the red yew of their screen. The girl smiled back in a half-surprised, half-speculative way, came and stood beside me and took the beaker from my hand. She filled it with yellow mead from a leather jug she had under her cloak. She drank some and then gave the cup to me, saying, 'Drink. It's from the King's own store.'

I drank, noticing the way the drops of rain had caught in her hair and on the fibres of her cloak. She brushed her body past me and went over to the King's cubicle, swinging her hips. I remembered her then as the woman the King had had his attention on during the feast of Samhain. It must have been he who gave her the big blue cloak. She bent and put the jug down beside the King. She had her back to me, but I could imagine the way her breasts would move under her dress. Hers were bigger than Emer's.

The King didn't even look at her or thank her, though Cormac did, absently. She turned quickly and came back to me, her hips still swinging, but pouting a little at the lips. I smiled at her again. The mead she had given me was far stronger than the mead usually in the vat, but I didn't have to drink it to know what she wanted.

Fiall and I got very wet before we found a place to be private.

## VI

The next day it was not so wet, though the ground was marshy. I was crossing in front of the Speckled House when Cuchulain came towards me from the Royal Hall. In the light of day, however cloudy, I could see no suspicion at all on his face, although there was a strange guardedness about it, a thoughtfulness, as though, for once in his life, Cuchulain wasn't quite sure what to do. His two beautiful hunting dogs were trotting at his side, looking gravely eager.

'I'm going hunting, Lugh,' he said. 'Will you come?'

'Surely,' I answered immediately. I felt oddly constrained. Cuchulain went past me and collected his hunting spears from the Speckled House. Then I followed him out of the dun, round the mud made by the chariots and many feet going in and out and across to the horse pen. The end of the green closest to the dun had been fenced off for the horses and the rest was being used by the Boys' Troop for hurley. The horses and ponies in the pen were ignoring the shrill shouts and yells and all were gathered around the tall, red-headed man standing in the middle of them.

'Hey Laegh!' shouted Cuchulain as we went towards the green. 'Have you got them ready?'

'Of course I have, you idle Hound-dog. If it wasn't for me there's many deer would be blessing the fact that the Champion of Ulster doesn't come hunting any more.'

'You're only angry because you're such a bad hunter yourself, Laegh. If you had your way, you'd go hunting wild boar from a chariot.'

'And why not? You could hunt the Great Sow herself from a chariot.'

Cuchulain laughed at that, silently, for his laughter made no noise. The Great Sow is another way of saying the Land of Erin. Cuchulain went on past the horse-pen to where the boys were playing hurley, myself still following. He leaned the spears against a fence post and put his arms comfortably on the top pole.

The boys were bunched around the little wooden ball, all yelling wildly and waving their sticks in the air. One half of them were trying to get the ball into the hole at the other end of the green and the other half were trying to stop them. Their camans thwacked together madly and one boy howled as he was hit on the shins. The mass seemed to be at deadlock.

Cuchulain watched them, smiling broadly. At last the shouting redoubled and one boy burst from the crowd, bouncing the ball skilfully on the end of his caman. He swerved nimbly past two far larger boys and ran close along the fence in the direction of the hole in the ground. Somebody else ran at him from the opposite direction. Cuchulain shouted as the two collided, the other boy going one way and the boy with the ball slithering on his back and coming to a stop at our feet. The ball trickled after him.

Cuchulain looked down on him.

'How many goals have you made, Follamon?' he asked.

The boy made a rueful face and said between his panting, 'None. They're going to win. They got one when they were attacking.'

Cuchulain made 'Ts, ts!' sounds and shook his head. Then with a swift movement, he bent and took the hurley-stick from Follamon's hand and picked up the hurley-ball in his left hand. He tossed it lightly in the air, bouncing it neatly on the end of the caman. Then he knocked the ball up high and as it came down, swung and hit it with one tremendous uncoiling movement which used every muscle in his body. The ball sailed across the field, fell to the ground and rolled gently into the hole. Half the boys cheered wildly and waved their sticks. Cuchulain handed Follamon back his caman saying,

'Next time you see you're going to collide with someone, get rid of the ball. With any luck you'll knock the other man over in the process.'

We went back to the horses as Follamon charged into the mass of boys. Cuchulain's grin had left his face in the sudden

79

way it had. He waved at Laegh, went to his horse and jumped on. Conin was ready to be ridden with two spear-slings hanging down on either side of his back. I made the steed-leap and rode his usual bucking to a standstill.

Without a word Cuchulain handed me a selection of his spears which I slid into their slings. Laegh opened the pen and we rode out in the direction of the forest.

Cuchulain set the pace and we rode hard for some time. At around noon we came to a small glade in the forest which spreads on south, and joins with the forest on the slopes of the Gap of the North. There was a little break in the trees which might possibly have been made by man. There, among the wet mass of last year's bracken and grass, with broken cow parsley and the draggled fibres from willow-herb looking somehow hopeless, Cuchulain yanked his dun riding horse to a standstill. He pulled it round and faced me fully.

'What weapons will you use?' he demanded.

I gaped at him. Conin moved tentatively for the bracken and I checked him automatically.

'*What?*' I said.

Cuchulain made an impatient gesture.

'Which weapons? Spears? Daggers? It's your choice, since it is myself that is challenging you.'

'But . . . why, man?'

He looked at me very slowly. 'Oh, I think you know well enough.'

'You mean . . .?'

'I mean Emer!'

So he had seen something.

'Cuchulain, listen! Nothing happened. Yes, we came near to kissing, perhaps near to making love, but you came in. Nothing happened beyond that, I swear it!'

His face twisted.

'You fool!' he said savagely. 'Do you think I'd care so much if she took a lover to amuse herself? Gods, Lugh! Do you think I haven't done the same thing myself? Oh, I saw something when I came in last night, but it was only the shadow of your two faces close together. It could have been a trick of the light. But she told me herself . . .'

'*Emer* told you?'

Pride fought its way through the pain in his face.

'Of course. But can't you see? It was the way she spoke of you. As if . . . as if she *cared* for you . . .'

I said nothing. What could I say then? My heart was thumping a little too loudly and my hands felt clammy. I had seen Cuchulain in the sword-fighting contests at Samhain which always ended at first blood and not once had he been beaten. He had that rare thing, true genius with the sword. In his hands a sword ceased to be a thing made only of iron, and became a live animal, answering to his will as his hand did. And I knew that his genius was one that extended to any weapon so that he would be as deadly with a spear as he was with a sword and as deadly with the sling hanging at his belt as he was with a spear. It was all bound up in the same understanding. And now he had decided to fight me.

'Cares for me,' I said, hearing my voice oddly thoughtful. 'Perhaps she does. I know that I was attracted to her . . . strongly.'

He made a half-choked sound.

'Maybe she does care for me,' I went on. 'I'm glad that I'm not in love with her. If I were I think that I would go off quietly, far from men, and find myself a bear to fight. Or fall on my sword.'

'Why?'

'Because she would never love me,' I said simply. 'Even if I were able to kill you, though I think I'd need all the armies in Erin to do that, she would follow you to Tir-na-nOg soon after. There would be no way I could have her because she would always belong to you. So it's just as well that there is no love between us.'

In the silence I could hear some bird calling, long and lonely.

'I brought you here to fight you,' Cuchulain said, his voice even harsher and deeper than usual. 'And that is what I am going to do.'

He snatched a spear out of his sling and held it out to me.

'Take it!'
'No.'
'Take it!'
'No.'

His arm dropped and he stared at me.

'Are you afraid?' he demanded, twisting his lip on the word as though it tasted bad.

'I'm not going to fight you, Cuchulain.'

'Yes you are!'

'No.'

'What are you? Some kind of coward? Afraid of being killed?'

No, said a little voice inside my head, only of fighting. Despite the cold and dankness of the air there was sweat prickling under my armpits. Did my fear show on my face?

'I'm not going to fight you, Cuchulain,' I repeated, wondering how my voice could stay so level. His face darkened with rage.

He kicked the horse forward and raised the spear for the thrust.

'Then I'll kill you like a sheep!' he shouted.

I held myself still, waiting. My mouth stretched at the corners as the spear-point quivered; eager, I thought, for the kill and the sweet taste of my life.

'No, you won't kill me, Cuchulain,' I heard myself say with absolute certainty.

The polished iron point wavered, the length of a finger from my chest. I put out my hand and pushed the spear aside.

'You'll never kill a man who won't fight back,' I said, wondering, even as I said it, how I knew with such certainty.

Slowly the spear lowered. Slowly Cuchulain brought the leaf-shaped blue head close to his face and stared at it, breathing heavily through his widened nostrils. He raised his deep eyes to mine and for a moment I thought I saw the shadow behind them, but it hid itself before I could see, or else was only fancy.

'No,' he said wonderingly, 'you're right. I can't.'

Then he put his head back and laughed, shaking with his silent laughter. He finished, swallowed and breathed in and shook his strong wiry hair back from his face, so that it was startlingly black against the chequered blue of his cloak.

'Come!' he said. 'Let's hunt.'

I followed his horse out of the dead wintry glade. I was glad he couldn't see me. I was shaking all over.

We hunted hard all that day and the next, almost into Cuchulain's own lands, but the deer we were after had changed their feeding grounds and we had to go far afield to find them. Cuchulain managed to knock down a swan with a slingstone from a flock that we found rising from a lake. It was still alive when the hounds found it and we picked it up, white against brown of dead bracken. Cuchulain wrung its neck briskly. He was very silent with me.

We doubled back north and found the deer in a small valley of Slieve Cuillen, browsing on the wet winter grass at its head. We let the dogs pick out a fine young stag from the outskirts of the herd, with the velvet still on his horns, making them very soft and young-looking. Cuchulain's dogs separated him from the herd as they scattered for the woods and as he leapt through the woods and slippery leaves of last summer with the dogs giving tongue behind him, Cuchulain and I separated, and rode tight-reined through the trees, spears at the ready.

He turned at bay by a many-boled silver birch. I hauled Conin on his haunches as Cuchulain galloped up and then something made me slide off Conin's back, shouting, 'I claim kill!'

I balanced the smooth haft of the spear in my hand, poised on the balls of my feet. The stag's nostrils flared red and his eyes rolled as he watched me: his flanks were heaving from the chase but he wasn't completely tired out. He would still fight. And Cuchulain would not help me because I had claimed kill and there is no interfering with a man's kill once he has done that.

I dodged to the left, so he readied on that side and then I ran in swiftly and threw at very short range: I found the

83

vein in his neck and the blood gushed. As he went down, still trying to kill me with his hooves, I felt a flash of burning, aching pity of the death of his beauty. One of his tines knocked against my foot as he rolled over in the last death-spasm.

We gralloched it and hung it on a tree-branch to drain that night. Next morning Cuchulain and I slung the carcass across Conin's back, with the swan tied on in front and one of its wings spread over the stag's back. Conin was unhappy but the weight prevented him from rearing and I patted him and gave him some salt. Cuchulain and I took it in turns to ride his dun riding horse, while the two dogs, rather full from eating the offal, trotted along behind. It rained most of the way back to Emain Macha and we reached it in late afternoon. Cuchulain on foot led Conin up the path to the gate which was, as always, a sea of mud. We had left his dun horse in the pen. I squelched through after, looking dully at the way Conin's tail swung, under the splash of white hide. The purer white of the swan's wing, even in the rain, made sharp contrast with the sodden brown of the stag and the emptied look of its belly. It reminded me of the way I had last seen Ailell: bodies collapse without the intestines.

Emer was standing by the gate. As I plodded past her she put out her hand and pulled me to stand before her. She said nothing, waiting for me to speak. Something in her face made me blurt out, 'I nearly fought Cuchulain.'

'I knew.'

'You *knew*?'

'Yes. It had to be . . . brought out in the open. Otherwise it would have festered and poisoned all three of us.'

'You told him on purpose.'

'Of course. How could I have kept it from him? And it is better this way.'

I was quieter now, in answer to her own calmness.

'Emer, if we had fought I am fairly certain he would have killed me.'

She smiled softly and, with an oddly motherly gesture, she pushed back the wet hair from my face and put the strands behind my ears.

'Ah, but then, I didn't think you would fight. Another man, perhaps yes. Most men can fight. But so few of them think before they do it. Not . . . not even Cuchulain.'

She turned and walked away, lifting her russet skirt clear of the mud, her soft leather boots making quiet sucking sounds as she went.


## VII


Winter passed. We had a cold snap just after Winter's Lap which the Romans celebrate as Saturnalia, but it thawed in a week. Conor sacrificed the ewe in milk for Oimell and not long after, spring began returning to the brown litter of last year's leaves until the trees were covered with a fine mist of buds or yellow catkins and men aching with winter-sickness began to feel well again.

I still hunted occasionally with Cuchulain, though Conall Cernach had ridden in during the frost after Winter's Lap. Cuchulain seemed to be ill at ease with me, as though no longer quite sure whether he liked me or not. I think it was because Cuchulain could never be friendly with a man who was afraid and he was not sure whether I had refused to fight with him because I was a coward or not. Cuchulain was always one who liked to be right in his estimation of men; never having felt fear, he suspected and did not understand the emotion in others.

As spring ripened and the roads became more passable, a sense of expectancy began growing in Emain and the tension between the two factions crystallized and became more and more taut-strung. Men would gather in knots to talk and they would break up with seeming nonchalance whenever someone not of their group approached. And as the seas became less stormy and the spr'ng gales abated, the stormy atmosphere in Emain thickened until it was almost palpable. A blind man could see that there was some kind of fighting or trouble brewing – and Cuchulain was a leader in it, whatever it was. But because of the new distance between us, I felt uneasy about asking him questions. Nor did I think he would answer them if I asked.

Then, one day, about two moons after Oimell, I was sitting in the Speckled House checking over my weapons. If there was going to be trouble, I wanted to be ready for it and besides, one way of adding to my small store of credit with King Conor was by fighting creditably. The fact that I loathe fighting unless I am actually in my fighting madness, when I do things I cannot forget afterwards, the fact that I have never become hardened to it, that had nothing to do with the matter. If Conor ever guessed I was afraid – well, I would be finished.

To my annoyance I found a few little specks of rust on my sword. I searched out some silver sand and began cleaning the blade before sharpening it on the stone outside. As I sat down in the doorway, to be in the sun, Cormac Connlonges came up to me, as though going into the Speckled House. I moved aside to let him pass, but he stopped and glanced from me to the sword and back again.

'Sharpening your sword, Lugh?' he asked. I nodded. Then I felt impatient: at last my curiosity got the better of me.

'I'm not a total fool, Cormac. When I see trouble coming in full armour with the speed of a war-chariot, then I sharpen my sword.'

'What do you mean, t-trouble?'

Cormac was no good at dissembling. His honesty shone out of him, even when he was trying to be careful.

I snorted and rubbed energetically at a spot of rust.

'What do I mean, trouble? When Cuchulain leads one party of chieftains and Conor another and the two groups are very very watchful of each other and the air between them gets visibly worse every day. When you know, and I know, that trouble is meat and drink to one Cuchulain Mac Sualtim, chief of the Sedantii, whether he knows it or not, and Conor knows it if he doesn't. What trouble?'

86

Cormac looked thoughtful. Then, seeming to make his mind up about something he leaned on the whetstone and said, 'If there were to be a break between some of the nobles and the King, would you be on the King's side?'

'Wouldn't you?'

'Not in this matter.'

'What is it? A plot? Is somebody bidding for the Kingship?'

Cormac frowned. 'No!'

'Then what?' He still hesitated. 'Cormac,' I said, 'I swear by all the gods, if you tell me what's brewing, it will never go any further until you give the word. But by Lugh Longspear Himself, what is going on?'

Cormac sighed. 'I suppose you might as well know. After Beltain everyone will. When you were in Connaught, did you hear anything of the sons of Usnach and Deirdre?'

I looked up in surprise. Yes, I had heard something, and more recently. Three years ago there had been all sorts of wild rumours flying around Erin about the sons of Usnach and some scandal concerning King Conor's woman. But it had been impossible to get a true tale from anyone who knew for certain.

'I heard something. Nothing I'd believe.'

'It's simple enough. Deirdre was . . . is one of the most beautiful women ever to be born in Erin.'

I grunted. I had heard those words very often before and always about different women.

'She was being brought up to be C–Conor's wife when she was old enough – she was the daughter of Fedlimid the Poet and there was something about a bad omen at her birth. So she was kept very close in a small valley with foster-parents and Levarcham the Druidess to teach her. Naisi Mac Usnach went hunting and came on the valley quite by accident; he saw Deirdre, fell in love with her and she with him and she persuaded him to take her away with him. So he did and his brothers helped and went with him.

'C–Conor chased them all round Erin until at last they went to Prydein, north of the Frontier Road, to King Brude there. Brude gave them shelter, but when he saw Deirdre he wanted her for himself, so he broke the Guest-law and tried to kill Naisi. They escaped and fled west again and now they're living somewhere among the Epidii, on an island. Or at least, that's the message Conall Cernach got from some people who owe him tribute in those islands. So that's what happened with Deirdre and the sons of Usnach.'

It was simple enough. I don't know how many songs there are about that kind of thing.

'So?' I asked.

'So. Few of us in Emain have seen Deirdre, but we all knew the sons of Usnach and they're fine men, and their tribes are good fighters too. Naisi was a particular friend of Cuchulain's when he was with Scatha, the woman-warrior of Skye, though they were never as close as Cuchulain was with Ferdia Mac Daire. But Cuchulain wants them back and so does Conall and Ferghus Mac Roich and myself. So we're trying to persuade Conor to allow them back at least, and perhaps even ask for three Druids to judge the case.'

'What if he refuses?'

Cormac looked unhappy. 'I'm hoping he won't.'

Beltain came closer and the dun buzzed with preparation for the feasting: Beltain is one of the four greatest feasts when all the household nobles and many of their tribesmen come into Emain if they possibly can and not just for the food and drink which Conor supplied from his own lands. They would bring the goods and slaves and cloth and jewellery they had bartered or stolen, as well as women for marriage-agreements. Emain filled up and overflowed, so that the pasture had to be enlarged as usual and the wagons were parked here and there with families fighting over who should get to the water first.

A little before Beltain Cuchulain rode down to Dun Delgan, his stronghold near the coast, to meet Goll the Trader, who came from Britain every year with a load of Roman goods.

Goll was the chief man of the Veneti traders in the Western Seas who were connected with a group of Greek and Phoenecian merchants in the Mediterranean. Although he could have remained in Londinium or Rome or Byzantium if he had wanted to, and left the hard trading to agents, Goll loved to trade and he loved the sea, and so he sailed a ship regularly from Londinium to Prydein and from Prydein to Erin and from Erin back to Londinium. He had arrangements with certain customs officials in the port, which simplified matters since his more valuable goods didn't have to go through customs at all, and he made a vast profit, particularly on the jewellery and the ready-made cloaks and furs.

This was the reason for Cuchulain's great wealth: Dun Delgan was near Baile's Strand which is sheltered and good for loading ships and Cuchulain loaned Goll some of his warriors to guard his pack trains through Erin. The protection of Cuchulain's name made things even easier for Goll. In return for these favours, Cuchulain was paid in some Roman goods and a lot of wine, which he traded with the south after Goll had returned to Britain and the amphorae he had sold were used up. Cuchulain also traded in his own right, selling Goll hunting dogs and metalwork and gold from the hills south of Tara, some of which he got by legitimate trading and some by raiding. Goll would only take a few slaves captured on these raids and those mostly women, because he said he didn't have the right kind of ship and also because he said they fetched a low price in the markets, being difficult to train.

Cuchulain liked to handle the business personally which was why he went down to his dun to meet the trader. A little while later he reappeared on the road to the south, with a smaller man than himself riding beside him on a fat pony, talking cheerily. A string of pack-ponies with Sedantii outriders guarding them stretched out along the road south, such as it was. Cuchulain provided the pack-ponies as well.

The two rode into Emain Macha to the accompaniment of shouts and jokes from the people outside and crowding inside who came to watch. It was all part of Beltain, but Goll the Greek Trader was somehow a man who invited jokes, being the way he was. However, his fantastic exterior hid a merchant who was the terror of the market-place. I never met anyone who got the better of Goll at bargaining, not even Cuchulain.

Goll was a very small squat man with a paunch. His face seemed to have been put together at random by some god in a playful mood and he was missing one eye. The other eye was as black as a cockchafer and seemed to have enough shrewdness for two. His hair had two parallel streaks of white in it and the rest of it was bright red; he was Greek, but he spoke Irish fluently and well, though with a definite accent. Goll generally played the fool – he said it made people less afraid of him and quoted a saying the Romans have about the Greeks: it was his favourite quotation and comes from one of their greatest Hero-tales. '*Timeo Danaos et dona ferentes*' – I fear the Greeks when they bring gifts.

The whole of Emain was turned into a full-blown fair by then and the dun echoed to the baying of dogs, the wailing of slaves and mad bargaining. It seemed unbelievable that one man could be at the centre of it all and still keep his head and drive hard bargains with everyone. Goll loved it. Every time a man approached him with a load of skins or weapons, the light of battle appeared in his one eye and he would settle to beating the man down to as few bars of iron or whatever as may be.

This year, however, Goll spent a great deal of what time was left over from buying and selling, talking with Cuchulain and Cormac and Ferghus.

The day of Beltain came and the dun was strangely quiet, considering the number of people there, though most of the men were out bringing in the cattle from the winter pasture ready for the festival, or building the bonfires for the night on a high point a little way from Emain.

I guessed that I would be asked to sing and so I was checking the tuning of my harp. The only disadvantage with using bronze strings, apart from expense, is that they have a tendency to go flat when the weather becomes warmer.

Cuchulain, with Goll at his side, came up to me, as I sat

with my back against the wall of the Royal Hall. We had hardly spoken while Goll was in Emain; nor had I met Goll, for having no cattle or gold or anything except Conin, Fiorbhinn and what I wore, I had nothing to buy or sell and no reason to trade at all.

I nodded at them both and concentrated on my tuning. They stood watching me for a while in a way that made me nervous until at last, without any preamble, Cuchulain said,

'Lugh, will you make a song for me?'

I raised my eyebrows. 'What kind of song?'

I didn't think that the mere desire to hear my music lay behind the request. It rarely does.

'A song about the sons of Usnach,' said Cuchulain, waiting for my reaction.

I raised my eyebrows higher. 'Oh?'

'Or at least, a song that'll make Conor think twice about them.'

'Why?'

'Because he wants Conor to think twice about them,' said the trader patiently. I looked at him. He was wearing a tunic of orange and blue stripes which clashed with the red of Cuchulain's, and a fine fur mantle, pushed back on his shoulders.

'What have you to do with it?' I asked, not rudely but for curiosity.

The trader shrugged. 'I provide the transport.'

'And I pay him,' said Cuchulain feelingly.

'My friend, three things are free: birth, love and death. The rest you have to pay for.'

'I won't quibble,' said Cuchulain. 'You might raise the price. Will you do it, Lugh?'

'What do you want me to do? Make an epic on the subject of the sons of Usnach? Sing their praises to Conor? – from what Cormac tells me, he won't like that. Say I'll satire him if he doesn't let them come home? What?'

Cuchulain thought for a moment.

'Could you tell the tale about somebody else, but make it clear that you mean the sons of Usnach? Something about someone who stole the King's woman because of love and was banished for it and then the King had bad luck from it. Something subtle.'

'Something subtle?' I echoed, looking at him in amazement. 'Subtler than you at any rate – you're as subtle as a dog-fight, Cuchulain. The King will think he'll be killed over it, or at least the man who's paying me is thinking about it.'

'That's the idea,' said Cuchulain.

'You *will* kill him? Cormac said this isn't a King-breaking.'

'Lugh, Cuchulain didn't say that,' put in Goll. 'He said, that's what he wants the King to think.'

I looked from one to the other.

'You're both fools,' I said. Cuchulain frowned. 'You can't force him into anything unless you'll go through with it.'

'We'll see to that,' Cuchulain said. 'It's a way of starting matters, that's all.'

'*Are* you leading a King-breaking?' I asked. 'Because if you're not, it looks very much like it.'

Cuchulain stepped up close and stood between me and the sun. He was angry and threatening, his hair starting to bristle like a dog's.

'Now listen here, Lugh! I am the Champion of Ulster, the King's Champion, the King's man. And there's no wish on me to be King, none at all! I'm happy as I am: do you think I'd be happier if I was King and loaded down with geasa? I have more power as I am. But I want to bring the sons of Usnach home, because they are my friends and because we need all the strong men we have against whatever your Queen is planning!'

I went very cold, very stiff. I didn't move, but I said, clearly and precisely, 'Cuchulain Mac Sualtim, don't you ever again speak of the Queen of Connaught as *my* Queen.'

We glared at each other for a moment and in that moment I came within a hairsbreadth of fighting him. Then Goll stepped forward and touched Cuchulain's arm, watching me shrewdly, and my anger broke and I turned away.

Cuchulain relaxed and I plucked a few notes from Fiorbhinn, still on my lap.

'Will you tell the tale, help us to bring back the sons of Usnach?' asked Goll.

I sighed. 'I don't know them. It's none of my business whether they come back or not. I say you're both fools purposely to alarm Conor like this.. But, Death of the Daghda! – I'm a bard and you're paying me for it. I'll make the song and you can pick up the pieces.'

Cuchulain put his hand on my shoulder and smiled.

'Thank you,' he said.

As he went away I no longer wondered why all his tribe loved him fanatically and men would follow him where they would follow no other man. He was mad, but he had the Hero-light on his brow and it was far harder not to follow him.

## VIII

I chose a good epic, altered it slightly and played it twice to get it to my satisfaction. By that time the afternoon was passing, and the warm sunlight becoming warmer coloured as the sun sank westwards. The herds of cattle were being driven into the special pens and they made the air mournful with their lowing while the servants and slaves hurried about, preparing the feast. Then, as the day closed, one by one every hearth in Emain Macha was put out, stamped out until no trace of smoke showed; the ashes were scraped up and slaves washed the hearth-stones down and scrubbed at the scorch-marks. There was a slight breeze and it dispersed the smell of wood and peatsmoke that always hangs around anywhere men live.

The bonfires on the piece of higher ground, not far away, were built and ready, like all the beacons across Erin. There was a beacon on Slieve Cuillen and a chain of them southwards to Tara. For it was at Tara and by the High King of

Erin that Beltain was begun.

People began moving out of the dun towards the Beltain fires. I too picked up Fiorbhinn, put her in her bag on my back and joined the drift.

The sun went down behind the hills and the sky flamed gold at its passing, striped like a King's robe with purple clouds. A skein of swans, strung out in the shape of an arrowhead and calling faintly across the air, flapped their way past in their flight to the north. It caught at my throat, that sight against the sky. The kind of thing every harper strives to bring to a lament: the beauty of the swan-shapes and the loneliness of their hooting, the blood of the dying sun and the blue of the mountains of sorrow. We strive and never attain it and yet the Earth Goddess calls the beauty out of herself and never tries. It is not for our benefit that she makes the glory of the bloody sun, but for her own satisfaction. The swans fly north, not for our sake, but because they must breed in their homes close to the Pole Star and feed their young on colours plucked from the crown of the north. If there had never been a hero born on earth, if never the Dagda had mated with the Morrigan as she stood over a stream so that she brought forth men and women, the swans would still fly north in the spring.

All this I saw in a single haunting instant and then nearby, someone moved impatiently and the moment died. Now that the sun had gone down the people waiting on the hillside turned so that they could see south, waiting for the beginning. Emain was dark and dead.

Darkness fell as the wake of the sun faded. The stars came out. The crowd of people was completely dark. I could smell them around me, hear the little restless spots of movement, the coughing and the cautious rustling of night-creatures here and there.

There was tension. It had been growing and gathering all day and now it became heavier until it was a great breathing animal, dominating the night. There was movement and soft footfall by the small laid-fire of rowan twigs and something was put down beside it. The swish of robes and the creak of

94

leather and then silence. We strained our eyes south for the spark of light from Tara, each one alone in the dark.

My thoughts flew back to Connaught. They would be standing as we were now, standing by the Cave of Cruachan and the Queen waiting with her new consort, whoever he was. Her face would be still as she looked north-east to Tara, her eyes as wide and unwinking as the jewels set in the wooden eyesockets of a god.

I pulled my mind away from the Queen. The very thought of her seemed to taint the night with fear – but it was already tainted. There is always that fear at Beltain: is this the death of the Earth? For if the Beltain fires are not lit somewhere, the year will surely die and the Earth with it. It is the fire which ensures the return of the spring next year.

Strange how in the silence and the dark, one becomes so much aware of one's other senses. I felt the stones in the grass vividly beneath the leather soles of my boots and smelt the crushed grass, the fearing people, the cut branches of the bonfires.

A spark appeared against the night.

Everyone let the pent breath out of their lungs. In the centre of the ring of bonfires someone stepped to the pieces of wood there and picked them up. There was a click as hard wood was placed on soft wood. We rustled round to turn inwards and watch. A steady 'Whitt, whitt' sound of leather on wood as the King pressed his weight against the firedrill and started sawing the bow back and forth, back and forth. He worked on in silence, grunting occasionally and breathing hard with effort.

A faint glow appeared in the hole in the wood and the King redoubled his efforts. Smoke began to rise and someone else blew gently to fan the smoulder. Little bits of squirrel's drey were placed around the smoulder and at last a tiny flame appeared. The firedrill went on twirling, but in the small light we could see the King's sweating face.

A rowan twig was put into the flame and as the light spread and divided into two and travelled slowly to the little pile of rowan twigs, guarded by a cupped hand, there was a surge as everyone bent closer to see.

The flame was put to the pile of rowan and the need-fire flickered up and lit the two figures of the King and Gennan Bright-Face. The King was naked and painted with sun-signs; Gennan wore horse-skins because his father was at Tara for the High King's Fire-Making. They stood silhouetted against the flames and then Gennan and King Conor stepped aside so that the people could see the fire.

A cheer broke from the throats of the whole crowd, a roar, a welcome. After the tension and the waiting and the fear of the dark, there was the licking Sun-fire, ready to call the Sun back again.

The warriors in full war-paint ran forward and picked up the torches lying by and lighting them in the need-fire, ran here and there lighting the central fire and the eight around it; Conall Cernach and Cormac Connlonges ran back to Emain, carrying two lit torches high above them to light every hearth in the dun.

The bonfires blazed and threw their shadows so that there might have been wolves in each one. Herdboys drove up the cattle and the hill-sheep and goats and their noises mixed with the roar of the flames. The warriors began to make a circle in between the bonfires, with all the people of Emain, free or slave, old or young. I caught my breath with joy for this was something we also did in Cruachan, the self-same thing. The drum-beat started up and the people began to clap.

I saw Cuchulain waiting beside one great bonfire with Emer standing smiling before him. His head was back and his black hair flying unconfined in the wind from the bonfire, quite heedless of the sparks falling about him. I looked in the crowd of people and saw Fiall, the girl whom Conor had tired of and with whom I had slept the night I nearly loved Emer. I dived forward and caught her hand and pulled her into place beside Cuchulain. Cuchulain caught sight of her and started laughing again.

At last the drum-beat was too much for us. Cuchulain began it and we started circling in and out of the bonfires, clapping and leaping and making our own steps to the beating, but all the time winding the dance-skein around the bonfires to make the earth fruitful. We danced faster and faster until it seemed the circle would break into chaos from its own speed, but then the herdboys drove in the animals so that they became mixed with the dancing. Each couple chose one cow or ewe or nanny-goat and drove it in and out of the bonfires once and these would be the most fertile.

At last the circle did break and we began to dance up to the dun, carrying torches and weaving complicated patterns of light as we went.

We were singing by that time, the Welcome song for the Risen God.

> 'You are the King of the East. (Hai!)
> You are the Slayer of Death,
> Chief of the Gods of the Day. (Hai!)
> You mount the hill of the sky
> And your spear is sharp in the cutting,
> The slashing and slaying of night.
> You are the Lord of the World.
> You are the Prince of Flame.
> You are the God of Light. (Hai!)'

When we had wound our way into the new-lit Royal Hall, the feasting began in earnest, with the great boar roasting on spits above the leaping fire, for boar is the most holy of animals; loaves and platters of meat going round and the two vats brimful with mead and ale; dogs waiting for discarded bones. The noise of it all was slightly hysterical, as though they were trying to convince themselves that they hadn't really thought the fire would never come back.

There came a slight break in the roaring, as though the people had now become almost certain that there was nothing to be afraid of. This was not Samhain, but its opposite, and opposites are sometimes very close together.

I was in Cuchulain's cubicle as I usually was, and Goll was sitting beside me. If he had been at the Fire-making I hadn't seen him. Now he nudged me and gave me a meaning

97

look. Cuchulain nodded at me.

I picked up my harp and made my way to the centre of the hall and the fawnskin for the bards. There was a tightening in my head, a tensing in my belly. My mouth felt dry. I am not usually very nervous when I sing, or so I tell myself afterwards. What I feel is not precisely nervousness, but something nearer to excitement, to battle-joy perhaps. That night I was also apprehensive because I did not know what King Conor would do when he worked out, as I was sure he would, what I meant by the tale I had chosen.

I sat on the spotted skin, and crossed my legs: it was hot and I was sweating though I was wearing a lighter linen tunic, green, with yellow and black embroidery. Fiall had made it for me because I gave her a bracelet. Fiorbhinn, my harp, was on my lap, in tune. This time as I looked round, the faces were not mere blurs, but each one meant something to me. Cuchulain, intent and laughing; Cormac worried and looking closely at his father; Ferghus making eye-talk with a girl; Duvthach arguing over something; Cethern fondling a favourite bitch.

I waited for silence and it fell as people noticed I was going to sing a proper epic for listening to, not music for talking to. Conor was watching me idly. I wondered what his reaction would be. Surely he knew what was going on.

I began to chant the Hero-tale, singing the dialogue in verse and making most of the story with my harp. I had chosen the most difficult of the three suitable stories to show off and it needed all my concentration. I shut Conor's slowly comprehending face away from me and fixed my attention on the placing of my hands and the pitching and emphasis of my voice. It was a long tale.

I pulled the wailing last chords and leaned back, flexing my fingers. As I looked at Conor I saw that he was stroking his beard and staring at me under his hooded eyes.

'And what was the reason for that, Lugh Mac Romain?' he said finally.

'Ask – ' I was going to say 'Cuchulain', but then I caught Cormac's expression and changed it to – 'ask Cormac

98

Connlonges, your son.'

Conor's cold eyes swivelled to his son's face and Cormac came to his feet, putting back his straight fair hair and reddening slightly.

'F . . . father,' he began, then stopped and took a deep breath to master his stammer, 'I am taking this chance to ask you a boon.'

Silence.

'I ask . . . that you permit the sons of Usnach to come safely home. Must Ulster lose Naisi and Ardan and Ainnle, three of its best warriors, its finest heroes, because of a woman? Let them come home.'

Again silence. Conor regarded his son thoughtfully.

'Who else is with you in this?'

'I am,' came Cuchulain's deep voice. Laere and Conall were a second after him and then all the other nobles who agreed with them. Many approved, but then Naisi, Ardan and Ainnle had all three of them been popular.

Conor's stare went round the hall. I could see him weighing up those for and against and calculating what was likely to happen if he refused openly. He must have expected it and thought about it before, for his answer came just a fraction too quickly for a man taken by surprise.

'Very well,' he said slowly. 'Since I am outnumbered in this, let them come home.'

Cormac's face split into an idiotic grin of relief. He began to thank Conor, but Conor turned away from him. About half the hall were cheering and congratulating Cormac and Cuchulain. I saw Goll bury his nose in a horn of mead and I went back to Cuchulain's cubicle, feeling a little left out, since I had never met Naisi. Cuchulain gave me a gold bracelet for payment, but I could not help but see that not all the men in the hall had been pleased by Conor's answer and that some of the strongest warriors and nobles were talking intently among themselves.

The rest of the feast went with even more of a swing than usual. Towards the end, when everyone was very drunk, the dancing began again. I joined in, and stood in the ring of stampers as Cuchulain and Cormac acted out the hunt; Cuchulain was the deer and Cormac the hunter and then changing over without warning so that it was Cuchulain hunting Cormac.

I remember that night so brightly, vividly, because of what happened after. Did I have any premonition? No. It is not given to men to know what happens next, or else perhaps they would all die of despair. The gods know what they are doing when they withhold foreknowledge. If I had known what was to come the shadow of it would have dampened my happiness.

The gold of that night is stamped deep in my mind. Cuchulain swaying and jumping with his blue-black hair swinging around his crimson-covered shoulders, his hands raised and splayed for antlers; Cormac shouting and laughing and leaning back as he mimed the spear-throw. At last the stamping circle dissolved into the circlings of a dance and the light like mead flowed around our ankles, mead spurting from the fire and laughter.

The next morning, with a headache splitting my skull in two I watched the long train of pack-ponies plodding down the road to Dun Delgan. But it was Ferghus Mac Roich who rode at its head with Goll, his shock of grey hair towering above Goll's striped red. I watched them go blurrily through the cool grey dawn from the sentry-walk of the wooden palisade around Emain Macha.

Cuchulain was walking there too, watching Ferghus going to fetch the sons of Usnach – and of course, Deirdre. He was near me, but he said nothing, frowning over the pointed log tops. When I asked him the reason, he said, 'Conor asked me what I would do if any hurt came to the sons of Usnach while they were under my protection. I told him that I would kill any man responsible. He looked angry.'

'Is he planning treachery?'

Cuchulain looked south to the forest-wrapped hills of the Gap of the North and Cooley. 'I wonder.'

The days passed with fine weather, the business of spring

over, and the increased cattle-raiding on the borders of Connaught. The fields were sown with barley and rye and spelt and the last cows were calving and the brood-mares dropping foals in inconvenient places. Time yawned long and waiting.

I went out hunting with Cormac. We found a fine tusker of a boar and hunted it for some miles, before it turned. Cormac dismounted with his boar-spear, but before he was properly settled, the boar charged him out of a clump of bushes. The spear wasn't straight and so instead of the boar spitting itself on to the spear with the force of its charge, the blade just glanced along the pig's side, tearing a great red gash, but not killing. The boar squealed with rage and swerved, or Cormac would have been killed immediately. It went on past him and spun round in its own length. Cormac tried to turn to meet it as I slid off my horse to help, but he slipped and fell full length.

The boar rootled around him as he flattened himself against the grass: as the boar's tusks curve upwards it must get them underneath the body and tear upwards. The boar was trying to roll Cormac over to get the necessary leverage.

I shouted and snatched a spear from Conin's sling. It was a light one and so I threw it at the boar at close range. The spear stuck in the hump of muscle behind the boar's head. It spun round again and charged straight for me. I had just time to place my own boar-spear's butt against my foot and wedge my other boot against a treeroot. The pig ran itself straight on to the spear and hung there, squealing and trying to get past the bar halfway down the shaft, to tear me with its tusks. Then it heaved a last time, vomited blood and died.

Cormac climbed to his feet. I think both of us were shaking, but he had stopped long before I had. I don't even remember whether he said thank you or not, but it wasn't necessary.

When we came back into Emain Macha with the boar-carcass slung across Cormac's horse, the space between the door of the Royal Hall and the gate of the dun was filled with servants and slaves and attendants and tribesmen. I could see from their tattooing which matched the shapes on Cuchulain's body, that they were his folk, the Sedantii.

Two chariots were standing with the horses shifting and fretting under the yokes. As Cormac and I stopped still by the gate and stared, Emer came out of the Royal Hall. Her face was unnaturally still, as though she had put on a mask. She was wearing a green dress of new cloth Cuchulain had bought for her from Goll the Trader and her belt was made of studded leather. She had on all her jewellery as part of her mask, the torc gleaming in the hollows of her collarbones, pendants and gold chains falling over her breasts and her wrists heavy with gold. Seeing her so brought a moment's awakening of the desire I had felt before, but the ache died away almost as quickly as it had come, leaving the memory. She was too far away like that, behind her fence of jewellery.

I went towards her and was about to speak, but she swept past me as though I was a servant and she the Queen. I don't think she saw me.

Cormac was by the gate, telling a groom to take away the horses and a slave to carry the boar into the hall. I looked across at him and raised my shoulders helplessly, though I felt hurt by Emer's disdain of me.

There was a harsh order shouted behind me. I turned and saw Cuchulain coming out of the Speckled House, carrying his spear, the Gae Bulg, which he so rarely used, and his sword. That sword was made by Culain and was said to be the finest blade in Erin, as it should be, since its maker was the finest smith in Erin. Its hilt was weighted with gold and had a grip of carved sea-ivory, and its name was the Cailid-cheann, the Hard-Headed One. On Cuchulain's back was his black shield, the Dubhan, over his cloak made of the fleeces of the sheep of Manannan of the Sea, glossy brown on the red of his tunic. His hair was bristling like a cat's when it scents a dog.

Emer had already mounted on to her chariot and her charioteer, Gaiar Mac Riangabra, who was still being trained by his elder brother, Laegh, because he had not yet found a lord, stood beside her with the reins knotted round his waist.

Laegh was standing by the big silver- and gold-decorated war-chariot, his sandy brows practically meeting over his long nose.

I went to meet Cuchulain and saw that he was very pale, so white that his black brows and dark eyes stood out unnaturally from his drained face. His lips were pressed together so that they too lost all their blood.

'What's happened, Cuchulain?' I asked, seeing he was angry, but not understanding why.

He stopped and stood stiffly as though holding himself in with difficulty.

'Well,' he said. I heard the shadow of a battle-cry in the crow-harshness of his voice. 'Conor asked me to do him a favour. I have refused and I am leaving. Is there anything else you want to know, because if you can't guess what it is he asked me, Lugh, you're a greater fool even than I took you for. Get out of my way!'

After a moment I stepped aside. He brushed past me and swung himself up on to the platform of his chariot. Laegh swung himself up loosely behind him.

'Dun Delgan, Laegh, and don't stop till we get there!'

The cavalcade swept out the gate of Emain Macha and clattered down the Road of Midluachair. In the centre of its storm rode Cuchulain, balancing easily on his chariot, his hand round the haft of his spear quivering white-knuckled with the strength of its grip.

I know that Cormac did not understand, but I was beginning to.

I don't think anyone has ever worked out exactly what happened at the arrival of the sons of Usnach. This is the story as best I can put it together.

Goll the Trader put in with his ship carrying Ferghus and the sons of Usnach and Deirdre and their attendants at a little sea inlet near to Tara. He simply put them ashore and went on south, carrying his merchandise to the east coast of Erin, and theirs around Dumnonia to Londinium on the other side of Britain. He could do this because he had a Veneti sailing-ship which could survive the enormous waves off the coast of Dumnonia.

Naisi, Ardan and Ainnle, the sons of Usnach, and Deirdre, the daughter of Fedlimid, went on to Tara and there Ferghus was met by Burach who called him to a feast and said that it was geasa for him to leave until he had eaten it. Ferghus was angry and protested, but Burach would not let him go. Ferghus had no choice but to go to the feast, since no man may break his geasa. However, he sent his two sons, Fair-haired Iollan and Rough-red Buinne on with Naisi and his brothers to give their protection. It still didn't really occur to Ferghus that Conor might break his surety.

Naisi was angry that Ferghus had forsaken them, though Ferghus had little choice in the matter because of his geasa. Cormac had left the dun of Emain Macha with Duvthach and some other friends of his; I think he wished to meet the sons of Usnach and Deirdre and all of them to come to Emain together. But Burach sent him a message saying that Ferghus was at Dun Burach at a feast: Cormac thought, as he was meant to think, that the sons of Usnach were still with Ferghus, and went to Dun Burach to join them.

Naisi and Deirdre with Ardan and Ainnle and all their people, pressed hard up the Road of Midluachair, by-passing Dun Delgan in their haste. They arrived at Emain at evening four days after Cuchulain had gone home. They rode into the dun and looked around them with tears in their eyes. Even I smiled to see their obvious joy and thought with longing of Cruachan. But Cruachan was getting further away from me.

So the little party rode in, unaware, thanks to the gods, of the future. Deirdre rode between Ardan and Ainnle and she was wearing a hooded cloak to hide her beauty. She dismounted behind Naisi, like a man, swinging her leg over the horse's neck and slipping down. She was dressed in boy's clothes. I caught a glimpse of her face and saw that she was truly beautiful; beautiful as very, very few women have beauty. But it was not her golden hair or bright grey eyes, or red lips that caught my attention, so much as the sheer love of life that shone from her. She thought only of herself and of Naisi and anything else was of no more moment than a buttercup she would step on and leave crushed in the grass. That was the greatest thing in her beauty: her careless love of herself and her life, like a dragonfly dancing above the water and recking nothing of the swallow swooping to snatch it in mid-air . . .

I watched them arrive and would have been as pleased as everyone else who liked them, if it hadn't been for what Cuchulain had said to me as he left. I am not a fool and I could guess what Cuchulain had meant, but somehow it didn't seem possible. The Dagda help me, I couldn't believe that a man could do such a thing, even such a man as Conor. Well, I have learnt better since.

Conor was not there to meet them, which struck no one as odd. After all, he might allow them to come back, but who could expect him to love Naisi very much? What I didn't notice then, but remembered later, was that none of the enemies of Naisi were present when he came.

They were shown to the smaller guest-house, standing apart from the Royal Hall, a hall in its own right, called the House of the Red Branch. When the boar I had killed and which had been hanging to make it tender, was roasted on the spit in the Royal Hall, meat was sent to them. Now that

Cuchulain and his tribe was no longer there, no one could occupy his Champion's place in the Hall and so I was sleeping in the cubicle used by Owen Mac Durthact, of Fermanagh. He wanted me to come with him to his lands and be his bard because his old one had died: I was considering the offer and he gave me sleeping-space as part of the process of sweetening.

In the middle of the night I was awoken by somebody's foot kicking me. I grunted and rolled over, opening my eyes, to see Owen getting up very quietly and drawing aside the screen. As he did so I saw Conor standing in the middle of the floor, ruddy in the light escaping from the fire. In his hand gleamed his sword. Other screens were pulling aside and other men were coming out quietly from the crowded sleeping cubicles. Owen looked round to see if he had awakened anybody and I blinked my eyes shut. His cloak was already pinned on his shoulder and his dagger on his belt. Then he went through into the main part of the hall, stepping over the sleeping shape of one of the servants.

The men all gathered quietly round Conor and left the hall. As soon as they had shut the door behind them I jumped up and, stepping over everyone, went from my place near the wall through into the rest of the hall. There I stood for a moment, undecided, as I buckled on my knife-belt and pinned my cloak. I went softly to the door, listened at it to see if I could hear voices and then opened it a fraction and looked out. There was no one there. I slipped through the gap and closed the door carefully behind me.

I looked round. The door to the Speckled House was open and men were crowding purposefully inside. I slid along at a crouch and hid behind a slave-hut. Shortly, they all came out and stood in a dark bunch, the heads of their spears glinting a little above their heads. Then they made for the House of the Red Branch where Naisi and his two brothers lay sleeping, and, with Naisi, Deirdre, the golden-haired daughter of Fedlimid the Poet.

I followed them, moving as quietly as I could. The men had lit torches now and they were walking fast. I slipped from slave-hut to storehut, stepping round the snoring shape of a sow with her litter in the middle of a scrap heap. I knew what Conor wanted to do: he would burst into the House of the Red Branch and simply kill all inside. I wondered if he had given orders for Deirdre to be kept alive. But Naisi and his brothers were as good as corpses already.

Something in me revolted at the thought. If I had any sense I would go immediately back to Conor's hall and forget I had seen anything. They were nothing to me: I had never even spoken to Naisi or Deirdre, and when they had ridden into the dun that evening my eyes had been so fixed on the insolent life in Deirdre's face that I had not thought to look elsewhere. Naisi and his brothers were only hazy shapes in my imagination, hefty warriors with black hair, and Naisi standing almost as tall as I stand myself. And yet I could not let Conor come upon them while they slept, trusting in Ferghus's absent protection, in Conor's good faith. I could not let their throats be cut like animals given to the gods.

Moving faster and holding my breath with tension, I moved between the shadows of huts, skirting round the Red Branch House, to come at it from the opposite side. I saw the men were spreading out around the door now. I guessed it must be barred from the inside. Naisi was not an entire fool and years of living as a hunted man had taught him caution.

On the opposite side of the hall I saw a little patch of light lying on the ground and realized that Naisi had taken down one of the shutters from the window-holes to let some air in, for it was a close night. I went up to the window, for once thanking my stars for my height which let me look in. Inside the fire was low, but the screens were mostly up and there were one or two guttering torches. I could see Ardan and Ainnle sleeping in another cubicle with the screen half-open. I dared not shout out.

I bent and picked up a handful of small stones. I threw it against the screen and saw some of the gravel hit Ainnle's cheek. He started up, drawing his dagger and looking round him and wakening his brother. The two stood up together and then they heard the speech and orders round the door.

They went and listened and what they heard told them enough. Ainnle gave a shout of rage and Ardan ran to one of the closed cubicles and dragged the screen aside. There lay Naisi fast asleep, with Deirdre lying snuggled close by his side and the two of them breathing together. Ardan shook his brother roughly awake and as Naisi opened his eyes, urgent whispers passed between them. Then Naisi too was on his feet and Deirdre sitting up. The screens were pulling back all around the hall and their people and attendants waking and lighting torches and searching for their daggers and weapons.

Then there came a hammering on the door and the order to open up. Naisi went close to the door, dressed only in his cloak wrapped round his waist, his scars standing out against his skin, some of them white, some of them purple and recent.

'Is it you, Conor?' he shouted.

A pause. Then, 'Yes, Mac Usnach, it's me. I've come for my woman.'

Naisi made a strange sound in his throat. I could not tell whether it was pain or rage.

He shouted again, 'The woman's mine, King, mine! Killing me won't get her for you. How many have you with you anyway?'

'Enough to get my rights.'

'Oh gods! Conor, listen! I'll fight you, fight you properly. In the sword-ring, with Druids. Whoever wins gets the woman.'

Silence. Naisi's face seemed to crumple. Deirdre had run to him and pressed herself against him, wrapped as she was, only in a deerskin. Unconsciously he began to caress her, to stroke her hair.

'Conor!' he shouted, 'Can't you see? Can't you think! Kill us this way and the stain will be on yourself, can't you see that? Let you and me fight this thing properly, with swords and our own strength. Just yourself and I, cleanly. Not this torchlight treachery!'

'I will have the woman,' came Conor's grey voice.

Naisi turned away from the door.

'Oh Deirdre,' he said, 'I'm sorry. He was my King. I trusted him.'

Deirdre said nothing. She stood high on tiptoe and kissed his lips quickly. Then she ran away from him into their cubicle and shut the screen. Naisi followed her, walking like a man in an evil dream.

Orders were shouted outside. Despite what I had seen, the sons of Usnach were nothing to do with me. Perhaps if I had been Cuchulain I would have found some way to stop Conor, or fought against him or threatened to withdraw my support for his Kingship. But I was not Cuchulain, not the man who had gone to Dun Delgan when Conor had asked him to take part in or sanction this thing, because he would not do it and nor would he go against Conor with force of arms. I was a not-very-well-known harper and bard, come fleeing from Connaught, with a curse probably snapping at my heels. I could have roused Naisi's friends, but what good would that have done? More blood would have run that night and enough was shed as it was.

They were butting a log of wood from a nearby fuel-pile against the door. The bar across it would not snap and so torches were tossed into the thatched roof. Conor was burning his own hall.

I stepped back from the window-hole, stepped back another pace, and then, as the flames began to lick hungrily around the thatch and the shouts and clash of arms began ringing through the night, I turned and went away. I did not run. I walked. It was not flight, but dismissal, disavowal. I disowned what was going on in the House of the Red Branch, the guest-house of Ulster.

Of course the noise woke the rest of Conor's household and they came running, snatching up their weapons from the opened Speckled House as they ran, and asking where was the attack?

Naisi and his brothers pushed the King's men out of the house and sallied forth themselves. And yet their friends stood, while Naisi, his people and the two sons of Ferghus with them were slowly borne down, back and into the burning house. They stood round: not carelessly, but rigid; they were shocked and stunned and there was no man there who could break their stillness, no man with the suddenness and fire needed. None, for Cuchulain was in Dun Delgan.

I tried to ignore the noise. I wanted nothing to do with this: it had a foul taste, a slimy feel, the smell of rot – or burned thatch. I hated myself for my cowardice, and hated the excuses I made for myself. The women cry 'Ochone!' for the dead hero as they would surely cry for Naisi, but whoever says 'Alas' for the man who would be a hero, and is not? I don't know. There was a feeling of fate in the air of that night, or perhaps it was only the stink of burned wood after all.

At last I could bear it no longer. I went back to the Red Torch that had once been the House of the Red Branch and stood among the people of Emain as they stared. What did they look like to Naisi as he fought for his life and his woman? Rows of eyes, like the surrounding wolves of a man lost in a winter midnight forest? They were all there, the nobles and warriors and women; the servants and charioteers and slaves. The dogs had all slunk away from the fear of fire. They just stood watching the red murder and never moved, the hands of the warriors nerveless round the hafts of their spears and the hilts of their swords. I stood among them.

Naisi and his brothers sallied, with Deirdre between them. They were driven because the burning thatch was falling from the ribs of the roof, falling and setting the hay and rushes on the floor alight and the red yew of the screens and the beautiful carving of the pillars and the structure of the walls. Most of their attendants and people were dead or dying. One of Ferghus's sons lay with his arms still locked against a son of Conor's, fair hair mingling with dark brown and both dead.

So now there were only Naisi and Ardan and Ainnle, with Deirdre between them. They put up their shields, making a shield-wall to protect her and the men surged around them. I saw that it was the pleasant-faced, rich Owen Mac

Durthact of Fermanagh who led, the man who wished to give me a place as his bard. When the brothers were at last overborne it was he who struck off Naisi's head. Then a high wail went up at last from Deirdre's throat and she fell down beside her tall lover and held his headless body in her arms and never heeded the blood spurting all over her. I don't think she had believed that he could die and leave her.

They had to tear Deirdre away from Naisi's body by main force. They bound her arms behind her and brought her, all bloody as she was, before Conor. Conor was simply standing there, looking up at the burning hall. His black-and-purple striped tunic was unsullied by blood or smirch for he had not taken part in the fighting. Owen had led it all. Owen stood beside his King now, with Naisi's head tied by its long black hair to his belt, the features with something of a baby's wide-eyed calm and the severed neck only dripping a little now.

Deirdre stood with her back to the flames. She saw Naisi's head, but it didn't mean anything to her. She looked dully at the hem of her dress. You could not tell its colour though I think she had put on her best dress for the fighting, being a vain woman.

Conor stared at her now, and said in a soft voice, 'So, Deirdre, you are back at last.' There was no gloating in his voice, only satisfaction . . . and something else. She still said nothing, staring at the mud between the hem of her dress and Conor's feet.

'Now you are mine, Deirdre, as you should have been at the beginning,' he said and his voice was gentle, almost pleading. In a shocked moment I understood that Conor loved Deirdre, loved her as Cuchulain loved Emer. He loved her, wanted her, had killed three of his best warriors for her, perhaps split Ulster down the centre for her, perhaps lost his crown and life for her and now he was asking her to love him back and forget Naisi.

'Deirdre, look at me.' The raw longing in his voice seemed to hurt the very air. All Emain watched and waited, many with hate in their hearts for what he had done, and now he bared his breast before them and asked for Deirdre's love.

Asked, not demanded.

Slowly she raised her head. There were no tears on her face. Her grey eyes were shocking in their deadness, their total lack of life. Can you wring water from a stone?

'I am back, Conor, you have me and I am looking at you. What more do you ask?' Her voice, like the rest of her, had once been beautiful.

'Yourself, Deirdre. Only yourself.'

A little silence, filled with the crackle of flames feeding on unheeded. Then Deirdre spoke again in the same dead-level voice, measuring out the syllables and letting them fall as though they were handfuls of colourless sand.

'You love me, Conor,' she said, 'and I loved my Naisi and he loved me. What room was there for you?'

Conor gave no answer and she answered herself.

'None. There was no room for you.' A spark suddenly sprang to life in her dead eyes. 'And so you killed Naisi by your treachery, your torchlight treachery. He was a hundred times better than you, though he was no thwarted *King!*' She spat the word out like a worm. 'And you ask me to love you? Oh, there's room for you now, King, room and more than room, for I'm thinking I will never love a man again. You have my body, King, but not myself and that you'll never get for all your might. It was Naisi that I loved; it is Naisi I love still and it is you I curse, Conor, by all the curses that there are and by every god ever worshipped! May your life never lack for sorrow and may . . .'

Owen stepped forward and clapped his hand over her mouth. Conor made the Sign of Horns with his fist and then gestured helplessly. She was led away, her step heavy and stumbling and Conor turned and walked off with the same tread.

Then, and only then, did men start forming bucket-chains and the women begin to look among the bodies for wounded they could tend with some hope of saving. There were none. I walked away from the mess and sat by the gate in the dark, with my back against the bank. My mind was whirling with images so that I could find no relief.

Hooves came cautiously up to the gate, and a man's footsteps too, leading the horse. There was no gate-guard, for the old man had gone with his son to help with clearing away the dead. I stood up. A sword scraped in a scabbard.

'Who is it?' I asked, moving back a pace and reaching for my dagger.

'Lugaid Mac Nois. Is that you, Lugh?'

'It is.'

'Open the gate, will you?'

'You're a friend of Cormac's,' I said.

'And Naisi's.'

I opened the gate for him. He mounted up and galloped away south to Burach's dun.

## X

I stayed on watch by the gate, dozing most of the time. I was woken by a messenger, a man who shouted he came from the Sedanta, and opened the gate for him. I slept again and only woke when dawn came. I stood up; my mind felt drained by tiredness.

The dead had been mostly cleared away and the flames of the House of the Red Branch completely doused, so that now there were only smouldering ruins. It could be rebuilt.

There was a sense of purposeful bustle which I didn't understand. After all, they had more need of rest than I, who had taken no part either in the fighting or in the clearing up. I watched for a moment and then went over to the Speckled House, where I found Conall slowly sharpening his sword on the stone outside. I hardly recognized him. There was no colour in his face but for his red splash of a birthmark, and deep circles under his odd-coloured eyes. He looked up at me and answered my question before it was asked.

'Someone got through to Burach's dun and told Ferghus

and Cormac what happened. Most of Naisi's good friends went over the wall of Emain. They're gathering to the south.'

Without a word I went into the Speckled House and got my sword and stabbing spear. The Speckled House was no longer speckled because the central lamp was out and the walls denuded of their arms.

Outside again I waited until Conall had finished and then started sharpening my own sword. There was really nothing to say. I was a little surprised that Cormac had managed to gather men so quickly, but I knew that Ferghus had lands near Burach's dun. Lughai must have ridden like the wind.

This would be my first fight in Ulster and it was against Ulstermen. I had fought against them often enough before, and killed them too: I had raided the cattle of Ulster just as Ulster raided the cattle of Connaught. There were a few herds belonging to homesteads near the border that must have been very bewildered cattle indeed, what with their ceaseless journeyings back and forth. But that fighting had been against more or less anonymous figures: they were people who sprang at you with mouth and eyes wide open, their yells lost in the sound of your own yelling; then when you had killed the man and taken his head and carried it back to Cruachan in triumph, someone would point to him and say that that had been so-and-so and you would feel doubly pleased at having killed such a redoubtable warrior. This fight would be personal: I knew many of the 'enemy'. I could see their faces already, no longer with friendly smiles, but snarling and lusting for my death: I would know them.

I looked at Conall and saw that he was thinking on the same lines.

I had no chariot and so I decided that I would fight on horseback. I wished I didn't have to use Conin, but there was no help for it. I had no other horse. Another thing I did not have was a shield. Conall knew and he lent me a spare one of his. I remember examining it and noticing its colour very clearly: it was painted red and the white bronze rim was honed razor-sharp. I would have to be careful not to cut myself with it.

The warriors of Emain waited outside the gates. We waited and waited. It was a beautiful day, full of summer. Warm with a pale blue sky and only a few sheep's-wool wisps of cloud against its blue. It seemed obscene to be waiting to go into battle under such a gentle, peaceful sky.

Standing beside Conall, I felt the sweat trickling down under my tunic. It wasn't that hot: I was afraid. I am always afraid before a battle. Not just of what will happen to me, but also of what I will do. Conin was cropping the grass on one side of me and Conall was humming unconcernedly on the other. He had a chariot. His charioteer was engaged in slapping flies off the horses' flanks. Everywhere it was the same: little spots of movement making the stillness more unbearable.

I began to think of what would happen. Of swords slashing and crunching through flesh and bone. How did it feel to die? How did it feel? And the pain. I had heard the screams of wounded men, dying men. Gods of the battlefield, Red-Robed Morrigan, if I die, let me die quickly. Lugh Brightspear, my namesake, don't let me show what I feel, don't let them see that I am afraid . . . Oh gods, why wasn't I born like Conall Cernach or Cuchulain? They don't know what it is to fear. They can go into battle with delight and kill in a red rage and come away with their trophies hanging on the sides of their chariots and never wonder how the people they had killed had felt when the sword came slicing down on them, or the spear thrust through their ribs.

And yet another, cold little part of me was laughing at the images in my mind and the thoughts chasing them: it knew that when the time came I would go into battle with as much swing and shouting as any hero and forget all about everything else until the blood-lust was quenched and the reaction set in. Was it pride? Or did I want to take my revenge on the people who had, in some obscure, roundabout way, made me sweat so beforehand?

Conall Cernach turned and grinned at me happily. As I always did, even then, I took refuge in wryness.

'A fine fight this will be,' I said, 'Ulstermen fighting Ulstermen. Ah well, I'm a Connaughtman: I might as well be at home – I'm still fighting Ulstermen.'

Conall looked puzzled.

'What do . . .?' he began.

A cry went up. Ferghus's army had been sighted. A grey and glinting cloud on the Road of Midluachair.

'Oh, it doesn't matter,' I said and spat to get rid of a bad taste in my mouth. Conall turned away and swung himself up into the chariot, his brawny arms flexing. Everywhere chariot-chieftains were doing the same. I turned with a sour pull to my mouth, and leaped on to Conin's back. I had no patience with his customary bucking and jabbed the bit unmercifully.

I pushed my hair back from my face, feeling it fine and soft under my hand. I had let it loose so it flowed down my back as a challenge to anyone who thought he could wear my head swinging by my hair from his belt. Most of the other warriors did the same. Perhaps it shows more than anything else how different is our fighting from Rome's. Free hair is a fine challenge, but it can also get into your eyes and cause your death.

Then, from a silent dustcloud, Ferghus and Cormac and their men became a thundering, creaking, shouting mass. The chariots of Emain started forward, and I kicked Conin to a trot and a canter and then a hand-gallop: I shouted and raised my stabbing spear, the shield up to my chin, guiding Conin with my knees. A slingstone zipped past my ear and that simplified the turmoil of my feelings so that instead of being pulled this way and that and distracted by thoughts, I felt the joy of fighting and battle and my one desire was to kill, kill, kill! After that and the rush of blood and the meeting of the two sides and the noise and confusion and guiding the bucking sidling Conin among the press while I stabbed with my spear, I had no time to think.

I remember only flashes: the surprised look of a man when I pierced his throat; little things, like the look of a dropped sword on the ground. Once in the middle of the fighting I saw a grey-faced greying man in a gold tunic, fighting three attackers on foot: my mind recognized him as someone I knew, though not who it was, and I drove Conin into the middle of the attackers and killed one and the other two disappeared somehow.

'I am Ulster!' shouted the man and I believed him, so I slid from Conin's back and gave him the reins.

I came against a man with a battle-distorted face and fair straight hair clotted with blood from a scalp wound: I think he was Cormac. Another time I found an empty chariot going by as the horses bolted, somehow avoided the hooves and knives and jumped on to it. One of the horses was dying from a spear-wound, the other was maddened with the smell of blood. I cut the traces of the dying one and let it lurch away: I fought from that chariot before I had to jump off again. I know I was doing something with my voice, although I didn't know what at the time, in the terrible joy of killing, in the contest of luck and strength and skill.

There was one man I fought hand to hand for a long time, in a small oasis all our own, sheltered by an overturned chariot. In the end I tripped him and pushed my knee in his stomach and cut off his head and tied his hair to my belt.

But at last there was no one around me trying to kill me. Everyone was standing about among the dead and ordure, their breath rasping in their hoarse throats, wiping their blades or just leaning on their spears watching the chariots and men disappear down the Road of Midluachair, the road to the south.

'I wonder where they're going?' said a breathless voice beside me. I turned and saw that it was Cethern, stark naked and covered in war-paint; blue woad and red ochre and charcoal all running together from the sweat and the blood. The sourness rose within me like vomit.

'Ach, can't you guess?' I said. 'Soon the Queen will have many more fine strong warriors than were born in Cruachan, all of them speaking hard Ulster Irish.'

He stared at me; I smiled with a strange sense of pity.

'You've exchanged yourself half the chariot-warriors of

Ulster for one sour-mouthed Connaught bard. May you have as great a satisfaction from the bargain as the Queen.'

I walked away from the churned field of the dead in front of Emain, the one head still banging at my hip. I bent over and wiped my sword on the grass and did the same with my spear-blade. The head slipped from my belt and rolled, dripping on the green grass, crushing a blue flower as it went. It was a man I knew well: his name was Donall and he had liked my harp-playing.

I picked up the head by its hair, looked at the snarling, frozen features and closed the wide eyes with a gentle forefinger. Then I threw it from me with all the strength of my arm.

## XI

As soon as I had stopped vomiting and shivering I went and helped dig the death-ditch. One thing I found on the battlefield: it was Conin, gashed with spears and lying on the ground, on his side, half-disembowelled. Flies were already settling on him though he sometimes shook his head feebly to get them off his nose and eyes. I felt choked with pity for him. I crouched by his head and let him smell me: perhaps he knew who it was for he opened his eyes. I put my hand over them so he would not see, drew my dagger and cut his throat. He twitched and was still.

A little later I saw his body tumbled into the death-ditch with the other horse-carcasses – it is geasa for Ulstermen to eat horseflesh, so they buried them – and the white flash on his rump a little brighter as the earth went on top.

It was evening by the time all the bodies of men and beasts had been thrown in and the earth put on top of them. Soon the Druids would come and make the prayers for the dead and hasten them to Tir-na-nOg with offerings of meat and drink. They say that Tir-na-nOg is whatever you want it to be. Is death so bad after all?

Next morning I washed and shaved, using Fiall's bronze hand-mirror. It was cool and clouded over after the warmth of the day before, but there was little wind: the smell of burning still hung over the dun. Owen had come and asked me if I would be his bard: I had told him, politely, no. Just as I finished and started to sharpen the bronze razor, a boy came running up to me. It was Follamon, the King's son.

'Lugh!' he shouted, 'Lugh, the King wants to see you.'

I dropped the razor and sighed. Fiall picked it up: she was sitting on a stone nearby and she smiled as I gave her back her valuable mirror with the complex red and white enamel pattern on the back.

'What did he want to see me about?' I asked.

'He didn't say. He's over by the chariot-sheds looking at the tally-sticks for our losses in the fighting.'

'That must be a pleasure for him,' I muttered.

Follamon frowned. 'Oh no. But he's not showing anything on his face. We lost a lot of men.'

'I know.'

'You must come. It's important.'

'I'm coming, Follamon.'

I swung my harp on my shoulder and started towards the chariot-sheds. Follamon came alongside.

'It was a good fight, wasn't it?' he said. 'They wouldn't let me join in because they said all the boys of the Boys' Troop were too young, but I'm not. I heard the noise: it was exciting. There hasn't been a fight so close to Emain for a long time. But it was a good fight.'

'You know, Follamon,' I said, 'there's only one difference between a good and a bad fight.'

'What?'

'Whether you win or not.'

He looked at me closely to see if I was laughing and was puzzled.

'Won't you make a song about it?'

'No, I will not.'

He thought better of asking why and was silent.

Conor was holding the tally-sticks in his hands at the end

of the row of chariot-sheds. I was suspicious. I stood a few paces off and waited.

Conor looked at me and through me.

'You asked for me, King,' I said.

He came to himself again.

'I did. I saw you in the fighting yesterday.'

'Yes.'

'Did you know you were singing?'

'I was *what*?'

He smiled a little under his beard. 'Singing. A song about willow trees . . . Why are you laughing like that?'

I swallowed and shook my head. 'Was that what you wanted to speak to me about, King?'

'No. Don't you remember, Lugh? You saved my life in that battle. And you gave me your horse when I needed it. Is it surprising I wanted to speak to you?'

I stared at him, remembering, now he mentioned it, the grey man in the gold tunic who had shouted that he was Ulster. So it had been Conor.

'Had you forgotten?' he asked.

'I . . . yes. I remember very little about the battle.'

Why on earth had I done such a thing? I had very little love for King Conor, especially after his betrayal of the sons of Usnach. I had understood him better afterwards when he spoke with Deirdre. Had that been my reason? Or was it something to do with the oath I swore?

Conor smiled again.

'Even if you don't, I remember. It is no small thing to save the King's life. Ibar!'

'Here!' There was a chariot coming down from one of the sheds, a fine chariot, drawn by two tough ponies and driven by Ibar Mac Riangabra, Conor's charioteer.

'Since you lost your horse to me,' said Conor, waving a hand at it, 'I am giving you a replacement.'

I couldn't say anything. I walked up to the war-chariot and all around it. It wasn't new, though it had been washed down, and it had probably belonged to a lord who was killed before he could get back to it. But it was beautiful.

The tops of the iron-bound wheels came up to my chest, with the platform between them, the length of a sword in width. The high wicker sides were painted black and silver and picked out in red and green; the handles were made of bronze and the yoke pole inlaid with silver.

I jumped up and stood beside Ibar, looking down on the ponies' glossy bay and black haunches. The bay tossed its head, jingling the horse-bronzes. It was a chariot Cuchulain would not have been ashamed to own and it was mine.

I smiled down at Conor and noticed, with a slight dampening of pleasure, that his eyes were hooded and keen.

'This is a chariot, King,' I said at last, 'that I could put to the harp on my back and sing from here to Rome.'

Conor nodded curtly. 'It's yours,' he said as he left.

Follamon was hopping delightedly from foot to foot.

'Oh, it's beautiful!' He grinned. 'That's a marvellous chariot. When are you going to try her?'

'Now. Would you like to come up?'

'Oh yes!'

He ran forward and I caught his arm as he jumped, and hauled him up. Ibar nodded to him, leant forward to touch the haunches of the ponies with the reins and we drove sedately out of the dun. The platform swayed and gave under me, like the back of a horse. It was built to roll over bumps and pot-holes and down hills without anything breaking and would do it too. Follamon balanced well and smiled at the slight breeze raised by the trotting ponies. He waved at a friend of his as we passed out of the dun and the friend stared with jealousy.

We went down the path to the home-pasture and the furthest end of it where there were stakes and dummies put up for a practice-field. There were no boys doing sword-drill there yet, so it was empty. Ibar stopped the chariot and jumped off, after handing the reins and goad to me. Follamon reluctantly jumped off too.

I felt the ponies' mouths, shook the reins. They walked

forward, then to a trot, a canter, a hand-gallop and finally to a gallop, but I slowed them again, judging their sensitivity, their stamina.

Ibar shouted for me to weave in and out of the standing stakes. I grinned, thinking of how often I had done that with mismatched ponies in a beat-up old chariot on the practice-field in Cruachan. Cruachan. The grin was wiped from my face and I concentrated on guiding the ponies at a hand-gallop between the stakes and round in a full circle on one stationary wheel and then back again. Finally I touched them with the goad and let them out to their full speed. They reached out, their manes flying, necks straight. We charged across the practice-field so that the wind watered my eyes and pulled wisps from my plaited hair and my tunic pressed against me. I slowed them to a trot as we came up to Ibar and Follamon, so that the two could jump on and then I goaded them to a gallop again, up the path and through the gates of Emain, bringing them to a pawing standstill by the charred ruins of the Red House.

I heard Follamon's gasp as I stopped them and Ibar looked at me sideways as the ponies began walking towards the chariot-sheds, snorting as they went.

'Hmf,' he said. 'I've met only one charioteer more dangerous than yourself.'

'Who?' I was breathing a little fast.

'Cuchulain.'

He had jumped down before I recognized it as a back-handed compliment. I called to one of the stableboys while Follamon thanked me and ran off, and got down myself, still smiling.

Ibar was watching me with his hands on his hips.

'You'll be needing a charioteer,' he said, 'I'll send my brother Gaiar to you now, since Laegh says he's taught him all he knows. It'll do him good.'

# XII

The death of the sons of Usnach completed the split in Ulster. There was more to it than that, for many nobles were dissatisfied with the way Conor ran things. Cormac Connlonges, Ferghus Mac Roich, Duvthach, Lugaid Mac Nois and others had all gone to the Queen of Connaught, where they were welcomed with open arms by herself and her new Ailell. They took their fighting-men and clans and herds with them and the Queen gave them all new lands – and made sure that the whole of Erin knew it. Bricru of the Bitter Tongue, he who had set Cuchulain and Laere and Conall Cernach fighting, he also went south. He had been living on the brink of a cliff ever since his disastrous feast and the argument over the Championship. Now he decided, with reason, that it would be wise for him to flee. He and Ferghus were two of the greatest nobles in Ulster and Cormac was the King's son and his first choice for the Kingship.

Most of the other great nobles were with Conor and all of those who had been enemies of the sons of Usnach. Their power in men and arms was greater than those who opposed Conor and they, knowing where their interest lay, ranged themselves solidly around the King. But Conor, who was a subtle man whatever else he may have lacked or been guilty of, saw that there were two main dangers to him, both incalculable.

The first was the Druids. Cavath had been absent from Emain Macha since before Beltain, and no one was fool enough to ask where he had been. But gradually rumours began cropping up here and there that there was a Druid-curse against Conor because of his conduct in breaking the Guest-law and disregarding Ferghus's surety. This curse took a different shape in every different place the rumour cropped up, but it made men uneasy. Conor had to prove that if the curse existed, it hadn't impaired his luck.

The second danger was more immediate: in the whole of the Land of Erin, the greatest man was not Conor, but Cuchulain. If Conor had Cuchulain with him, then he could laugh at all the rest: Cuchulain alone had the fire and the leadership to lead a successful King-breaking. If he put himself at the head of Conor's enemies then Conor was in very serious trouble. And yet, though Cuchulain was not a subtle man, whatever else he may have been, he stayed in his dun and came out neither for nor against the King. He was a friend of Naisi's, but he was also the Champion of Ulster.

In the days after Conor gave me the chariot I often wondered idly whether it was given from policy or reward: perhaps he would give me the lands Ferghus or Bricru had left behind and use me as a foil to Cuchulain. But the King himself gave no sign.

In all things to do with the sons of Usnach, Conor was unlucky. He now had Deirdre as he had wanted and he kept her in a little hut close to the Royal House, so she could not escape. I think he had expected to have to fight her into submission, being an Ulsterman and not looking on women as we do in Connaught, but she never fought back. Even when he hurt her sorely and on purpose, she did nothing, but remained like stone.

Sometimes she was allowed to sit in the sun outside her hut and spin, though there was always someone near to see that she didn't try to run away. She never moved from the little bench, but span and span and sang strange wailing little songs.

I passed her one day, after this had been going on for half a month, and I pitied her for her loneliness. What it must be like for her, alone and haunted by her memories of Naisi, with no one to speak to her and tell her she was beautiful. For she was beautiful, despite the fact that she had not washed her hair or reddened her nails since the night when Naisi died. Her pale blue dress with green borders woven into it hung around her and she was far thinner than she had been. And yet still she was beautiful, only now her beauty was like the beauty of statues that the Romans make, that are more beautiful than women, but cold.

She was singing, singing a lament and the music of it had a strange quality, as though it came on the wind from a land where the trees were crippled and the earth diseased and men walked around dead with their flesh rotting off their bones . . .

I stopped.

'Deirdre,' I said, with no very clear idea of what I was going to say after that. She ceased her eerie singing and it seemed that the sun came out again from behind an invisible cloud.

'Who are you?' she asked. There was no sign of interest in her face or voice, but her eyes turned from their terrible staring at nothing and fixed on me, so that I felt uncomfortable.

'Lugh,' I answered. 'Lugh Mac Romain.'

'I remember your face,' she said. 'I wonder where? It doesn't matter. Sit down beside me.'

I hesitated only a second before I did as she asked.

'I remember now. You were looking through the window.'

'Yes,' I said, wishing now I hadn't said anything. The deadness of her voice made my hackles rise. No voice should ever sound like that.

'Ainnle said something about that. He said someone threw stones at the screen to wake him. He wondered who it was. It was you, wasn't it?'

'Yes.'

'Otherwise we would have been killed in our sleep. Naisi would have, but not me. I'm glad you did it. Naisi always said he would rather die fighting than asleep. Naisi died fighting. I'm glad. He always said he would rather go to Tir-na-nOg with blood fresh upon him. But he hasn't got his head.' She giggled inanely. 'I wonder how he sees. Owen has his head. He's pickled it and got it hanging up in his dun. I know, because the King told me. Naisi's head. I used to stroke it. Now it's hanging up in Owen's dun.'

She giggled again. Then she clasped her hands to her stomach and started rocking herself back and forth, back and forth, the distaff falling from under her arm and rolling on the bench.

'Oh Naisi . . .' she said softly, 'Oh Naisi, Naisi, Naisi. Oh my Naisi . . .'

She seemed to have forgotten about me. I stood up, but she stopped as I did so.

'Deirdre,' I said suddenly, 'is the King . . . cruel to you?'

'Oh yes,' she said, with no change of tone. 'He does it on purpose to make me fight him. But I ignore him. I don't think of him, I pretend I'm with Naisi again. I don't even look at him. That's why he does it. He hates it when I ignore him, he hates it when I pretend he isn't there.' She giggled again, nerve-rackingly. 'Poor King . . . But he killed my Naisi. Oh Naisi.'

I went away from her, but as I went round the Royal Hall, I heard Conor's voice raised, speaking to her and so I turned back to see.

He was standing in front of her, legs straddled, arms folded. I couldn't see his expression because he had his back to me, but his voice was hard.

'Who is it you hate most, Deirdre?' he was asking, though he must have known the answer.

Deirdre ignored him. He leaned forward suddenly and slapped her face.

'Who do you hate most?' he demanded again.

This time Deirdre did answer him and still her voice had nothing in it. 'Yourself surely. Unless it be Owen Mac Durthact who killed my Naisi.'

'Well, Deirdre, since you're worse than useless to me, I'm sending you to him for a while.'

That broke her calm.

'You'll send me to *him*?' She didn't shout. 'To that pig's-dung butcher? You'll make me lie with *him*?!'

'I won't,' said Conor brutally. 'He will.'

She was silent. Conor shouted orders to the old hag he had in attendance to her. I walked quickly away, knowing there was nothing I could do, feeling physically sick.

Conor had her dressed in her best clothes, though they no

longer fitted. He put her on his chariot and began to drive to Owen's dun at top speed, driving the chariot himself. He laughed at her stricken face and said that she looked like a ewe between two rams. Then, with the horses going at a full-out gallop, she threw herself head first off the chariot.

When Conor had fought the horses to a halt and come running back, he found her dead with her skull broken open and a smile on her face. The outriders said later that Conor crouched by her body for a long time, weeping like a child for a lost toy.

They buried her near where she died and did not mark her grave.

# XIII

As he had said he would, Ibar sent to Dun Delgan for the youngest of his brothers to come to Emain and a few days after Deirdre died, the young man rode up the path to the gate of Emain. When I came back from weapons-practice with Conall, who had beaten me soundly in a mock-swordfight, Ibar brought him to me where I was washing myself down with water from a bucket of water Fiall had brought from the spring. I had forgotten he was coming because of something Conall had told me, which was worrying me.

'Here's my brother,' said Ibar. 'He'll be your charioteer.'

I looked round to see Gaiar Mac Riangabra, who had been Emer's charioteer, standing beside Ibar. I looked at him properly for the first time: he was medium size with mousy brown hair and a broad face, sprinkled with freckles. He had an upper lip something like a frog's and his hands were chunky and square, but I had seen the way they handled the reins with the delicacy and sensitive strength inborn in all the sons of Riangabra.

Ibar left us and we stood looking at each other: I had not thought of saying no to Ibar's offer and not just because I was unlikely ever to get a better charioteer than a son of Rian-gabra. Now I wondered what kind of man Gaiar was.

Gaiar was the first to speak. He had narrowed his blue eyes as he interpreted the clan-marks tattooed on my chest and stomach. Of course, they were the Pigs of Cruachan, the Queen's clan.

'You're from Connaught,' he said.

'I am. Didn't your brother tell you who I am?'

He shook his head.

'My name is Lugh Mac Romain,' I told him. 'I am a harper, and I was foster-son and nephew to the Queen of Connaught.'

His eyes widened.

'Then you're the man who . . .'

'Killed the King. Yes.'

He glanced at a pebble by his foot and kicked it away. He seemed to be thinking: I said nothing because I knew that in the end it would be he who would decide whether he was going to be my charioteer. I needed a charioteer badly and from what Conall had told me, I hadn't much time to find one. Also I liked the look of him, and the way he had driven Emer's chariot.

'Can I try your chariot?' he said at last.

We took it out on to the practice-field: first I drove it and then gave the reins to Gaiar, who was obviously itching for them, and stood beside him on the swaying creaking chariot while he outdid everything I had done with the chariot, looking as though he had hardly noticed, talking to the bay and black ponies all the while and barely using the goad. We spent most of that morning on the field so that we would know each other's minds on a battlefield: Gaiar galloping past where I stood poised, slowing a little to let me grab a handle and swing myself on, and then swerving on down the field. Gaiar took as much pleasure in it as I did, but he was far more careful of the horses. His skill had been taught him by his brother Laegh, but the love he had for the horses was part of his nature.

We led the sweating horses back up into the dun and as we

climbed the slope Gaiar asked me how soon we would be driving into battle together.

I didn't look at him. Gaiar took it for granted that I was as eager for fighting as he was, though I thought he had not been in a real battle before from the way he spoke about it: he was only recently come to manhood.

'I've been speaking to Conall Cernach,' I said, 'and he told me this: have you heard of Gerg of Rath Ini on the borders of Ulster and Connaught?'

Gaiar frowned and nodded. 'Yes, but I never met him. Cuchulain didn't like him so we never visited him.'

'Well, his daughter, Ferb, is going to marry Maine Morgor, one of the Queen of Connaught's sons.'

Gaiar looked blank. 'But why?'

'Conall told me that Conor sees only one reason: Gerg is transferring his allegiance from Ulster to Connaught and his daughter will seal the bargain.'

'Oh. And is Conor going to raid him?'

'Probably.'

'Will we be in the raid too?'

'If the King asks me.'

'But you think he will?' Gaiar was holding the bridle of the bay anxiously.

'Yes.'

A long slow smile split Gaiar's face and he fondled the bay's soft muzzle, dreaming, no doubt, of his defying death to save me from my foes on the battlefield. I left him there, feeling angry and not quite sure why.

Emain was always quieter in summer: most of the great lords were in their duns, raiding each other or Connaught, hunting, breaking horses. They would go to Tara for the great summer fair at Tara on the Feast of Bron Trogain and they would go home again for harvest and bringing in the herds until Samhain brought them all together again. If there had been a war on, or even a big raid, then they would have come together gladly until the harvest, but for the most part they preferred to carry on their own feuds and cattle-raids from their home-duns.

Now Conor needed a small force of men, quickly, without calling in the tribes. And so he decided to use the ragtag and bobtail of the foreigners staying in Emain at the time; among them, myself. There was a woman-warrior, Cathrach Catuchenn, who had lost her heart to Cuchulain as had many women before her and after; there were three short men of the Sidhe-folk, who had been cast out by their own kind for some reason; there was a young man who claimed he was of the old stock of Ulster, though he had only his sword and horse and spoke a dialect from the far west; there was a strange small yellow man from no-one-knew-where, with eyes that went slanting up in his head, little slits in his flat face. All he would say was that he came from the Land of Silk, from the Uttermost East to the Uttermost West and spent all his life doing it.

Conor asked me to join the troop too, to Gaiar's delight. I took Fiorbhinn to Gennan Bright-Face and asked him to look after her until I came back. It reminded me of Iollan Hen.

'And if you don't?' he asked, watching me closely.

I shrugged. 'It won't concern me. Keep it or give it to some harper.' Then a thought struck me. 'Gennan, have you seen my . . .?'

'Your death? No,' he smiled, 'I haven't seen anything.' It didn't sound genuine, but he would say nothing more.

I felt uneasy for a while, but I forgot about it quickly in the preparing for the raid; sharpening my sword and stabbing spear; borrowing Conall's red shield, strengthening the straps and sharpening the edge; trying not to think about what was coming and telling myself that if I fought creditably, Conor might reward me with some land. Gaiar washed and polished and oiled the chariot and the harness until everything shone bright enough to dazzle. He was shining with happiness when we set out for Rath Ini with all Conor's troop, close to the King's side as befitted my rank, leaving dust hanging on the still summer air behind us as we went.

We had left Emain Macha very early in the morning, in the dark before sunrise, to catch Maine Morgor by surprise at his wedding. We travelled the paths across the hills and through the forests, made by cattle-reivers, and quite firm since there hadn't been much rain recently.

I had known Maine Morgor. I neither liked nor disliked him: I had hunted and raided in his troop, but not as much as with Dalaigh or Murcael Mac Gelban, or his younger brother, Maine Andoe. He was built on the lines of Conall Cernach and so many others: a big, brave, fair-haired fool of a man; unthinkingly courageous and arrogant, with a liking for finery. A useless King he would make. But then it would be Findabhair who would become Queen when the Queen died. When the Queen died. How could the Queen die? It seemed impossible that her laced blue eyes could ever be staring with death, her body stiffening and cold. And yet she was a woman and could die.

So thinking I rode down with Conor, King of Ulster, and his troop of warriors to Rath Ini set in a valley of the hills: pride high in their minds and their weapons burnished and sharpened until they could dazzle the sun and cut a hair on water. I was with them, but somehow not of them: Gaiar was by my side, nursing the ponies across the rough parts, his ugly face gentle as he controlled them. Images flashed through my mind, my hand was sweaty on the haft of my stabbing spear, a feeling like a tight band round my head. I had not put on any war-paint since I was no longer entitled to wear the paint of Cruachan and I would not put on the paint of Ulster. I counted the little throwing-spears in their sheaf strapped to the wickerwork side for the hundredth time. There were about half a dozen – there had not been time to make more.

We came sweeping down from the hill path into the little valley. At one end of it there was a waterfall and a stream going past the dun, a clear rippling stream. But the dun was shut, the cattle and horses all taken into safety. We must have been seen as we came by some herdsman or other. There were heads looking over the fence at the top of the rampart.

We rode onto the home-pasture: Conor raised his arm in the signal to stop and the flat piece of worn-down grass became a mill of rearing ponies and horses and creaking chariots, as the charioteers flung their ponies back on their haunches. Gaiar stopped the ponies without any flourishes and smiled at me. Then he yawned and I knew he was afraid. Well, that made two of us.

I looked up at the sky. It was close and warm, but the sky was grey and full of rain. I sniffed and thought I could sense a cooler breeze. Around us the dun and its wooded hills seemed ominously quiet: the birds had been put to flight by the noise of our arrival. Gaiar was putting the knives on the hubcaps of the chariot; all around charioteers were doing the same.

I looked across at Conor: he was talking with Cathrach while Brod put the knives on the wheels. Ibar had been kicked by a horse two days before and so Conor was being driven by Brod, a cousin of Ibar's. Cathrach was standing on her chariot platform with her hands on her hips, smiling: she had a scar running across her cheek which seemed to improve it, pointing at her magnificent dark eyes; a big strong woman. Gaiar shook the reins and brought my chariot up closer to the King. Cathrach drove off to talk to someone else, leaving the King standing, legs straddled and one hand to his beard.

He looked at me as I came alongside and then back at the rath.

'Well?' I asked.

'Buan has just told me what he saw.' Buan was a short man, more than half Sidhe-folk, and he was Conor's best scout. 'Maine brought a whole troop of men with him for his wedding and as well as them there are Gerg's men in the dun.'

I raised my eyebrows and looked back at Rath Ini. 'We're outnumbered?'

'We are.'

'We can hardly go home.'

'Hardly.' Conor bit his lip: he had made a grave error in underestimating the number of fighters there would be in the rath. He knew it now, of course.

Cathrach clattered up, grinning.

'When are we attacking?' she demanded.

'If we attack as things are,' said Conor thoughtfully, 'they'll have the advantage.'

'What's wrong with that?' said Cathrach. 'Makes it more fun.'

Conor ignored her and asked me, 'How would Maine Morgor react if I insulted only him?'

'He'd lose his temper,' I said, 'and do something rash. But very honourable.'

Conor nodded.

He turned to Brod and spoke some words in his ear. Brod straightened up the ponies and shouted. They snorted and went from a standstill to a trot to a canter. Conor's crimson cloak spread out behind him as his chariot drove for the gate of the rath. Stones and throw-spears whistled down around him, but Brod made the chariot circle and weave, turning this way and that, showing the left side to the gate as an insult. Conor shouted something up at the people trying in vain to hit him: the words 'Maine' and 'Coward' came back and then Brod had turned the chariot and they came flying back over the green grass. The chariot structure creaked as Brod fought the ponies round in a circle to face the rath again. Conor smiled at me. For the first time I didn't feel suspicious of his smile, but thought: treacherous he might be, but he is brave. In that moment I even liked him and the gorgeous gold-shot tunic no longer seemed strange on him.

Belatedly I remembered my shield, took it from my back and arranged the holding strap on my shoulder and arm. Just as I got it settled, the rath-gates slammed open and a crowd of fighters came out, all chariots, resplendent and glittering with wedding finery. They looked to be exactly one troop: Maine had come out without any of Gerg's clan to strengthen him.

Behind us Conor's foreign troop shouted in answer to Maine's cry of 'Cruachan!' Incongruously familiar, that battle-cry. How often had I shouted it in raids and battles? Gaiar and Brod leaned forward in the same movement and touched their goads on the ponies' haunches. There was a surge as they started forward and a jerk that nearly unbalanced me as we went over a large stone and then the chariot was bowling forwards across the grass, faster and faster, the ponies quickening to a gallop. I swayed in time to the movement, facing forwards; I took a holly-spear from the sheaf and made ready to throw.

The bunch of chariots rattled towards us: I threw four spears into them in quick succession, saw two men go down and then there came a mingled redoubling of crashing and creaking and neighing and roaring as the two groups met.

As always, having sweated and thought too vividly all the way there, as soon as the actual fighting began I forgot it all. When everyone around you is trying to kill you, your imagination cannot function: you're too busy just trying to stay alive.

The press was too thick to manoeuvre in the chariot. Gaiar had run out along the pole and was balancing there, keeping better control of the ponies. I shouted his name and he looked over his shoulder. I jumped down and waved my arm away from the fight. He fought the ponies round and took the chariot away.

A man leapt for me, his sword arm raised, to catch me unawares. I shortened my spear, bent and stepped in under his guard, spitting him on the spear like the boar I had hunted with Cormac. I remember glancing at him as I pushed him off the spear with my foot and deciding not to take his head. After that, as with most fights I remember very little, except the tiny details that remain with you when the great things have been forgotten. I know that my arm ached and that the shoulder-strap chafed my shoulder and that I got a painful cut along my ribs when I didn't dodge fast enough.

At last a chariot came past and I saw Gaiar's face shouting above the spinning wheels and blades as he hauled the ponies on their haunches. I reached for the handles and swung up and we pressed on to the gates.

They were open, but the men of the dun were trying to close them to us, but there were Ulstermen outside pushing against them. Gaiar stopped the chariot because there was no way through without cutting down Ulstermen with the scythes. My mind suddenly went cold: I dropped my stabbing spear in the sheaf, swept out my long sword and sawed through the leather hinges of the gate, where they were perished with damp. One gate crashed to the ground, open, leaning crazily against the two posts. The blade of my sword was bent: I straightened it as best I could with my teeth as Gaiar drove on over a man who got in the way.

Then we were all into the rath and fighting in a mixture of men, women and pigs and stampeding cows, for all the livestock was gathered in makeshift pens in the rath. and they easily got free. Chariots crashed into storehuts and the noise sounded as if all the sky-demons and Bocanachs and giants of the deep were gathered together for singing. Then Gaiar stopped the chariot and ran down the pole to comfort the horses; I put away my sword which was now blunt and took my stabbing spear, but there was no one nearby for me to kill. The redness faded, leaving me feeling hollow and realizing I was cut along my ribs. A drop of wet fell on my hand and I looked up.

The sky was grey, no longer filled with noise of battle. Three more drops fell on my face, cooling me further. In a moment it was pouring with rain. All around warriors were catching their breath and looking about them. A few torches were tossed into thatch, but they burned sourly and soon fizzled out. The people of the rath and what was left of Maine's troop had retreated into the hall itself, leaving us outside, though judging by the number of bodies, there were many fewer of them. Many fewer of us too.

Conor drove up to me, driving the ponies himself. His greying hair and beard were turning into strings and his wonderful tunic was clinging to his limbs. I grinned a little at the sight, despite the pain of my ribs. There is something very ridiculous about finery reduced to bedraggledness by rain, though I knew I probably looked worse with a long rent in my tunic.

'They're inside,' he said, pulling a hair from his beard.

'We'll fire the thatch . . .'

'In this?'

It was stalemate. They were inside the hall and we were outside in the pelting rain. We could no longer use our chariots, but neither could they and we couldn't fire the thatch to make them come out.

Cathrach Catuchenn came striding up to Conor's chariot and said in her loud voice, 'What do we do now, King? Wait until the rain stops?'

I looked up at the sky hanging over us.

'You're hopeful,' I told her.

She looked as though she was going to spit at me. 'What says the King?'

Conor was gazing at the closed door of the house musingly.

'We wait until nightfall. Then we attack in the dark,' he said.

It seemed to me like a good idea. Cathrach nodded reluctantly and went round to tell everyone and I jumped down from the chariot to forage for something to eat. I wondered what the people inside the house were thinking. Did they expect another attack immediately? Perhaps a pause would lull them into a false feeling of security.

I went cautiously up to the wall of the house and felt it. It seemed very firm and it was oak-planked. I didn't think it could be hammered in.

A pig ran across my feet: I gave chase and caught it and cut its throat as it squealed and struggled between my knees. I carried it back to the chariot and found that Gaiar had discovered an empty storehut. There was a dead man lying by the hut. I bent over him and turned him over, before dragging him away and saw he had half his face missing. I thought suddenly that that could quite easily have been me. I started to shiver with reaction . . .

After a while I was able to go into the hut, though I thought miserably that there was more fighting to be done later. Gaiar comforted me a little by looking almost as pale as I felt: he tried to smile at me as I came in and then he concentrated on getting a fire going with some peat he had found stacked in a corner.

We singed the pig meat and ate, though neither of us was really hungry – and neither of us would have admitted it to the other. Really, it was comical.

Gaiar got up when we had finished and put his cloak round him. He had brought mine in as well.

'Where are you going?' I asked.

He blushed a little. 'There might be some horses still alive on the field,' he said, 'I don't want to leave them . . .'

I let him go. I had a look at my sword-cut, though strictly that was Gaiar's job, and it seemed to be clotting properly. I wondered whether the men inside the house would make a sally. I thought they would, knowing Maine Morgor as I did. He was not one to wait inside a hall to be killed; unless he was dead already he would come out. Or perhaps he was waiting for the Queen to come and relieve him: the rath had been shut up by the time we arrived – he might have had time to send off a messenger.

I went outside again, pulling my cloak around me, for it was still raining and likely to go on for the rest of the day. While we had been eating, Conor had got some men to make up a ram from one of the fence-posts on the rampart. I didn't think it would be much good: the doors of the house looked very sturdy and barred inside. It was ominously quiet. The only sound coming from Gerg's house was the sound of a woman keening all by herself, 'Ochone, ochone!'

'It's Gerg's people we must deal with now,' said Conor to me. 'And however many of the Connaughtmen there are left.'

He looked at me sideways, as though he had only that moment realized properly that I too was a Connaughtman.

'Were you friends with Maine Morgor at all?' he asked casually.

I had to smile at it.

'I never had much to do with him. I knew his brother Maine Andoe better. He's a good warrior and a fine strong man. But . . . not subtle.'

'And I am?' he spoke sharply.

'Yes. A very subtle man, Conor.' He didn't seem surprised, but simply looked me over very thoroughly as though I were a horse.

'And there's more to you than meets the eye, Lugh,' he said.

I smiled and bowed slightly. 'I take that as a compliment, King.'

'You may do so. What was it you came about?'

I hesitated about telling him of what I had thought, that Maine might have sent a messenger to his mother: Conor, that subtle man, had probably thought of it already. I shrugged a little.

'Knowing Maine as I do, I think there'll be sallying.'

'You forget, Lugh, that I am a subtle man,' was all the King said before he moved away.

I saw what he meant a moment later.

Without any warning the door slammed open and three men came running out, their weapons in their hands and no shields to slow them down in the Hero's Sally . . . And they tripped, falling headlong over the log Conor had had set across the threshold. They were dispatched immediately and their bodies kicked out of the way.

The next ones jumped over the log, but were killed with stones and throw-spears. The ones after them carried shields which slowed them down so that only one man completed the circuit of the hall and got back safely. Conor marched up and down arguing with all those who wanted to attack the hall immediately. Soon the sallying stopped.

I went back to the shelter of the storehut, wishing suddenly for my harp, but I had left her in Emain Macha. My fingers longed for the touch of the bronze strings and I sat on the ground, looking at my hands for a long time. I hadn't noticed before that, in addition to the sword-callouses every warrior has, my fingers were hard at the tips.

It was still raining and a drip of water was falling in the corner where some thatch had come off. I dozed in a mixture of swift-running thoughts and memories of battle. I remember thinking that the monotonous noise of raindrops was like the sound of my fingers when I tapped out the beat of the chariot-ponies' battle-shod hooves on the sounding board of my harp.

## XIV

I was awoken by Gaiar shaking my shoulder. The firelight was much more vivid and it was darkening outside, still raining, though the big drops had lessened to a small hissing rain. The dripping corner was now a pool of mud and the fire had burned down. I was cold and stiff.

'What's happening now?' I asked, standing up and wincing as I pulled at the wound in my side.

'The King is going to attack soon now,' said Gaiar. He was looking at me oddly, a little tight around the lips.

On impulse I said, 'What is it, Gaiar?'

He looked down, shaking his head.

'Nothing. I . . . Is it always like this? Fighting, I mean . . . I . . .'

'Yes,' I said quietly, 'it's usually like this. Glorious too, of course, but the aftermath is always the same.'

'There was a horse I knew . . . with a white blaze . . . I had to kill it . . . I didn't think it would be quite like this. I thought the songs and Hero-tales . . .'

A horse, not a man, I thought; but said, 'I know. You thought the songs and Hero-tales were the whole truth instead of only half of it. Well, believe me, Gaiar, and I'm a harper: I know where those songs and Hero-tales come from – a very little truth, a lot of invention and dreams.'

'But Cuchulain . . .'

'Cuchulain. Yes, Cuchulain makes it all seem true, though he'd be puzzled if you told him so. He believes it's true.'

'Aren't you like him?'

I almost laughed, but he was quite serious: perfectly pre-

139

pared, was Gaiar, to see in me the sort of man Cuchulain
was . . .

'No. But you'll get used to it,' I promised, knowing it was
a lie for myself at any rate. 'You're not unusual: most
warriors feel this way after their first battle, but it soon fades.
Soon you won't even notice the dead.'

Gaiar plainly didn't believe me, but he shook himself and
said,

'I'm sorry. I didn't mean . . .'

'Ach, let be, let be, Gaiar. I know what you meant and
didn't mean. We can't all be like Cuchulain.'

I left the hut with my shield and spear. There was a group
gathered near the house and more bodies lying around than
I had seen last. It was still dusk of the long summer's day and
I could see Conor by his ruined splendid tunic. No one had lit
torches.

I pushed myself through the crowd to Conor. He was
shouting at them.

'By the gods of my people!' he said. 'I wish now I had
brought my own men with me. You're no good at all. You
want to go home? Well, if you leave this matter unfinished
there will be no harper up and down the land who doesn't
make a satire on it, and not a one of you will ever be able to
sit among fighters again.'

I thought it was his own reputation he was most afraid for:
if he had to leave now there would be whispers up and down
the land that the Druid's Curse was beginning to work on
him.

Someone caught sight of me and yelled, 'What does the
Connaughtman say?'

It took me a moment to realize it was me he was speaking
about. Conor watched me shrewdly. I shrugged my shoulders
and said,

'For me it is a matter of indifference. I will do what the
King does. None of you have sworn any oath to him, you are
not bound to stay. I am. But at any rate, I've heard tell of
the riches of Gerg's rath and his women. If none of you have
any honour or pride, surely you have some desire for riches?'

140

There was silence. I had said what Conor wanted me to say, but I thought detachedly that it was not myself who said it. Nothing would please me better than to go home now without any more fighting. I had no quarrel with Gerg or Maine Morgor, but here I was perfectly prepared to kill them both. I was afraid again, yet I knew that if Conor had to go home now I would feel as shamed as if I had suggested it. I didn't know why. Perhaps something to do with the possibility of lands from Conor, perhaps Maine Morgor's being the son of the Queen. My reasons were too complicated for me to unravel.

There was a movement in the crowd. The little yellow man came forward and bowed deeply three times to Conor.

'I will not insult my honoured ancestors,' he said with a singsong accent. 'I will not lose Face here. Therefore I fight for you.'

Another silence. Then Cathrach's low voice came distinctly.

'If we'd had Cuchulain to lead us, we wouldn't have had to wait until nightfall.'

Conor heard, as he was meant to, and I thought for a moment he would attack the woman.

'Cuchulain Mac Sualtim may not be here, Cathrach Catuchenn,' I said coldly, 'but he will certainly hear about this night.'

'Let's get on with it then!' she snapped, turning away.

The ram was brought up by men swearing and slipping in the mud, but in the end it wasn't needed. The doors slammed open and men came pouring out. I don't think they had expected us any more than we had expected them and so there was a kind of hiatus as the two sides stared at each other. Then Maine, at the head of Gerg's people and the remnants of his own, yelled again and charged forward and the whole degenerated into boiling confusion.

Most of the time we were simply pushing. It was not a fluid battle: the two troops were trying to go different ways and so we pushed and they pushed and gradually, oh, so slowly, we pushed them back into the house, treading and tripping on the things underfoot. Then we were in and it turned from a simple battle into a nightmare.

Rath Ini was a rich house with a great bronze vat full of mead by the door called the Ol Guala. There was gold and silver all around; the rushes being trodden into slush now had been laid over with fragrant herbs for the wedding feast.

I knew all this in a flash of clarity when we penetrated into the house: I saw the embroidered hangings on the walls and the fine drinking horns lying scattered and the women shutting themselves into a cubicle as we broke in. Then someone trampled on the fire and it was a struggle in the dark, lit only by a few of the torches high up out of reach and not bright enough to let you tell friend from enemy so that if someone fell against you, you killed him on principle.

I heard Maine's voice shouting 'Cruachan!' and I answered him with the same battle-cry and then remembered and changed it to the Ulster shout: 'Macha! *Macha!*' But the rest is nothing but a dark heaving and threshing and confusion. I was in a fog not only of physical darkness, but my mind cut off from itself, so that I killed and killed and joyed in the killing . . .

Then I came up against Maine himself and he was berserk too, still foaming at the mouth like a mad dog. He was using his sword and he leapt at me, hammering blows on me and battering at my shield. I saw him close to my face and recognized him. I stepped backwards, tripped on something soft and cracked my head against a screen. There were coloured lights and someone pitching forward on to me, dying somehow on my spear. Then muffled dark.

It seemed only a moment later when I came to again and pushed Maine's body off me and sat up, but the fight was over. The house was full of carnage and destruction, a nameless mess.

I felt very sick and my head split down the middle and I ached all over. I pulled myself to my feet and voided my stomach, though there was nothing in it. Then I stumbled outside, heading vaguely for the sound of voices, and found that it was daylight. The rain had stopped, but the light hurt my eyes. I blinked and made out Conor and a little knot of men standing by the gate. I went over to them, walking very carefully like an old man, so that my head wouldn't fall off.

There were sounds of surprise and pleasure at seeing me and Conor said something. Gaiar came running up to me.

'I thought you were dead too.'

It was hard to think.

'Not quite,' I croaked.

There was a rag bound about his arm still oozing juicily, but he seemed quite cheerful. I joined the group. There were pitifully few. Most of Conor's foreign troop were dead, though Brod had reappeared, looking pale with circles under his eyes and blood clotting his hair. The little yellow man was dead, having, I am told, fought better than a man twice his size. So was Cathrach Catuchenn who had loved Cuchulain. It was the best way for her, since Cuchulain wasn't interested.

Conor blurred in my eyes. His beautiful tunic was entirely ruined. No doubt the women of Emain would unpick the gold from the cloth and weave it up again into another gold and linen tunic, fit for a King, to point up the greyness of his beard. His thumbs were in his belt as he looked round at us, numbering us and knowing that the victory was not worth it with this number of men lost. The Romans would call it a Pyrrhic victory.

The whole ruined rath was silent, but for the cries of the women and the noise of the animals being rounded up. Conor would spoil the rath and it was well worth the spoiling, but the spoil wasn't worth the fight. And the death of Maine would surely bring closer the day that must surely come, when Ulster and Connaught would be at each other's throats. So I thought then and the gods withheld foreknowledge from me.

We spent most of that day resting, spoiling the rath and rounding up the cattle, sheep and horses. We slept that night near the rath, rather than spend the night among ghosts. Next morning we sent some of the warriors and charioteers with the herds, to take them by a different route and the rest of us bowled north together. Already, up above the dead in Rath Ini, the crows were waiting for us to leave. Well may they call the crow the Mistress of the Battlefield: most of us come to her in the end.

## XV

We were not halfway back to Emain, moving slowly, when we saw chariots coming towards us across a stretch of heathland, their outriders spaced out along the flanks of the hills. We drew together and as we came near enough to see details the two leading chariots detached and drove forward to meet Conor. The chariots halted side by side, Conor's horses standing still, the other horses frisking a little under their yokes.

Gaiar walked the ponies up close to them: the two leaders were two of Conor's many bastard sons, Niall and Feradach Mac Conor.

Niall was saying, 'Maeve is coming north with her household. She was staying close to the border and someone must have got through to them. Cuchulain sent us word to say she had gone through west of Slieve Fuad – it was Cormac who told him. Feradach and I decided to bring out our clans and give you some support, though you never told us you were going to do this.'

'Are these all that are left?' asked Feradach in wonder.

'They are,' said Conor dangerously softly, 'and they have fine spoils and more coming to them.'

Niall looked hard at us. Conor turned his horses himself and then gave the reins back to Brod. He had escaped the battle nearly scatheless, which is often the way: either you come out whole or not at all.

Gaiar turned the horses too as Niall and Feradach rolled on. As I realized there was going to be another battle, I felt suddenly unbelievably tired. My head was still aching and I

144

was cold and sick from it. I couldn't think of the battle ahead. It was all coming too close together.

We went back the way we had come, squelching through grass and trees. As we by-passed Rath Ini a flock of crows rose up in alarm and then settled down again. Feeling slightly drunk, I thought I heard the sound of a lament in their wings, like the birds of the gods who sing men to sleep: but the men in Rath Ini would never wake from their sleep; cattle would no longer graze on the pastures . . .

I shook my head and thought of the lament I would make when I got back to Emain. There is something very satisfying in making a lament: somehow I find that putting sorrow into music cleanses it away. I considered how I would begin it and the way I would put the verses together – and then I remembered that there was still a battle to come. My stomach clenched. Perhaps the lament would never be made, or sung only in Tir-na-nOg or the House of Donn. I was afraid. And of what?

I felt dizzy and nearly fell from the speeding chariot, but I grabbed the side and held on. The feeling passed away. Gaiar hadn't noticed: he was talking low-voiced encourage-ment to the ponies, looking as though he had forgotten everything of Rath Ini and everything to come.

We knew the way the Queen would take to Rath Ini and we went that way. Sure enough, we passed through a thin wood and as we came out from between the trees into a clear space, slowed to a walk through the mess of leaves from last year and this year's bright green, we sighted her army, as it were the mirror-image of our own, chariots creaking across the flat sloping ground, disappearing to the axles in fern and high summer grass. There were three troops of a hundred and fifty with the Queen, outnumbering us.

They stopped when they saw us and formed the chariot line, with the horse-riders spread out between or riding beside the chariots for reinforcement to some great lord, or horse-men in groups of three. The Queen had brought most of her clan with her, both men and women-warriors, all those who lived in Cruachan and travelled with her. I knew nearly every one of them, had fought with them, hunted with them, drunk with them. There was Buac Mac Banblai who was one of the Queen's best councillors and there was Cur Mac Daltach who had tried to make me into a great warrior.

The two troops of Niall and Feradach and those that were left of Conor's lined up to charge. It would be difficult through the thick summer growth, but no more difficult than, say, over heather. As we prepared for the charge the sun came out from behind the clouds and the chariots shone dazzling on green, with a kind of fierce splendour like the colours shown by goldfinches when they begin to fight. The bronzework and paint of my chariot, where it wasn't dented or splashed with blood from the previous fighting, was a pleasure to the eye: I looked at the ponies as they stood unhappily. They were sweating and the enamelled ornaments on their harness jinked as they tossed their heads.

I straightened up. All along the line of chariots, just under the eaves of the wood, people were settling their shields comfortably, transferring their stabbing spears to their left hands and reaching down for their throwing-spears. I had only two left. The charioteers were checking the reins and whispering at the horses. I saw several of them swallow hard and cross their fingers and it suddenly occurred to me to imagine what it must be like to be a charioteer: very few of them have any weapons or armour except a knife for cutting tangled traces and the charioteers' band of saffron cloth across their foreheads. It is dishonourable to kill an unarmed charioteer, but who notices little details like that in battle?

Conor rolled forward a little, and I saw the great chariot of the Queen roll out from the line of her forces, flashing gold and enamel and painted with red, her horses two red-coloured animals with white-rimmed eyes and mealy mouths. I could see her at the distance, her long gold hair with the carefully bleached streaks of grey in it, some strands of it plaited and pinned round her head. Her face was dead white from the powder she put on except for the patches of ochre on her cheeks, so that she looked as though she was wearing war-paint, although I knew that she never did, except to dance in.

A little behind her red-robed figure standing so straight and fierce in her pride, was the chariot of her consort and it was a little smaller and painted blue. The man standing in it next to the charioteer was a big broad man with brown hair and a moustache and he wore the great gold torc of the King, the New King. I looked at him closer as the line of chariots gave a little ripple of readiness. He was checking the strap of his shield and for a moment I could not see his face. Then he looked up and, as if pulled together by a string, my eyes met his, and I knew him.

Dalaigh. Big smiling Dalaigh, the man who carved toys for children, who collected sword-tricks. When we were boys he always tended to follow my lead, and he still preferred that. He was one to be led by others, he loved the Queen with a mixture of awe and veneration like most of the men at Cruachan, and did whatever she said, and yet sometimes he would become obstinate about something and then there was no way to shift him. Dalaigh, consort of the Queen of Connaught, husband to the woman in the red chariot. Dalaigh – Ailell now.

I couldn't understand my own emotions. We had been friends when still in the Boys' Troop of Cruachan until I left when I was twelve to start the full bard's training. When I came back we had become spear-brothers; I had saved his life in a cattle-raid and he had saved mine in the retaliatory raid from Ulster; now he was the King, now he no longer had the name Dalaigh, but he wore the name of Ailell that a dead man had left behind. He loved the Queen. I had often wondered who was the new consort to die in seven years' time, now I knew. And it made me angry. I felt betrayed, although it had been the Queen who had sent him her token, the little carven finger of bone which sets the seal of Fate on the man who receives it and becomes the Queen's Consort: he lives brightly and as best until he is killed and his body scattered over the cattle-pasture to make the earth fruitful.

Dalaigh, that man.

He was staring at me very hard and a slow flush spread up his neck. I could see it quite clearly in the bright sun and then there was no time to see anything clearly again, because Conor's arm had come down and pointing against the Queen and he was shouting something. The battle-horns of Cruachan, those high metal monsters who bellow and squeal, were being blown by two men on either end of the chariot-line. The Ulster battle-horns had been left in Emain, since this was not a proper hosting. Ulster shouted the battle-cry in answer and Connaught threw theirs back.

'Macha! *Macha!*'

'*Cruachan!*'

The two lines started towards each other, the high wheels only a little encumbered by the green-growth. As we came within range I threw my remaining two throw-spears, badly because of the hurt and anger welling up inside me. The speed picked up to a canter; the bracken was crushed under the wheels, so that they turned up green blood. We had a slight slope in our favour, but the whole of the Connaught line was swerving round slightly and they were longer than the Ulster line. They were trying to outflank and drive in from the sides. A spear whistled past.

There was a little gasp beside me. I looked and saw that Gaiar, ugly-faced young Gaiar, was slowly crumpling up and letting the reins fall from his skilful hands, draping across the haunches of the ponies. They swerved nervously. There was a spear stuck under his ribs, a light throw-spear of fire-sharpened holly: even to this day I can remember the way the knots in the wood looked as Gaiar slipped to his knees and then slid quietly against the side of the chariot. His mouth was open and his eyes rolled up. For the first time I noticed that they were bright blue, blue as cornflowers with none of the milk mixed with the colour to lessen the blue-ness . . .

I scooped up the reins with my right hand. For a moment it was as though the line of charging horses and chariots was moving too slowly, as though through water, like the undersea armies of Tir-na-nOg . . . They speeded as I looked and I saw the man who had thrown the spear and he was the man leading the curling round of the line into ours, with his own people. I had known him well in Cruachan: his name was Murcael Mac Gelban, I remembered quite clearly, and the whole of the betrayal and anger and black, black sorrow coalesced against this one man, with his lime-washed hair sticking out from his head, pointing and laughing at the death of Gaiⱬr; the death of all that promise which had made his brother say that he would be the best of all the sons of Riangabra – all gone. And now this man was bringing round the line of chariots to crash into our flank . . .

I made a noise like a crow. I switched hands on the reins and pulled the ponies so that they were headed directly for Murcael. I had thrown all my throw-spears. I took my heavy, broad-headed stabbing spear in my right hand and took aim for him.

I threw, but the chariot jerked. Murcael's charioteer fell down, but there was no time to see whether it had been my spear that had done it . . . No time, but to swing the ponies back on line, directly for Murcael's chariot, yet time enough to see Murcael's eyes open wide as he saw death driving towards him in full panoply. I saw he recognized me. He grabbed for the reins, dropping his spear and tried desperately to haul the ponies out of the way, but they were crazed and it could not be done in the time remaining . . . No time at all, for I could see the very fronds of the bracken as they broke under the iron-shod wheels of the other chariot, see the red of the ponies' distended nostrils as they saw and swerved and feel my ponies swerving from destruction and through the black rage that had caught my mind in its coils, a little voice went yammering, something my ears were closed to . . .

The teams went swerving past each other and as they did, Murcael's chariot jack-knifed into mine. I had my knife from my belt and as the two chariots crashed together, I threw myself across the gap at his throat. Even as I did it, and caught him, and cut the throat and watched the red come fountaining, the little yammering noise in my head made itself heard: it's not worth it, it shouted, *not worth it*!

The chariots rolled over. The traces broke and the sides crashed and I was thrown over with the ruin of the careening wreckage. Quite clearly I felt my thigh-bone snap like a rotten hunting spear, but there was no pain from there, only the general pain of death. My mind could wonder sadly what would become of Fiorbhinn my harp, but there were whirling bright scythes above me and a heavy weight. Then the sun did die and the aged stars fell through my head and darkness and the end of the world came and it was over for ever . . .

## ☙ Part Three ☙

# The Sidhe

## I

In the beginning there was pain. Pain and strange dreams and then black; red-hot agony and then black, so that it was as though I was swimming in a black sea that burned at the surface and I could not break through. I would swim desperately through the smother and come close to the surface; then I would feel the pain and whimper and turn round and burrow back into it, where at least the pain was only a red thread running through everything. But there were strange monsters in the depths of the darkness; things that looked like the Queen, mutilated animals, enormous dragons that chased me so that I sweated and cried out and fought to escape, because I knew they all came from the pain . . . Yet when I reached the deepest part, where not even the dreams pursued me, I knew that I had only to go down a little further and I would break through to . . . where? As soon as I reached that place, fear would catch me and hold me; I would turn and start struggling for the surface again and the pain that at least told me that I was there, that let me know I was alive, although I did not quite know what that meant. I had always been swimming through the seas of my mind and there was no other world; there would always be a red pain over and through everything, so that even when I was nearest to the . . . other place, on the other side of the abyss, I could feel it pursuing me and I longed to escape.

Sometimes the pain was less red and sometimes it was

worse: sometimes I felt that I was a fire and sometimes the snows of winter would weigh me down again through the bitter depths.

Once or twice I came to a twilight zone where the pain was everywhere. I could smell the smell of wood burning and people near; shadows would come from beyond my dreams and do mysterious things with me and the place where the pain came from, so I might go deeper into the black, or the red would worsen until I longed only to escape, to get away from it, anything to be rid of the agony. But that passed too and there was no time and nothing but the contrast: the difference between the red and the black.

Then came a time when the twilight zone was nearer and the red dimmer: the black no longer seemed so inviting and I knew that worse things than dreams moved in it and beyond was something I didn't understand. Often now there was a bitter taste in my mouth, strange alien shadows and smells. I came closer and closer to them and the twilight receded . . . came back . . . receded again, further away. It relinquished me reluctantly, as the waves of the sea lap longingly at the shores the tide is pulling them back from, unwilling even to leave just one pebble behind, so that they foam and return, but each time move further back.

So the strange dark sea I was in left me and went back, but I knew it was there, had been there and would be there always. That was a familiar enemy: it was the strangeness of the pain that frightened me. The only worse thing I ad ever felt was when I got a spear thrust in my arm during a raid and Dalaigh had to use a hot iron on it. But this was grinding and dull with a sharp core to it and it was not for a few seconds, but for ever and ever.

And then suddenly I broke through a skin and awoke, opening my eyes. There was sweat on me, but no heat and no chill; the pain was there, but it had always been there. It was stronger at first and I caught my breath, but in a little it settled down. I became piercingly aware of myself: I knew I was sore in many places, but the source of the red was my right leg; I could not move it and indeed, when I tried the muscles in it, it hurt so much I bit my tongue.

I was lying beneath what felt like a hide of some kind, perhaps a goatskin and I felt the fur soft against my skin in some places and rough in others. Under me was the shorter smoother fur of a deerskin. There was pressure of bandages on the sore places. I could move my fingers and did so, stroking the furry deerskin: I was pleased at that; feeling something so definite and real as fur gave me a sense of steadiness, an anchor against the distortions I remembered and could not quite separate from reality.

My sight had cleared. I was looking up at low ceiling beams. They were laid in a strange way, parallel instead of radiating from the smoke-hole and they were so low that even in the dim warm light I could see the knots and wood-grain in them. They were stained black with smoke and between them was dried bracken and turves. Various things hung from them: dried meat and herbs and leather vessels. The place reeked of people and animals and smoke, mainly peat-smoke, and there was very little light.

People were speaking and a cow lowing somewhere a little further away. I could not see them because I was lying on my back and my head was too heavy to turn. With difficulty I concentrated on what they were saying and found to my vague fright that I could not understand them. Whatever the language was, it was not Irish. None of the words were familiar. I had never heard it before.

Suddenly my mind distorted, seeming to swoop sickeningly. I am in Tir-na-nOg, I thought confusedly and I will starve because I cannot ask for water, and they will kill me. With a great effort, I moved a little, trying to escape.

There was movement and a swish on earth and hay. A shadow was thrown across me and then the person bent over me and I saw a face between mine and the black roof beams. I was afraid and flinched back, and then, because of the feeling of the deerfur beneath my fingers, I swallowed drily and the world steadied again.

153

I caught my breath, but not with pain this time. Thoughts and memories came together in my mind and I knew where I was.

It was a woman bending over me, a woman with her black hair plaited down her back, but slipping under her arm as she bent down, and shining with the gold thread entwined in it. Her face was pale and the lines on it were not lines of age, but tattooing as the Caledones of Prydein, north of the frontier, tattoo themselves. Perhaps it was not quite as thick as that, but still it was like a mask: straight overcrossing lines in some places, on the cheeks and temples, curls and lozenge shapes in others. Her eyes seemed terribly deep because they were encircled with blue lines, blue spirals, starting under the eyebrows and spiralling in to the inner corner of the eye. They were totally different from the patterns on my own naked body. They were the tattooing lines of the Hill-people, the Dwellers in the Forest, the Fir-Bolg and the Sidhe-folk. The Tuatha de Danaan, the People of the Goddess.

I was afraid again, formlessly, because of the Queen. She is the Goddess-on-Earth, they are her people, what would they do when they found out? What would happen ... Did she make the pain in my leg, did she? And would she come back and hurt me more? The world lurched and I clutched at it.

'Are you in pain?' she asked softly. The words sounded strange in her mouth, but I could understand them. I breathed out with relief. I had been so afraid of not being understood, of the Queen and her people ...

'Close your eyes once for yes and twice for no,' said the woman. From her voice I realized she was young, perhaps only a girl. The mask of blue lines and the firelight made it hard to tell.

'Do you understand?' she asked and waited. I wished I could find energy to speak, but it was too much effort. I tried to concentrate on what she wanted. I closed my eyes once.

The girl smiled. 'Good. Are you in pain?'

I closed my eyes once.

'Where? In your leg?'

Yes, I said with my eyelids. She nodded approval.

'Are you thirsty?'

At the mention of the word I realized just how dry my mouth was, how hard it was to swallow. I closed my eyes.

'Wait, and I will bring you something to drink.'

She moved away over the rustling hay. I followed her with my eyes and got the impression of a long piece of undyed cloth around her, from her breasts to her feet. It was fastened with outlandish pins which glinted like the wire in her hair.

She came back quickly, holding a leather cup. She put her thin arm behind my head, lifting it from the pillow and the rim of the cup touched my lips. I drank greedily, spilling some. It was milk with something bitter at the back of it. She let my head fall back on the pillow and put the cup down while she cleaned up the spillage with a wisp of hay. Then she smiled at me again.

'Do not fear. You are in a sidhe and we know who you are. We will take care of you until you are better. You are safe.'

Even as she said this, I felt my eyelids close. There must have been something magic in her voice, or in the drink. I slept without dreams.

## II

When I woke up again it was lighter in the sidhe. At first I couldn't remember where I was, or what was the pain in my leg, but then it all came flooding back to me. I moved a little and croaked. The girl was there again, holding a cup and with someone standing behind her, holding things. She was dressed differently this time, in a leather jerkin and a short kilt, so that her legs were bare. I thought her too thin when I saw her that way – she had hardly any breasts at all and the high cheekbones stood out clearly. But there was a gold spiral fastener on her jerkin.

155

She smiled and asked in her lilting Irish, 'Do you feel better now?'

I made a noise which meant yes. She understood and came forward and knelt by the pile of skins and bracken.

'We must disturb you a little,' she said softly. 'You must say if it hurts too much.'

She nodded into the shadows and two men of the sidhe stepped into my view. They wore only leather kilts and their tattooing, and they were dark and shut-faced like the Fir-Bolg I had seen at Cruachan, though the men of the sidhe are not tattooed the same way as their women. Both saluted me with fist to forehead. I felt too weak to wonder why.

I was more helpless than a baby and the things that must be done in such a case were done by those two young men quickly and gently and without a trace of any expression showing on their faces. It hurt me to be moved, despite the pads under my hips and shoulders which protected the pressure on my bones from causing sores. I couldn't even try to help them and I hated it: to be so weak and helpless that everything must be done for you, it made me angry, between resisting the pain of my jarred leg. I felt like a log of wood, a heavy boulder to be moved, an object for which everything must be done.

When it was over and I lay back panting and sweating and feeling ashamed for no reason, the girl gave me the bitter milk to drink and I slept again.

Days passed in that way and gradually I gained strength so I could help a little. I felt proud of each new achievement of effort, like a baby learning to burble. I spent less time sleeping and more time lying awake and looking at the ceiling. At first I was content so, but then I began to be . . . bored, lonely. The girl never spoke to me more than necessary.

One day, when she had finished feeding me soup from a wooden bowl, I said before she could leave, 'Who are you?'

'I am a woman of the sidhe, one of the People of the Goddess.'

'No . . . your name.' It was still difficult to talk because of weakness, but it was getting better as the days passed. Only I could not talk for long.

'I am called Otter.'

'Why?'

'Because I like to swim in the little beck near here. It is very pleasant in summer. Sometimes I spear fish, though Wolfling is better at that.'

'Wolfling?'

'He is my brother.'

I knew enough about the Sidhe-folk to know that that simply meant he lived in the same place with her and was probably related in some way. All the Sidhe-folk are related to each other: they know only their mothers and the men are held in common by the women. The People of the Goddess. I knew their Goddess. She had golden hair and white-veined blue eyes and she lived in Cruachan and would kill me if she could find me . . . The nameless fear sickened me for a moment and then I pushed it away.

'He is a very good hunter,' said the girl, Otter. 'Much better than any of the other brothers, even the grown men among them. He can hunt like a wildcat on the side of a mountain.'

That meant he was more silent than the touch of Lugh the Sungod's bright spear. Wolfling. An odd name for a boy. Well, Lugh is odder, I thought to myself. Why Lugh? I didn't know and it was tiring to think. The two names danced together in my dreams as my eyelids shut, Otter and Wolfling, the Wolf hunting the Otter who turned into a girl and the girl into the Queen and the Queen cursed the wolf and he became a boy without a face who passed away like a shadow.

The next day I felt much stronger than I had. There was still pain in my leg and I dared not move it, but I found my thoughts were clearer. I think they were no longer drugging me so heavily – the milk tasted different.

Childlike, I looked forward to Otter coming with the broth she fed me: I liked her fine bones, despite her thinness, though I still couldn't get used to her mask of tattooing. And she was the only one who had spoken to me in Irish, though sometimes other women had come and tended me. Or rather, a woman gave the orders and examined me, but men did the rest. They were the People of the Goddess: I soon got used to the idea. I never thought to puzzle over the fact that I was never treated as a man of the sidhe would have been, but always with deference and respect. And a kind of distance, as though my presence was dangerous.

When Otter appeared, carrying the bowl of broth, I smiled at her and managed to prop myself up almost unaided. Despite the small mocking voice inside me, Otter was pleased.

'You are stronger,' she said. 'That is good.'

She would not let me feed myself, but spooned the broth into me with a wooden spoon, like a mother a child.

'Otter,' I said, between mouthfuls, 'how did I get here?'

'Into the sidhe? I know, but I cannot tell you because I was not there. Wolfling was. He was hunting and when he came upon the traces of Queen Maeve's army he followed them and watched the battle.' I flinched at the Queen's name, but of course she could say it because she was a woman and it had no power over her. Any woman can Intoxicate. And she was one of the Tuatha de Danaan, one of the Queen's people in her capacity as goddess. Goddess and woman.

'I will call my brother Wolfling,' she said, 'and he will tell you what he saw at the battle.'

'Now.'

'No, you must finish this soup to make you strong. You have plenty of time.'

When I had obediently swallowed all she gave me and she had gone to fetch Wolfling from outside, I stopped and thought of what she had said. Plenty of time, plenty of time. I hadn't considered how long it would take to recover from whatever injury I had got from the crash of chariots, the splinters and heavy, whirling weights. Plenty of time. How long?

'I am called Wolfling,' said a voice beside me.

158

I turned my head and looked at the boy squatting next to the bed. At first I couldn't see his face because it was in shadow; then he moved his head restlessly, tossing back a wisp of black hair escaped from his pigtail, and I saw his face.

It had been a face like one of the other of the Sidhe-folk, long and fine, with deep black eyes and darker skin than the Celts. But there was a terrible scar all across it, white and old and puckered where edges of skin had been sewn together in an attempt to repair the ruin. It ravaged all the left side of his face and there were two smaller scars on the right. I stared at the boy and he looked down.

'Wolfling?' I asked softly.

'A wolf did it,' he explained dully, 'when I was a boy. The wolf was killed. They expected me to die, but I didn't, so they said part of the wolf's life had gone into me to make me live and they called me Wolfling. I have another name, but only I know it.'

I nodded. Suddenly, I understood what it was like for this boy, how he must know what that stare meant and anticipate the question before it was asked. Have learnt to hide what he felt about it. Walked quietly, so as not to be noticed too much and laughed at – children are cruel. And learnt to hunt better than anyone as an answer to those who pointed.

'Your sister, Otter, told me you were the best hunter and tracker.'

The boy flushed under the scar and looked pleased.

'Grasswind is better . . .' he began.

'She said you followed the . . . Queen's army and watched the battle.'

'Anyone can follow an army. It's the easiest thing there is. It's harder to count how many were in it from the footprints.'

'Can you do that?'

He shook his head. His Irish was better than his sister's: less careful and more fluent.

'Where did you learn to speak my language so well?' I asked curiously.

The boy smiled. It stretched the scar and made it seem worse than ever, for the muscles on the left side of his cheek could not smile so well as those on the other. It made him look lopsided.

'The Hound taught me,' he said. 'He's the best tracker *I* know.'

'The Hound?'

'The Sedanta, of course.'

'*Cuchulain?*'

'Yes.'

'How did you come to know him?'

The boy shrugged. 'He is half Tuatha de Danaan himself. He is not afraid of us.'

I remembered the story then. Conor's sister, Dechtine, had disappeared one day. A year later she came back with a baby which she gave into the care of her brother as a gift to Ulster – the baby Cuchulain. No one knew exactly where she had gone – there were rumours that Lugh Longspear had taken her himself.

'You,' said the boy suddenly, 'do you think that when you leave this sidhe three hundred years will have passed?'

He asked it so abruptly I didn't know what to say. Strangely enough I hadn't thought of it. Now I did and a chill went down me, as I thought of the many songs sung of those who had entered the faery-hills and not come out again until a hundred years after.

'For some it may be three hundred years,' I said carefully, 'but Nera of Cruachan went into the Sidhe of Cruachan for a year and when he came out again it was the same day.' I wondered if he had been taken in by what I said. I thought not, but he didn't show it. His face was even more impassive than his sidhe-brothers', because of the scar.

'You wanted to know about the battle between the Queen and the Men of Ulster?'

'No. I know all I want to know about the battle. I want to know what happened afterwards, how I came to be here.'

The boy nodded thoughtfully. 'It isn't a long tale, so Otter won't be angry with me for tiring you. I will tell it to you. Some of it was seen by a Fir Bolg who told me.'

He settled down comfortably with his legs crossed. I noticed that he had his back to the light so his face was in shadow.

The battle was over quickly, a brief vicious clash and the crows were already settling by mid-afternoon. The Queen's household camped close by and Conor led his men back to Emain Macha. Ailell rode back to the field with surgeons and Mac Roth the Herald, to look for Connaught wounded on the field. They knifed those of the Ulster wounded who were still alive.

And then Mac Roth came up to Ailell who was talking with Cormac Connlonges. He drew Ailell aside and spoke to him quietly. Ailell turned white and after a moment he told Mac Roth to show him where the body was.

Mac Roth led him to the other side of the field where lay the tangled wreck of two chariots. Two bodies lay, one above the other, both covered with blood.

Ailell pulled off the corpse of Murcael Mac Gelban and found me lying there, half under the chariot ruins, soaked in blood. Mac Roth, whose business was to remember such things, had known the closeness between Ailell and myself when Ailell was only named Dalaigh.

Cormac knelt down beside me and rubbed off some of the blood, to be sure.

'This is Lugh Mac Romain,' he said.

'You knew him?' asked Ailell.

'Yes. He saved my life once, when we were hunting. And he helped me with his harping . . . in a certain matter with my f–father.'

'He died well,' said Mac Roth.

Cormac felt my neck sadly, hopelessly. He stopped, checked, listened at my chest and then looked up.

'I don't believe it,' he said incredulously, staring at the mess of the chariot.

'What?'

'He's still alive.'

161

They brought horses and dragged the chariot wreckage away. Ailell ordered the best of the Queen's physicians to come over, whose name was Errge Mac Blar, and he, when he saw that my leg was broken in two places and one of them above the knee, simply prayed to Dian Cecht, the gods' physician, and set to work. He set the fractures as best he could and searched the wounds as deeply as he dared, and then he splinted and bound the leg, dealt with the other wounds, though by some miracle I had not been hurt very badly anywhere else and said he could do no more.

'What shall we do with him now?' asked Cormac. 'Bring him into camp?'

'No!' said Ailell. 'If the Queen gets to hear of this, she'll kill him.' He called Errge back and put him under bonds of geasa not to tell anyone who I was.

Afterwards Ailell stood chewing his moustache for a long while, trying to think.

'You're the K–King,' said Cormac, 'surely you can order someone to look after him?'

'King?' Ailell laughed shortly. 'No. Maeve is the King and I am her Queen. I am the Corn-King with only seven years to live.'

Cormac looked down. 'Is there no one who will do what you order because . . . because of what you are?'

'I could order slaves to look after him secretly, but then he would die. I know something about healing: he needs more than just someone to wipe him down when he gets the wound-fever. And he will get the wound-fever.'

'Then he'll die,' said Cormac helplessly.

One of the small Fir Bolg slaves who had brought the horses to drag away the chariots had been squatting quietly nearby, listening to this conversation. Now he came up to Ailell and made a gesture of obeisance to him and said, 'My lord King, is this man a friend of yours?'

'He is,' said Ailell. 'Why do you ask?'

'You are the King. Who is he?'

'Why do you ask?'

The Fir Bolg said nothing.

'His name's Lugh Mac Romain,' said Cormac.

The man sucked in a breath. 'I have heard that . . . that the Queen is angry with him.'

'Yes,' said Ailell.

'Is he badly wounded?'

'Yes. See for yourself.' Ailell was getting impatient now.

'I see him,' said the Fir Bolg. He stood silent a moment, rubbing his fingers in his greasy sheepskin kilt. 'If my lord will call upon the Tuatha de Danaan to help him, then they will care for this man as they would for my lord.'

'How do you know?' asked Cormac suspiciously. The Ulstermen are more afraid of the Sidhe-folk than Connaughtmen.

The man shrugged. 'I know.'

'Perhaps you'll bewitch him?'

'The Tuatha de Danaan do not bewitch,' said the man contemptuously. 'And this man could walk safely in the nemeds, the Holy Groves, and take no harm.'

Cormac was about to ask why, though it is because, being a bard, I am accounted a member of one of the three branches of the Druids and so have every right to walk in the nemeds. But Ailell interrupted him, saying, 'Call them.'

The Fir Bolg cupped his hands round his mouth and whistled thrice, like a bird, but not like a bird.

'They will come,' he said.

'How?' demanded Cormac.

'There will be someone watching this battle.'

'We searched the forest for ambushes . . .' Cormac began.

The Fir Bolg's face showed nothing, but he said, 'The Tuatha de Danaan are not Ulstermen. And you need not search the woods for Ulstermen. If they are there they will already have been killed.'

Hidden in the tree from which he had watched the battle and heard some of the talk, Wolfling knew what the call of the Fir Bolg meant. He dropped to the ground and ran to his sidhe. He brought back four men and a priestess: shortly

163

afterwards they had put me on a litter and so I was brought slowly by stages into the sidhe.

I was silent when he had finished. He waited, arms folded over his bent knees.

So Dalaigh – no, Ailell – found me, I thought. And the Queen doesn't know I'm here. The thought was one of infinite relief to me. Somehow, having seen her in the battle-line had brought her nearer to me. She had haunted my dreams while I hovered between life and death, her pale long face smiling, the veined blue eyes staring at me with that indescribable look in them, the light behind them veiled behind the tracery of white on blue, so that I could not, dared not understand it. As I thought about it, I saw her face near me again, hanging between me and the rafters.

I moved to break the fancy and jarred my leg. The pain went coursing up through me, making me gasp. I wondered when I would be able to walk properly again. It was a miracle that I had survived the crash of the chariots, but I knew well that I had been hurt, grievously hurt. How long would it be before I could go back to Emain Macha? And what would happen in the meantime?

'It seems I owe my life to Cormac and . . . Ailell.'

The boy shook his head. 'The Mother says you could not have died, for it was not your time.'

'What do you mean?'

The boy shrugged. 'It's what she said. I heard her.'

'Wolfling,' I asked, struck by a new idea, 'Wolfling, would you teach me your language?'

He seemed surprised.

'Why . . . I . . . I must speak to the Mother about it first.'

He came swiftly to his feet and bumped into Otter. Quick words passed between them and Otter frowned and then nodded. Wolfling went towards the dim source of the fire-light, but walking stiffly as though he was hiding a fear, awe.

Otter helped me to lie flat again. I was suddenly very tired, but I forced my eyes to stay open.

'What's wrong with my learning your language?' I demanded.

She looked away. 'Nothing. Sleep now. The Mother will ask the Stone Goddess and She will decide.'

'Why's it so important?' I knew of the Stone Goddess.

'It is not important.' Her voice caught, though her face showed nothing.

'You are too fond of your secrecy, you Sidhe-folk,' I said bitterly.

'And have we not reason to be? This was our land and you took it.' She wasn't angry, but sad, gently sad, like the dew on a dead moth. 'You even took our gods and now you hate us and fear us and kill us when you dare. You tell stories of our entrapments and enchantings. Once we were great, but now we are secret. What else can we be, now we are not great?'

I felt sorry for her then: I felt with her the sadness of a greatness stolen and diminished. We have kept the story of their greatness in the songs, but I make songs and I know what they are made of. I moved my hand and touched her small rough hand with its tracery of blue lines. She pushed back her small plait and, taking my hand, tucked it under the goatskin cover. My eyes closed of themselves and then, moth-gentle, I felt a hand smooth back my hair. Hay rustled and I was alone again.


### III '


The Mother spoke to the Stone Goddess and She did not say no. Wolfling came to me with the news next day, smiling with his stiff scarred face. We worked out a system for learning the difficult Sidhe-tongue and I began to learn. The teaching wasn't continuous: for one thing, at first I quickly found learning tiring and had to sleep; for another, Wolfling being a very fine hunter already because of his skill at tracking and stalking and his knowledge of the habits of game, he was often sent off on hunting expeditions, or would go by himself, roaming far afield and telling no one but myself what he did. As time drew on and I grew stronger and more accustomed to the dull pain of my leg which sometimes grew worse and sometimes only stayed the same, I envied him his freedom. I longed to go walking and running in the hills, to ride a wild horse into obedience to my will: rope a bolting colt and stop him in the wild spring round-ups of wild horses. I had been thought skilled at that, and because I could sometimes think with the horse, I knew what one would do next and when a new-broken colt was ready to be ridden.

Fighting I did not think of, but after a long time, many days, weeks, a month had passed, even that became attractive to me and I thought of riding a chariot in the wind, weaving between the sticks on the practice-field, feeling the horses' mouths with my hands on the reins. I sat looking into space for a long time, near mad with restlessness and boredom and knowing that an incautious move would hurt my leg.

People would come and sit by me sometimes and ask me questions of what the Ulstermen did and how they thought and were they good hunters and fighters . . . ? They all asked about Cuchulain and as I got better at the language, I tried to tell them what they wanted to know. In return they told me how they lived and told me stories of their past: the people of the sidhe had a dreaminess, a fey quality, and after a while I grew to understand what it was that made them so. They lived half in the past, half in the future. The present for them was something they could not, or did not want to, understand. Some of the women among them would tell long stories of the future, of white and red dragons and the foreigners who would come and grind down my people as we had ground down the Tuatha de Danaan. And after a while I came to accept this as normally as any one of them.

They are very different from us, the Tuatha de Danaan. They are so secret I sometimes think they don't even tell themselves what they are thinking. Contrasted, the Tuatha de Danaan.

For one thing, their halls, which they call a sidhe, are not shaped like one of our halls, or square like the house of a Roman. Instead of being round, they are long and low with turf-rooves. From the outside they look just like a long-barrow or death-house of some Hero in the Olden Days. Inside the house is divided lengthways into three by two rows of pillars going the whole length. There is a central aisle and a space on either side where they sleep and store their food and gear. At the other end, beyond the middle door are the animals, the goats and pigs and little scrawny sheep. And it is all very small, very close together and it stinks of peat-smoke and animals and humans.

The Old Mother, the Wise Woman of the sidhe, slept in a cubicle by the fire, formed by hanging up curtains and those curtains were beautifully woven out of dyed wools, and em-broidered with spirals and lozenges and Earth-signs. It glinted with gold, yes, gold and the women all wore at least one small piece of gold on them, whether a semi-circular fastener or a lunula or only a slender chain. The men wore only their kilts and capes against the cold. But the women dressed in jerkins which were built to push out their breasts and nip in their waists. Sometimes they wore a single piece of material held with gold fasteners and swayed around the Mother sitting in the middle, next to the fire, and sang strange eerie songs, winding round and round like a spiral, like a skein of silken rivulets. And this to the sound of a goat bleating at the other end of the house.

Once I asked Wolfling about it and asked why they didn't exchange such wealth for more cows and sheep to improve their stock. He was shocked.

He pointed at Otter who was working at a loom nearby, her small breasts moving under her jerkin as she passed the shuttle to and fro between the clay-weighted threads and her fastening catching the firelight and warm sunlight from the open door. The sidhe was almost empty as it usually was in the daytime.

'You see that fastening she has on her jerkin?'

'Yes.'

'It is older than Emain Macha.'

I stared.

'All the gold you see was made when we were great,' he went on, 'in the days before the Iron-Folk came, when all the land was ruled by bronze and the Druids traded with Achaea and Minos in gold and amber and jewels. There is a dagger in this sidhe which was made in Achaea. It has pictures of lions and men hunting them on the blade.'

I stared at him. It seemed so incongruous in the small dark house.

'What was Achaea?'

Wolfling shrugged. 'A land far south and east of here. There has been no trade between us since the days of the Kings.'

'The Kings? You are the People of the Goddess,' I protested.

'The Kings were slaves of the Goddess and the people were slaves to the Kings. They built the Stone Circles in Albiu, that the Romans call Britain, and they made their tombs for their heroes and they put up single stones to the honour of the Goddess.'

'And then?'

'You came. The Iron-Folk. Have you not noticed: bronze is softer than iron? That's what happened.'

Again I understood their sadness, as I had with Otter. Their songs were sad too, though they weren't a wholly unlaughing people. Serious perhaps, but they laughed, particularly the children.

'Is that what you sing about?' I asked.

'Yes,' said Wolfling softly.

That was close to what the Ulstermen call Lughnasa, but what we and the Sidhe-folk call Bron Trograin, the Earth's Labour. The sidhe became subtly disturbed. Women would go off in groups into the forests and peat-bogs and come back bearing herbs and mushrooms, especially the red white-spotted mushrooms which grow under birches. A small, bronze-bound chest was brought in, covered with damp earth. It was shaped and disguised as a tree-trunk which was what it was hollowed out of, but when they opened it, it was full of fine soft stuffs and bright things wrapped in supple leather. The women began brewing liquids in wooden vats, because they only had the one bronze pot for the whole sidhe: that, and the milch cow, made them wealthy among the Tuatha de Danaan. Once the men were shut out of the sidhe. The women debated about me and in the end they made me drink a sleeping draught and I slept the day through.

Otter disappeared for long periods of time and would come back looking white. I asked Wolfling about her and after some hesitation, he told me that she was to be made a priestess at that Bron Trograin. She would learn the sacred songs and the manner of cursings, the secret script and the manner of making certain drugs.

Bron Trograin came with a crying of joy. The children were blessed and the girls brought one by one to the Mother where they drank a small sip of a dark liquid and then went and lay down outside.

Some of the women, the priestesses, were wearing the strangest clothes I had ever seen. They wore long flounced bell-shaped skirts to the ground, with tight nipped-in waists and tight bodices which left their breasts bare. I asked Wolfling about it and he said only that these were the sacred clothes, made to a certain, traditional pattern. The priestesses in their swaying flounces sang and wove their paces in a complex stately pattern Wolfling called the Maze Dance. The men sat silently watching.

At first I couldn't see Otter anywhere, though I looked all round the sidhe, searching the leaping shadows for her pointed face. At last I saw her, stretched out before the Mother's cubicle, lying wrapped in the cloth she had woven during that summer. She lay there twitching and mumbling while the dance went on around her. Every so often one of the women would bend down and make her drink from a small leather flask.

I touched Wolfling's shoulder and he turned his scarred face to me.

'What's that she's drinking?' I asked.

'It's the Queen's Drink, the Drink of the Goddess. She is drinking it pure, undiluted and . . .'

'*Pure?* But it'll poison her, she'll . . .'

'Oh no.' Wolfling smiled, looking a little envious. 'She has drunk it neat, more and more, every year since she was a child. It won't kill her. But she'll see fine visions. Perhaps the Goddess will speak to her,' he added wistfully.

I thought of the Goddess-in-flesh I knew and shuddered. The Queen's Drink: the Drink that could open the gold-pillared halls of Tir-na-nOg and likewise the House of Donn.

Suddenly the air, the whole sidhe, seemed to be full of her, pulsing with her. I was afraid, afraid of something I knew too well. The Queen's Drink. I knew the visions you could have when you had drunk it, the strange beauty, the great horror, the feelings and sights and smells that flamed through you so that each sense was mixed with the other and you saw music and felt smells. And the Queen. She was so beautiful, rich as cream and the very thought of her and her magic drink made my skin crawl with fear. And she was here. Not herself, but her magic, her centre, what made her what she was, the goddess using the woman cruelly, so that only bleak greed and hate came from her eyes, the will and the urge to suck, suck, suck life to replace what she had lost.

'What is it?' asked Wolfling sharply, 'are you seeing a vision?'

'No,' I said shakily. 'No. I don't want to watch.'

'But . . . but soon, when the Mother comes and makes her a priestess and we have killed the pig in thanks and they have made the Birthing Dance, soon the *men* will drink Her Drink.'

'*We* drink it?'

'Of course. Always. This is the Earth's Labour and we may see . . .'

'No!' I almost shouted. He stared, the smile fading from

his face. 'No, I won't drink the . . . that stuff.'

'But the visions . . .'

'Visions? I have no need for visions out of a flask. And I'll not drink *her* Drink.'

At that moment there was a shout from all the women. The curtain was drawn back and the Old Mother stepped out. She was wrapped in furs, but on her shoulders gleamed a close-fitting cape of gold. She stood in front of Otter's prostrate body and touched her shoulder gently. Otter sat bolt upright, the whites of her eyes showing and the taut skin on her cheekbones accentuated by the firelight. She began to sing, no, chant in a high monotone, the words falling over each other in riddlesome meanings. I stared at her, unable to look away, though I longed to, because, hearing the way she spoke her prophecies, I knew they were true and I could not understand them.

At last there was quiet and Otter was gently laid back. The chanting and singing began again and I watched until the pig had been sacrificed and the shadows merged and became dreams. I know that feasting and loving went on around me and the Drink made for wildness, because all these things disturbed me. And then I was given a cup of mead and as soon as I had swallowed it I knew it had the Queen's Drink in it and so I dreamed after all. They were bright and vivid with colours, but it is geasa to say what they were, and so I will not.

IV

It was a few days after Bron Trograin, when all the debris had been cleared away and everything was as normal, and I could detect no change in Otter except that all the men, even Wolfling, now saluted her when she looked at them and took care not to step in her shadow. I said to her, 'I want to walk.'

She stopped what she was doing. 'Walk?'

I was sitting up. I leaned and touched the bandages hold-

171

ing the splints to my leg and showed my teeth.

'Yes. Walk. Before I completely forget how it's done. When do the splints come off?'

'The Old Mother is going to examine you soon and if she thinks the bone is set she'll take them off.'

'I don't think I'll be able to move my knee.'

'How does it feel?'

I shrugged. 'It hurts.'

'Still?' she frowned.

'Not badly. But all the time. And my skin itches.'

'That will be better when the splints come off. And your knee will be stiff, but I will massage it and put ointment on it and soon it will bear your weight again.'

'Otter,' I said, suddenly longing, 'what's it like outside now?'

'Summer, warm, the edges of the woods are gold with toad-flax. But soon the trees will be changing.'

'I love the woods when they change. They become a rustling fire . . . I wish I had my harp, Otter. I could bring summer in here if I had one.'

'Magic?' she asked, only half-serious.

'No, music. When I'm singing, I can see it all, passing in front of my eyes . . . I can make my own visions, Otter, without the help of the Queen's Drink.'

'That is a true gift of the Goddess,' she said.

I moved restlessly, incautiously, and a little spurt of pain shot up my leg, igniting others on the way and then dying down. I was used to it by now, used to bracing myself against the constant nag of it, the sudden shock of it. It wasn't as bad as it had been, but it was still there. I felt a sudden surge of anger and frustration. I leaned forwards again and pounded the bed with my fist.

'I'm prisoned here! I can't get out! How long is it since I last saw the sky, Otter, how long? A month? Two months? I want to get well, Otter, I want to ride and walk and run again and feel wind on my face and go hunting . . .' My voice died away. I saw the look in Otter's face and I wanted to hit her and kiss her both at once. I dropped my arm and relaxed my hand.

'Never mind, Otter. Never mind. I think I'm going mad, so let me be.'

'But I . . .'

'Just go!' I shouted at her. She drew back, her lips tight, her eyes blazing in their spiralled sockets. She got up and turned away without another word and I watched her walk across the smelly floor and out into the sunlight.

The next day Wolfling returned from a hunting trip and came and told me all about what he had done on the hunting trail. He said he'd seen Cuchulain riding out with some of his tribesmen, the Sedantii, inspecting his herds of cattle. Wolfling asked why Cuchulain no longer stayed at Emain Macha and I explained what had happened that spring and summer. He nodded and said he had heard something of it, but wanted to be certain.

Then I looked up and saw a small shape coming towards me, flanked by two women: one of them I recognized as Kestrel, the woman who had borne both Otter and Wolfling. The little woman in the middle was the Mother. Wolfling made obeisance to her and didn't look at her, but I looked, because I am not one of the Tuatha de Danaan. She was wrapped in furs, even in the warmth of summer and she had a small brown head like a sparrow's – even to the short sharp nose. She stood by my bed and dismissed Wolfling with a curt nod of her head. Wolfling disappeared very quickly.

'Otter tells me you are unhappy,' she began. Her voice was old and a little cracked, but firm and with something of kindliness in it. To my relief there was nothing of the Queen there, apart from the sense of the Goddess.

It was on the tip of my tongue to say – why shouldn't I be? I've no cause to rejoice. But I didn't say that because of the Goddess.

'Old Mother,' I said instead, 'I am not used to lying still so long. And . . . I have no harp.'

She nodded brightly, like a bird. 'We must see. I am going to take off the splints and bandages now. You were very lucky, and some goddess or god must favour you.'

'*Favour* me?'

'You should really have been killed, you know. But you survived both the crash and the wound-fever. My magic is potent, but the strength must be there. I think you are a hard man to kill, even if your time had come.'

'My time?'

'We all have a set limit to our lives and yours was not yet.' Even as she said it I felt she wasn't telling me the whole truth. She pushed back her furs and nodded to one of the women.

Kestrel, Otter's mother, pulled back the goatskin so that I was naked under their eyes. I felt uncomfortable, though it had never bothered me before. The Mother looked at the bandages and told Kestrel to undo them. She and the other woman carefully did so. I may as well have been dead for all the notice they took of me . . . I pushed the thought away as unlucky.

When at last the bandages were removed, the Old Mother looked down at it for a moment. I could not see what the scars looked like, but although she did not look anywhere but at the leg, I felt acutely conscious of the way my body was made; the way the tattooing patterns of my clan curled on my chest, flanks and stomach, fine blue lines in an intertwining pattern unlike the close colour of the Caledones of Prydein, or the criss-cross marking of the Tuatha de Danaan. There were white lines and marks of scars, I knew, and at least three new purple ones.

The Mother bent and began to examine how the breaks had healed, her light old fingers running up and down and pressing deftly here and there. She flexed the knee which was practically rigid and told the other woman to massage and anoint it. Then she stood for a moment, thinking.

'You should try to walk now,' she said, and still I felt there was something she wasn't telling me. 'Not today, but tomorrow perhaps. Exercise will tell us . . .'

'What will it tell you?'

'What I want to know.'

She went away then, while Kestrel put on new bandages to support it.

174

'Kestrel,' I asked, 'tell me the truth. Have the bones knitted?'

She looked up. She was a fierce woman, well named, small and clear-eyed, with no time to waste on pity.

'They've knitted perfectly firmly,' she said.

'Then why does it still hurt me?' I demanded.

'I don't know,' she lied and went away.

Gradually the muscles strengthened and gradually I could put foot to ground. With Otter's help I stood up. The world lurched and the ground seemed to drop away from me. I was very weak, not just from the injury but from lying still so long. I was worried. I didn't speak of it, but the usual pain seemed to worsen when I stood or tried to walk until finally it forced me to sit down again. I didn't know what it was supposed to feel like. Otter watched me with concern: she had come back to me and never mentioned my shouting at her.

This had been going on for many days and I could only just stand when Otter asked me,

'Does it still hurt you very much?'

'Yes,' I said unwillingly. 'It's worse in one place, much worse.'

She said nothing, but went away. Shortly after she came back with the Mother. Together they unwrapped the bandages. When they saw the scars, Otter gave a little exclamation.

'What's that? Mother, I thought you said there was no more sickness in it?'

'This isn't sickness,' said the Mother. She picked up a knife, there was a sudden burning sensation and then relief.

'Look here,' she said and I opened my eyes. Between finger and thumb she held a bloody splinter of wood, as long as a thumb. 'This worked its way to the surface and made a boil. Do you know what that means?'

I shook my head, suddenly afraid.

'It means that the wounds weren't searched properly when the bone was set. I must do it again.'

'Do it again?'

175

'Until it's done you'll never be able to walk with ease.'

My stomach clenched inside me. I licked my lips and swallowed in a suddenly dry throat, hoped it wouldn't be noticed. I knew that I was sweating and I knew the Mother understood the reason and I was ashamed. But I could imagine . . .

'Is it . . . necessary?'

'Yes, child,' said the Old Mother kindly, 'it's necessary. If you want to be well again and see the sky.'

'Then get it over with,' I said harshly and thought bitterly that it was all to do over again. All over again. Lugh Long-spear, bright namesake – *why*?

The Old Mother rolled up the furs and pinned them with gold pins: her arms were knotty and blue-veined with a patch of tattooing on the back of the hands. My mind felt oddly divorced from the sickness of my body, coldly analysing her movements and the lack of expression on her face. A drink of poppy-juice was brought me to deaden the pain and leather put in my mouth to bite on. Through a fog I watched her as she picked up a sharp bronze knife, bent and began to work. Long before she had finished drawing out splinters I had dived back into the familiar black sea away from the pain, and the bitter poppy-scented waters were washing round my mind, so that I could not feel . . .

When at last I climbed my way back from the darkness I opened my eyes and saw Otter looking down at me. Her face looked pale and pinched and she seemed like a giantess for a moment and then things slipped back into perspective. The pain in my leg had suddenly become like fire: as though before it was only a beating on the soundbox of a harp with the occasional string plucked; now it felt as though it was being jangled discordantly, a white-hot noise of pain.

'You will get better now,' said Otter softly. She lifted my head and gave me the milk I had drunk before with the herbs added to it. With her face close to mine I noticed something I had never seen before in any of the Tuatha de Danaan.

'You . . . you've been crying, Otter,' I said. My voice

176

sounded slurred, from a great distance.

She shut her eyes a moment and shook her head. Then she bent and kissed me, quickly, on the lips. I was already slipping back into a drugged sleep and I could only wonder vaguely why she had done it.

## V

They say that a man can get used to anything. I think this is true. When I first woke up in the sidhe, it had seemed alien to me, unbearably unlike anything I had known before. The pain had been another foreign thing, something unknown, intruding itself always, bound to me because it was in me and inescapable. There had been long nights when I had lain awake listening to the quiet breathing of the Sidhe-folk: the grumbles and harsh sounds of the old ones, the cries of the young ones and the pain an ever-present accompaniment to it. After a while I had even got used to that, but never to the feeling of imprisonment; I never ceased to long for a wider horizon than the smoke-blackened beams and the shadows of the lines of pillars in the dimness of the banked-up fires. I did not think in those nights: I could not, because I needed solitude and because my harp was in Ulster and, bound as securely by my injuries as I would have been by an ankle-chain, I could not go and get it. Sometimes the longing to escape, the desperate need to get away, run away, be free of everything, would fill me, clog my lungs until I thought I would cry out. Then some hay in a corner would rustle as someone turned over or someone else would get up to go out to the cess-pit and I would be brought back, if not to normality, at least to the semblance of it. Even that I got used to, so that some cold part of me would wait until the choking longing for freedom had risen to a peak and then died down again, knowing it would. Perhaps I did think in those long nights and longer days, but I never came to any conclusion then. I seemed to be suspended in time and in my

177

mind, like some Hero sleeping in a sidhe for a hundred years – and it would occur to me that I too was sleeping in the sidhe and I would wonder idly whether that was true. It didn't really seem to matter, beside the longing I had to get out.

But, as I said, a man can get used to anything. When I recovered from the first shock and blood-weakness of the second searching it seemed that I had reached a new compromise: at the same time some things seemed to fade more into the background murmur of thought, like my worries about the Queen, while others pushed themselves to the forefront. Among them was the tension I felt between Otter and myself. With Wolfling I got on better than ever and he used to talk to me for long periods of time, teaching me many things of hunting skills and he used to show me how he would chip an arrowhead. First he would find a large core of flint and knock one end off. Then he would use that flat part and knock off chips which he would carefully examine: when he found one that satisfied him, he would begin to chip it into shape, using the natural flaws in the flint and making in the end a beautiful blue stone arrowhead with a serrated edge. I used to watch him, fascinated, knowing that I could never begin to approach his skill with stone, just as he could never approach mine with a harp. Each his own craft. But Otter would come and watch me and I would know she was watching and yet feel reluctant to look at her; she would talk to me and try and amuse me and I felt uncomfortable. I still don't know why it took me so long to work out what was wrong with her – she made it plain enough and the whole sidhe, including Wolfling, knew exactly what was happening.

As the scars healed under the Mother's watchful eyes and my right knee began to lose some of its stiffness, I ventured to try and walk again. I had to learn the skill anew: first Otter and Wolfling or Otter and Kestrel, her mother, would hold me up and help me as I learned to totter and then limp as my legs got stronger and the world no longer lurched when I stood up. I felt like one of the children forever underfoot,

178

toddling or crawling or fighting: a thing seemed impossible, then possible and then I did it and felt as though I had won a fight with eight men. It was childish and I knew it and found myself amused at it all, and yet I was still very proud when I managed to walk unaided to the nearest pillar. Goats have never seemed so beautiful to me as when I walked unsteadily, from pillar to pillar and with many pauses for breath, to the other end of the sidhe where the animals were kept penned up.

My clothes had been too torn to be mended and my jewellery, including my torc which marked me as a nobleman, had been robbed from me when I lay on the battlefield, as well as my sword and the head of my second spear. I had nothing at all except myself and the belongings and my harp I had left in the care of Gennan Bright-face in Emain Macha. So Otter brought me a white sheepskin kilt and hide belt and a woollen cape for when the cold weather should come. But when I looked closely at the clothes they seemed peculiar: the sheepskin was very clean and white and freshly cured. I was sure it hadn't come off the back of one of their own sheep which were small, few and scrawny without much wool. That meant someone had run the risk of raiding some chieftain's sheep-flock for my sake. And the cape was brown, but the brown was not dye: it was the natural colour of wool from a black sheep and interwoven in the material were spirals of white wool.

I couldn't understand why they were treating me so well. Normally no man of the Iron-Folk was allowed into their sidhe and they would be more likely to knife the wounded left on any battlefield than to take one in and heal his wounds. They would do a lot for the Consort of the Goddess, but not against the Goddess, the Queen. I wondered if they knew what I had done, and I was sure they did, because the Tuatha de Danaan know everything that happens. I often tried to speak to the Old Mother, but each time she was busy, or asleep and would not talk, though I often felt her eyes on me, watching what I did. As I grew better and stronger at walking, I would come and sit down by the fire: the Sidhe-folk would always make a place for me and leave space on either side. I listened to their sad songs and tales and stored them in my memory for further use, tales of the gods and the First Battle of Magh Tuireadh, between the Tuatha de Danaan and the Fomor, and Lugh Brightspear, my namesake, who led the Tuatha de Danaan after Nuadha lost his arm. It was strange to hear them speaking of Lugh: they spoke of all the gods more as people than gods, as though Lugh Brightspear was simply a great man who led them and not the Sun-lord.

Otter's mother, Kestrel, who was one of the elder priestesses, would often talk to me. She would find me things to do and I was glad of some distraction while I was exercising and moving about to strengthen myself. It was rainy weather and she would not allow me out in case I caught lung-fever and died after all their care. To tell the truth, she rather overawed me and I meekly did all she said. I thought she was paying so much attention to me because she liked me.

Then, one day, not quite a month after the searching, when I was sitting plaiting a leather thong for a sling and she was sitting spinning nearby, she began to talk of Otter.

She told me that Otter was only lately come to womanhood, but that she was very likely fertile; she understood the uses of herbs almost as well as Kestrel and knew where to look for each particular one; she understood the magic which made crops grow and she knew how to make cows fertile and she was a priestess. All the while Kestrel told me this, her dark eyes would flicker to me and then away again to a man sitting chipping stone in a corner, a woman milking their milch cow for milk for a sick child. If this hadn't been the sidhe I would have thought she was trying to arrange a match.

At last I broke in, 'Why are you telling me all this, Kestrel?'

She looked away. 'Isn't it the custom even among you Iron-Folk to give a gift to someone who has saved your life?' she said.

'Yes,' I admitted, 'sometimes.'

'Otter saved your life. Oh, yes, the Mother made her magic, but in a case like yours, it's the nursing that counts almost as much. And she's my daughter and well-skilled in healing. She may even have a touch of the Sight. My mother had it, but I did not get it from her. She may inherit that.'

I surreptitiously made the Sign of Horns. It was hard to get used to the Sidhe-folk's way of taking things like the Sight so calmly.

'Otter saved my life,' I agreed. 'What gift do you say I should give her?'

She rounded on me.

'You fool!' she hissed. 'You typical man. Haven't you seen my daughter trailing after you, desiring you, trembling after a touch of your hand and hiding it because you're one of the Iron-Folk and with you it is the man who asks the woman? Pah! You're too thick-minded to see when a woman will have you for the asking!'

I gaped at her. I truly hadn't realized it, being pre-occupied with other things.

'What should I do?' I asked. I regretted it as soon as it was out – my mind was still slowed.

'Lady Moon give me strength! What should you do? What do you think you should do, you great dolt? Haven't you sired any bastards yet?'

'How in the name of Donn should I know? No woman's come chasing me to support her child – yet. And what's my sleeping with your daughter got to do with a gift . . .?' I stopped, beginning to understand.

'Look around you,' said Kestrel coldly. 'How many children do you see?'

There were children underfoot, but they did seem few. And there had been one child born dead while I had been in the sidhe.

'Not many, eh? Did it occur to you to wonder why?'

'I thought they died. Children do.'

Kestrel shook her head. 'We're isolated here and we haven't made exchanges of men for a long time. You can see it happen with cattle: if you don't bring in new bulls, the stock goes down. Well, that's what is happening to us.'

'And you want . . .'

'I want you to get Otter with child. Otter first because she wants you, but then any others who want you.' She smiled, wrinkling her eyes, 'I might myself. It would be the best gift you could give this sidhe: an infusion of new blood, some tall strong children with big bones and good minds for the hunt.'

There came into my mind a picture of Conor's stud and then it vanished in anger.

'You want me to service your herd?' I demanded slowly.

She blinked her crinkled small eyes at me. 'If you put it that way, then, yes.'

'By the Dagda,' I said, letting the sling slip through my fingers, 'by whose authority do you want this?'

'My own,' she answered calmly.

'Then listen to me, Kestrel, woman of the Tuatha de Danaan: I am not a bull to be put at some cow in heat. You said it, remember? I am one of the Iron-Folk and my father was a Roman and by every god that lives, *I'll* choose, not you.'

She stared at me, seeming faintly amused.

'I really don't know what you're making such a fuss about,' she said, 'After all, you're the one who has the enjoyment and afterwards, no trouble with the babe.'

She genuinely could not understand. Nor could I really: I wasn't sure why I felt so angry. Perhaps if Otter had come to my bed one night I would have loved her, though she was thin and so delicate-boned I would have been afraid of hurting her. No, what angered me was this old woman's – she was old-looking, though probably not much older than thirty – calm assumption that I would do as she said and give the sidhe lots of fine children. Disport myself with each woman there in turn and so refresh their bloodstock . . . It was irrational, but gods, I was angry.

'Is this how you deal with your men, here in the sidhe?' I asked. 'And is it customary for a mother to pimp for her daughter?'

Her eyes flashed and she put down her spinning.

'How dare you!' she spat. 'How dare you, you Iron-man! Here I offer you a great honour and a pleasure and you throw it in my face with spittle about pimps. By Edain Echraidhe and the three Morrigans, you will regret that!'

She stood up and walked away towards the Old Mother. I watched her, afraid and already regretting my anger. I felt suddenly very alone and unnecessary in the dim sidhe, with rain pattering on the turves above and seeping under the hide across the door. I was cold and there was a small nagging ache in my leg which came from the wet. I picked at the bandages and felt the longing to be free rise in me until my hand bunched into a fist and quivered. I was homesick, but homesick for what? Emain Macha was not my home and I was a stranger there. Cruachan? In Cruachan, the Queen who followed me even in my dreams, she waited to kill me for what I had done.

The hide lifted and Otter came in, carrying a basket which seemed heavy. Her hair was flattened on her head by the wet and she seemed tired. She smiled at me, but I could not smile back and I looked away and knew that her face fell. I picked up the half-made sling and savagely started pulling it to bits. Someone came and stood between me and the fire. I looked up, and there was Kestrel, standing over me wrapped in her cloak. Her face was like a carved skull, covered with fine-coloured leather and her eyes burned.

'I curse you . . .' she began. I made the Sign of Horns and sneered,

'Oh, curse me, woman. Then there'll be fine daughters I'll sire for you, every one of them squinting and sterile. I've curses baying on my heels already, woman, a few more will make little difference, so save your breath for finding more bulls.'

She stopped, surprised. I had dropped the honorific I had been using up till then, but there was something more.

'Curses?' she asked. 'For what?'

'For what?' I could scarcely credit it. I had thought the news of my killing of the King to have gone far and wide by now, especially among the Tuatha de Danaan who are always the first to know anything that happens.

'For what I did a year ago come Samhain,' I said, speaking as to a child. 'I killed the King.'

She stared at me, but not with horror. And then she started to laugh. I watched her sourly, misunderstanding.

'Yes,' I said. 'Hardly any need for you, is there?'

'You fool,' she said, serious again. 'You fool!'

She moved away then, brushing the floor with her feet, thinking. A fine time to make an enemy, I thought to myself, when I still can only just walk far enough to greet the goats and come back. Bandaged and bound, I thought, and I have no weapon. Then I shrugged. If she chose to kill me, she would kill me. After all, she was skilled in herbs and it was Otter who gave me food and the medicines I still had to take. I was too weak and my leg was healing too slowly and I was dependent on these People of the Goddess for everything. For the first time in a long while it was brought home to me just how different they were, with their secrets and their Mother and the way they lived.

'What was my mother talking to you about?' asked Otter, putting down the basket near to me. I saw seed-pods and early fruits and wet leaves in it.

I didn't think. I was afraid and still angry and lonely and so I said, 'She wanted me to father a child on you and she cursed me when I said no.'

Otter's pointed face was different: it seemed to have gone stiff behind the mask, like the face of a dead man, and her eyes old. She turned silently and went over to her mother and they went outside together. I could hear their voices rising and falling, shouting and quieting again. After a long time Kestrel came back in alone, without Otter, but I could not read her face behind the tattooing. The Mother watched and understood. She beckoned me over.

I hesitated and then stood up and limped painfully to her curtained-off space. She was too old to do much, though she healed the sick of the sidhe with her magic. She was holding a sick child in her arms now: she had been speaking a charm to it, but now the child's mother brought the cup of milk while the little boy whimpered and turned his head. The Mother sprinkled herbs and dropped three drops of a dark liquid into the creamy yellow. She made the child drink and then gave him back to his mother. I watched from where I had sat down on the floor near her, stretching out my right leg whose knee was still too stiff to sit cross-legged. I had talked a little with the Mother, but I always had the impression of trying to converse with a marshlight. Sometimes I would begin to understand something of the way the mind of the Sidhe-folk worked and then it would flit out of my reach so I would be as much a stranger as ever.

'Why did you refuse Kestrel?' asked the Mother gravely.

I spread my hands. I felt I could speak honestly with her, though I sometimes felt as much in awe of her as any of the menfolk of the sidhe Though she was small and dried up like a withered leaf, brown under the blue of the tattooing and her hands scarred with work, she had power.

'I don't know, Old Mother,' I said, feeling tired. 'Pride. Some small matter like that.'

'It is a pity.'

'Did you wish it?'

'No. I am not blind. But it would be good for the sidhe: Kestrel is right in that. No, I understand your reasons. I think perhaps better than you do yourself.'

'What will you do?'

'Nothing. It's the best thing to do, when in doubt. Nothing. But I'd ask you . . .'

'What?'

'To be kind to Otter. And to remember that I, who have the Sight, see many things – and an end.'

# VI

The next day was wet and a day like all the others. They merged into one another to my mind's eye, stretching behind me and before me with seemingly no change either past or to be expected. Kestrel ignored me, but once when I caught her staring at me, I was stunned by the cold enmity in her. I made the Sign against the Evil Eye and I know she saw, because her eyelids dropped and she turned away. Otter moved about like a shadow, sadly. I had not seen her come back again, but from the mud on her bare feet she had been wandering in the forest she knew well: the mud was leaf-mould, not peat-bog or hill-pasture.

Some of the men were strengthening the roofing against the winter, which had to be done every year, and the man on the roof was the one who saw the hunting party come back. They came into the sidhe, tired and muddy and very wet, but with a wild pig and a little fallow-deer on two poles. Wolfling was among them and while their leader, Owl-eye, who could see in the dark, went and knelt before the Mother, Wolfling came over to where I sat, with the news bursting him, and squatted down beside me. He poured it out.

'There's been messages going to and fro between Cruachan and Daire of Cooley and the Queen wants the Bull of Cooley and she's sent to Daire to ask for it and Mac Roth went on an embassy to him and he should be coming back in a few days and if he says yes, then Owl-eye says King Conor will be in bad trouble with the Hound still at his house-place and likely to go over to the Queen and . . .'

'Yes?' I said.

'You're not listening!' accused Wolfling.

'Try beginning from the beginning,' I suggested.

Wolfling grinned and rubbed his scar ruefully. 'I don't know what started it, but I heard a rumour . . .'

'What started what?'

'I told you. The Queen of Connaught wants to borrow Daire of Cooley's Brown Bull for a year to service her herds and improve her stock.'

'I see,' I said. And I did see. Sourly, I remembered my conversation with Kestrel – so others had trouble with their stock. Still, I had heard tales of the Brown Bull of Cooley: it was said that Cuchulain and Conor coveted the bull and blood-feuds over it had only been avoided when the Druids ordered Daire to lend the bull to both Cuchulain and Conor for payment. But I knew the Queen: there was more to Mac Roth's embassy than stock-breeding.

'They say she's promised Daire lands in Connaught, riches and her own friendship in return for the use of the bull,' said Wolfling.

I nodded.

'Did you know?' asked Wolfling, disappointed.

'No,' I said. 'But I thought there would be something like that involved.'

'Like what involved?' Wolfling was puzzled.

'The Queen is trying to draw Daire away from Conor and on to her side. She thinks she has Cuchulain of Muirthemne and now she's trying for the land north of Dun Delgan, on the Cooley peninsula. She's trying to surround Emain.'

'That's something like what Owl-eye said.'

'Quite.'

'And there's a rumour that the Queen and Ailell have quarrelled.'

'Ailell has quarrelled with the Queen?' I repeated, sitting forward. It was almost unheard of.

Wolfling nodded. 'I don't believe it,' he said, 'but Owl-eye says that the new Ailell is stronger than the old one was and very stubborn. He thinks the Queen will overcome him in the end, but it will be difficult.'

I thought of Dalaigh and his patience and his skill with children's toys. And then of his delight in sword-tricks and his obstinacy. I could believe it: he seemed very quiet and easily led and so he was – until he made up his mind about something and then it was impossible to shift him and there was no knowing what he would do. There was sadness at the thought of his losing his name and becoming simply Ailell.

Wolfling was speaking again.

'Daire will agree, won't he?' he said.

'He might.' I smiled a little. 'Either way I can tell you what's coming – and I haven't got the Sight to make riddles with.'

'What's coming?'

'War.'

The Mother heard the same news from Owl-eye and came to the same conclusions as myself. She asked me about it because I had been recently both in Connaught and Ulster. I told her all that had happened and what I thought of it and she listened and nodded wisely.

'It depends, all of it, on which way Cuchulain Mac Sualtim decides to jump,' she said.

'Only he knows that,' I answered.

'Yes. He's Champion of Ulster, but his father was one of the Tuatha de Danaan. He might go to war in defence of Daire if Conor went against Daire for the sake of the bull.'

'You have the Sight, Old Mother,' I said. 'What can you see?'

She smiled, an oddly young smile. 'I am not Fedelm of the Sidhe of Cruachan,' she said. 'My Sight is blurred and un-predictable and I cannot read the glinting of a bright sword-blade waved in the sun as she can. All I can see is blood-red.'

She sent her best hunters and trackers south and north and contacted her sisters in other sidhes: the Tuatha de Danaan generally remain neutral in fighting – they have no interest in it, though they'll fight to hold what's theirs. If that seems strange, not to love fighting, well, they have enough to do to stay alive in the first place than to risk their sparse flesh to swords and shields.

Word came back soon after, carried by runners by word of mouth, or whistled long distances like birds in the special whistling code of the Sidhe-folk that they use when hunting.

At first Daire had agreed eagerly: he was a fat, excitable man who would always rather act than think and was in any case rich and greedy for more riches. Then, apparently, two servants had made rude remarks that if the Brown Bull weren't given willingly, then it would be taken by force. It was supposedly an accident, but its result came pat: Daire did an about-turn and refused point-blank to lend the bull, no matter how much the Queen paid and no matter how much persuasion diplomatic Mac Roth could use. So the envoys came home without the bull to the Queen and the waiting Ferghus and Cormac.

The Queen of Connaught began mustering for war, calling in all her tribes and those who owed her fealty. She sent messengers to the kings she had made alliance with: to the Kings of Leinster and Munster, Cairbre Naifer of Tara and Curoi who did not want to come.

For two weeks the chariots and wagons streamed into Connaught as fighting men and all their families, which they couldn't leave behind to the risk of raiders, came to the Queen's summons.

Ulster had been sitting in the north for too long: the Ulstermen had come to Erin later than the other peoples of Erin, across Northern Britain and across the sea in fighting coracles and Veneti boats. The rest of Erin feared them because of their power, though they only held the dour north. But they had connections with Prydein, north of the frontier road and Conall Cernach held land among the islands and inlets of the west coast.

So Connaught's army grew as the tribes streamed in and noblemen brought their households and clients: Ferghus and Cormac and those Ulstermen who had followed them into exile were prominent in Cruachan. They were determined to get satisfaction from Conor for the death of the sons of Usnach and I have heard it said that they were the ones who finally goaded the Queen into the war. I doubt that, because of what they did after, but it's possible.

At last, after about half a month of gathering, and with the further-flung tribes still dripping into Cruachan, the Queen went to consult Fedelm of the Sidhe of Cruachan. Fedelm read the glittering and told the Queen that there was

189

blood-red on her army and that Cuchulain of Muirthemne would oppose her coming. That she knew already, for the Road of Midluachair drives through Cuchulain's lands before dividing to go to Emain Macha and Cooley. And Cuchulain would not willingly permit any army to pass through his hunting-runs in any direction while he or any of his Sedantii were alive.

The morning after that meeting, the Queen's red chariot bowled out of Cruachan and along the eastward road, and the great spread-out slow army ground its way through the countryside after her, like a clumsy, overweight serpent. From the start there was trouble: it was, from the start, too big an army and only the Queen could have thought she could control it. For example, the King of Leinster had brought with him the men of the Gailiana from the land near the Hill of Howth. They were three troops of the best fighters in Erin, drawn from all around and they were vowed, each of them, to the Morrigan, Goddess of the Battle-field. As a sign of her protection they all went stark naked into battle, wearing only their jewellery and war-paint and they drank the Morrigan's Drink which makes men mad. But the Queen was forced to split them up among the rest of the army, because of the jealousy they caused among her nobles.

The second day after they set out the chief men of Connaught and Leinster and Munster consulted together to select a Leader of the Host: they were all afraid of each other and of the Queen and so in the end it was Ferghus Mac Roich who was chosen. They thcught he would be safe, not only because Conor had ousted him from the Kingship of Ulster (which he never really wanted anyway), but, more important, had ignored Ferghus's surety for Deirdre, Naisi and his brothers, and so it was Ferghus's duty to avenge their deaths.

But as soon as Ferghus was confirmed as the leader, he delayed the whole army by leading them the wrong way and he sent a messenger to tell Cuchulain of the force rolling towards him. Cuchulain called out his tribesmen that same day and sent a messenger to Conor as he set out for his southern borders. But no word came from Conor and the messenger did not return.

'Why not?' I asked. I was speaking to the man who brought the news: a hunter called Deerkiller. He made a spreading gesture with his hands.

'I am not the King of Ulster. But I heard a rumour of what he has done to close Emain Macha and the Gap of the North.'

'Yes?'

'I do not know this of my own seeing. I heard it from a man who spoke to one of the Tuatha from a sidhe near Emain Macha. But if he spoke the truth, then I think that Conor will not come soon.'

Perhaps Conor realized the odds against him and was holding back until . . . Until what? Until the Queen's army laid waste Muirthemne and Cooley and came to hold the King's place to ransom, until some plan of his came to fruition? No. No King would dare do a thing like that: there is no shorter life than that of a northern King whose people believe he has lost his luck.

'Well, what has he done?' I asked.

Deerkiller looked over his shoulder and made the Sign of Horns. We were sitting in my usual corner of the sidhe and it was as private as it ever would be.

'Men *say* . . .' Deerkiller whispered, 'they *say* that Conor has laid the Curse of Macha on any man who goes south from Emain without his permission and he has not given permission to anyone for any reason. No one knows why he has done this.'

The Curse of Macha lays the weakness of a woman in childbirth on a man, so that he cannot move or eat and so dies. It is a death-curse and the strongest a King can put on anyone without the help of a Druid. No one would dare venture south with a curse like that hanging over them.

Deerkiller told me something of his hunting and told me of the many berries in the bushes and undergrowth, the coldness and dampness outside after the warmth of summer, and how the farming tribes of the thin-soiled hills were bringing in the harvest.

'Was it a hot summer?' I asked him. Deerkiller looked at me in puzzlement, his long face shut except for the expression round his eyes.

'It was warm, yes. Very warm sometimes.' And then he looked at the bandages still on my leg and his eyes showed his understanding. I hated that. When he left I got up and limped to the door-opening where the hide was hooked up, out of the way, and looked out. There were four uneven steps up, because the sidhe was dug below the level of the ground to about thigh-level, to make the walls less high and the whole sidhe less noticeable. Outside I could see the tree-tops and the bramble hedges forming the stockade around the sidhe, hiding it, and deep blue and purple clouds piling up in the sky. There was a cold damp north wind, smelling faintly sour. I stood looking for some time, until I felt cold, but something made me afraid to climb the four steps, out into the naked world: I had been long in the sidhe and grown used to it; the closeness of other people, closer even than in the Queen's Hall, without even the semi-privacy of a cubicle: the smell of animals sharing the same roof, the dark, the smoky semblance of warmth, the sense of hidden things. Outside it was autumn now and unless my nose had been badly blunted by peat-smoke, there was snow on the way, coming down on the sidhe and the Queen's army and Cuchulain's tribe of fighters preparing to defend Muirthemne.

There was this to the army: the Queen was at the head of a nucleus of fighters and chieftains only. The main part of the army was there to give weight, but it would do what it liked: only she knew what she would do with the fighters she had round her.

To a Roman this is something that seems strange. They are used to trained armies, complete in themselves, marching twenty miles a day on well-made roads, not tracks dignified with that name. When the Queen had come to help her son she had come only with chariotry and cavalry, which moves very fast: now she had her tribes with all their gear, with wagons to slow things up and get stuck in mud, with women and boys and children being new-blooded on the war-trail. And every one of those tribes and clans had feuds with at least one other and more would grow up: when one clan caught up with another it was blood-feuding with, swords would be out and the chief men and elders would walk around each other with their hackles up and it would take three Druids three hours to sort out the mess. So when the Queen's army reached the borders of Muirthemne and the true fighting began, what reached Cuchulain's lands was the best part of her army and the rest was strung out for miles behind them, being kept from going off south and north on their own errands only by bogs, hills, forests and their own inertia. They spilled through waste and wild places, got stuck in bogs and lost in forests and quarrelled interminably: it was the price the Queen paid for getting the warriors and the veterans, all the fighting men and women of the tribes.

On that day, as storm-clouds built up in the north with their promise of snow, the Queen's army reached the borders of Muirthemne. And on the west of the River Boyne is the pillar-stone of Ard Cuillin, which marks the southern-most limit of Cuchulain's lands.

Only about half of Cuchulain's tribe had reached him from his summons and so, much to his disgust, he couldn't give battle of any sort to the Queen when they came to the pillar-stone. He and Laegh went there the day before and as they looked at the place with its woods and hills, Cuchulain called up one of his fast riders. He had already sent word to Conor of the threat coming to him: now he sent word that those of his own people who weren't fighting should take the cattle and drive them further north into the hills and forests, because he knew he could not prevent the Queen from pass-ing the pillar-stone. When the man had gone, he and Laegh stayed by the pillar-stone, near a small stream which came down from the hills to join the Boyne further south. It was a small pillar, with one or two spirals on it and it resembled a group of them further upstream.

'The rest of the Sedantii should have gathered by the day after tomorrow,' Laegh said in answer to Cuchulain's question.

'That's what I thought myself,' Cuchulain said. He was leaning against the pillar-stone paring his nails with his dagger and whistling softly between his teeth. 'So we must delay the Queen until I can begin to make her ... uncomfortable.'

'And how do you propose to do that?' demanded Laegh. 'She'll be ready for you to try and fight her on the border.'

'Indeed she will,' said Cuchulain, smiling. 'And so we will stop her without the need for any fighters at all, Laegh.'

'How? By standing in her way and asking her politely to stop because she's trespassing on your land?'

'Have you got the little axe for cutting replacement chariot-poles?' asked Cuchulain.

'Yes, Cuchulain, I have,' said Laegh patiently, 'but we haven't broken a pole yet.'

Cuchulain grinned and sheathed his dagger. 'Get it,' he said.

Mystified, Laegh brought the little axe from the chariot and they went into the woods a little way. There Cuchulain chose out an oak sapling and started to cut it down.

'You use holly for chariot-poles,' Laegh pointed out.

'When did I say I wanted a chariot-pole?'

He cut the sapling down and carried it out into the open ground by the stone, where the two chariot-ponies were grazing contentedly on the grass by the stream. There he sat for an hour carving scratches on the thin sapling with his dagger. Laegh watched him for a while and then went bird-hunting for the pot with his sling. He was carrying a rabbit when he came back to find Cuchulain engaged on bending and trimming the sapling into a ring. Convinced that his chieftain had gone mad, Laegh helped Cuchulain push the ring down over the thick part of the pillar-stone, which was not too tall or wide, and they stood back and looked at

Cuchulain's handiwork.

'There,' said Cuchulain with deep satisfaction.

'I see it,' said Laegh. 'A twisted oak-sapling with scratches on it and a lot of time wasted for nothing.'

'That, friend Laegh, will stop the Queen.'

'Oh yes?' said Laegh sarcastically. 'And how? I suppose you'll use the oak gad as a handle to uproot the stone and then throw it at the Queen.'

'I'd do that, if I could, but since the strength of Oghma isn't given me, I must make do with Ogham instead.'

'*Ogham?* I didn't know you could write Ogham. Only Druids can do that.'

'Scatha taught me what Cavath left out – and other things besides.'

'Is it a spell?'

'Not exactly. Maeve is expecting me to be here with my tribe in full battle-fury to bar her path – and naturally get killed doing it, right?'

Laegh nodded and Cuchulain enlarged on his brilliance.

'Well now, when she comes she'll be very wary and she'll stop when she sees what I've put on the stone and just in case it is a spell, she'll get someone to read it. And who will she ask?'

'A Druid?'

Cuchulain shook his head. 'She doesn't trust them. No, she'll ask Ferghus and Ferghus will read my name and what I've put there and just in case I do come out and fight her, she'll stop here the night as I've told her to.'

Laegh grinned.

They went south to the dun of one of Cuchulain's clients where Cuchulain spent the night in one of the women's bed.

That night it snowed: Cuchulain was warm in bed with a willing girl; I slept in the sidhe, disturbed only by dreams of the Queen, but the Queen's army shivered under leather and their wagons and chariots and heartily cursed the fact that it is best to fight in autumn when there is plenty of forage still and your own harvest has been taken in.

Next morning I woke late: Deerkiller had gone to scout out the Queen's army which was quickly coming nearer to the sidhe. Wolfling had gone with him which depressed me. Since the quarrel I had had with her mother, Otter had scarcely spoken to me and I had had to live with Kestrel's looks, which, if she had had the Evil Eye would surely have killed me by now. I could talk to others of the sidhe and help them a little in their tasks, though I was not skilled in the things they did, and I would never have admitted the fact, but I was lonely for Otter. I liked her: she seemed to me to be different from the other, rather managing women of the sidhe. I had the impression that she was hiding something of herself behind the mask of her tattooing.

I heard shouts outside and high-pitched laughter. I went to the door, lifted the hide and looked out. It was cold and damp and the ground was covered about two fingers deep in soft wet snow, mixing with the leaf-mould and clinging to the leaves still unfallen from the trees. The children of the sidhe were trying to scratch up enough snow to make snowballs to throw at each other, bare brown legs squelching in the slush they made as they ran about. I watched, feeling a little envious.

'Put this on, or you'll be cold,' said a voice behind me. I turned, and there was Otter holding the dark brown cape with the white spirals that I had been given. She smiled at me, half-shyly, and I was reminded of the fallow deer who used to come out of the forest sometimes, nibbling the sweeter grass, with every sense alert, every tendon strained. She had something of that fleet quality.

'I felt like joining them,' I said for lack of anything else.

She shook her head and smiled. 'The Mother says she will take the bandages off today for the last time.'

'Then it's healed?'

She looked down, her long eyelashes making shadows on her cheeks. 'Almost. Soon you'll be able to leave.'

'I will? When? How soon?' I held out my hands to her. 'Oh Otter, I've been here so long . . . I want to get out . . .'

I looked at her more closely. 'Otter, do you want me to leave?'

'Come inside, it's cold.'

'That's why you brought me the cape.' I took it from her and put it round my shoulders. '*Do* you want me to leave?'

She looked up and I could not understand the look in her eyes.

'Could I stop you?' she asked. She turned away and I followed without quite meaning to.

Her mother, Kestrel, stared as we came back into the main part of the sidhe together. Kestrel was on her knees near the fire, pegging out some skins ready for scraping and drying and then tanning. She saw us together and came swiftly to her feet, angry.

'Otter,' she said, 'I told you not to go with that man again.'

Otter stood still and drew herself up. Standing behind her, I could see she was quivering.

'I am your daughter,' she said in the most formal mode of address, 'and you are my mother. But I am a woman now, in my own right: I can have children and I am a priestess. Therefore you may not tell me whom I may be with. Only the Mother can do that, and you are not she.'

Kestrel stared, but I knew enough about the sidhe now to know that Otter was speaking the truth. After a girl has had her first flow of blood she is a woman and among the Tuatha de Danaan every woman is a Queen of her own. Kestrel knew it too. She took breath to speak, but Otter whisked round and walked to the other end of the sidhe, her long pigtail swinging against the leather of her jerkin.

I looked back at Kestrel.

'Wait, Iron-man!' she hissed. 'Wait for what I will bring you.'

She went back to her stretching out of the skins, stabbing the pegs into the earth floor as though it was my chest.

A little later, still pale, but otherwise the same as always, Otter brought me to the place where the Mother sat in a pool of light let into the sidhe by the half-raised hide over the door. It was a bright day, though I thought that the snow wouldn't melt completely until nightfall.

So for the last time I waited while the Mother unwrapped the bandages and examined the scars with her quick fingers, pressing and prodding and stretching. At last she looked up with her bright black eyes.

'And I said this summer that if you could recover from this, you would need Dian Cecht to doctor you.'

I smiled. 'With you, Old Mother, there was no need for Dian Cecht.' She acknowledged it with a bow of her head. 'Is it healed now?' I asked.

'Almost,' she said, just as Otter had. 'Then you can leave.'

'Old Mother, is there any way I can repay you for . . .'

'No,' she said, 'this wasn't done for payment. We ask nothing, we of the Tuatha, and what we need you cannot give us. But I thank you for your thought.'

'But . . .'

She shook her head and then she hesitated. 'Perhaps there is something you can do.'

'What?'

'You are a harper?'

'Yes.'

'Perhaps you would remember what you have learned here and sing it to your own people. So that the knowledge will not die. That would be payment.'


# VII


The snow which had furnished the children of the sidhe with scanty snowballs, helped Cuchulain as much as if Lugh Longspear had desired it. The army of the Queen pressed on eastwards to the ford of the Boyne and Cuchulain and Laegh followed the track, making a rough guess at the numbers and the horses, from the prints in the snow.

Cuchulain told Laegh to overtake the army as it trailed

198

slowly on its way: they drove fast in a great semi-circle by secret ways through the forest that Laegh knew well, for this was country he and Cuchulain had raided over often. They had arranged to meet the gathered Sedantii north of the Boyne.

As they forded the river, they were attacked by two young men, the sons of Nera, who had been scouting and were delighted to catch Cuchulain alone and at a disadvantage. They learnt better as Laegh wove the chariot dexterously between them and Cuchulain fought and killed them without even bothering to swing his shield from his back.

When it was over Laegh stopped the horses and jumped down to join Cuchulain as he surveyed the scene of the fight, breathing a little fast.

'Hmm,' said Cuchulain with deep satisfaction. 'Laegh, have you got the axe for cutting poles still, or did you leave it behind at the pillar-stone?'

'Are you going to leave another message behind for the Queen?'

'I am,' said Cuchulain happily.

When the Queen's army came that way, ready to ford the Boyne, they found four stakes set in line across the ford. On the stakes were impaled the heads of the two sons of Nera and their two charioteers, facing towards the Queen, the blood dripping still. On each stake, Cuchulain had engraved the first two letters of his name in Ogham.

The Queen camped her army there for the night. Ferghus told her stories about his old pupil, which he more than half made up, though one of them was true enough. That was the story of how Cuchulain got his name, which means Dog-of-Culain: how he came late to Blacksmith Culain's feast and, being attacked by the guard-dog of the dun, threw stones at the dog and then killed it by catching its forelegs when it jumped for his throat and dashing its head against a stone. Culain had been very upset at the loss of a good guard-dog, no matter how tremendous the feat of a small boy to kill it, and so the boy had offered to take the dog's place until such time as he was able to train the blacksmith a replacement

199

for the dead dog. The Druid Cavath who was at the feast, told him then that his name would be 'Cuchulain', meaning Dog-of-Culain. The boy promptly protested at that, saying he liked his old name better, but he agreed to it when Cavath told him the name would be famous – as anyone could guess about a boy who could kill a wolf-hound with his bare hands and afterwards argue with a Druid.

The next day the Queen went on eastwards to find a better ford for her army, which was not blocked by Cuchulain. Also she suspected an ambush. But, being fearless herself, the Queen underestimated the effect the grisly barrier at the ford would have on her men. They refused to pull the stakes down because everyone knows that a head put up on a stake is an offering to the Morrigan and she will curse any man who steals her offering. The whole army passed by there and wondered who had done it and decided there was probably a large army of Sedantii ahead, all fearsomely armed and vowed to the Morrigan, which meant they would be impossible to beat.

The Queen walked straight into a trap: a narrow place, blocked up by trees and stones. The scouts the Queen sent beyond the blockage were killed and as her men struggled to clear the obstruction, slingstones and spears whistled down on them from men hidden on both sides. It took them most of the day to free themselves.

The next day they crossed the Boyne into Ulster.

While Cuchulain played wolf on the flanks of the Queen's ponderous army, I stayed in the sidhe, becoming stronger, going outside sometimes now, though not outside the compound.

On the day when Cuchulain blocked up the valley and maddened the Queen's army while they struggled to get free, Kestrel disappeared from the sidhe, taking with her a flask and two food-wallets. On the next evening, as the Queen camped on the other side of the river, a woman of the Tuatha de Danaan came to her and what the Queen heard from her made her angrier even than she had been when a slingstone had killed her little dog, Baiscne.

Next day, as the rest of the army trailed over into Muirthemne and the vanguard headed by Ferghus and Ailell pressed on for Dun Delgan, the Queen rode out of the camp with an attendance of twenty men and rode like the wind north to Slieve Fuad and Kestrel, the woman of the Tuatha de Danaan, was with her.

The snow had melted, but small lumps of brown slush remained. Winter was coming on fast, after a summer I had hardly glimpsed. The goats in the stockade bleated and butted each other and as I watched from the doorway, wondering whether to go out, Otter came to me, carrying a leather basket for the collection of berries. She had my cloak over her arm and smiled as she gave it to me for me to put on. No other woman of the sidhe would have done that for a man.

'Wolfling is back,' she said. 'He came back last night with Deerkiller. The Hound has already been fighting the Queen, but her army passed Ard Cuillin three days ago.'

'Has Conor come yet?'

'No. There's been no word out of Emain, but the Sedantii are bringing in all their cattle. They won't have finished by the time the Queen comes through.'

She went up the steps and I followed her with difficulty, holding the two stone door-pillars and pulling myself up. Otter watched me.

'You should use a stick,' she said.

'I am not an old man.'

I walked beside her across the compound, through the cold wet mud. The Tuatha de Danaan only wear soft boots in the very coldest weather and my feet were very soft from lying down so much. I still limped badly, though there was only a little ache in my right leg from the wet. I looked down at it, without intending to, wondering how this had happened to me.

The first time I had seen it without bandages I had been shocked. It was wickedly seamed with scars, where the muscles had been torn in the crash; where Errge Mac Blar had probed and left the job unfinished; where the Mother had searched the wound again and left it clean. Also it was twisted because the bone had been set a little out of place, and aside from breaking the bone on purpose and setting it again properly, there was nothing that could be done. No one was likely to take that risk – it was a miracle that it had not got gangrene as it was. Perhaps that had something to do with the magic filth the Mother had put on it: among them was a mouldy leather poultice, which Otter told me the Mother always put on wounds that looked doubtful and which almost always stopped them sickening. Some of the scars of the second searching weren't even properly healed and the others were purplish and young.

Looking at it now, it didn't seem to be mine. I felt strangely about the scars: I was angry and embarrassed by them and the twist in the bone that turned the foot out slightly; embarrassed by the way it forced me to walk.

'Why are you frowning like that?' Otter asked as we pushed through some goats. 'Does it hurt?'

'No. Only the sight of it.'

She seemed taken aback and looked at me anxiously. I wondered why I had snapped at her like that and smiled a little, embarrassed. It came to me that I had not smiled very much since the chariot crash and that when I had, the smile had been different from the way it had been before.

Otter stopped by the gate in the hedge. I hadn't been outside the compound before: I wondered briefly if I would turn into dust from old age as I stepped out of the spell of the sidhe, like the Heroes of old who had spent a night in the sidhe. The forest and the sky surrounding us and the shoulders of the hill seemed oddly changed, as though I were viewing them for the first time with some other man's eyes. The sky was grey but it didn't look as though it was going to rain very soon. I shivered quickly: it was a stark land and a distant sky: I hadn't noticed that before, though it had always been so.

Behind us, the sidhe looked exactly like the long barrow of an ancient Hero, except for the door in it and the people and goats around it in the compound. A little fear brushed my back: it was as though I was the hero, killed in a chariot crash long ago and now I was come out again, the world had changed forever.

I turned to look at Otter, to convince myself that it wasn't true. She had gone. My stomach went hard, but I saw her, standing by the hedge of brambles, picking blackberries. I limped over to her and helped, getting pricked and missing all the juiciest ones. She laughed at my ineptness and waved at a nearby tree-stump.

'Sit down,' she said. 'You'll tire yourself.'

I limped over to it and sat down, a certain sourness turning down the corner of my mouth for a moment. She was right. My right leg had begun to ache already. It was something I was already learning: to be careful of it always, to allow for it, to rest it when I could.

We were in a small clear space between the hedge of the sidhe and the crowding forest and there was fruit still hanging higher up where the children of the sidhe couldn't reach. A pig trotted complacently under the branches, snouting for acorns. There was an oak-sapling near the hedge from some last-year's squirrel's store, somehow uneaten as yet. Strands of dead convolvulus showed among the thorns, where there would be green leaves, and white bell-flowers of the bindweed and the yellow bee-mead flowers of honeysuckle: in summer the sidhe would be almost impossible to find. I sniffed the air, cold and damp, but clean and not crowded with other people's breath, spiced with leaves and nuts, mushrooms growing nearby. Everything seemed bigger and more vivid, even colours brighter, the hill more aggressive. Fancies, I told myself, only fancies of freedom.

Suddenly I longed to escape. I longed to stride a horse and go galloping across country in pursuit of deer, I longed to ride a chariot in just those few glorious seconds between the end of worrying about a battle and the fighting itself, when the whole world seems centred upon you, when life seems like a song and you the great one at the centre of it. I thought of Cuchulain and his fight with the Queen, a fight which would go on in the woods and at night, by ambush from hillsides and traps laid on the edges. I wanted to fight with him, help him against the Queen. There would be a war where the desire to kill would outweigh my fears, my weaknesses.

It was autumn, near to Samhain: a year ago, soon, I would have killed the King and called the curses of every goddess on me. The chariot crash was probably part of that, but I wondered why no news of a full ceremonious cursing had reached my ears, why I had not been driven out of men's houses because of the bad luck I might bring. It was strange the Queen had not called me back to her with magic, which was something I had been sure she would do. For nothing had come from Cruachan that concerned me in particular, no curses, nothing. It was as though I had never existed, much less killed the King untimely. Well, I would teach the Queen I existed: as soon as I was fully healed I would leave the sidhe and go and join Cuchulain and help him against the Queen, tell him all I knew of her and her people and how best she could be defeated. But first I needed to be whole.

I looked over at Otter, with the yearning spilling over into my voice.

'Otter, when will I be able to run again, to fight, drive a chariot, ride? When will I be whole again?'

She stopped picking berries and came over to me slowly, saying nothing, and then, as though she had made up her mind, braced herself to do something she hated, she said, 'Not . . . not soon.'

'When?'

Again she hesitated.

'You will never have much strength in your right leg.'

'What do you mean?' It was a stupid question to ask: the cold part of my mind that never stops calculating and goes on regardless of what I want to think, had guessed it a long time ago. But I had deliberately buried the knowledge, hoping if I didn't believe it, it would turn out not to be true.

'Listen to me.' Otter crouched down beside me, so I was

looking down into her small, tanned, blue-tattooed face with the eyes too deep for it.

'Listen. You will always have a limp until you die. You will find it difficult to run fast; hunting for any length of time on foot will be harder still; your balance will be bad in a chariot and you will not be able to fight well because you will be slowed down and easily killed. You must understand that. You will never be the same again as you were before the crash: you've healed about as much as you ever will and there are some things you can't do any more. You must accept it, or . . . or you'll destroy yourself.'

I don't know how long I stared at her. I had known it really, but I had hoped . . . Now I knew. It was a bitter truth. Always to be slow, always to have to take every chance to rest, because otherwise it would ache . . . I was young: this coming Samhain would only be the sixth since I had been a first-year warrior, since I had received my weapons and the tattooing marks on my skin. I was just entering into the bright world which anyway lasts only until death or illness puts a stop to it, in the flower of my strength; too tall perhaps and with little spare flesh, but what there was was all muscle and tendon – Oh, I was strong! And now the scars on my leg would always be chains, even when I had got back the condition I had lost in my illness, always slowing me down, marking me out, making me unable to do the things that others did. Still confined.

At last I looked away from her face, flinching from the pity I saw there. I stared at my hands, watched the way the tendons worked as I clenched and unclenched my fist; stared down and saw just how seamed and torn with scars my right leg was, the way the foot turned out at rest. Not much, I thought, just a little.

Suddenly I couldn't bear to be near anyone. The place seemed full of people and I hated them all, even Otter.

I stood up suddenly, pulling the cloak around me, and limped into the forest, along the path the Sidhe-folk had made driving the pigs to and from the oak-trees. Otter followed me, but she stopped after a few steps. I think she understood something of my need to be alone.

I went on and on, not thinking or even bothering to look where I was going. I was unarmed, without even a knife at my belt, my feet unprotected, and I never noticed when I scratched my legs on brambles or stepped on stones and bruised my feet.

I walked and at last my leg ached enough to stop me. I was still weak and I felt very tired. I stopped under a great oak and sat down on one of the big knobbed roots, sat down and rested my bearded chin on my hands, stared at the brown oak-leaf litter and noticed where it had been rootled up by swine looking for acorns.

I don't know how long I stayed there, thinking. I didn't think all the time, but in bursts, in among inconsequential thoughts of other matters, of the past, of the Queen. It seemed she was concerned with this too: and if this was a result of her curse, then her cursing showed great imagination. I had thought death the worst thing that could happen; now I had looked at death, I changed my mind. It didn't really hurt all that much. I remembered the dull breaking sensation when my thigh-bone was snapped in the crash and the slow unreality of it; the bitter reality of the results was something far different. I was young: I could not imagine life without the full use of my body.

I could no longer fight, that was clear. I almost laughed at the bitter irony of it. I, who was always so afraid of fighting, because I could picture so clearly what I did to other men happening to me, now I could not fight and this was something I had never pictured happening to me.

Suddenly I longed for my harp, Fiorbhinn: she would have helped me as I sat and stared unseeingly at the floor of the forest, while the stark branches darkened above me. My thoughts were circular, revolving around, but always fearful, rejecting.

There was a scuffling among the leaves. A russet squirrel darted from tree-bole to bramble, watching me and trying to decide whether I was a tree-stump or a hunter. I stayed still, hoping it would come nearer.

The squirrel darted forward and grabbed for a nut. It took it in its paws, shook it to make sure it was sound and held it in its mouth to carry it off. It walked a careful few steps, dropped the nut, looked for it and splayed leaves in all directions as it searched. I smiled and must have moved, because it leaped round and chattered at me. Then it picked up the nut and fled into the undergrowth.

I looked up; it was getting dark and I was stiff from sitting still for so long, so I stood up and started back to the sidhe. I went slowly because I had to stop every so often and rest my leg, and when I came back to the oak again, I realized I was lost. It was growing darker, so I couldn't follow my own tracks to the sidhe and although I wasn't many miles away I knew I could easily spend hours exhausting myself and going for miles in circles. For a moment I panicked. I had no weapons and I knew well enough there were wolves, wild boar and bears in the forests. But it was not the first time I had slept out. I thought for a moment and decided not to try and find the sidhe that night, but to sleep as best I could, perhaps up a tree and find a way back in the morning. My stomach growled and I remembered I hadn't eaten since that morning. I cursed my foolishness: anyone might think I was some idiotic first-year warrior eager to prove my manhood by going alone and unarmed for the night into the forest.

I searched my mind for my forest craft, and what Wolfling had taught me: I was a fool. I could have thrown a stone at the squirrel and had something at least to eat, though squirrel-meat tastes unpleasant and especially so raw. I had no means of making a fire and had neither the energy nor the time to make a firedrill. Oh, Lugh Mac Romain, I told myself, was there ever such a lack-wit as yourself?

I looked at the oak-tree and wondered if I could climb it, but I thought not: not with my lame leg to hamper me and besides I might fall out if I went to sleep. Instead I picked up some stones to serve me as weapons and I uprooted a small ash-sapling to serve me as a club and a stick. I even tried to chip the stones I found to make an edge, but after I nearly got a chip in my eye in the dimming light, and had had no effect on the stone anyway except to make it smaller, I gave that up. I settled down in the hollow of one of the roots, wrapped in my cloak and trying to ignore the ache in my leg.

I had almost dozed off when I heard the whistling. I raised my head and listened carefully. It was like a bird-cry and not like a bird-cry, long and then short like a curlew and then a series of up and down sounds.

I remembered Wolfling in the sidhe, patiently teaching me how to whistle the signal which carries far through the woodland and further over bogland. I stood up and whistled back. The forest was dark and there was a rustle of feet over the leaves – probably a badger. Then the smaller trundling and battering-ram stealth of a hedgehog who need not go quietly for fear of predators, the very quite rustling of mice.

Among these soft noises I could not hear the sound of feet and I thought I must have been mistaken at the whistle – it really had been a bird. But of course, the Sidhe-folk are the quietest hunters of all in the forest, their hard bare feet make only the faintest of rustlings. I whistled again, straining my ears. Was that the sound of one of them? Or was it something, someone else I might not wish to meet? I had not been very afraid before, but now I was, straining my eyes in the tree-striped darkness, listening and hearing very little. I sniffed and thought I smelt something, but I could not be sure.

There was a rustle and someone stepped out of the under-brush. I stiffened and reached for a stone.

'It's Wolfling!' hissed a voice and I saw the small figure come forward.

I relaxed.

'How did you find me?' I asked.

'I tracked you.' Wolfling sounded very angry. 'What possessed you to go wandering off into the forest like that? Don't you know *any*thing?'

I said nothing. He was right: I should have known better. But I hadn't thought of it: which is no excuse, as the wolf said to the lamb he ate.

'Come on,' Wolfling muttered after a moment. 'I suppose

you had . . . reasons.'

So Otter had told him. I would not look at his face in case he pitied me.

'Yes,' I said neutrally, 'I'm coming.'

It was not really very far to the sidhe and we soon got there. As we came to the gate in the hedge I stopped and said, 'Wolfling, I'll leave tomorrow.'

'Why?' His voice was guarded.

'I don't want to stay any more. I want . . . Lugh's Spear, I don't know what I want. But I can't stay. I'll stifle, I think, if I do.'

Dimly I saw Wolfling's scarred face turned up to me. I wondered what the expression on it was.

'The Mother will be asleep by now,' he said at last. 'So will everyone else. You'll have to tell her tomorrow.'

'I wanted to leave as soon as possible.'

'Otter will be . . . unhappy.'

'I know.'

'You could easily help, you know.'

'I know.'

'Why don't . . .?'

'I don't want to talk about it, Wolfling,' I said warningly.

He was silent for a moment, fidgeting.

'Once,' he said in a very soft voice, 'once I admired you. I still do. I don't know why.'

'Nor do I, Wolfling,' I answered harshly and went forward to the gate. He trailed after me like a boy who has been whipped. The gate was opened to us and at the door of the sidhe stood a small, ageing woman. It was Kestrel. She laid a finger to her lips as I opened my mouth to ask her where she had been and beckoned me to bend down to her.

'You must be quiet,' she whispered. 'I'll show you where to sleep.' She took my hand in her bony fingers and led me inside: the sidhe seemed even more crowded than usual and I had to pick my way over legs. Kestrel led me to a narrow space between two other sleeping bundles and as I sat down and prepared to curl up to go to sleep, she asked very softly, 'Are you hungry?'

'Yes,' I admitted, 'but it doesn't matter.' I couldn't understand why she was being so kind: I suppose I must have been tired or I would not have thought she had forgotten what she said when Otter was friendly with me again. She gave me some bread and a drink of heather-beer and I never thought to ask her why. When I had finished there was a bitter taste at the back of my mouth which reminded me of the time when I was very ill. But I was too tired to think it out and too tired to wonder why there were the dim shapes of two curtained-off places instead of one. Or why I heard a horse neighing nearby just as I dropped off.

# VIII

The army of Erin spilled into Muirthemne and spread out across its woods and hill-fields and cattle-pastures. It was some of the richest land in the north and Cuchulain had been wealthy with many herds of cattle. Not all of these had been driven into the woods and so as the army spread out, herds of cattle went along with them, driven along and getting mixed with the main part of it. Then different groups did start going off in different directions so that the countryside was full of marauding bands of raiders, burning and looting.

Cuchulain watched and heard this happening and he burned with fury for his ravaged land. He raided and attacked mercilessly in small groups on the edges of the army, surrounding raiding bands and leaving their heads in piles, but he knew he couldn't stop the Queen. For that he needed Conor and the full strength of Ulster. And Conor did not come. Cuchulain began to realize that since he couldn't give battle he would have to devise some other, better way of slowing the Queen. It never occurred to him to go over to her: she had ravaged his land, burnt his crops and heather, stolen his cattle, killed his people. He would never forgive and he would take his revenge on her. Until that time came he could only whittle her down from the outside and wait and hope for Conor's arrival.

The army was delayed by a river in flood and when Uala, one of the Queen's best men, was swept down to the sea by the flood, Ailell gave orders to camp until the snow-swollen waters subsided. Cuchulain made this difficult and planned a night-attack, but meanwhile he took counsel with his old men as to what he would do when the Queen asked for a parley, as she surely would do soon. But the Queen was not with the army and it was Ferghus and Ailell who were in command.

That same day as the flooding river delayed the army of Erin, I slept on past sunrise, very deeply and without dreams. It was, I think, a sense of danger which woke me, for I woke suddenly and turned over. There had been a smell, familiar to me and bringing the sense of unease. It was musky and unmistakably feminine.

I opened my eyes and looked straight up at the person standing beside me – and caught my breath back in my throat with a gasp. And yet it was almost inevitable to me, that it should be so. It never occurred to me to doubt the evidence of my eyes, or wonder if this was another fever-dream.

The Queen of Connaught was standing there with a warrior on either side of her and a small terrible smile of satisfaction on her lips.

I sat up stiffly and stared at her, looking only at her beautiful cruel eyes, but seeing all the rest of her with my skin.

She was wearing a long russet robe to her feet; it had spirals embroidered on it in black and gold and there were two gold pins fastening it at the shoulders. It was belted with a belt of enamelled gold plates, linked together, and the centre of the great buckle-hook was studded with amber. She wore a black and red cloak, fastened at the shoulder with a brooch of gold and carnelians. Her golden hair, carefully bleached as I knew it was, to hide the few strands of grey in it, was partly plaited and coiled round her head, held in place with jet-headed pins, and partly allowed to flow down her back. Deirdre's hair had gone down her back in a still waterfall too.

But the Queen was not Deirdre and where Deirdre's face had been full of impudent life and then shockingly dead with sorrow, the Queen's face was not of life and not of sorrow. It was whitened and reddened in the correct places, but somehow it was ageless. There were lines at her eyes and her forehead and lines telling tales on her neck. There was a cruel line sweeping from the proud curl of her nostril, around her mouth, and the whole of her long face was filled with pride, so that it needed no expression: it was just there. And yet the whole face, the whole body of the woman was still beautiful, still capable of rousing lust and keeping it at arm's length until she chose.

Maybe it was her eyes that did that, that cast the spell of beauty. I have never seen eyes as beautiful or as cold as the eyes of the Queen. They were deep blue, blue as a dusk sky, but there was the tracery of white across the blue, and mingling with it, raying from the pupil and making a net of moon-strings across the night that looked from her thoughts . . .

A smile continued to curve her lips.

'Lugh Mac Romain,' she said, caressing the word with her teeth, 'Lugh Mac Romain. Did you think to escape me, by any chance, Lugh Mac Romain?'

I heard my heart beating and felt my stomach lighten. My face felt stiff.

'No,' I said.

'No?' she repeated, raising her darkened eyebrows just a little. I shivered again at the well-remembered sound of her voice: deep and throaty, old and young. How should I forget it? Had I not heard it often enough in my dreams? No, I hadn't thought, really, that I could escape her.

'No?' she said again. 'Can it be that you are wise, O harper? I have heard tell of your skill with music, your friendship with Cuchulain Mac Sualtim. Ferghus speaks well of you and Cormac too. Well.'

'Well?' I asked.

She bent and took my hand and touched each fingertip with her forefinger. I snatched it back, the touch of her revolting and exciting me at the same time. She laughed, and she had a beautiful laugh, as beautiful as a whirlpool.

'I think we will start with your hands, Lugh Mac Romain. Perhaps we will remove a few joints, perhaps we will simply crush them . . .' She put her fingers together slowly and deliberately. I watched her, fascinated, like a rabbit at a ferret. I could almost feel the pain in my fingers. My mouth was dry; I was sweating.

'Well, I have you, haven't I?' she said, still smiling.

I forced myself to answer. Anything to break the spell her voice cast on me.

'You have me, Queen.'

She frowned. 'You've changed, Lugh Mac Romain. There's something stronger in you. Perhaps I'm glad – it should make matters more . . . interesting.'

'Perhaps,' I said. Matters. My belly squirmed at the thought of those 'matters'.

'It is just as well you are so wise and changed, Lugh. For now I have you, I will not let you go. I may play with you, but I will not let you go. I have my men here and we will play with you here, perhaps, and kill you, maybe. Or perhaps we shall take you away. But you will not escape.'

She lifted her skirt and her right boot and kicked me lightly, contemptuously. Then she turned and walked away. Three Connaughtmen looked down at me impassively: I knew them all, but they didn't show it if they recognized me again. Ill-luck is catching.

The Queen walked to the part of the sidhe where the Mother sat on a pile of skins, with her furs draped around her. The Mother saluted, her fingers to forehead and then to mouth, and the Queen bowed in acknowledgement and salute of her own. The Queen stood before the old woman, the top of her hairstyle brushing the roof of the sidhe (I had to keep my head bent when I stood up) and the whole place seemed to centre round her, as a hall of my people does on a fire at the centre. I noticed that the men of the sidhe knelt to the Queen when she looked at them, but that the women did not.

'Old Mother,' said the Queen in the language of the Tuatha de Danaan, and even I could hear the contempt in her voice, 'I will kill him here, or if you prefer, I will take him and kill him in my camp.'

'Maeve,' said the Mother, naming the Queen's name as she had a right to do, 'I cannot prevent you taking his blood on yourself, but you will not bring it on my people.'

'Your people? They are *my* people. You are the Tuatha de Danaan, the People of the Goddess. I am the Goddess.'

'You will not kill him here. Nor need you do it at all.'

'I'll have satisfaction for the insult he put on me.'

'Is that your right?'

'My right?' demanded the Queen, and I could hear the pent fury in her voice. 'You question my right?'

'It is possible he did not know.'

'How could he fail to know?'

The Mother spread her hands. 'Is it necessary?' she asked.

'Necessary? Yes, it's necessary. I say it must be done. I will not be insulted.'

'Is that all you care for?'

'Ah well, Old Mother, if it comes to that: he is lamed.'

'True.'

'Therefore I will take him and kill him.'

'I ask you, Maeve, Goddess, let him go. He has been punished.'

'No,' said the Queen, low and vicious. 'No, he has not been punished. But he will be.'

I saw Otter looking at me, her face white as marsh-cotton.

The Mother's voice hardened. 'The bad luck will be your own, Maeve,' she said.

'What do you care about my bad luck, Old Mother? That is my own affair.'

'No,' said the Mother, 'it is our affair.'

'Will you keep him from me?' asked the Queen in a dangerous voice.

'No,' said the Mother, sighing. 'You are the Queen,

Goddess-in-the-flesh, She-Who-Intoxicates, Maeve. We are only the Tuatha de Danaan, the People of the Goddess and – you are the Goddess. We do not deny him to you. How could we? But we sheltered him at the request of the Corn-King and he is our guest.'

'At *whose* request?' demanded the Queen in a voice that swept from the seas of the north.

'Then you did not know?'

'Know? Of course not. He daren't tell me, that spineless bastard, that half-wit, pig-headed . . .'

'He is the Corn-King and he has honour while he lives,' said the Old Mother and her voice was hard.

'Do you tell *me* of the honour of Ailell?' hissed the Queen, leaning forward so that her long beautiful face was close to the Mother's.

'I do,' answered the Mother.

There was dead silence, broken only as a turf on the fire settled more firmly. Then the Connaughtmen shifted uneasily. They were bored by this long conversation in a language they didn't understand and uncomfortable in the concerted gaze of so many of the Faery-folk.

The Queen straightened up and she laughed harshly.

'It matters not who brought him here, or why he is here and certainly, your feelings do not matter, Old Mother. I am the Goddess and I do what I like. I will take him and have him and do what I will with him – outside your sidhe, since you are afraid. For his life will be short and his death long and there is nothing you can do about it, Old Mother, nothing! For am I not the Goddess?'

'You are the Goddess,' said the Old Mother after a short silence. Old? Rocks are old and a man may break himself against them: the Mother's voice was like that. 'You will do what you will though the land sicken for it and the people die. You will have your men and treat them as you will and in it all you will not care, so long as all do your will.'

The Queen's white mask slipped and I saw her livid with hate. But she caught it back.

'I am the Goddess,' she said, saying each word clearly and

spacing them out.

'That I know,' said the Mother coming to her feet remarkably quickly for one so old. 'And it cannot be changed.'

'No, it cannot.'

'Therefore I must give you the man. When will you take him?'

'I must ride immediately. I'll leave half my men here and they will bring him on more slowly, on horseback.' She showed her teeth. 'After all, we don't want him to die before ... I wish it. Tuachel here will see to it.'

She turned and beckoned a tall, mousy man over from his place by the door and gave her orders. He was Tuachel, a man I knew and did not like, because he was completely the Queen's man, without even the semblance of his own will.

'You will do as this man says, Old Mother,' she said, 'and if there is any trouble ... I will know and I will not forget.'

'You have no need to threaten me,' said the Old Mother as the Queen swept to the door. Then she said in a loud voice, 'My blessing on you, Maeve, and may you and all of us be protected from the consequences of your actions.'

A tic flickered at the side of the Queen's mouth as she glared for a moment and then left swiftly.

Tuachel took out his long knife and came deliberately to where I still sat amid straw and skins. He squatted down on his haunches and let me feel the cold blade of it kiss my throat under my beard. I refused to move. He was as I remembered him: light brown hair, moustache and pale hazel eyes, too small for his reddish face, and no chin.

'Don't imagine you can escape, Lugh Mac Romain,' he said overloudly. 'We'll be leaving soon so you can say your farewells. For good. And don't alarm me or ...' He let the knife prick a little.

I looked up at him and felt my mouth stretch.

'Put your knife away, Tuachel Mac Buan,' I told him. 'You know what the Queen will do to you if you harm me or kill me before she has the pleasure of doing it.' It was strange to talk Irish again after so long.

He didn't move, so I turned aside the blade with my finger

216

and came to my feet. He stood up too, stiff. He was afraid of
the Tuatha de Danaan, I thought, pleased, but he's more
afraid of the Queen. It amused me.

I turned my back on him and limped over to the fire near
where the Mother had sat down again and was staring at the
fire-flames, her bony hands folded on her lap. Kestrel was
watching me, triumphant, and I knew that she had told the
Queen where I was, and yet I couldn't feel angry with her.
She had seen her daughter's love being taken from her and
she had done this without realizing that by doing it she had
lost her child's love forever. I understood the fear she had,
which had made her do it, and I felt sorrow, not hate. My
fault? I supposed so.

'Old Mother,' I said, 'I would speak with you.'

She made a small gesture of welcome with her left hand
and allowed it to return to her lap.

I sat down at her feet, moving my still stiff right knee into
a comfortable position. She was so small: there was not
much difference in the level of our eyes. I felt Tuachel and
his men watching me and knew they were envious and
apprehensive of my ability to speak with the Tuatha in their
own tongue.

'Speak,' she said. I thought she sounded kindly.

'Old Mother,' I said, 'why did you defend me against the
Queen, against the Goddess?'

'You are our guest,' she said. I shook my head.

'There was more than that in it. You said something about
ill-luck. Do you know what I did?'

She began to answer and then her eyes narrowed shrewdly.
For a moment I felt as though I were naked under them
again.

'Tell me,' she said.

'I killed the King. I killed Ailell.'

I expected the reaction I had got from Iollan Hen (where
was he now?), the reaction I had got in Emain before Druid
Cavath had made it clear that he thought I wasn't a danger
to Ulster. I expected the gasps, the stares, the Signs against
the Evil Eye. I expected them all the more because I was

among the People of the Goddess and it was the consort of the Goddess, the Corn-King, whom I had killed.

Nothing happened. There was no reaction and I could not understand it. The Old Mother nodded, her face mysterious in the small light.

'Tell me how it happened.'

And so I told her the story, all of it, from beginning to end. Halfway through Tuachel tried to interrupt and take me away, but the Mother stopped him with a look and he subsided, making the Sign of Horns. I made a good story of it, because that is my way: I was trained to tell any story well.

'I understand,' she said when I had finished. She was quiet for a while and I could hear the noises of the animals and the low buzz of voices from the other Sidhe-folk. The noises were unimportant to my ears, as the smells had become to my nose. I knew I would die soon, unless I could escape somehow, but in her presence I remained strangely unmoved. In her I felt that death was a natural part of the scheme of things and mine was relatively unimportant. Later, I knew, I would begin to imagine, and the imaginings would be ten times worse because I knew what would happen to me and I had seen the Queen doing the same to other men who had angered her enough.

At last the Old Mother said abruptly, 'You have told me your story, son of a Roman, and now I will tell you one of the People of the Goddess. You won't understand, but remember it.' She began to speak in a chant, like a sacred song.

'There is the earth and there is the sky. The earth brings forth the plants and the animals, people and the food for the people; the sky fertilizes her and warms her. The Earth is all-knowing and all-powerful, but the sun is bright for a while and then every year he wanes away and dies and is reborn, every night he sleeps while the Earth never sleeps.

'So we have a Goddess among us, who mirrors the Earth and we have a King for seven years who mirrors the Sun. This way the Earth is kept fertile: this is why the King dies, why the Queen never dies, but simply passes the Goddess-hood on to a new body. She is the Goddess: that part of her

218

is separate from her person and her actions. And the King is the Young God who dies and he must die at the right time, by the right hand. If he does not, no matter what has happened, then curses and ruin follow, the land is blasted, the seed is withered, the Earth frowns.' She paused. 'Don't you understand?'

I shook my head.

'Understand this at least, then. It is not for the Queen to kill you in this way, for she is life. On the battlefield, yes, for then she is the Morrigan in human form, but this way – *NO!*'

I stared at her. None of it made sense. I could see she was speaking in some kind of riddle-talk, trying to get me to understand something important without actually saying it. The secrecy of the Sidhe-folk, I thought. I had known something of what she said, it was part of my training.

'Why have you told me this, Old Mother?'

'Why? We were great once: once the Queen would not have spoken like that: it is against all custom. We give to the Queen, because she is the Goddess, but you are our guest and . . . In anything unconnected with the Queen, we will always help you.'

She drew over her head a small hanging thing on a leather thong. She beckoned me to bend my head and when I did so she put it round my neck and it hung, swinging. I took it in my fingers and looked at it. Whatever it was, it was inside a tiny leather bag, painted with signs I could not understand, which were not Ogham or any other symbols I knew. Inside was what felt like something hard and carved. I recognized only one of the signs, which was painted in purple: it was the Earth Mother sign, a warning against sacrilege.

'What is it?' I asked.

The Mother smiled kindly at me: her wizened face breaking its mystery for a moment and looking at me like a mother.

'It is a token. Always wear it round your neck – it may give you protection, but any man or woman of the Tuatha de Danaan you show it to will help you to the utmost of their ability. And they will know who you are.'

'How . . .?'

'Kneel, and I will bless you,' she said.

So I knelt and felt the pressure of her thumb as she made the Sign of Four on my forehead.

'The horses are waiting,' said Tuachel. 'Hurry up.'

I stood up and looked round at the watching faces of the Sidhe-folk I had lived among for so long. I felt a rush of . . . kindness? towards them. They had taken me in and made me one of them for a while and saved my life. I was grateful. But there was no way I could repay them, because soon all their work would go for nothing and I would be dead at the hands of their Goddess . . . No, I wouldn't think of that.

I saw Otter standing dead-faced, her eyes like holes in her head. Without quite intending to, I walked over to her and kissed her, and she responded to me like fire – and then became like stone.

I went with Tuachel, up the four steps of the sidhe. I needed help to mount the horse because my riding muscles had quite gone, and so we rode sedately out of the compound and into the forest, where the other seven men joined us. It was a bright day, I remember, the trees painted with autumn, fire from the dying year . . .

# Muirthemne

## I

We did not ride fast, for Tuachel could easily see from the way I sat the riding horse I was given that I was not yet fully recovered. Once outside the sidhe, he stopped the group who surrounded me completely while he bound my hands in front of me with a leather thong, not looking at me as he did it. They all levelled their spears at me as though they were afraid I would kick in my heels and be off through the trees before they could do anything about it.

Truth to tell, I did consider it, in a way, but my mind seemed numb and I watched while Tuachel bound me and only thought that that would make it more difficult for me to stay on the horse. Everything around me seemed to have stopped and I let them do what they liked, as though I had no more will than Tuachel. One man was given special instructions to guard me: I knew him well. His name was Rinn and we had gone bird's-nesting together when we were both in the Boys' Troop of Cruachan. He was younger than I and I wondered if he would show he remembered me. I don't think he had recognized me at first and when he did realize who I was, he looked away shamefaced. When Tuachel handed him the reins of my horse to lead me, he leant across quickly and felt the leather binding my hands.

'They're too tight,' he said. 'If it rains they'll shrink and cut off the blood to your hands. I'll loosen them next time we stop.'

'Why?' I asked.

He seemed embarrassed.

'I like your harping,' he said. 'And Iollan Hen was kind to me and . . . well . . .'

'How is Iollan?'

'The Queen wanted to kill him when you . . . when you left. She said he helped you and he said he had. But then he reminded her that he was a harper and if she killed him she'd have the satires of all the harpers in Erin to reckon with. She left it at that, but she hasn't forgiven him and he's not been well.'

'Is he with the army?'

'Yes. He must be mad: you know how old he is, and his bones stiffening day by day, but he insisted on coming. His sons Raen and Rae have taken his place as the Queen's harpers since you left, but they aren't as good as him, no one is . . . Except perhaps one man.'

'Who's that?'

Rinn looked at me: his square face was a mirror for everything he thought. When he was surprised his eyes would widen and his upper lip would pucker – as it was doing now. He was comical to see.

'Haven't you heard of the man?' he said. 'They say he has the makings of the best harper since Amergin of the Men of Mil.'

'Well, who is he?' I asked impatiently.

'You.'

I must have been the comical one then, because Rinn smiled.

'I promise you it's true,' he said. 'We've heard of you even in Cruachan where the Queen won't even let anyone mention your name . . .' He trailed off as he remembered why he was talking to me and the fact that he was holding the reins while I rode with my hands bound.

'Sad, isn't it,' I said. 'Fame and then oblivion.'

He reddened. 'You won't die unavenged,' he began, 'Cuchulain will . . .'

'Cuchulain!' I hawked and spat. 'And what good does that do me, dead and stinking with bits of me scattered over the countryside . . . Do you know what the Queen said to me, Rinn, do you know? She said she would start with my hands, my precious, harp-playing hands . . . And you hold out crumbs of revenge as comfort! Next time use the swine-feed you call your brain before you try comforting me again!'

He flushed deeper, hurt and angry now. 'I won't try again!'

'Don't,' I said, more quietly now. 'Believe me, Rinn, it wastes good breath. Just talk about something different, something far away from now, so I can rest my mind from thinking.'

'I don't know what to talk about,' he said in a small voice.

'Don't you? Well then, Rinn, say nothing at all until you do.' I spoke more kindly, but I felt very tired. 'I'm not fit company for any man, even leaving aside the question of your own safety.'

'My safety?' Rinn was puzzled now, his brow above his flattened nose wrinkled and his jaw pushed out.

'You've forgotten the Queen,' I said. As I had expected, he recoiled and we rode along in silence, broken only by the irregular sound of horses' hooves moving slowly and cautiously through thick forest, the sound of the other men talking quietly amongst themselves around us. There was the fine spicy smell of autumn in the air and it was intermittently bright through the trees, so when the wind came and cleared a cloud from the sun's face, the God Lugh's Spear would stretch down through the half-clad tree-branches and impale a yellow beech-leaf or a red-brown oak-leaf as it fluttered down to the ground. It was cool, but not cold, and when I forgot the pain of the thongs round my wrists and the presence of the men guarding me, I could even feel something like happiness. It never lasted, because then the horse would lurch and my hands would hurt more and I would flex them to try and ease it and the fact of what would happen to me would clang down again like an iron cage.

By the time we stopped for a few minutes by a stream to water the horses, my hands were growing numb. I said nothing, but Rinn noticed again that they were becoming swollen and loosened them enough to let the blood flow. This time he didn't try to talk. I felt sorry I had been so vicious with him: he meant well and could not help the fact that he wasn't very clever and didn't know how to carry out his well-meanings. But I would have snapped at anyone. Had I not reason?

We rode down the hillside and into the thick wooded valleys by nightfall, but we found a small clearing where a great oak had come down and brought two other trees with it. Their rotting stumps already had a sapling from an acorn growing up and the place was thick with underbrush, but it was good enough to leave the horses there to graze and Tuachel had his men light a fire under the trees in case it should rain during the night. They were raggedly leaved and small shelter.

Tuachel brought out the supplies and they singed some strips of dried meat on the fire for their evening meal. I sat chewing on the leathery stuff and staring at nothing, not really thinking. I knew I must escape, but I could see no way to do it. Tuachel had two of his men on either side of me, tribesmen of his, whom I didn't know, and he didn't untie me to let me eat. The night was damper than the day had been and I was cold and glad of the fire. They made me sleep close to it and Tuachel tied a bit of rope to my wrists and slept with it attached to his wrist.

I slept little that night. I was cold and the ground was hard and thoughts chased themselves round and round my head: plans for escape which were obviously impossible, wondering about Iollan, trying not to think of the Queen . . . I had to escape and I decided to do it or die trying tomorrow. But still sleep escaped me, so I turned carefully and stared at the banked-up fire and let it trance me into something very like sleep.

I awoke in the grey dawn, shaken by Tuachel. A mist had come down and was close about us, clinging and damp and blotting out trees only a few yards away. The horses were invisible, though I could hear their neighing and movements. The mist made things close to seem very clear: as I sat up and scratched, the seamings on my right leg stood out in new relief and I was reminded of what I had forgotten while I was asleep. I smoothed down the sheepskin kilt over it unconsciously and then found myself amused at that. I was sore all over from the unaccustomed exercise of the day before. Tuachel looked at me, worriedly: I saw that his nails were bitten down to the quick, as I remembered them. He always was nervous.

'Do you need anything?' he asked at last.

'Nothing,' I said, trying to pull my cloak around me with cold hands. 'Except what you can't give me.'

'What's that?' asked Rinn, as I had thought he would. I smiled a little at him.

'Cut the thongs,' I said, 'and turn your backs until I have slipped into the forest. That's all.'

'The Queen . . .' began Tuachel.

'I know,' I said, cutting him off. 'The Queen would be . . . displeased. I said you couldn't give it to me, didn't I? After all, why should you die so that I can live?'

'I . . .'

'Don't worry, Rinn. Did I say it was your fault?'

'But . . .'

'Shut up, Rinn,' said Tuachel, hurrying off to see to the horses. 'Just make sure he doesn't escape.'

Rinn hovered around, biting his lip and fiddling with the buckle of his sword belt. I watched him as he paced: sounds came from the clearing where Tuachel and his men were harnessing the horses, but the mist was so thick I could hardly see the ones who were stamping out the fire, and the tree-trunks were like still ghosts.

Finally Rinn burst out, 'I don't understand!'

I watched him interestedly. 'What don't you understand?'

'About the Queen . . .'

I shrugged. 'It's clear enough.'

He shook his head. 'No, it's not. If she'd cursed you, I could understand that. When the news broke and all the rumours said that it was you who'd killed the Old King and

Iollan Hen had helped you to escape, we all expected famine, disease, a blasted land. At the very least, we thought the Queen would sacrifice a horse and curse you in its blood: we half-expected the Druids to be called in to help with the cursing. We thought the bards would go out with tales to sing of what you'd done, to bar every door to you, even Ulster. And then Samhain came and there was a new King and we just mimed the King-Killing as we do in the other six years, no one could understand it. It was almost as though the Queen was afraid to curse you: she won't hear your name said in Cruachan, but she didn't even kill Iollan Hen. Now we find she means to kill you, but she won't do it by a curse, or even sacrifice you for appeasement to the Earth.' He made the Sign of Horns.

'Well?' I asked, wondering what all this was leading up to.

Rinn looked carefully over his shoulder and all around. For a moment no one was looking our way. He leant close to me and drew his dagger and started sawing away at the leather thongs.

'You'll have to knock me aside,' he hissed, as my mind started catching up with what was going on. 'I'll wait a moment to give you a start and then I'll start shouting and I'll send them off in the wrong direction.'

I stared at him, and then, as my hands came free, I understood what he was doing.

'Do you realize . . .?' I started.

'It'll be all right,' said Rinn. 'I'll explain you knocked me aside.'

Sweet Edain, I thought to myself, the man really believes it. He truly thinks she'll believe him. For a moment it was on the tip of my tongue to tell him, but just as I took breath, the cold part of me took over: I too became cold. I knew what would happen to Rinn, but . . . Can I help it if I love life?

I came quickly to my feet, pushed ineffectually at Rinn and then headed off into the forest. But even as I slipped between two trees and saw Rinn swallowed up by the mist, heard him shout and the answering shouts from the other men in Tuachel's band, I stopped and thought. I was lame. I knew

226

they would immediately hunt through the forest for me: I couldn't outrun them, and I hadn't a good enough start.

They had no dogs with them, it being a war-party. So I limped a little way, found a place where several oak saplings had grown together, making a screen, and dropped under it, flattening myself to the ground. For a moment, the voice of Cur Mac Daltach echoed in my ears: 'Lie down boy! A little dirt won't hurt you and if you squat on your backside like that your ugly face will scare the deer away, you cack-handed harping half-wit! And didn't I tell you to find downwind first . . .?'

It made me smile to think of the days when the worst worries of my life were the possibility of a beating from Cur Mac Daltach or the laughter of the Boys' Troop of Cruachan, because I was going to be a harper. And it wasn't very long ago either.

Footsteps, running and more shouting around the place where Rinn was. Voices raised, Tuachel cursing, Rinn explaining. Then a shriek: the smile raised by the thought of Cur Mac Daltach was wiped off. I shut my eyes. Rinn.

Dead leaves crackled and branches broke: I heard Tuachel giving orders that everyone spread out through the woods, *everyone*. He was furious and I heard his voice crack, muffled by the mist. I could picture the way he would be biting his nails and looking around him with his light-coloured eyes. Thinking of the Queen, no doubt. Well, let him.

I waited until they had gone past, fanning out through the woods. It never occurred to Tuachel that I hadn't immediately run away as fast as I could. When the wood was quiet again and the disturbed birds settling down, I came cautiously to my feet and crept forward to the deserted encampment. The horses were neighing unhappily, but I could hear no sound of anyone there. I hesitated before coming out of the shelter of the underbrush, but I couldn't go walking in the forest as I was: I had to have warmer clothes than the ones the Sidhe-folk had given me and I needed at least a spear to protect myself from the wild animals, and a horse to carry me.

At a half-crouch, ready to fling myself flat again if anyone should move, I crept out into the cleared space. And stood up straight. Tuachel hadn't even left anyone to guard the horses, unless you counted the man lying on his face with sticky substance soaking into the leaf-mould around him.

Knowing already what I should find I went up to him and turned him over. It was Rinn. The blade had gone through his neck. I closed his eyes and for a single insane moment I wanted to take Tuachel by the throat and throttle the life out of him. But Tuachel was not there, and even if he had been there I don't know whether I would have done it. And there wouldn't even be a blood-feud for Tuachel to deal with. Rinn was a lesser member of a small clan: they would have to take Tuachel's word for it that Rinn was killed by a boar or a Sedanti. What I had said earlier was true: why should he die so that I could live? No reason at all.

I looked around me again: no sounds, no one but the horses. I needed Rinn's clothes and he no longer needed to be kept warm: working quickly I started to strip his body. The tunic was bright blue – Rinn liked the colour blue. And he was a fine hurley player, with a skill with a caman I hadn't often seen: I had cheered him as he raced down the pitch with the ball and his square face wide open with pleasure and . . . Ach, leave this thinking and thinking, I told myself; you think too much for your own good. What is there is dead meat, with the awen gone from it and Rinn has gone most likely to Tir-na-nOg and is playing hurley with Oghma – as if it mattered.

I dressed myself quickly in Rinn's clothes: when Tuachel came back he would know what had happened but I couldn't help that. I was going over to take one of the horses when I heard a breaking twig, someone coming back. I snatched a spear and limped quickly into the forest and hid. I waited there a moment and then I started off, heading south and west for Dun Delgan.

After a long time walking I came to a stream, where I washed myself. The bearded reflection that looked back at me in the still pool caught from the flow by some stones, it was a stranger. It took thought to remember that the man was myself, that leaner, older man, with the bleak eyes. Lugh Mac Romain.

I drank deeply of the water, breaking the reflection into ripples and walked on by its banks, knowing that in time it would flow into the sea by Dun Delgan. I slept a little way from it so that the sound of its flowing wouldn't drown out the sound of any pursuers. For it was only a matter of time, I knew, before Tuachel picked up my trail and set about hunting me. And he was horsed and I was afoot, and lamed. At times it seemed hopeless and useless to keep on walking, and when I lay down to sleep, hidden in the undergrowth of the forest, I wondered if a wolf would find me that very night and put an end to it all, quite unforeseen, thus spoiling the Queen of her prey. But then I remembered that wolves would not be wandering in these northerly forests: they would be further south, where they could feast themselves on the bodies of the men Cuchulain had slain. As I dozed off in the rustling, night-moving forest, I thought of the grey wolves, dining on the fields of battle, and I thought that even wolves had packs.

II

For most of the next day I followed the stream down. I was coming into Cuchulain's hunting-runs and there were cleared spaces and rough pasture for the cattle, mostly on the sides of the hills. I came to farming country, where here and there I could see the thicker pillars of smoke from burning farm-steads. I skirted widely round them, but the forests were thick and there was bog too.

It was early afternoon when I came upon the hunting party. We saw each other across a tiny cleared space and I dropped down out of sight. I could hear them spreading out, beating the underbrush and calling to each other in Ulster accents. I peeped behind some brambles and saw that the

229

patterns of their cloaks were like those used in the north. They might be Sedantii.

I stood up, unarmed, as two of them started coming towards me, stabbing at the undergrowth with their stabbing spears.

Three spears immediately levelled on me from all sides and I showed my hands were empty and shouted, 'I'm a friend!'

One man came close to me, his spear at the ready, reached out and grabbed my dagger from my belt. He didn't relax.

'What are you?' he asked.

'Are you Sedantii?' I asked in turn.

'We might be.' He was frowning, a large, heavily-built man in his prime, with a broad red face and a bushy black beard. His eyes were bright blue and were watching me shrewdly.

'I want to see Cuchulain,' I said.

'Why?'

'He'll tell you who I am. We know each other well.'

'Do we?' There was heavy sarcasm in his voice. 'Do we indeed? For an Ulsterman you talk uncommonly like someone from Cruachan. Do you serve Maeve?'

'*No!* I . . .'

'Then say her name. Maeve.'

I couldn't. Why not? I don't know, but when I opened my mouth my tongue was rooted and my throat closed. Yes, I was afraid.

'I tell you, I'm not of Connaught any more.'

'Any more?' He raised his eyebrows. 'What's your name?'

'Lugh Mac Romain,' I answered. 'I'm a harper and I've played for King Conor in the King's Hall at Emain Macha.'

'Have you indeed?'

'By Edain, you must believe me! The Queen's men are hunting me to kill me and . . .'

'Take off your tunic.'

'What?'

'Take it off. That!'

The spears moved menacingly. I looked at the hard faces

of the Sedantii and pulled the tunic over my head. The Sedantii gazed in silence at the tattooing on my chest and stomach. I looked down too. There they all were, of course, the Wild Pig of Cruachan, the Earth-Mother sign in the male aspect, the Crow of the Morrigan, all the signs of a Connaughtman of the Queen's Clan at Cruachan. Well, so I was, of course. I didn't need to look in their eyes to know they wouldn't believe me.

I lifted the tunic to put it on again, and when the hunters stiffened, I said tiredly, 'A man gets cold standing naked to the waist.' I pulled it over my head and buckled the belt. I waited.

'Well, Man of Cruachan,' said their leader, almost good-humouredly, 'I *have* heard of Lugh Mac Romain, the harper, and he died this summer in a chariot crash. So how about trying to tell me who you really are and why you thought you could get away with this.'

I could almost have laughed, if they hadn't looked so ready to kill me, if it hadn't seemed so hopeless, there in the forest with a hunting band of seven all around me. I felt my shoulders sag and longed to take the weight off my leg. Never stand when you can sit, never sit when you can lie down, lean on something if you can do neither. Otter told me that once, in the sidhe. There was nothing to lean against. I shifted my weight.

'What shall I say?'

'Try the truth,' suggested the heavy-built man kindly.

I shook my head. 'I've already tried that,' I said, 'and you don't believe me.'

He laughed. 'Try something new, Connaughtman,' he said. 'And stop wasting my time.'

I shook my head. 'Take me to Cuchulain,' I said.

'Why should we?'

'He's . . . I'm his friend.'

'That's something serious you're saying there, Connaughtman. The Sedanta's choosy about his friends. And you don't look much like the sort he chooses. Apart from your being from Cruachan. And a spy, most likely.' He thrust his face close to mine and glared at me. 'Why shouldn't we kill you?'

'No truth I speak will stop you if you want to kill me.' He raised his spear to stab. I heard myself say, 'But Cuchulain will kill you when he finds out who killed me.'

'Why should I believe you?' he asked, his eyes narrowed.

'No reason, but that I swear by the Earth and the Sea and the Heaven of stars, may they all destroy me with the gods of my clan if I speak untruth.'

The man drew back. It was a strong oath: you do not bind yourself by it lightly. I saw him waver and there was doubt in his eyes.

'Guard him,' he growled and beckoned one of the men out of the group. They drew aside and talked. I looked down at the men still standing round me: they were mostly stocky huntsmen and warriors, tough and efficient, honed sharp by Cuchulain's constant raiding and counter-raiding over the border into Connaught and Leinster. I moved slowly towards the nearest tree and rested my arm against its white-lichened trunk.

'What's the matter with you, Connaughtman?' asked one of them, a small curly-haired man with a half-healed scar on the hairline. 'Can't you stand?'

'Not for long,' I replied coldly. 'The chariot crash lamed me.' They all looked down, saw the turn of the foot, the stiffness. None of them said anything. My mouth felt sour: of course not. If I had had my harp, they wouldn't have treated me this way, since everyone knows that harpers may not be harmed. I savagely thought of making a satire of these men, particularly their leader, and see if it would raise blemishes on their faces. But after all, they were only doing what Cuchulain had trained them to do.

The heavy-built man came back, stumping decidedly. I waited tensely, keeping my face still.

'I'll take you to the Sedanta,' he said reluctantly, 'and see what he has to say about it. But if you've lied to me . . .'

I raised my eyebrows.

'. . . then you'll die. Same if you try to escape. Now, put

your hands behind your back so I can bind you.'

Oh, it was funny, it really was. To run so hard, only to be taken prisoner by tribesmen of the very man I hoped would help me. Yes. Very amusing.

While he was tying my hands I asked, 'What is your name?'

'Facen Mac Mornai. I lead this hunting party. Any objections?'

'Would it matter if there were?'

'No.'

'Quite,' I said, feeling my mouth stretch at the sloe-sweet taste of this joke of the gods. But it was only for a little while, until they found Cuchulain. It was no hardship really. Facen finished tying me and tested the thongs to make sure they were firm but not too tight. He said over my shoulder, 'Well, you've still the marks of tying on your wrists, so perhaps that tale about the Queen of Connaught chasing you is partly true.'

'It's all true,' I insisted. 'I escaped from them yesterday morning and I've been in the forest ever since.'

'A regular Suibhne,' sneered the man with the cut on his head. 'Do you know that song by any chance, harper?'

I showed my teeth and started to sing:

'Sad it is to wander where the wild swan wanders;
To hunt the shores for dulse, the brambles for berries;
To sleep in a bed of moss and have no roof but leaves;
To walk by silverfish streams and shun the places of men.
Bare are my bones, like the rocks of the mountains:
The wolf is my brother, my brother the deer,
And sad am I alone in the cold wet of autumn,
In the leaf-stripping wind and the tapping of twigs . . .'

There is no mistaking the voice of a trained bard: the men looked at one another and shuffled their feet while I smiled very sweetly at Facen.

He jerked his head and we started off through the forests, south and east now. They went slower to help me since they soon saw I could walk no faster. They had gone hunting on

233

foot to leave the horses for the Sedantii playing wolf on the flanks. Even so, they were in a hurry to get back to Cuchulain. They had a small fallow-deer and a couple of rabbits on a pole between two of them, which left four to guard me – not that I wished to escape. But they didn't know that, or didn't believe it.

They pressed on until it was too dark and then they made camp, lit a fire and let me sit near to it. After they had bound my feet, they untied my hands so that I could eat.

The small man with the cut on his forehead seemed a bit sheepish about his sneer earlier on. He managed to sit near me, and as we gnawed at the dried meat they had brought with them, he asked me if I had really been to Emain. I said that I had, and he asked me to describe it to him, because he had never been there. I told him some of it and then I asked him about Cuchulain. He told me all of what had happened up to when they had left Cuchulain five days before. He said they had sent back a wild boar to Cuchulain which was why there were only seven of them, not nine, and he told me his name was Conn Mac Gege.

That night I slept deeply, being more secure in a group of men and warm by the fire, and besides I was very tired. The next morning they left at early dawn, when there was still some mist about. They bound me again, though I think they were beginning to trust me, especially when I made no attempt to escape. The man on watch had been quite close to me and it would have been hopeless anyway, even if I had wanted to.

We travelled on slowly, skirting any open ground, some of the men grumbling at the slowness of the pace. Conn came by my side: he chatted on, asking me questions about the nobles at Emain Macha and what manner of man this Ferghus Mac Roich was, and how the King looked, and what respect the Sedanta had among all these fine warriors. I told him that Cuchulain was accounted the best of them all, which made even the King fear him. Conn looked happy about that and told me a great deal about Cuchulain: what a good chief he was and how he always knew how many of his cows were going to calve in the spring; how once, when there was a cow calving with its calf caught sideways in the womb, Cuchulain had straightened it better than the best of any of the cowherders. It was a small cow, Conn explained, and only Cuchulain had an arm and hand small enough and strong enough to do it. I noticed later that it was the same when any one of the Sedantii spoke about Cuchulain: their faces lit up and he could do no wrong. Which was remarkable, when you thought that Cuchulain was not many years older than me and often left his tribesmen to go off on expeditions to the Western Isles of Dalriada, with his friend Conall Cernach, or south into Kerry, spending a good part of the year at Emain.

I grew to like Conn as we went on south and after a while, he put geasa on me not to try and escape and loosened the thongs round my wrists slightly. But as we walked, I felt more and more uneasy: I felt in my skin that we were being tracked and trailed, though when I looked behind me I could see nothing there, except sometimes moving leaves which may have been the wind. Once or twice the birds were put up behind and in front of us, and I could not shake the feeling that we were being followed. Perhaps by the Sidhe-folk, though they would not have disturbed the birds.

Facen and some of the other hunters were becoming uneasy too: he headed for the thicker forest where it would be harder to catch us.

We were in a slightly thinner patch of forest when we heard horses' hooves, coming towards us, a crackling of movement. We stopped and the hunters' spears pointed round and then, before we could either run or hide, two troops of horsemen came down on us from opposite directions at a fast trot and encircled us. Facen shouted and the men formed a ring, bristling spears and knives like a hedgehog.

The ring of horses halted. I had taken a place in the circle by accident and force of habit and the man opposite me looked down on me, satisfied. It was Tuachel, relief shining from his pale eyes and his sparsely bearded red face grinning inanely.

Facen was cursing in a long monotone.

'Don't worry,' I growled at him. 'It's only me they're after.'

'Then it was true?'

'Of course it was true!'

'Then they'll have to kill us to get you.'

'Don't be a fool,' I snarled. 'What good will that do? It won't even be remembered in song – the only harper present will be dead.'

'Sedantii!' began Tuachel, not looking at me now. 'Who is the leader among you?'

Facen set himself and stepped forward.

'I am,' he answered gravely, out of the depths of his barrel-chest.

'Well then,' said Tuachel, leaning on his horse's withers to bring his face closer to Facen's. 'You see you are surrounded and outnumbered and we have horses?'

'I'm not blind,' said Facen. 'What do you want, since you haven't killed us?'

'We want your prisoner,' said Tuachel casually. 'That's all. Then we'll let you go.'

I was standing still, listening, afraid and tense, knowing what the outcome would be, thinking desperately how to avoid it and knowing that there was no way to avoid it. I felt the cold touch of a blade against the heel of my hand and a release as the thongs fell off. I looked sideways with my eyes and saw Conn standing next to me. I liked him then even more, with a sudden rush of hope and an equally quick in-flow of dampening thoughts. I could predict what Tuachel would do – I would have done the same – and even if I had my hands free, I would easily be run down and speared by the men on the quick little forest horses.

'Why do you want the prisoner?' asked Facen, stroking his beard. 'You'll only have to feed him.'

'That's our business,' said Tuachel. 'It doesn't concern you.'

'Perhaps I say it does.'

'Then we'll have to kill you and all your men and take the prisoner anyway.'

'And if we hand him over?'

'Then we'll let you go.'

'How do I know you'll keep your promise?'

'You can put us under geasa if you want.'

'Hmmf.' Facen appeared undecided. He knew what the odds were against his hunting band and he also knew of Cuchulain's desperate need for fighting men, which he could ill-afford to lose over some Connaughtman who may or may not have been who he said he was. Tuachel now had twice as many men as he had, at least. On the other hand, Facen loved Cuchulain and admired his courage and his honour and wanted to copy him in everything, almost like a boy sometimes hero-worships the warrior whose spears he carries. Facen knew what Cuchulain would have done and he knew what would be best to do, and he couldn't decide.

I could read all this so clearly in his face, and understand the difficulty he was caught in, even sympathize with it – if it had not been myself that his decision concerned.

He talked in a low voice with his hunters and I listened, but found myself distracted every time a horse moved or champed on a bit.

'We should fight,' said Facen reluctantly. The others growled dubious agreement, except for Conn who argued far more vigorously that fighting was the only honourable thing to do. I felt keenly that the others were more interested in getting back to their wives and clans and cows and less in the fate of one Connaughtman who had slowed them down and got them into the situation anyway.

Before they could decide, I interrupted, saying, 'Listen. If you fight, you'll have no chance and you'll all be killed and they'll try and capture me alive – though I'll try and make sure it's dead – and the end result will still be the same.'

'Who wants you in Connaught?' asked Facen. 'The King?'

I smiled mirthlessly. 'If only it was. No, I told you: it's the Queen of Connaught who wants me and she's been balked of me once already. She'll not be pleased with a second time.'

'That settles it,' said Facen. 'We're not giving you to the Queen – whatever you've done to make her angry.'

I could have spat with impatience, though they thought they were doing me good by resisting.

'Yes, but if they let you go and you go hotfoot to Cuchulain and tell him about me – well, there's a chance he might be able to do something about it.' A chance? What chance, even if he wanted to? Cuchulain was great, but he couldn't work miracles and I knew how badly the Queen wanted me, I had seen her, after all, and seen the greed in her eyes. Something? Yes, perhaps he could slip into the camp some dark night and put a knife into me when I could no longer do it for myself, or even ask that it be done. But he was still my only chance at help. If he wanted to help me. Which I doubted – after all, hadn't I very nearly slept with his wife, Emer?

'You mean we should hand you over without a fight?' Facen asked incredulously, not noticing, or at least not commenting, on the fact that my hands were freed now. 'But . . .'

'It'll come to the same thing either way,' I said. 'And you might escape to get to Cuchulain.'

'I'm not . . .'

'In the name of the Morrigan, what are you arguing about? I'm not offering, I'm telling you!'

Before he could say anything more and before I could stop myself, I raised my voice and said, 'Tuachel, if I come over to you without fighting and swear not to try and escape again, will you let these men go?'

He drew breath, but he hesitated and spoke to his second-in-command. There were twice as many of them as there had been before: he must have found a raiding band and made them accompany him.

'Yes,' he said.

'Swear it.'

'I swear it.'

'Swear it on the Morrigan and the Earth-Mother and the Queen herself,' I insisted.

He flushed. 'Do you think I'd break my word for . . .'

'Yes. Swear!'

'I swear.' I waited. He went bright red. 'All right! I swear by the Morrigan and the Earth-Mother and the Queen herself that if you come to us without fighting and swear not to escape again, I'll let the others go. Does that satisfy you?'

'Yes!' I shouted, hoping that at least he wouldn't break that oath. He waited, they all waited, all watching me, for me to come out and walk over to the Connaughtmen. And my knees felt loose and my bowels too and I wondered if I would stumble. I clenched my fists and prayed to Lugh Longspear to hold me up, promising him the first head I took after that – forgetting that I would take no more heads again.

I walked forward, between the dead bracken and old blackberries, rotting and wormridden, and saw between the trees a buzzard flying. The fighting, of course. Who was it feeding on, I wondered. Anyone I knew?

One of Tuachel's men dismounted and tied my hands again. My arms felt stiff from being bound so long, but I knew I wouldn't be able to relieve them soon. That thought made it worse.

'Your promise, Tuachel,' I reminded him. He looked regretful that he couldn't take such a lovely set of heads back to the Queen.

'You can go,' he said. 'But if you try to attack us and get him back, we'll kill you all.'

They turned without words and filed south-east into the forest. Conn hung back and gave me the sign for good luck, the Sign of Horns reversed. I watched him go, my face stiff, not just with dirt and beard.

239

# III

We rode into the main camp of the Queen's army a few miles south of Dun Delgan at about midday. The clear parts of the country in the plain of Muirthemne were scattered with small enclosures built by the various tribes, but the Queen's was the northernmost. It was surrounded by a hedge of thorns and a hastily-dug ditch, but it was irregular in size and the ditch was unfinished. Tuachel spoke quickly to the guard on the makeshift gate as we passed through. He made the Sign of Horns as I passed him. In the camp were wagons and leather tents and campfires scattered here and there, the horses picketed wherever there was room, and piles of dung already accumulating in odd corners. There was a stream, very dirty, where some women were washing clothes and filling pots for cooking; men and boys were practising with their weapons or herding the pigs and cows they had raided; children dashing about playing games of catch; Fir Bolg digging cess-pits and graves. The Queen had entrenched because she had been settled there for some days and was trying to come to some kind of agreement with Cuchulain – which was hopeless from the start until she found out what he wanted.

We rode slowly and carefully through the camp, picking our way, the hooves of the horses sounding on the logs put down on the worst of the boggy parts. I kept seeing people I knew from Cruachan and wondering if they would recognize me: I saw Lugaid from a distance and thought I saw Ferghus's bush of grey hair and Cormac's flax for a moment. It was a grey muddy day, so that the colours of the nobles' clothes were bright splashes against it.

We came to the trodden patch by the fire in the centre of the camp, where the Queen's tent was pitched. It was a big round tent with smaller attendant tents around it where Ferghus and Cormac and the Ulstermen slept, and two wagons for carrying the Queen's gear parked nearby. Tuachel and his men dismounted. They let me slide down stiffly.

Tuachel and two others marched me into the tent: I ducked my head under the flap and then blinked in the fire-lit dimness.

It was roomy inside, with a fire in the centre filling the place with smoke. The ground was covered with hay and some dried leaves and herbs and scattered skins and a pile of them to one side which looked as though it served the Queen and Ailell as a bed. Not quite opposite the flap was a place slightly raised with branches and covered with hay and a cover of catskins sewn together. On this sat the Queen, dressed as I had seen her last, but with a beaverskin cloak wrapped around her. A crow stood on her gloved fist like a falcon and she was stroking it and whispering to it and feeding it little bits of raw meat.

Two of the men stood on either side of me. We waited for the Queen to please to notice us. It was very quiet in the tent; I could hear my own breathing mixed with the breathing of the other men. A few drops sounded on the leather roof, drumming like impatient fingers and then spattering down continuously as it began to rain. Some men came in, crossed the tent and stood by the Queen. They were Ferghus Mac Roich and Dalaigh – no, Ailell. Ailell looked away when he saw me, stroking his moustache. Ferghus only glanced at me at first: so that I wouldn't stare at Ailell, I concentrated on him. At first he seemed to be as he always had been: big, strong, a great deal of iron-grey hair and a weathered oak-like face. Then I saw that there was a subtle difference in him. The way he looked sidelong at the Queen, the way his hand moved out casually and just touched her shoulder and away again. What had I thought when I saw her in the sidhe? Still able to provoke a man's lust, she was. I wondered where was Cormac.

Ferghus had not recognized me properly when he first came in: now he looked again and his mouth opened in a gasp. I smiled faintly: it must be strange to see alive before you a man whom account had killed.

My leg ached. I shifted position surreptitiously to ease it. I wondered how long the Queen would keep me waiting, but I was not going to speak first.

At last she stopped smoothing the blue-black feathers of the crow and looked up at me. Her magnificent eyes swept up and down my body, sizing me up, measuring me, as I would do a horse I was about to buy. I became acutely conscious of my stained blue tunic and breeches and boots, all the wrong size for me, my beard and general dirt. I had forgotten when I last had a proper wash.

Her eyes narrowed.

'Unbind him.' Tuachel looked momentarily surprised, but he cut the thongs. I eased my wrists and waited, suspicious.

'Ailell,' said the Queen, 'have you those irons I told you to bring?'

'They're by your seat,' said Ailell.

'Put them on him.'

'Why?'

'Because I order you to.'

They were facing each other now, Dalaigh angry, the Queen ice-cold, perilous.

'You know he was . . . he is my friend,' said Ailell.

'You are my consort,' said the Queen. 'Do as I say.'

'Your consort?' demanded Ailell. 'Hadn't you better tell Ferghus, then, when next you go disporting in a wood?'

'How dare you!' hissed the Queen. 'You helped this man when you knew my desire: you who are nothing without me, you who will be nothing in a few years' time. *You* dare disobey me?'

'He is my friend,' said Ailell, beginning to waver, hesitate. 'You're the Queen, but . . . I still won't.'

'Do as I say.'

'No. I can't.'

They stared at each other for a moment, Ailell half-shamed, half-determined, the Queen blazing coldly. Then Dalaigh dropped his eyes and walked out of the tent.

The Queen settled herself like a ruffled cat and started to

preen the feathers of her crow again. It bated and cawed and she fed it with another piece of meat. Then she transferred it to her shoulder where it stood, grooming its unclipped wing-feathers.

Silently she handed the irons to Tuachel who put them on me and locked them. They weighed my hands down, cold and rough against the bones of my wrists. I shifted position again.

There was another stretched-out silence. At last the Queen began to talk to Ferghus Mac Roich.

'Do you see this man, Ferghus?' she began.

'Yes, dar . . . yes, Queen.'

A smile, a faint inclination of the head.

'You see how he looks? Tall, like one of us, but dark and his face is Roman. Like his father. His father had that nose like the beak of an eagle.'

'My lady?' Ferghus was puzzled. The Queen's old love was not generally known.

'Yes, I knew his father once, Ferghus. His father said he was a Roman merchant, but I found out later that he was a Roman spy. I gave him my love and after a while he spurned me when I asked him to become King. What do you think of that, Ferghus?'

Ferghus said nothing.

'He ran from me when I sent him my token, ran and went back to Britain. When he returned many years later, I knew him again and took him prisoner. I asked him why he had betrayed my love and he told me that he had always loved me and still did, but that he could not become my King: he was a Roman, he said, and Romans always command their wives. It would have been against his honour, he said.' Her voice was bitter, bitter as bile. 'He escaped me and ran as far as Brugh na Boyne. I sent my men to catch him, but it was only the following morning when they caught him and killed him. For that night my sister was in the Brugh, awaiting the first man to come for her as a propitiation to the Goddess, and he came to her and got on her a boy-child. This man.'

Now she turned again and gazed unseeingly at me, so that I felt I was invisible to her.

'And his son in his turn betrayed me. So alike and yet not like. For Lucus was a short man, I remember.'

I realized, with a sense of shock, why my mother had named me Lugh. It is the way we would shorten the name Lucus for our own use, just as Caractacus is the way a Roman lengthens Caradoc for his use.

'So like,' she repeated. 'Lugh, why did you run away from me?'

I did not answer.

'I gave you the greatest honour a man may have: to be raised to the side of the Mother-of-all, to the Goddess, and quicken her for a little while and make the land fertile and then carry the ill-luck of the land with you when you die seven Samhains after. That is the honour I offered you, Lugh, the Kingship. Why did you run away?'

I stared. I felt as though I had been hit again under the ribs: it numbed me and froze my brain. I breathed carefully and tried to understand.

'You never offered me the Kingship!' I blurted.

She frowned.

'I sent you my token. How could you mistake it? You were born and bred in Connaught, Lugh, I tried to bring you up to this, though you were always against me. Lugh, for all you are half-Roman, you could not have mistaken my token!'

'But I never got it.'

'Don't lie to me!' she hissed, leaning forward and showing her teeth. The crow on her shoulder half-spread its wings uneasily and she calmed it without thinking. 'I had the woman of the Tuatha de Danaan put it in your harp-bag. You could not have missed it.'

And then I understood. In a flash of memory I saw the old Ailell, the man I had killed, searching guiltily in my harp-bag. He must have seen the woman of the Sidhe-folk put it there and thought that if he could kill me, he would rule for another seven years. I remembered the way he had gone casually to the fire and dropped something in: of course, it had been the token of the Queen which settled down and burnt up so I could never receive it. That was why he had tried to kill me.

And it explained why, when I had killed him instead, and fled to Ulster, I had not been cursed nor the land blasted. For, although no man may kill the King without suffering the Wrath of the Goddess, the New King is the one who must Kill the Old King at some time during Samhain. I had been the New King when I killed Ailell: it had been my right and the time did not matter. We had fought and I had killed him by my own strength and fighting skill and so, when I had fled Connaught for a fearful crime I had not committed, I had been the King of Connaught. I had been Ailell.

It was a strange thought: I Ailell. I the doomed King, to quicken the Goddess and die in seven years. But now it was not possible: I was lamed and the King must be perfect and unblemished in mind and body, like a sacrificial animal, or the land sickens with him.

I stared at the Queen still, seeing her blue eyes hard, hard as winter skies, her mouth set straight, the cruel line sweeping round it deepening in her pale face.

'You betrayed me. So I took a new Ailell, and now I think I am glad for he is more easy to lead, to control. It will take time, but I will succeed. You would have taken more taming, I think.'

But for Ailell, I would have been her consort by now. In a way I was glad that the token had been burned: it is no life for any man, to be bound to a woman who will eat him like a she-spider and then throw away his empty husk in seven years' time. The way she spoke of taming me made me feel a little sick, in the midst of the numbness: it was as though I were some dog to be taught to walk to heel.

If I could explain to her what had happened, surely she would . . . lessen her rage against me. I was not proud enough to stand silent and refuse to explain; but I was too proud to beg for mercy.

'Listen, Queen,' I said, 'I never got that token. I truly

245

didn't know.' Did that sound like whining? 'Ailell, the Ailell then, he found it and burned it before I ever saw it. He tried to kill me later and that's how it came about that I killed him. I thought I had killed the King untimely – and so I fled. That's how it happened. You must believe me.' Yes, definitely a whine. Well, it was said now.

She came to her feet, slowly, the folds of fur around her, and hit me across the face with her heavy-ringed hand, once, twice, three times.

'Liar!' she spat.

I licked away the blood that was running from my cut lip. She hit as hard as a man.

'It's true,' I said.

'Fear, I expected,' she said softly, 'but not craven lies.'

I shut my mouth.

She waited a moment and then said, 'Well, Lugh Mac Romain, now let us have the truth.'

I drew myself straight and took breath. It was like the Sedantii all over again.

'The Sky is over our heads, the Earth is under our feet, the Sea is round about us: I swear by all these and Lugh the Sungod, my namesake, that I speak the truth.'

Tuachel growled suddenly. He nodded at his men: they held me while he kicked and hit. The Queen watched and then made a gesture to stop. The men let me drop. I sat up slowly, my head singing and my ribs and stomach throbbing with the blows. The Queen was looking down on me with a smile that might have withered a flower.

'And even if what you say is the truth,' she said in a soft voice. 'Even if you weren't lying when you said you never got my token, I think that if you had got it, you would still have fled, Lugh, son of the Roman.'

Seeing her like that I was afraid, like a child of the night. But then my anger rose up against my fear and won, for once, and I said, 'By the gods of the . . . Ulstermen, you speak . . . truth!'

Her smile froze.

'Take him and put him in a tent where he won't escape,'

246

she hissed. 'Let him think on what I will do to him and in the sight of all the camp.' Then to me: 'You will beg for death, Lugh, and it shall be my pleasure not to give you that gift. Think about it.'

They hustled me out, still shaky, and pushed me into the smallest of the nearby leather tents where they attached the manacles to the central tent-pole and then went out and dropped the flap. There was a guard outside.

I sat, hunched up in the darkness, and it seemed that the sides were pressing in on me and there was no escape, no escape. No escape from the Queen. No escape. The numbness, the pride whatever it was that had held me together until then suddenly melted away, leaving me naked in the darkness. I pictured the Queen's face looking down on me as her men did their butchery and smiling, for I knew she enjoyed such things. I could feel what they would do, see it: the blood bright against the dark. I tried to shut my mind from the thoughts, telling myself that it was bad enough suffering once, that it hadn't happened yet, perhaps never would . . . If I had had my harp I could maybe have kept the Hounds of Annwm, the Hounds of Donn from pursuing me, but my harp was still in Emain. My fingers longed for the strings, for the release that music gives, so that your soul goes flying up with the music and your fears are exorcized on the wings of a song.

The Hounds of Donn came back to me. I pressed my arm against my eyes, heard a chink, and wanted to be sick.

'Oh God,' I muttered, thinking of Lugh of the Sun and praying to him to kill the darkness. Especially the darkness inside me. Death in battle is one thing; this was something different. I was young. If my laming was bitter, this was more bitter still: to die as a pleasure for the Queen, in the full sight of all. The fear of it lay in my belly like a stone. I wanted to weep, but could not because of my pride, because I was ashamed of being so frightened.

But admitting the fear seemed to help. I calmed a little and my muscles relaxed. The stone in me didn't go away, but it seemed less overwhelming. I laid me down on the damp earth, pulling my cloak around me, with my arm awkwardly under my head, quiet in the leather-smelling darkness.

I lay quite still, so as not to rattle the iron links to the tent-pole, and heard a bird chirping somewhere near. It was a blackbird, singing for no reason other than it simply wanted to sing. The notes fell bright and ringing and I listened.

Time passed. The little trickles of light dripping into the tent through seams grew even less and ceased altogether. The sun went down behind the soft-drizzling clouds, dusk fell. The bird flew away.

It was later that night: I had been given some porridge and bannock and also allowed out to the cess-pit, with a spear-head against my spine all the while.

It was cold without any fire but the one outside in the middle of the group of tents, and I wrapped the cloak more closely about me. Then I heard careful sounds on the opposite side from the tent-flap. I shifted over there. A voice hissed, 'C–can you hear me, Lugh?'

I smiled a little, a sudden rush of hope in me.

'Yes. Is that Cormac?'

'Shh. Listen, Lugh, I heard about . . . you and the Queen.'

'It must be all over camp by now.'

'It is. Cuchulain knows too.'

'Then they got through.'

'Who got through?'

'The Sedantii I told . . . well, anyway, what does he say?'

'I don't know. He's walking very c–carefully. He wants something of the Queen, but she doesn't know what it is.'

'Do you?'

His voice had a touch of puzzlement in it.

'No. But the Queen's sending Mac Roth the Herald to him again tomorrow to see if he'll make any agreement at all with her. She'd agree to almost anything to get him off her back.'

'Anything?'

'He said he'd try, that's all.'

'Why are you telling me all this?'

248

'Why not?'

'Why not? What if Cuchulain can't do anything?'

'If he can't, then . . . I'll get you out of here myself.'

I was silent a moment.

'If the Queen catches you she'll . . .'

'No, she won't. I'm not a Connaughtman. And anyway, you saved my life. In the boar-hunt, remember?'

'The boar-hunt. I see. I'd forgotten about that.'

'I hadn't.'

There was the sound of someone coming near. I heard the suck of Cormac's boots as he stood up quickly and walked on, and the voices of the two men as they met. After that the night was disturbed only by Cuchulain's nightly attack.

The next day passed almost without moving. I kept myself occupied by reciting the songs I knew to myself. In the morning I was fed the same porridge by the relief guard. He didn't speak at all in the time he took to put the bowl down and leave: the disfavour of the Queen is an infectious thing.

The camp seemed very active, and four times I heard the unmistakable squeaking sticky sound as chariots departed and returned. The last time was mid-afternoon and in late afternoon three guards came to fetch me. I knew them all: we had been in the same Boys' Troop, like with Rinn, and had gone hunting together, but they pretended I was a stranger. I covered up my hurt by telling myself that it was only to be expected.

The Queen was not in her tent, but outside it: it was a cloudy day, but it hadn't rained yet. She was sitting in her fine chariot, all carved and painted red and studded with gold and carnelians along the pole to the two red chariot-ponies with mealy mouths, champing at the bits. The cushions were made with bird-feathers, like the cloak of the Chief Poet in Ulster, Athairne. There was smooth-faced, brown-haired Mac Roth with his white herald's staff and sea-ivory hilt to his sword, standing at her left hand, and Ferghus Mac Roich standing at her right. My heart suspended, not daring to hope.

The Queen glared at me as I stood before her. There were

little white patches round her nostrils.

'Why does he not show me reverence?' she demanded of Tuachel.

The two guards pressed my shoulders down and made me kneel to her. I had to look up at her now, kneeling stiffly in the mud.

'Tell him,' she snapped at Mac Roth.

'Cuchulain Mac Sualtim, Chieftain of the Tribe Sedanta, has made an agreement with the Queen of Connaught, Goddess of the People, on condition that you, Lugh Mac Romain, once Ailell, are not killed until the Queen returns to Cruachan,' said Mac Roth.

I looked down into the trampled mud and closed my eyes. I felt like a harp-string that has been tightened and tightened until it was near to breaking and then been loosened again, a stretched leather thong let snap back to normal. True, the time was only postponed, but a lot could happen between now and the Queen's return to Cruachan. Perhaps I would be able to escape . . . If Conor won, then almost certainly I would be recaptured . . .

I raised my head and tried to keep my expression even, from breaking into a silly grin of relief.

'So I will not kill you – yet,' said the Queen in a tight voice, 'since he will send his charioteer Laegh Mac Riangabra into camp to make sure you are alive and arrange for the combats.'

'What combats?' I asked.

'Does it concern you?' enquired the Queen. 'You have a lease of life until we finish with Ulster. What more do you want?'

'More? Not much, Queen, though you won't give it. But I would like to know what Cuchulain agreed to in order to buy so much time from you.'

'You are impudent, Lugh,' she said. 'And I agreed to keep you alive, only. You were not his only reason, nor even the most important one.'

I smiled a little. 'I know that, Queen,' I said gently. 'What was the agreement?'

She nodded to the guards to take me back to the tent. As I came clumsily to my feet again, she said contemptuously,

'He's a fool. He agreed to fight one of my men at a time each day, and while the fight lasts, then we can go forward. You made the arrangement, Ferghus, after he scared Mac Roth away. Does he think he can keep it up day after day after day?'

The guards were listening too.

'I tell you, Queen,' said Ferghus, 'Cuchulain's not ordinary. I had the training of him in battle-skills. He's got a feel for swordplay I never saw the like of in another man and it's the same with a stabbing spear or any other weapon. He's like a man out of a song.'

Ferghus shook his grey head in wonderment.

The relief was draining out of me, to be replaced by a sick sadness for Cuchulain, putting his own body between the Queen and Conor sitting riddlesome less than a day's hard ride northwards, in Emain Macha. I knew that Cuchulain could not possibly survive because what he was trying to do was quite simply impossible for a man of spillable blood and breakable bone.

'Oh, listen to a man who knows about songs, Ferghus,' I said. 'Let any bard tell you, men in songs never step out of them.'

Seeing the expression on his face, I felt as though I had struck him. Without waiting for the Queen to dismiss me again, I turned my back and walked towards the little tent. This time it was my guards who came with me, not I with them. I tried not to hear them talking curiously about Cuchulain: wondering what kind of man he was. I knew.

# IV

Cuchulain had been camped on a hill when Mac Roth went out to him again with the Queen's new offers of lands, wealth and her friendship if he would only come over to Connaught.

'Well, Mac Roth,' said Cuchulain from his chariot, with his tribe around him, 'is that all your Queen can think of to offer me? I have broad and fruitful lands here in Ulster – if you and your army would get off them. I have plenty of wealth – if you would return the cattle you reived to me. And I have no need and no wish for the friendship of your Queen.'

'Is there no bargain you would agree to?' asked Mac Roth.

Cuchulain grinned. 'There's one man with you who can answer that question: if he comes out to speak to me, then I'll talk. But if any other man comes out to me – ' his smile broadened – 'I'll kill him.'

So Ferghus had gone out to him and with him a brash young chieftain called Etarcomal, who bordered with Cuchulain. Ferghus did manage to come to an agreement with Cuchulain and started back to the Queen. But Etarcomal hung back, picked a fight with Cuchulain and got himself killed. Ferghus came rushing back, furious at this breaking of his protection – a thing he had been touchy about ever since the death of the sons of Usnach – but Cuchulain explained, with Etarcomal's chariot-driver backing him up, that Etarcomal had picked the fight. Ferghus, who had never liked Etarcomal in any case, tied the stripped body to his chariot and brought it back to the Queen and Ailell.

'Where was your protection this time, Ferghus?' the Queen asked acidly.

'It was Etarcomal who picked the quarrel, when I told him

not to,' said Ferghus angrily, 'and Queen, Cuchulain could have killed me as well – as he'll kill your champions. So don't speak to me of surety, when you send out young fools who can't keep their side of it!'

The Queen turned away in contempt. But Ferghus no longer slept with her, and from that small quarrel came something greater.

I remained a prisoner in the camp of the Queen and heard about Cuchulain's fights the way most people did – by rumour, which naturally never hesitated to improve on a bald killing. I was put in the charge of two men I had had very little to do with while I was still at Cruachan and they were told they would die if I escaped or died without the Queen's permission. For that reason they loathed me at first – and who could blame them?

The two were twins, born in the one birth, and they looked so much alike each other, I had difficulty telling them apart in the beginning. They were called Brocc and Brod Mac Magach: they were both big, heavy warriors, with low brows and thick curly brown hair all over their heads and chins. They both had dark brown eyes like hunting dogs, and big hairy hands and they never seemed to worry over who owned what: they swapped tunics, cloaks, spears and boots without even seeming to notice which belonged to whom. Their cloaks were of the same dirty yellow and their tunics of the same filthy green, though the one Brod wore most often looked as though it had once had red stripes which had run in the rain.

At first the only way I could tell the difference between them was by smell: Brocc always, no matter what time of the day or night, smelt of mead and sour ale.

On the day Cuchulain fought Natchrantal, the Queen moved her army on. The tent was unpegged around me, while I stayed manacled to the tent-pole, feeling remarkably foolish, suddenly surrounded by watery sunlight and commotion. At last Brod undid the chain around the pole, while Brocc gripped my arm until I thought he would break

253

it. Then I was hustled to the nearby Queen's wagon where Fir Bolg slaves were loading in the tents from around the central fire. Seeing them I was reminded of the Sidhe-folk, for the Fir Bolg are also of the Tuatha de Danaan, but slaves used for menial jobs. The chain was attached to a rung in the side of the wagon for the purpose of harnessing unused ponies, and captives to be sold as slaves.

I protested at this.

'I'm not the Queen's slave,' I said. 'I'm her prisoner.'

Brod held his fist under my nose.

'I don't care. The Queen says that's where you go, and that's where you go. So shut up.'

I shut up, leant against the wagon to take the weight off my leg and watched the frantic activity as camp was broken. In the distance I could see Natchrantal riding down to his fight with Cuchulain. The whole camp was full of shouts and curses as slaves dropped things and pack-ponies bolted and chariots sank two fingers deep in the trampled mud. Some slaves, newly captured, were attached to the other side of the wagon – I could hear their wailing and lamenting – but to me it was almost pleasant to stand in the light of day and see something more interesting than my own thumbs twiddling.

I heard the whinny of horses and the squeak and squelch of a chariot coming by. I looked round and saw the Queen's red chariot with her red ponies pulling it coming close up to the wagon: the Queen in a blue long-sleeved woollen dress, embroidered with purple and red and a red cloak over it fastened with Sidhe-gold, and the gold outshone by her hair. She brought the chariot alongside where I was leaning and looked down on me over the painted wickerwork side and the high spoked wheel. She seemed truly like a Goddess to me then, catching the sunlight in her hair and eyes.

'Well, Lugh?' she said. She was still angry.

I swallowed. 'Well, Queen?' I asked.

'I hope,' she said acidly, 'you are enjoying yourself?'

I bowed a little, ironically. 'I thank the Queen of Connaught for her concern.'

254

The cords of her neck stood out above her red cloak and gold torc. She snatched the reins and goad from her chario-teer and goaded the ponies from a standstill to a hand-canter. Mud spurted up from under the ironshod wheels, spattering me and getting into my eyes and mouth. When I had stopped spitting and wiping my face, I found Brocc looking down on me, a puzzled expression on his stupid face. He goaded the oxen and we plodded on through the mud.

Where was the Goddess? Nothing there under the gilt but a sour vindictive old woman, a greedy, hidden crone. What a Goddess! They were sacrilegious thoughts, but it made no difference to me any more. Her magical dazzle had been washed from my eyes by the mud spurting from under her chariot wheels.

As Natchrantal was one of the Queen's best warriors she expected the fight to take some time. In fact it took Cuchu-lain somewhat less than an hour to kill him, but in that time, the Queen had taken a raiding-party and gone northwards to Dun Sobairce. Cuchulain followed her north, but turned south again with his tribe to screen Dun Delgan as the main part of the army followed. Coming south to rejoin her army, the Queen managed to slip past Cuchulain. But the Sedanta caught up with Buac Mac Banblai, the Queen's trusted Lieutenant, who was driving the Brown Bull of Cooley southwards, along with fifteen heifers: they had a brief argument and Cuchulain killed Buac – but the rest of the raiding-party managed to get through with the bull.

If the Queen had really only been interested in the Brown Bull, that would have been the end of the matter: as every-one with wit to think had suspected from the beginning, she wanted to strip Ulster of wealth, kill Conor and burn Emain, so that all of Erin would follow her sway. But why hadn't Conor answered such a naked challenge, such a clear danger? Why had he put on the Curse of Macha to close Emain?

As I trudged along beside the wagon for the short while the fight lasted and we went forward, I was beginning to understand.

That night the army made temporary camp, without a stockade of any great thickness – just enough to keep the animals from straying. The Sedantii did not attack, though we could see their few campfires dotted around the surrounding country, like the eyes of shadowing wolves. I spent the night under a wagon with Brocc and Brod taking it in turns to watch over me.

Brocc got half-drunk – against the cold, he said. His brother heard him singing and came out of the tent and took his mead-jug away from him. Brocc was very hurt at this and grumbled loudly to himself. Finally he demanded of me, 'Donchoo think it's a sh . . . shame?'

I was only half-awake. I must have muttered something which sounded like agreement.

'It was only a li'l bit, jush a li'l bit. Anyway, I'm not drunk. Am I?'

I said that of course he wasn't.

'And you wou'n try'n es . . . escape, would you? 'Cause I'm not drunk in . . . the . . . slightes'!' He nodded his head very wisely at this and I said that I wouldn't dream of trying to escape. Something made me add that even if he fell asleep I wouldn't try to escape because I knew the Queen would also be unkind to him if I succeeded. I didn't think it necessary to mention the fact that my wrists were chained to a wheel-spoke.

Brocc was silent for a while. Then he said seriously, 'You know? You're a nishe . . . nice man.'

The next day Brocc waited until his brother wasn't looking and then, half shamefacedly, slipped me a little leathern bottle. I cautiously unstoppered it and tasted some: it was vile, but drinkable, so I swallowed a couple of warming mouthfuls and handed it back to him. Brocc was conspiratorial for the rest of the day and passed it to me as often as he thought of it when his brother wasn't looking. I was touched by his generosity.

The Queen's army never went much further than a mile or two each day because Cuchulain always killed his man far quicker than the Queen expected. And so most of the day

256

consisted in breaking the camp of the night before, moving forward a little way while foraging parties ranged out further and further, though there were supplies in the wagons from the harvest. When word came that Cuchulain had killed again, they made camp, dealt with the animals and raided peat-walls or cut wood for the fires. The nights became colder: Brocc had an argument with his brother about whether I should be allowed to come near to the fire they shared with five other men and one or two women belonging to Brod. In the end Brocc won the argument by pointing out that if I froze to death one cold night, the Queen would be just as angry as if they had let me escape. So they built the fire near to me and I warmed parts of myself for the first time in days. One of the men suggested that I sing, in payment: I was reluctant at first because I had no harp, but one of them produced a little reed pipe which he blew as an accompaniment and so I sang them songs. When Brocc was properly drunk he would teach me some songs I had never heard before, singing loudly in an incredibly bass voice.

I asked everyone about Iollan Hen the Harper, because I had expected to see him in camp. They were reluctant to tell me, but I persisted until a man I had known before I left Cruachan told me quietly that two days before I came into camp with Tuachel, Iollan had taken sick with camp-fever. He was an old man and the fever was a burning one. He died the next day. They had dropped him into one of the grave-pits, but had not found his wonderful harp to put by him.

'He didn't have it,' I said. 'He gave it to me the night I left Cruachan.' I realized then what he had been telling me when he gave it to me: that he would not live to see me again.

The Queen did not go near Dun Delgan, with its newly repaired walls lit by torches and surrounded by thorn-hedges and man-traps in case the Queen should try a sneak-attack. But the Queen did not: she knew if she attacked and burned Dun Delgan Cuchulain would never rest until he had taken a complete revenge – which would include her head. The Sedantii shadowed the army which moved more slowly every day, and Cuchulain kept on fighting.

I went with the army, seemingly forgotten by the Queen: Brocc had now become quite friendly to me, and even Brod was less brusque. I was in worse case than I had been when I came into the army: my leg seemed almost to be improved by the walking, but I now had shackle-galls where several pounds of metal pressed on my wrists and I caught a kind of camp-flux which meant I had to stop and squat down every few hundred yards. It was consoling to see that Brod had the same trouble: Brocc remained irritatingly free from it. Brod explained his brother's immunity easily:

'You see,' said Brod, 'the flux-devils get into Brocc's belly and fall splash into a pint of mead. They drink as much as they can, but their heads aren't as strong as Brocc's and so they get pissed – and Brocc pisses them out with the mead. Isn't that right, Brocc?'

'That's right,' said Brocc, who always agreed with his brother when he didn't understand what was being said.

The wagon lurched and stuck fast in a mud-filled rut, sunk up to its axle. Brod cursed and jumped down. I did the same, while Brocc went to the heads of the oxen and started coaxing them on with goad and curses.

Brod and I went round to where the wheel was stuck fast and heaved and pushed until our muscles cracked and sweat started trickling into our eyes. At last we stopped for a moment, gasping. As it will at such times, it began to rain, softly and wetly. The wagon was settling more firmly into the rut. I looked at Brod and he looked at me and we were both ready to weep from sheer frustration and fatigue. This was the fifth time the same thing had happened.

Horses and oxen passed us by, and a group of Fir Bolg, walking silently in the rain, heads down. Brod ducked around the wagon to relieve himself again, while I leant against the side and wondered what I was going to do about it. My world had come down to the fate of one wagon. I shouted to Brocc to let the oxen rest for a while and then we'd try again.

'Do you want help?' asked a voice next to me, in slightly

accented Irish.

I turned to see who it was, screwing my eyes against the rain. There was a small-built boy of the Fir Bolg standing there, slimy and mud-covered with a kilt around his middle and nothing else. His face was so dirty I couldn't recognize him. And then I saw the scar which ripped at his cheek, the partly-obliterated tooth-marks and the stiffness of his face and I knew him.

'Wolfling!' I gasped.

'Shh. Your guard will hear you.' He spoke in the language of the Sidhe-folk and I slipped easily into thinking in that tongue.

'What are you doing here?' I asked, 'Is Otter . . .?'

'Otter insisted on coming too, though I told her not to,' Wolfling said, 'And as for why . . . We've been trying to find you since the Queen took you.'

I couldn't think of anything to say.

'I see. Where is Otter?'

Wolfling pointed further up.

'Somewhere there. She'll come to you tonight if you get away from the rest. We couldn't talk to you alone before – you were always with those two bears or by a campfire.'

'I'll get away,' I promised. 'But they still chain me to a spoke of a wheel at night – look.' I held up the shackles. Brocc and Brod hadn't taken them off because they hadn't got the key, though I thought Brocc would have liked to. I'd have been more useful with the wagon that way.

'You can't escape yet. The Hound's too far away to run to . . .' He broke off. I looked and saw Brod coming back.

'Go and get some other Fir Bolg,' I ordered Wolfling in Irish. 'And if they argue, tell them it's the Queen's wagon.'

He nodded, trying to look sullen, and ran off to another group of Fir Bolg. I heard them talking in low voices and knew as surely as if I could make out the words, that Wolfling was telling them who I was.

A little later the small, nearly naked Fir Bolg slaves had helped us to lever the wagon out of the rut. We went on after the tail of the army.

259

Brocc started to sing the song about the Blacksmith and the Druidess and Brod and I joined in. The troop of warriors directly behind us took it up and added flourishes of their own. The day brightened and the rain slackened off: it was quite bearable, if you forgot the mud and the filth and the tiredness and the wet and the itch of vermin and the having to stop every so often. We were halfway through another song when a troop of horsemen rode up, wrapped in bright greasy cloaks which kept out the rain. Tuachel was at their head, biting at his nails with worry. Well he might, I thought, as I started a new verse: the Queen's army riddled with sickness and already thinking longingly of its home-duns, men dying of disease and accident, vicious quarrels breaking out between clans which promised half a dozen new blood-feuds for the Queen to sort out . . . Well might her lieutenant worry.

Tuachel saw me properly and his small eyes narrowed.

'What are you doing sitting up there, Lugh Mac Romain?' he demanded. 'The Queen ordered that you were to walk beside.'

'He had to keep stopping to shit,' said Brod in explanation. 'So we let him ride so we could go faster. We didn't think . . .'

'Get him down and do as you're told. When the Queen says a thing she means it. Do you want to be cursed?'

He was only taking out his gut-gnawing worry on someone who couldn't hit back: the pettiness of it made me furious, apart from the fact that the mud was now up to the ankles, on the best bits. The song faltered and died and everyone watched to see what would happen. They all knew about me, of course.

Brocc leaned forward with his curly beard jutting out.

'What's it to you if he rides?' he growled ominously. 'He's entitled to ride if we let him.'

'Are you disobeying me?' Tuachel's voice, unfortunately, squeaked.

'Belt up, Brocc,' muttered Brod.

'Why should I? I don't see . . .'

'It's the Queen's orders. Do what I tell you or I'll tell her,' said Tuachel.

Brocc half got up. 'Do you want a fight?' he asked.

Tuachel kicked his horse forward, reaching for his spears which were in his spear-slings. For a moment I was tempted to let it go on, but then I remembered what would happen to Brocc when he killed Tuachel. And he had given me some of his mead.

'Leave it, Brocc,' I said. 'It's not worth fighting about.'

'But . . .'

'Stop the wagon.'

The oxen came dumbly to a halt. I got down slowly into the squelching mud, feeling my bowels churning with flux and anger. Tuachel pushed his horse up close, leant down and chained me to the slave-ring on the side, once more. He was taking no chances, I told myself. Petty, only.

'And stop that singing!' he shouted as he cantered off slowly up the army, the horsemen bunched around him.

I watched him go. The army squelched on a few yards. I threw back my head, filled my lungs and, at the top of my voice, added some new verses of my own to the song we had been singing before, only this time I added some verses on the subject of Tuachel. The warriors picked it up with a roar of approval and as we plodded northwards through Muir-themne, crushing Cuchulain's woods, I knew it would be all round the army by evening. What a petty revenge. For a petty thing.

That day as we made camp, Brocc and Brod conferred together about me while they pitched their leather tent and tried to find a dry spot to light a fire. They couldn't get the tinder to light.

When the tent was pitched and they had given up trying to light a fire, Brod came over to me and said, part embarrassed, part truculent,

'We've been talking . . . If you promise not to try and escape you can come and sleep in our tent.'

I thought of Otter and Wolfling, but there was no believable way I could think of to say no. That evening, after eating cold oatmeal cakes and some salt meat, I lay down to sleep on the hide they had spread on the floor of the tent to try and keep out the wet. I planned to get up in the night to relieve myself – as I would certainly have to anyway. I couldn't escape because I had promised and because I wouldn't know where to run anyway, but I could talk with Otter at least.

Brod took the first watch. I had dozed off when I woke to someone shaking my shoulders. I sat up quickly, wincing as I jerked my shackle-galls.

'Someone's come from the Sedanta to see you,' said Brod's voice. I got up and followed him cautiously in the dark, lightly scattered with lamps and the occasional bonfire where someone had been more successful than Brod at getting one going. I could see the dim shape of a man standing by the wagon, waiting. He was holding a firepot which gave off a little light. Brod waited a little way off while I went up to the man.

'Is that you, Lugh?' he asked.

'Laegh?'

'None but.'

'What are you doing here?'

'Cuchulain sent me.' We squatted down on our haunches and Brod came over to us. When I said I wanted to talk to Laegh privately, he fastened me like a dog to the wagon and then wandered off to the girl he probably had secreted somewhere, telling me to call when I wanted him.

Laegh was silent for a moment. 'He's not taking any chances.'

I shrugged, though he couldn't see me. 'The Queen threatened him with death if he let me escape. The Queen is noted for keeping promises like that and so he won't give me any chance to escape.'

'Very nice.'

'Reasonable. Laegh, why are you in camp?'

'Two reasons. Don't you remember, when Cuchulain made that agreement, he said I should come in and see you sometime to make sure you were still alive? Apart from that, I came to find out from Lugaid and Ferbaeth and Ferdia Mac Daire who it is Cuchulain's fighting tomorrow.'

'Who is it?'

There was the noise of Laegh spitting.

'Ferbaeth,' he said, as though the word tasted bad.

'*Ferbaeth?* But Laegh, Ferbaeth was with Scatha when Cuchulain was there, along with Naisi and Ferdia. How did she . . .'

'Lugaid said the Queen gave him to drink of her cup and promised him Findabhair. I understand about Findabhair, but what does he mean by the Queen's cup?' I understood then, of course.

'Oh come on now, Laegh,' I said, 'don't you know what the Queen's name means?'

'She Who Intoxicates.'

'Well then.'

'You mean, she's drugged him?'

'Of course she has. Why not? It'll put Cuchulain off his stroke and Ferbaeth might be able to kill him.'

'The bitch! That bloody-begotten, death-drinking, cursed bitch . . .!'

He trailed off. I made the Sign of Horns.

'How is Cuchulain?' I asked.

'Not good. He has a couple of bad wounds and several scratches. There's one in his shoulder that might go sick. As I said to Facen, if he could just rest for a while, he could last out. It's the having to keep going that's sapping him. He still manages to win, but it's getting closer.'

Only Cuchulain could do it, I thought, but it won't last. His luck will run out – perhaps his friend will kill him.

'Facen was the one who . . . er . . . captured me, wasn't he?'

'That's right,' said Laegh. He laughed. 'Facen will treat you more respectfully when you meet him again. When he got back to Cuchulain and told him what he'd done with you . . .'

'What did Cuchulain do?'

263

'Beat him up for being so stupid. Then brought him round with his own ale – a waste – and said it could have happened to anybody and invited Facen to hit him back, because on reflection Cuchulain thought he did the right thing.'

'Did he?'

'Of course not. They're the best of friends again now.'

I had to smile. It was so typical of Cuchulain.

'Listen, Lugh,' said Laegh, 'Cuchulain told me to tell you this: "I can't actively help you to escape because of the agreement with the Queen which I can't break honourably until she does. But if you do escape, come to me and she won't get you back again."'

'Is that all?'

'That's all.' There was a short silence and Laegh moved restlessly. 'I must go back to him now or he'll think the Queen's taken me prisoner and come spitting spears to fetch me.'

'Yes, of course,' I said.

He disappeared into the dark. I heard him cursing as he tripped over something and then no more. I did not at once call for Brod to release me: I wanted to think and it was a long time since I had been alone.

Someone touched me on the arm. I twisted round, tense, staring into the murk.

'It's me, Otter!'

My breath let out, and I held out my hands to her, happy she was there. I could just make out Wolfling standing beside her. Her hard fine hands touched mine and then she found the wrist-irons: she felt them silently and the galls underneath.

'They chain you like an animal,' she said in a tight voice.

'No,' I said. 'Like a slave.'

Her hands gripped tighter and then released me.

'Don't speak like that.' Her voice, speaking the Sidhe-tongue was very low: only Wolfling and I could hear her.

'Why not?' I asked. 'It's true. And I would rather be a slave.'

'We'll help you to escape.'

'How?'

'I don't know. But there will be a way.'

'It's ironic, you know,' I said thoughtfully. 'If I escape then the Queen will kill the two men guarding me.'

'Good!' said Otter fiercely.

'But they've been kind to me.'

'*Kind!*'

'Yes. Ask Wolfling what happened this morning when I was riding on the wagon.'

Otter was silent. Then she took my hand again and pressed a small leather pouch into it.

'What's that?' I asked.

'It's medicine. If you take a little of that in your food, it'll help you get rid of the flux.'

I tried to thank them then, but Wolfling hissed that someone was coming. The two disappeared into the night as if they had never been.

It was Brod, coming to see if I had finished talking to Laegh. I went back with him to the tent and slept soundly in the warm fug of other people's bodies, with the little bag of herbs stowed in the breast of my stiff and filthy tunic.


# V


A few days before Samhain the Queen gave orders that the army fortify a camp for Samhain Eve and the Miming of the King-Killing. I helped dig into the thick soil on a mound, while Cuchulain camped on another mound on the other side of a small stream. He did not dig in, but he sent north again to ask Conor what he was doing. There were several camps of the Queen's army, all close to each other, and the main one had a ditch and earth bank and a thorn-hedge on the top, so it was almost a dun.

The Queen also ordered Brocc and Brod to put up a little tent for me alone and she told them to watch me more carefully. I wondered what that meant: the Queen had sent the cattle she had raided on south – perhaps she was preparing for a big attack on Cuchulain and didn't want me escaping to tell him.

So once again I spent my days solitary and bored, surrounded by leather tent, with plenty of time to meditate. I used the medicine Otter had given me and it worked well; I gave some to Brod who was badly ill with the flux and it helped him too.

The night before Samhain Eve proper, I was sleeping half-wakeful in the tent. There was a psst-sound from the opposite side to the flap. I moved over there and listened.

'Lugh,' said Otter's voice, 'you must escape tomorrow night.'

'Why?'

'Wolfling has found that the Queen intends to kill you instead of miming the King-Killing at Samhain.'

'But . . . but she can't! She said she wouldn't, it's part of her agreement . . .'

'I know that. Wolfling says he was listening to her talking to Tuachel: she said it would spite Ailell who has been getting too independent recently and it would shake Cuchulain – she knows he's badly injured and she wants to make him doubtful.'

'All she'll do is make him furiously angry.'

'I know. But you must escape.'

'How? You're . . .'

'Take this. I'm sliding it under the tent.'

I felt around and found something metal coming to meet my fingers. I picked it up and tried to examine it in the blackness.

'What is it?'

'It's a file. For those irons the Queen put on you. You can't escape with your hands bound.'

'Have you a plan?'

'No. I don't know what to do. I can drug your guards, but I didn't expect the Queen to fortify and I don't know how we can get out of the camp.'

266

'Why not drug the gate-guard?'

'I can't. I can't get close enough to them: I think the Queen may have seen something of me in the incense-flame, for she's given orders that none of the Fir Bolg are to go anywhere near the gate.'

I bit my lip. It would be too hard to get out of the camp by anywhere but the gates, with the bank and ditch and thorn-hedge: we would have to do it after dark and that would mean they would have been shut: on Samhain no gate-guard was likely to open any gate just on one man's say-so.

To be so close to freedom and have something like that stop you – I should have tried to escape before, instead of asking Otter and Wolfling to risk themselves like this, but there had been no chance. One of the brothers was always near enough to hear the scraping of a file. The tent might muffle a little of the sound.

I closed my eyes and forced myself to think: my mind's eye scanned over all the possibilities and they were all hopeless and there was no way out and . . . Cormac. Cormac might help. He had said he would.

'Can you get Cormac Connlonges to come to me?' I asked.

'Why?'

'He may be able to help.'

'He won't believe me – I'm one of the Tuatha de Danaan: he's an Ulsterman and they hate us even more than the rest of Erin.'

'Tell him . . . tell him he should come because of the boar.'

'All right.' Her voice sounded doubtful. 'Should Wolfling and I come back as well?'

'Yes. We should make a plan. He may be able to think of something.'

'Haven't you?'

'I don't know. I never had to before.'

The flap moved. I shifted across the tent and lay on the file, to hide it. Brod stuck his head in.

'Anything the matter? he asked suspiciously.

I opened one eye and mumbled, 'Wassat?'

'Were you talking?'

'I've been asleep,' I said, hoping Otter would stay quiet.

'Oh. You must have been dreaming then. Try and shut up. It gets on my nerves.'

When he had gone I moved over again to the full extent of the chain and whispered 'Otter?' There was no answer: she had gone.

It was a long time before I heard the soft sound by the tent again. I was stiff from sitting in an awkward position, waiting. But this time it was Cormac's voice.

'What is it, Lugh?' he asked, his voice wary.

'The Queen will kill me tomorrow,' I said, without preamble.

'She'll *what*?'

'Tomorrow.'

'But she agreed . . .'

'When did you ever know the Queen to keep her promises?'

'How c–can I help?'

Oh Cormac, I thought, what a disadvantage you're at: so transparent in an opaque world. I told him the problem with the gate-guard. When I had finished he was silent for a while and then he said, 'I'd k–kill him for you, but I'd rather not. There must be some other way.'

I could hear Otter whispering urgently to him.

'But that's dishonourable,' he said, too loudly. Wolfling shushed him.

'What's dishonourable?' I asked.

'The . . . the Sidhe-woman wants me to send the guard a drug to make him sleep.'

'Cormac!' I said, exasperated. 'It's dishonourable to help the prisoner of the woman you're serving. If your honour's so important then you'd better leave now.'

He was silent for a while again.

'Listen,' he said at last, 'no matter what happens, I'll see that the gate-guard either isn't there or lets you through.'

He had given his promise: I knew he would die rather than break it. He would make a more honourable King, at least, than his father: indeed, he had been Conor's first choice for the Kingship after him, before the death of the sons of Usnach. As it was, I supposed that Follamon, the last son born in wedlock, and still in the Boys' Troop of Emain Macha, would be the next King.

When Cormac had gone I lay awake, trying to plan how we could escape: but really you couldn't plan it. All you could do was follow events as they happened and make them work for you. I would have to escape in the evening, because the Miming of the King-Killing would take place not very long after sunset. Only this time it wouldn't be a mime. It would be a true sacrifice.

That night I dreamt of the Queen: I woke shouting at the top of my voice and remembered her face out of the slippery images of the dream, but I couldn't remember what the rest of the dream was.

The next day the camp was full of noises as the animals were driven in from the other campsites and bonfires made ready for Samhain: it was a cold day in the final stages of autumn, wet, and smelling of mud and leaf-rot, and for once I was glad of the tent and the noise. To hide the sound the file made when I tried scraping away with it, I had to wait until something was going by the tent which made enough noise: a cart or a herd of cattle or a fight. I worked in bursts, listening and watching: holding in the longing I had simply to break through the tent and run away. The day began darkening and I worked more desperately, sawing away with sore fingers and gritted teeth against the noise. No one came in and there was no food: the Sacrifice goes fasting to his death, I thought, very economical. The sun set, the bonfires were lit from the Queen's wer-fire; soon, soon now they would come for me and it would all be over, finished in blood on Samhain – there was at least a pattern, for the thing had begun in blood, on Samhain. One year ago I killed the King and became King of Connaught myself for a little while, before the crash, before my leg was lamed and the world changed.

I was sweating and filing away with the now blunted

metal on the link of the chain. There was just a little strip of metal left which I could not get a purchase on . . . There were voices outside. A voice I knew well.

'I have brought you some mead,' said Otter, 'as a gift.'

'Wait!' That was Brod and I knew the tone of his voice. He used it to his captive girl: soft and wanting only one thing. 'What are you doing tonight, Faery-woman?'

'What would you like me to do tonight, Iron-man?'

I moved over and lifted the flap. In the dusk, already torch- and bonfire-lit, I saw Brod holding Otter while she looked at him as though she wanted to sleep with him. But in the stiffness with which she held her body, I knew she was afraid. I wanted to go out to her and throw Brod aside, calm her . . . Brod pulled Otter towards him. Brocc was drinking down the mead. Otter struggled for a moment and then began to relax, but Brod reached out and snatched the mead from Brocc and drank the other half down. Otter watched, her lashes shadowing her face as I had seen them before, satisfaction under the dark semicircle.

She turned and whisked into the darkness. Brod made to follow her, but then he shrugged and came back. He saw me looking out and our eyes met: he said something quiet to his brother and came and closed the flap gently but firmly, and wordlessly. I knew then, if I hadn't known before, that what Otter had told me was true.

Time passed slowly. I was bending and twisting the little strip of metal, widening the gap: I cut my thumb and scarcely noticed and kept rubbing until at last, the thing broke and I could work the links loose and stretch my arms for the first time in days and days and I had forgotten how long. I stretched out until my muscles creaked.

There had been no sound from either Brod or Brocc for some time. I went and looked out: they were propped up against each other, almost asleep: Brocc, who had drunk the most, was snoring softly, but Brod kept trying to open his eyes. I waited, my heart beating under my tongue: slowly, very slowly, his eyes closed and he breathed deeper.

I lifted the flap and stepped out of the tent. I felt them

over in case they had the keys to the irons chafing my wrists, but they hadn't: I took Brod's dagger and stuck it in my belt and dragged both of them into the tent. Just as I ducked my head to come out again, I saw Otter, followed by Wolfling, running towards me.

'They're coming!' gasped Otter. Wolfling had his knife out: I saw white bronze shine in the light of a nearby fire.

A troop of men were coming: I could see the group of them as they passed purposefully by one of the chariots. A horse shifted quietly, nickering to itself. They were dressed, as I could see in glimpses, in the ceremonial gear for accompanying the Old King, in crow's feathers and black leather; they had their spears, glinting in the dark.

I grabbed Otter's wrist and hurried to the nearest shadow, a corner between a tent and some piled-up barrels. Wolfling ran after us: we crouched together in the tiny protection, knowing they had only to look our way and we would be seen, but they were too close for us to move somewhere better.

Tuachel was leading the troop: he stopped when he saw no one on guard and a shiver went through the troop as they stood up straight and looked round alertly. We cowered down, trying to make ourselves as small as field-mice. Tuachel went inside, shouted out. Somebody took a horn and blew three short blasts: the signal for alarm.

'Come on,' whispered Otter. 'Let's walk away quietly: we can't fight them, they're too many . . . Quickly!'

I could think of nothing better. I let her take my hand and followed her between the barrels, very carefully so as not to knock them over, precarious as they were and treacherous too in the small light.

'Look, Tuachel!' someone shouted. 'Over there!'

I twisted to look over my shoulder: one of the young men at the back of the group had seen us. He was pointing in our direction. Otter ran forward, dragging me after her. I stumbled, hampered by my leg and kicked the bottom barrel. The pile fell, rolling over the space between tents and into the horse-pen nearby.

The troop was thundering towards us, spreading out to avoid the barrels – they were Gailiana, I realized, Fianna-men, the best fighters in Erin. Otter dived between two tents, I followed and then discovered that Wolfling was not with us.

'Wolfling!' I hissed, pulled away from her and looked out beyond the side of the tent to see where he was.

He had turned against them, and I saw that his foot was hurt in some way. One of the barrels must have rolled on it. His knife was out and flashing; one of the Gailiana screamed and fell. I snatched at my dagger and started forward to help, but as I did so, a spear thrust by Tuachel stabbed down into Wolfling's chest and out the other side. His back arched in spasm, he lay still. Tuachel pulled the red spear out.

A breath was taken in beside me. Instinctively I grabbed Otter and held her close to me, my hand over her mouth. She struggled and bit, but I held on desperately, knowing that any sound she made would be death for both of us.

Tuachel stood over the body of Wolfling (so much blood in such a small-sized boy?) and gave his orders carefully, shouting. The Gailiana fanned out at a jogtrot, spears at the ready, to search the camp. Tuachel looked down at the body, bent as though about to take the head, then saw the scar on Wolfling's face. He looked disgusted and drew back, and strode off through the camp, looking to either side of him.

Otter tore free of me and ran over to Wolfling. I followed her cursing, dagger out, feeling every moment the spears of the Gailiana at my back. I could hear the sound of fighting somewhere.

She threw herself on the body of her brother, caressing it and crying over it and drinking the blood, as is the right of the nearest relation. She cried strangely, with short sharp crying sounds like those of the white seagulls which come inland when the sea is foul. I waited a little, for her to wash some of her grief out, dagger itchy in my hand, nervous and impatient, yet shocked and hurt by Wolfling's death, so that

I could not quite breathe although no one had hit me. It was such a pitiful wreck of a body, with a previously wrecked face, lying crumpled and torn . . . His features were already beginning to fall out of expression, drawn down by their weight.

I bent and closed his staring eyes. As I did so, Otter sat up with blood on her face, threw back her hair and started to keen, crying out with her whole voice,

'Aiieee! Aaieee! O-o-ochone! Ochone! Ochone! Aaaiii!'

I grabbed her, picked her up and shook her, slapped her face until she stopped and started to cry, weeping as though she would cry herself away in her own tears . . . She had already scratched her face and the grazes were beginning to show blood. She was like a boiled corndoll, with no stiffness in her. I slung her over my shoulder, as I had once done with a girl I caught when cattle-raiding, and turned to go through the camp in the direction of what I hoped was the gate. But they would have shut that by now: we were caught like rats and the alarm was out and they would run us down soon . . .

Tuachel was standing there, spear ready. I stopped and for a split second we stared at each other. Then Tuachel dropped into a fighting crouch, and I set Otter down on the ground and reached for my dagger.

Even as he circled me I thought: this is it, he has a spear and I only a dagger, I cannot win and he will kill me, but better to die on a spear than by the Queen . . . I thought of Wolfling and the way his back had arched and wondered if it was better . . . Oh no! Far better to live . . . !

With his spear, Tuachel had the reach on me: bloodied it was already with Wolfling's blood . . . Wolfling's blood. Tuachel had killed Wolfling, coldly with his spear, had killed a boy who had had only a bronze knife, killed him with a long stabbing spear . . .

Something exploded inside me and the world slowed down. My mind thought for me, while another part of me watched in faint amazement. If I stayed apart from Tuachel, he would surely kill me (and there was no fear in the

273

thought). Therefore my only chance was to fight close. But in trying to get close, I might well spit myself on the spear. Therefore I must trick him somehow.

So I lurched to the right, as though my lame leg had played me false: Tuachel leaped to the right and stabbed, but I jumped somehow the other way, in under his guard and knocked him over. His spear was no use to him: he dropped it and scrabbled for his knife – they always do that, my cold voice said, it would be far better to go immediately for the throat. My knife was pinned against him, I could not use it, and with my left hand I was holding his right, preventing it from getting the knife. We rolled over, kicking and struggling.

Suddenly a pain shot up my right leg: he had kicked it with his booted foot. It put me off and he grabbed his knife free and stabbed down . . .

I had already rolled. It whistled past my ear and into the ground and my hand closed on his as he tried to get it free. I stabbed at him with my knife and felt material part under the edge, but he sucked his stomach in, came to one knee, wrenched his dagger out of the soil and threw himself on me, the point an inch from my jugular vein. I slashed at his face with the manacle on my wrist, but I could feel myself weaken: I had not got my fighting strength back and it was telling on me. I was panting like a broken-winded horse and my sight was blurred and my leg hurt me.

Then there was a shadow across us and a thump of flashing metal. Tuachel choked. Otter had stabbed him in the back, being a woman and, thank the gods, caring nothing for Fair Play. I threw him off, because the shock numbed him for a moment. He started to climb to his feet again, but I stretched across, snatched up his spear and from a crouch, stabbed down with it viciously, till I could feel the point touch ground.

As I picked myself up, panting for breath and spitting the sour-tasting stuff out of the back of my mouth, I heard a curse. Otter was demented, hair flying, her patterned face smeared with blood and tears and spittle, stabbing at

274

Tuachel; he was not dead yet, but writhing a little. I stood up straight and hit Otter carefully with my closed fist. She was thrown back and lay there in the mud against an empty tent, crying. I bent and pulled out the spear. Blood gushed; Tuachel died. I cut off his head with the spear-blade and then, taking the head by the hair and carrying the spear, I went over to where Wolfling lay, and stuck the spear in the ground. On the top of it I stuck Tuachel's head, as a mark of why I had killed him. No, not I: Otter and I.

She was still lying where she had fallen, crying and crying; like a lost child she was, lost in a cold bog where marsh-lights are to fool you. I had feared I may have knocked her out, or even killed her, but I had only bruised her jaw. It would be swollen the next day. I crouched beside her and raised her up: she was crying too much to make a noise; her head hung back a little, her mouth open and her eyes half-shut and I felt like weeping for her; for the tearing of grief she felt I could almost feel myself.

'Otter. Otter. Hush now.'

She gasped for breath. I held her against me, looking round for anyone who had heard the fight. We had to get out, we had to get out. Far away, where the Queen was, I heard a horn blowing. Only Otter knew where the gate was: I had no idea which of the three possibilities Cormac would have cleared for us and cursed myself for not finding out.

I thought Otter's sobs had quieted a little. She seemed more relaxed, though she was shaking. I held her thin little shoulders and, as she looked up at me, I bent my head, on impulse, and kissed her. At first she was surprised and then she responded, and then I knew, as I had not properly before, that she wanted me, she would have me now . . .

I broke away quickly before I too should get out of control and held her more gently.

'Otter,' I said desperately. 'Think. In the name of the Mother-of-all, think! Where is the gate?' She shook her head. 'Otter, where is the gate?'

Still nothing. I shook her, not hard, but to clear her head. 'I . . . I'll sh . . . sh . . . show you,' she whispered at last. I

275

helped her to stand up and she looked round as though she had lost her bearings. She straightened herself and pushed her hair out of her eyes, wiped the mud and blood and dirt off, and even tried to smile. My heart hurt for her as it had not done before.

Otter started off through the camp, picking her way between the restive animals and sleeping men, steering well clear of the bonfires and torches, stepping softly through the shadows, listening with pricked ears for pursuers. Sometimes she would drag me down into the shelter of some tent or chariot as a man went by.

Gradually, fearfully, we drew near the gate, but as we did the shouting did too. There had been uproar growing through the camp, increased when they found Tuachel, and men had been running hither and yon, tripping over each other and fighting on slightest provocation, through which bedlam we picked our way like cats through mud. It was Samhain, you see, and the rumour had gone round that Cuchulain's Druids had called up Spirits to attack the camp. The closer we came to the gate, the more the tumult grew, and through it all, the Gailiana jogged implacably, scouting around like well-trained hunting dogs, quartering the camp.

Between the gate and the tents there was a stretch of open ground. Beyond it, where the makeshift gate was, I could see a dim flurry of fighting. I wiped the sweaty grip of my dagger on my tunic and made ready to fight again, but as I did so, Cormac killed the last man and opened the gate. His men spread themselves out. I smiled. He had fulfilled his promise.

I stepped out, sticking my dagger in my belt so they wouldn't kill me in the excitement of the moment and called: 'Macha!'

Cormac came to meet me, wiping sweat from his face with his arm, his sword held in his hand.

'Lugh?' he asked cautiously.

'It is. With Otter.'

'I had to k–kill the gate-guard after all: there were a

couple of Gailiana there too and we had to kill them as well. What happened to you? Why are you . . .?'

Quickly, I told him what had happened. He pursed his lips in a silent whistle.

'That was a good head to take. Where is it?'

'I left it by Wolfling to show the reason. And I didn't take it on my own, Otter helped me.'

'Oh.' He was unhappy about that. Before he could start talking about Fair Play, I interrupted; 'Listen, Cormac, the Gailiana are after me. Can you delay them?'

'Of course. I'll kill . . .'

'No. Don't kill them: you'll have to kill the whole Gailiana. Say I didn't pass this way, that no one has and . . .'

Otter grabbed my arm and pointed. Shouts rose, and a thrown spear clattered to the ground a few yards short. We had spent too long talking – how stupid can you be? To spend . . . Ach, what does it matter?

I helped Cormac haul the gate to and as he prepared to hold them off, his men grouped round him, I hissed at him, 'Don't get yourself killed, in the name of the Sun, it's not worth it.'

'But I . . .'

'You've paid your debt, you bloody hero, just get out of it! Go on!'

He seemed puzzled and about to argue. I grabbed his forearms, as though he was trying to struggle with me, and then hit him hard. He fell back.

Next moment Otter and I were out, with the gate shut behind us. It took them seconds to get it open and they thundered after us, shouting and throwing slingstones. But I could not run, only lope and as we ran downhill towards Cuchulain's little camp beyond the stream, I realized that my leg would slow Otter disastrously. She was going slowly for my sake.

She pulled me zigzagging through the low bushes and scrub that had not been cleared, brambles and gorse clawing at our legs, tree-branches whipping our faces. She said, 'You drop out of sight, I'll lead them on.'

'But . . .' I started to argue, just like Cormac.

'They won't catch me. Hide, then go to the Hound. I'll join you when I've lost them in the forest. Quickly!'

So when we were out of sight, temporarily, behind a great clump of gorse, I dived underneath, into the prickling bushes, stifling curses at the sharpness of the thorns. I lay still while the Gailiana passed me by, almost close enough to touch, running like wolves.

I waited for a long time until the noise of their passing had gone, until I could hear the noise from the camp of Erin, where it seemed a full-scale fight had broken out. Then I crawled out, stood up shakily and took a deep breath. I walked unsteadily until I found the stream by sound and crossed it at the ford. It came to my knees and it was very cold, cold that sent a pain into my body. I scrambled up the other bank and climbed cautiously up the mound, hoping I wouldn't get a Sedantii spear in my guts after all.

My mind was still bemused and half-dazed: there had been too much happening too fast; I could not get used to the idea of being free, though the metal of the wrist-irons still weighed down my hands. I could not get used to the fact of Wolfling's death either. I was dog-tired and numb and I needed time to rest, time to think. Above all, I thought suddenly, I need Fiorbhinn. Perhaps I would ride north to Emain Macha and fetch the harp. Or perhaps I wouldn't. With the Curse of Macha still on Emain I wouldn't be able to leave, and I wanted to be with Cuchulain until Conor finally decided to bestir himself. For it was obvious enough to me now what Conor's reasons for delay were, and they made me love him none the more.

I stopped before I came into the circle of firelight by the waiting shape of the chariot and the figure of a man, sitting very tired, by the fire. Was Otter all right, I wondered, has she shaken them off yet? Or is she dead too? Perhaps, said the small drunken thought, perhaps I am as well and don't know it yet. I was too tired to know.

# VI

'Stop! Who's that?'

I recognized the voice and smiled wearily. It seemed logical, though why, I wasn't sure.

'It's all right, Facen,' I said. 'It's me. Lugh Mac Romain.'

'*Lugh!*' he came closer and peered into my face, and then he slapped me heavily on the back. I staggered a little. 'I never thought you'd escape from that bitch. How did you . . .?'

'Is the Sedanta or Laegh Mac Riangabra here?'

The man sitting by the fire unfolded his skinny length and came over.

'Who is it, Facen?' he asked.

'Lugh Mac Romain,' said Facen with relish. 'That's one thumping I owe the Sedanta.'

'Lugh!' Laegh grabbed my arm and propelled me towards the fire. He looked closely at me. His face broke into his gap-toothed smile.

'It *is* Lugh. Great gods, man, I didn't think you'd do it.'

I made a tired gesture. 'I had help. It's why the army of Erin is at present engaged in fighting itself.'

'I wondered what the uproar was. How did you do it?'

'Cormac helped and . . . somebody else.' I had suddenly remembered what the Ulstermen thought about the Sidhe-folk, and I decided it would be better not to mention her for the moment. Besides it was Samhain.

'Where's Cuchulain?' I asked, to change the subject.

Laegh's grin faded instantly to be replaced by a worried expression which looked as though it was habitual. He turned away from the fire and gestured towards a shape huddled under the chariot, looming ominously fire-touched in the dark.

'Don't wake him,' he said.

'It's all right,' said Cuchulain, moving. 'I'm already

279

awake. I can't sleep. Is that Lugh Mac Romain?'

There was a strange quality in his voice and the way he asked questions. Very abrupt and yet husky, as though it pained him to talk too much.

I went over to him and squatted down. He sat up on his elbow and peered at me, his eyes unnaturally bright. I could see him quite well in the light from the fire.

He was very much changed. Firstly there was the growth of several weeks' beard on his chin and under it his face was clearly thinner than it had been. The eyes were deeper, his hair wild and coming out of its confining plait, too wiry to be held down. There was a cut still crusted with new-clotted blood along the side of his face, just missing the corner of his eye.

'So it is yourself,' he said thoughtfully. 'You've changed.'

I was taken aback. To me it had not been myself that had changed, but the world. But when I thought of it, I realized that I had indeed changed inside in some way. I could not tell why or how. Perhaps it had something to do with my laming, perhaps with the Tuatha de Danaan. Perhaps something different.

'You've changed yourself,' I said. 'You don't look well, man.'

He laughed. It was a hard laugh and completely false.

'Oh, that's only old Mother Laegh worrying for nothing. I've had worse in me.'

'You may have,' retorted Laegh. 'But not several together. Gods, for a man like yourself, you're unbelievably stupid sometimes, Cuchulain.'

'I'm all right,' said Cuchulain in a dangerous voice. 'I just can't sleep.'

'And where's the wonderment in that?' demanded Laegh. 'You've got three bad wounds in you, one that's going sick if I'm any judge and half a dozen little ones. One at a time and you'd scarcely notice the half of them, but all together . . .'

'Well, there's nothing I can do about it, so in the name of the gods, stop nagging me, Laegh!' growled Cuchulain, turning over carefully and lying down again. 'Anyone would think you were my catamite.'

Laegh whitened and walked over to where the Black Sainglenn was standing, a little way back from the fire, one leg cocked.

I followed him over and he said abruptly in a low voice, 'Don't mind what he says. He never means it any more than I mean what I say to him when he's losing a fight.'

'Must he go on with this . . . this lunatic single-combat agreement?' I asked after a while.

Laegh raised his arms in despair and let them fall.

'What else can he do? He has to delay the Queen and he agreed to do it indefinitely. He must go on. The Queen would have been at the gates of Emain by now if it hadn't been for this thrice-three-times accursed agreement.'

I could believe that.

'He looks feverish,' I said.

'Dagda's arse, he *is* feverish!' Laegh clenched his fist and pounded it against the other palm. 'But he won't rest. Says he made an agreement and he's got to stick to it until Maeve breaks it. Just a few days' rest and he'd be all right to go on until Conor arrives . . .'

'Until Conor arrives?' I asked, raising an eyebrow.

Laegh looked at me closely.

'So you've had the same thought?'

'It makes sense, doesn't it? Cuchulain is rich and powerful and he can make men follow him by crooking his finger. So he drains off the Queen's strength, delaying her and killing her best while disease and hunger help him along. And then, finally Conor comes down and wipes up what remains.'

'After the Queen of Connaught has rid Conor of that worrying man, Cuchulain Mac Sualtim. Yes, I know. Oh, curse Conor, may his guts rot! May he sleep in a sidhe and wake up to find a thousand years gone . . . Ach, what's the use? Cuchulain will fight himself to a standstill though he knows as well as you and I what Conor's up to. And why? Because he's Champion of Ulster, that's why!'

We went back to the fire. Laegh watched me, frowning.

'Why are you limping?' he asked.

281

It seemed so strange that he didn't know, I almost laughed.

'Didn't you know? My chariot turned over in that fight after Conor's raid on Rath Ini. I was in it at the time, and among other things, it broke my leg.'

'But . . . Then by rights you shouldn't be alive at all – who looked after you?'

I hesitated. Then I said, 'Ailell found me a physician who set the bone as best he could – though as you can see, it's a little crooked still.' I smiled with a sour twist to my mouth. 'Still, I'm grateful to him that it wasn't more so. And then I was taken in and cared for.'

'By whom?'

'The Tuatha de Danaan.'

He gaped at me. 'The . . . the *Sidhe*-folk?'

I nodded, enjoying his incredulity. He made the Sign of Horns, as I had expected him to.

'But . . .'

'As you see, I didn't sleep for a thousand years. Though sometimes I wonder.'

'The Tuatha de Danaan? But they're dangerous, enchanters, they bewitched you . . .'

'Dangerous? Yes – but so are you, Laegh, and Cuchulain. They are . . . shall we say: less overt about it than you are? Enchanters? Perhaps. But their enchantment saved my life at least once and probably more often and it healed my wounds. As for bewitching me – do I seem to you bewitched?'

'I don't know. You're changed, but I think . . . I think it isn't enchantment.'

'Well then.'

'But still . . .'

I grew impatient.

'Ach, stop acting like a child frightened with stories of the Tuatha. Don't you know that Cuchulain, your beloved chieftain, was born in a sidhe and probably has some small man of the Sidhe-folk as his father – or even Lugh Sunspear Himself, whom everyone knows, lives in a sidhe.'

'Well, perhaps. But still, they're uncanny the way they . . .'

I gazed at the stars. 'Laegh,' I said warningly, 'don't look behind you.'

Of course, he turned round. There stood Otter with four men of the Tuatha de Danaan standing behind her. The darkness behind seemed somehow suitable to them, and certainly they used it as a man might use a great cloak. None of the pickets had heard them come.

Laegh reached for his dagger, but I put out my arm and clamped his hand to the hilt.

'Otter,' I said, 'this is Laegh Mac Riangabra, charioteer to the Hound of the Sedantii. Laegh, this is Otter, woman of the Tuatha de Danaan. She was the one who helped me to escape and her brother died in the attempt. Any quarrel you have with her, you have with me.'

It was pure bluff, since I knew I could not fight him fairly and win. And yet I meant it and would have fought him if he had drawn his dagger. But to my relief he relaxed his hand from his dagger-hilt.

He bowed his head stiffly in salute. Otter did the same. Her face was wiped clean and she was perfectly composed.

'The Gailiana?' I asked her anxiously, speaking in Irish for Laegh's benefit.

She made a little chopping gesture. 'Dead.'

'And yourself?' I went towards her, but she remained stiff.

'I am well.'

'Otter, what's wrong?'

'Wrong?' she repeated softly, in the Sidhe-tongue. 'Wrong? Have you forgotten my brother so soon?'

'No. I haven't forgotten Wolfling.'

'Then why don't you weep?'

'Weep?' My voice sounded strange, even to my ears. 'I can't. But when I have my harp again, I will make a lament for him. I will make it as beautiful as my skill knows how. And that will have to do, Otter; I can give you no more.'

'No?' She lifted her head and her eyes met mine, and I read there a new message, or perhaps it wasn't new and I had only just noticed it properly.

'What are you saying?' demanded Laegh suspiciously.

I looked at him. 'Nothing that would interest you,' I said coldly. He subsided and went and added some twigs to the fire.

Cuchulain shifted and moaned softly in his sleep. And then I thought of something I could do for him, something that would help Ulster too, though what did I owe Ulster?

'Otter,' I said with urgency, 'is there a sidhe near here?'

'Of course there is,' she said, surprised. 'It's the Sidhe of Muirthemne and it's only a little way into the forest. These men come from there.'

'Would they take the Hound in and care for him for a little while, say three days. Without . . . without harming him in any way?'

Her eyes widened and for a moment her face looked almost mischievous.

'The Hound?' she said. 'In the Sidhe of Muirthemne? Of course they will, and ask nothing in return. The Old Mother of that sidhe will do everything in her power to help the Sedanta.'

'Can you take him there? Quickly, this night? And show me where it is so I can find him if we need him?'

'Yes. But only you must come. I do not trust this . . . Laegh.'

'Nor he doesn't trust you.'

She accepted it.

'We will need to drug the Hound first,' she said thoughtfully. 'He may not come willingly.'

I nodded and turned to Laegh.

'Listen to me, Laegh. You remember saying just now that if only Cuchulain could be got to rest for a while, for three days only, he'd be able to go on until Conor bestirs himself.'

'Yes?' Laegh sounded suspicious, looking from me to Otter and back again.

'If you would let me take him to a sidhe where they'll look after him . . .'

'*No!*'

'In the name of all the gods of Ulster, Laegh, be reasonable! Didn't you listen to what I said before? The Tuatha de Danaan helped me; they cured me as far as they could, and Otter's brother died to save me from the Queen's men. Who do you think put together the wreck that crash made of my leg? Look at it, Laegh!' I thrust it forward like a sword. 'Would they have cured it if they intended to curse me? Why should they have helped me? They'll help Cuchulain, if you'll bend your stubborn belief in harpers' tales and let them do it.'

'Don't you believe them, the harpers' tales?' Laegh was defensive.

I smiled at him, pitying. 'Laegh. Have you forgotten? I'm a harper myself.' And I remembered what I had said to Ferghus and before that to Gaiar: well, it was true. Who is less impressed by the blacksmith's magic than the blacksmith himself?

'If you let us help the Hound,' put in Otter proudly, 'then I will swear to you that we will care for him to the best of our skill and do him no harm of body or mind or soul. To this witness the Morrigan and Edain of the Horses and Earth-Mother Herself.'

'They will not break that oath, Laegh,' I said quietly.

Laegh turned away.

'So be it,' he said.

Otter felt in the breast of her jerkin and brought out a leather bottle she always carried with her. She gave it to Laegh.

'Put three drops in a cup of mead. Taste a little yourself – it will not send you to sleep from that amount – and then give it to the Hound to drink.'

So, reluctantly, Laegh did as she said and Cuchulain drank the drugged mead down like a trusting child. It seemed a pity to have to do it that way, but I knew Cuchulain well enough to know very clearly what his reaction would be to any suggestion that he should rest. There never was a man harder to help.

Otter sent the men from the sidhe into the forest and by the time they had come back with cut ash-poles (naturally the Tuatha de Danaan would not use spears which had iron heads) Cuchulain was sleeping quietly, his chest rising and falling deeply. Laegh stood by him watching as the men constructed a litter out of the ash-poles. He shook his head at the Sedantii when they came to see what was going on and when he had explained quietly to Facen, they left us alone.

A little later Otter and I walked off cautiously through the woods, followed by the men bearing Cuchulain on the litter like a dead warrior home from the battle . . . I made the Sign of Horns against the bad luck of the thought. Samhain night: there should be spirits abroad in the forest, for it is time for gathering in, when all the cattle and animals are brought in and all the clans past and present as well. And they would be doubly restless, this land being strange territory for most of the ghosts. But although I stared through the shadowy trees and bare branches pricking the white stars, I saw no spirit, no Bocanach or Bananach: only an owl flying on silent wings covered the stars for a moment and a short while later some small furry thing in the forest screamed its death-scream. For now I knew the Tuatha de Danaan: I could speak to the ghosts in their own tongue, and I had the protection of the little bag with the Earth-sign on it under my tunic. And so I felt that the unseen things no longer threatened me.

We came suddenly to a tiny clearing in the thickest part of the forest, though it was not very far from the cleared area where farms on the hills had shaved off the trees. Otter whispered quickly to the guard at the gate in the hedge and we went into the little compound. I did not go into the long turf-roofed sidhe: something choked me at the thought of going back into those smoky, smelly, close surroundings. Having escaped once, I was irrationally afraid that if I returned I might not be able to come out again. Or else that I would wake and find myself in the old sidhe once more, still bed-tied by my broken leg.

After a while Otter came out again.

'He is comfortable now,' she said, 'and the Mother will care for him as . . . a Mother.'

'How will I find my way back?'

'If you need to come here, just whistle the Calling, the way . . . the way you were taught.'

It had been Wolfling who taught me.

Otter took me back to the edge of the forest: she seemed stiff and distant. I didn't understand why, but I didn't ask. At the edge of the forest she left me and slipped into the shadow before I could say anything. I shrugged, feeling a little hurt, and then walked slowly back to the camp. Night was slipping away. I would have little sleep, but tomorrow being Samhain the Queen wouldn't move anywhere and it wouldn't matter if I slept past sunrise.

When I came back to the fire it was almost as if I hadn't left. Laegh was sitting by the fire with his head cradled in his arms. He looked up as I approached.

'Well?' he asked.

'Cuchulain will be . . . at least rested at the end of three days.'

'If it's not three centuries.'

I said nothing. Laegh was just speaking for the sake of argument.

'Who will keep the Gap of the North tomorrow?' he asked.

'No one will need to. The Queen won't move – tomorrow is Samhain Day.'

'Samhain Day. Of course. Tonight is Samhain.' He passed his hand across his eyes. 'I'd forgotten.' He snorted. 'Samhain. No wonder the Sidhe-folk came.'

I was about to say that that had nothing to do with it, but decided not to. For one thing I wasn't so sure it didn't myself. I went and sat down by the fire, wrapping my cloak around me and rubbing my leg which was aching dully. I yawned. The sky was beginning to grey towards the east and the sea. It had all passed so quickly it was difficult to believe. I began to doze off where I sat.

'Why doesn't Conor come?!' Laegh burst out suddenly. I looked up and said mockingly,

'Oh, you know the answer to that already, Laegh. Conor wants to be rid both of Cuchulain and the flower of the

Queen's army, and he has constructed a very neat plan which will kill them both with the one sling-cast. So let the two kill each other and warm the cockles of his filthy heart!'

I pulled the cloak closer around me, lay down and went to sleep, while Samhain Day lightened above me.

## VII

I woke later that day, heavy of eye and body, aching and cold. Laegh had gone to exercise the horses: they needed the rest after days of pulling a chariot, but he could not let them become stiff with inaction either. Conn Mac Gege was sitting cross-legged by the fire, carving something and whistling between his teeth.

I sat up groggily and yawned.

'You've slept late,' Conn said cheerily. 'But Laegh told me how you escaped from the Queen, so it's not surprising. If you're hungry there's fresh oat-cake on that stone there and some oatmeal and dried meat in a leather pouch in the chariot and there might be something left of a hare I killed the day before yesterday.'

I grunted and climbed to my feet. As I chewed on one and a half oat-cakes which were all that was left on the cooking stone, Conn told me where Laegh had gone. I was still hungry when I had finished the oat-cakes, so I borrowed a griddle from Conn and made some more and ate them with the remains of the hare: I hadn't eaten since evening two days before and I'd felt distinctly hollow.

Conn whittled away at his bit of wood, whistling and making the odd comment about matters, as they occurred to him. He was making a little peg-doll and I was reminded sharply of Dalaigh before he was Ailell. I didn't think he had time to make toys for the children of Cruachan now.

'Who is it for?' I asked, pointing at the small thing with a half-eaten oat-cake.

Conn smiled almost shyly.

'It's for my little girl, my Befind. Cotred – that's my

288

eldest boy – broke her old one and I promised I would make her another. She was very upset about it.' He looked up. 'She's just like her mother, that way: very soft and gentle. Cotred's hunting-bitch whelped and we thought the runt of the litter would die, but Befind and Ness – she's my wife – looked after it and it lived. It's the most intelligent dog of the lot now, but it always follows Befind. Cotred's jealous of that, but I told him it was only right.'

'What does he look like?' I asked.

'He's aged eleven, but he's not big – I'm not myself. It doesn't worry him: his hero's the Sedanta and he's all impatient to become a man and fight for the Sedanta himself. The Sedanta was going to arrange for him to join the Boys' Troop of Emain Macha, but they had their three fifties already, so he's waiting until the next batch become men and leave the Troop.

'Befind will miss him when he goes, but she can help my wife with the baby – she probably won't even want the doll by the time I get back. She'll have come to want to look after the babe instead.'

It was a peaceful, clear day, that day. In the Queen's camp there were games and feasting going on, but I had no wish for anything of that sort. Conn, who seemed to have a talent for that kind of thing, fiddled at the locks on the shackles with a bone needle until they clicked and opened, showing the raw, rubbed patches. My hands felt wonderfully light after the removal of the chafing metal: Conn said I should wash them and leave the galls to dry out by themselves.

Afterwards it was very pleasant to sit with Conn and Laegh and some others of the Sedantii who had no duties and were not watching the Queen or the Gap of the North and talk of small things: families, and the question of whether the brown speckled cow would have a live calf this time. I listened to the talk, saying little: I felt detached from it, from the small concerns, satisfying and important and apple-sweet to the taste, from the talk of wives and families and cows and horses.

The day slipped away surprisingly quickly, for it seemed slow when it was passing. I had no watch to keep, though I offered, and so I lay down to sleep not long after sunset, beside the fire. For the first half of the night I slept deeply, but then I dreamt the old terrible dream of the Queen which I had dreamt so often before and so often after. I woke suddenly, my eyes flicking open of their own accord and for a moment the world lurched as it had in the sidhe when I stood up for the first time after the crash. My sight cleared and I saw the clear cold stars of the cool autumn night, pinpricks against a blue-black so deep and so great I felt like a blade of grass beside a mountain. I stared up at them for a long time, my brain wakeful and as clear and far away.

The change Cuchulain had remarked in me, which had altered the world in some indefinable way to my eyes, it had left my soul as free as the note released from a harp-string. Connaught lay to the south across the stream; Ulster waited in the north for the Queen's army to be whittled down to manageable size; Erin lay around me and yet, now I understood that I was not a comfortable part of it all, I no longer worried. This was no new discovery. I had been gradually discovering it ever since Ailell's body had collapsed over me that Samhain night a year ago, the bowels slipping out like fish from his belly; and I had pushed him off me and sat up and thought, even while I was still shaking with reaction and panic, of how I could escape the Queen's wrath. I had lost something which I now could not even remember and grown something else in its place. I was the same man, but more than just one year older: I had recognized that, wish though I might to be like Cuchulain, a man living in the right time and place, I was not like him and never would be. A strange thing to realize: to realize that for all my new-found understanding I was jealous of him, jealous of the luck that kept him whole for all his wild recklessness, jealous of the Sedantii and their small-talk of wives and children and livestock, when I knew that I was myself and always would be. It had taken me that long to know it.

Even so, I slept no more that night: the Queen's dream, in which she had come and robbed me of something I knew was precious beyond price – though what it was I did not know – it had shaken me too thoroughly; also my mind was thinking too fast and brightly to let me relax and shut my eyes. In the end I gave up the quest, stood up and went and sat a little way from the banked-up fire, still wrapped in my cloak, and looked at the bulk of the northern hills and the Cooley mountains.

The light changed and a cold wind blew salt from the sea. I sniffed it. It had a smell that fitted with my mood. I had never seen the sea close to, never stood beside it, though I had often enough seen the line of grey-silver through hills and trees in the distance. Even so, I knew now what I would do. Iollan had been right a year ago, though he would never see me take his advice: he too had gone.

Cold grey changed into a pink blush along the line of the east, but too many clouds had come into the sky from the clear night, on the back of the east wind. I didn't see the sun as it came up, but I knew when it lifted free of the horizon as though I were myself riding the golden chariot of my namesake – even though I knew now I had been named for my father, Lucus – and I smiled. The hills of the north were very clear, very close – a sure sign of rain. Suddenly, seeing their heavy strength, their dour acceptance of the fact that it was rain that made them so clear to the sight, I realized that they were beautiful. They had the strong unbearable beauty of the last few chords of a Hero-tale as the Hero dies: heroes always die. It is the most mundane thing they do and yet somehow it is a greater tragedy at their ending than it is for the rest of us: perhaps it is more their youth and the frustration of their promise and the inevitability of their end that hurts the heart with beauty in the harp-song, more than the fact of their end. And watching them, I felt that the hills knew this.

Hooves drubbed the ground. I stood up quickly, tensing. Was the Queen coming on? But the sound was coming from the wrong direction. A man on a small horse passed by, pawed to a stop by the camp, slid to the ground. Laegh had awoken already and he was talking hurriedly to the man as I came up.

'How many are there of them?' Laegh was demanding.

'That's the strange thing. They're very few – certainly not an army nor even the vanguard of an army. There's only about a troop of them and not half of them in chariots and Finn says – he's got long sight, he can see like an eagle – Finn says they're too small, there's something odd about them.'

Laegh thought for a moment.

'How many people are there in camp and near here that can be spared from watching the Queen and the north?' he asked Conn. Conn counted up on his fingers.

'About twenty to thirty men.'

'Wake them all and tell them to mount up, ready to move.'

'But Laegh . . .' said the man, '. . . this can't be an attack.'

'I know,' said Laegh. He turned to me. 'Will you come, Lugh?' he asked.

'Certainly. If you want me.'

'I think we may need you,' he answered cryptically. 'Borrow a horse from the spares.'

I went and found a stubby little brown pony with hooves like cauldrons and a mouth like iron, but he was gentle and willing and not too fiery: I still had very little grip on a horse. I mounted up with difficulty and trotted over to the group of horsemen, where I rode to Laegh's left side. There were about thirty-five, since some had to be left behind to man the camp and look after the horses, and most of the rest of the tribe's fighting force was scattered across the country in clan-groups. The Queen would probably not move until she was sure she knew where Cuchulain was and unless the Tuatha de Danaan had told her themselves, which I knew they wouldn't, she would not know yet. And it was still only just after dawn.

We rode quickly to the Road of Midluachair and stood in line across it. Soon the troop could be seen coming down the road at full pace: if they had come from Emain Macha they must have been riding and driving half the night.

They came nearer: I blinked and rubbed my eyes, wondering if lack of sleep might be affecting my eyesight; the others were doing the same and talking between themselves in stunned voices.

The troop was nearer and there was no doubt about it: most of them were on horseback and they were mostly small . . .

Laegh gripped my arm and whispered, 'It's the Boys' Troop!'

I couldn't say anything. I stared, and it was true. They came riding through the grey dawn on their little shaggy ponies; some on the borrowed spare chariot-ponies of their fathers; some of them actually riding beat-up spare chariots and half-mended wrecks. They came riding along with their boys' weapons: a brave sight, unreal, and as wild and untouched as geese threaded across the sky.

They slowed when they saw us and came to a ragged stop some yards away. Their leader stopped them by flinging up his hand in a gesture that reminded me of nothing so much as Conor, and then made the ponies of the old unpainted chariot he was riding come towards us. Mechanically I rode forward a few paces with Laegh, so we were practically side by side.

It was Follamon, the King's youngest son. He was grinning, despite all his efforts to keep his face straight and serious (and noble and Heroic). He was red-haired and very fair-skinned, but his face was puckish rather than good-looking. I remembered him standing beside me on the chariot as I practised before the Raid on Rath Ini.

'Hey, Laegh!' he said. I don't think he recognized me. 'Where's Cuchulain?' Then, looking round with irrepressible pride: 'We've come to join him.'

'He's resting,' said Laegh. 'What are you doing out of the care of your wet-nurses, you babes-in-arms?' He said it in such a way as to rob it of all sting.

'Well, we've come for Ailell's head and his crown along

293

with it,' said Follamon. He was perfectly serious: my face wanted to smile, although it was not in the least funny.

'You what?' said Laegh, leaning forward and blinking. 'Ach, if you've come for a game of hurley, you've come to the wrong place. Get you back to Emain and tell King Conor that we want Ulster – not Ulster's best part.'

'Conor doesn't know we've come,' said Follamon, frowning in a way that reminded me, despite the difference in looks, of the King. 'My *father* put the Curse of Macha on all the grown fighters of Ulster not to move south of Emain until he gave the word, but *we*'re not grown fighters, we're boys, and so we crept out last night.' He grinned. 'He can't come out after us himself and he can't send his men because that would mean raising the curse and letting them all out, so there's nothing he can do.'

It was only then that Laegh realized how serious they were.

'Oghma give me strength!' he said. 'Do you think you're going to attack Connaught? Why they'll die of laughing, not sword-cuts.'

Follamon looked stubborn. 'I swore an oath.'

Laegh stopped. 'You . . . swore . . . an . . . oath?' he repeated very slowly. 'You didn't take it as geasa upon yourself too, did you?'

The boy looked mulish. 'Yes, I did. We all did.'

'You took it as geasa on yourself, that you would not return without Ailell's head?' Follamon nodded and all his troop with him, so they would have been funny if this geasa did not mean death and if it were not death to break any geasa. There was total silence from all the Sedantii. Laegh looked as if he had been hit in the wind.

I thought of telling them what they had done to themselves, but they were so bright and serious and full of the Hero-spirit distilled from the tales they had heard – I could not. I stayed as silent as the rest.

The boys began to shift uncomfortably.

Conn leaned across from where he sat a little behind and to the right of Facen.

'We can't stop them,' he said quietly, 'but we can go with them.'

'To death,' said Facen. The others muttered.

Laegh looked at me wildly.

'In the name of Oghma, is there any way they can be freed from this geasa they've taken?'

I thought desperately, had been thinking ever since the word was mentioned. I scanned my memory for any of the Brehon Laws that would exonerate them, release them from the death-trap they had walked into.

'Follamon,' I said, 'how did you take the geasa on yourself?'

'Why?' he asked, frowning again. 'I'm not going to unsay it. Anyway, I know how to take on a geasa.'

'Did you bind it by three-times-three Names?' I asked.

'Of course I did.'

I let my hands fall and shook my head at Laegh.

'Could anyone break it?' he asked. 'Break the Curse afterwards?'

'We don't want it broken . . .' put in a small dark boy near to Follamon. 'We want . . .'

I turned on him savagely. 'Be quiet, you little fool!' I spoke more quietly to Laegh. 'Druid Cavath might, if you could get him to agree.'

'And if you try to stop us by force . . .' said Follamon loudly, 'we'll fight you. And we outnumber you five to one.'

'He's right,' said Facen. Conn was white by now and so was Laegh.

'We'll have to go with them,' Conn repeated. 'We can't let them fight alone.'

I could see Laegh beginning to waver, because he wanted to fight with the boys too. But I thought of what Cuchulain would do when he came back out of the sidhe and found his tribe's fighting force lying dead by the bodies of the Boys' Troop: I would have to die in it too, because Cuchulain would get himself killed taking his revenge and Emer . . . Emer would not live long without him, as I had said so long ago last winter, in the woodland clearing, when he wanted to fight me. And the Queen would sweep on and take Emain Macha and there would be no inch of land free from her in Erin and it was something I could not stomach, that she should win.

I leaned forward.

'No!' I said fiercely, 'No, we cannot go with them.'

'Why not?' demanded Conn harshly. 'They're only boys, we could . . .'

'We could do nothing! How many of us are there? Thirty-five? Of the boys? A hundred and fifty? Fight an army with a hundred and eighty-five fighters, most of them half-grown. We will simply be killed.'

'Yes, but . . .'

'Yes, but – what? When we are dead, we'll have no more trouble. But what will the rest of the Sedantii do? Come roaring down on the Queen to take revenge, that's what! And what will happen to them? Yes, they'll be killed too. And Cuchulain comes back and what does he find? All his warriors dead and stinking. He'll have nothing to live for but to get revenge and he'll take his revenge – Oh yes, our deaths will be paid for in blood and three times running over and then . . .? And then Cuchulain will be dead too and the Queen will overrun Muirthemne and all your hunting-runs, and your wives will be raped and your children killed and your cattle eaten and your farmsteads burnt and Emain Macha will paint the sky red in the north for a little while and then there will be no more Ulster, but only the fatness and satisfaction of the Queen of Connaught!'

They were staring at me, all of them. The anger rose in me like vomit.

'Well?' I shouted. 'Go on. Go and fight. What are you waiting for, you honourable fools? Fight!'

Shamefacedly, some of them almost weeping, they stood back, cleared the road south to where the Queen waited. The Boys' Troop of Emain Macha rode through, heads held high. With Laegh I watched them go, and my anger had been spurted from me and all I could feel was a sick, numb pain, a quiet rage that those . . . fools had done what they had done.

We went slowly back to camp and Laegh called in all the Sedantii from round about, told them what would happen and why we wouldn't fight, took note of the numbers there and told them that he would personally kill the first man who tried to slip away to join the boys. I sat apart from them, with my head in my hands, trying not to hear the sounds of fighting, trying not to see the images against my lids.

Some of them escaped, but more than half of them died, though they took three times their number with them to serve them in Tir-na-nOg. Follamon, King's son, he died too, with the small dark boy whose name I never learned: I remember his red curls dabbled in filth where he lay across the body of a man twice his size whom he had killed while already death-wounded. For that night we went and searched for the bodies on the small field which had held the battle and we laid them in shallow graves and began to build a mound above them. Cuchulain could finish it later, if he lived. Meanwhile the weight of the earth would keep the wolves and carrion-birds off them, and their spirits from walking.

At the end of the third day, when the grave was more than man-high, though still irregular and unfinished, I knew that I could hold the Sedantii no longer. So, as evening came on and they began changing the watch on the Queen's camp and the north, and recovering from their grief at the death of the boys, I slipped away from them and went into the forest.

# VIII

She had been waiting for me. As soon as I stepped under the eaves the undergrowth moved and she stood up. She smiled at me and when I did not smile back, she began to turn away.

297

I caught her and turned her towards me again.

'Otter, do you know what has happened?' I asked. She nodded.

'The Boys' Troop.'

'Otter, how do I explain?'

'You can only tell him. He will understand why you didn't let the Sedantii fight.'

'Will he?'

'He must. He has led men and he knows what that means. He will understand – or if he doesn't, then he's no longer the Hound and no longer the Sedanta.'

'I hope you're right.'

'I am right,' she said quietly. She took my hand in her two hands and smiled again. This time I found myself answering to hers. 'Come. He is rested now, though not well again, and he will last.'

We neither of us could think of anything to say as we walked to the sidhe where Cuchulain lay.

This time I braced myself and went into the Sidhe of Muirthemne, because I would not be beaten by mere darkness, and because Otter still had me by the hand. For a moment I choked on the smell and thick black, which brought the memories flooding back, but then I became used to both and it was only a sidhe: smaller, but the same as the other one, the one where Otter came from. Someone rose from close to the fire at the opposite end and came towards us. I knew from the furs and clothes and lunula she wore that she was the Mother, though she was younger than the Mother in Otter's sidhe. Also I recognized that invisible regal circle which surrounded her, as it had surrounded the Mother of Otter's sidhe, as it surrounded the Queen too, though I was loath to admit it. This was something that needed no reinforcement of ceremony. It was simply there, as the hills are there, regardless of what grows on them.

'Is he awake?' I asked.

'No,' she said. 'But he will wake.'

She and her women led me to a heap of skins close to the

fire: Cuchulain lay there, curled up under his sealskin cloak. His mended crimson tunic lay near him and his boots by the pile of bracken. He had pushed himself half out from under the covering. There were bandages on him, holding a pad to his shoulder wound and under them I could just see the tattoo on his shoulder blade, which, like the one I wore on mine, proclaimed which tribe he belonged to.

He looked oddly innocent and childlike, lying there, his dark hair flung tangled to one side. In sleep he looked a lot like one of the Sidhe-folk themselves: which wasn't surprising since he was, after all, half-Tuatha de Danaan. But he had none of their other-timefulness.

'Old Mother,' I said, wishing I were better at thanking people, 'I thank you . . .' She smiled and shook her head. For the first time I noticed that she was unusually tall for a woman of the Tuatha de Danaan. I tend not to notice comparative heights of people because I am so tall myself.

'Do not thank the Tuatha,' she said. 'They do what they will for whom they will, if they so desire it. There are few men of the Iron-Folk whom we will allow into a sidhe, but for those we permit there is no stinting and we ask nothing in return.'

She spoke Irish to me, with scarcely any accent. I blinked in surprise, but she was still speaking.

'His shoulder wound will not turn sick again so long as he keeps the bandages on. He is strong. He will be able to fight until Conor arrives, though after that . . . I do not know.'

She went to him and pulled the sealskin back a way.

'Wake up now, little Hound,' she said softly.

He grunted and turned over, then opened his eyes and sat up, pushing the hair back from his eyes and looking at me under his long straight brows. The Mother moved back into the shadows.

'How long have I been asleep?' he demanded.

'Three days,' I told him.

'*What?*' He leapt out of bed, his eyes blazing. 'Do you mean to tell me that nobody's been keeping an eye on the

Queen all this time? Great gods, Lugh, if you've . . .'

'Save your breath, Cuchulain,' I said. 'The Queen's still there.'

I indicated his clothes and he put them on, moving cautiously and swearing when his shoulder wound stopped him pulling the tunic over his head with his customary haste.

When he was finished and had dragged his fingers through his wild hair, I went to the door. He followed, swinging his cloak on his shoulder as he went and jabbing in the fist-sized gold brooch with a vicious movement.

Outside the sidhe in the compound, he looked back with a sudden grin.

'You don't mind being in a sidhe?' I asked.

'Why should I? I was born in one.' One of the young men appeared from the dark and went ahead of us silently, through the forest. I knew we were being followed, and somehow I knew that it was Otter following us.

'Well,' said Cuchulain, 'tell me what's been happening.'

I hesitated. I didn't want to tell him what had happened to Follamon and the Boys' Troop. I knew what he would do.

'No one did anything on Samhain Day – that was the day after I came to you.'

'It makes sense,' he commented cryptically.

'But the next day . . .' I hesitated again. It was a horrible thing to have to tell anyone, though I didn't realize quite how horrible before I actually had to tell it. I had a sudden vision of Follamon, the last time I had seen him: lying straight and cold and stiff in the grave beside the other dead boys, his puckish face like wax. So different from the way Cuchulain would remember him: when he had slid to Cuchulain's feet, the hurley ball following him and Cuchulain had shown him that he hadn't forgotten how to use a caman, because Cuchulain would really never be anything but a boy playing hurley on a battlefield.

So I braced myself and told Cuchulain what had happened, telling it baldly and without description. Cuchulain went pale, then red, then deathly white. His eyes seemed to burn holes like the Sidhe in his face, his mouth compressed to a bloodless line. It seemed that the very hair on his head lifted like a dog's hackles.

He said absolutely nothing until we came within sight of the camp near the boys' grave, where were all the Sedantii standing waiting.

Cuchulain stopped before they saw him and turned to face me, his face like a wooden god they carve in a living tree-trunk. I stiffened likewise.

'It was you prevented them from fighting with the boys, wasn't it?' he said.

'Yes.'

'Why?'

'Because if I had not, Cuchulain, there would have been no tribe for you to come back to, save bones and ravens with full crops.'

Very slowly, he nodded.

'Yes. Yes, you were right. But I could not have done it, though you were right.'

I said nothing.

'Once I thought you a coward, Lugh Mac Romain,' he said slowly. 'But I think you are not that. Once I thought you more than half-mad with the Poet-spirit. But you are not – quite.' He paused. 'I have never met a Roman, but now I think, perhaps, you are a Roman, Lugh, son of the Roman.'

He walked towards his tribe. I wondered at what he had said, but he was wrong again, though I didn't know why.

'Get the chariot ready, Laegh,' he ordered as the shouting and greeting from his tribe died away. As I came up with him he said to me, 'You and I will avenge them, Lugh.'

I said nothing, but smiled a little, bitterly. Cuchulain's eyes went to my slightly twisted right leg and then to my face. For a moment I saw pity in his eyes and hated him for it, before he turned away to get his weapons and order his tribe to mount.

I watched them leave for vengeance in a night attack on the camp of Connaught and wondered which I felt more deeply: the desire to be with them or relief that I would not have to fight. As I stood watching, from near a little spur of woodland and a fallen tree-trunk, somebody touched me fleetingly on the arm. I spun round, my hand dropping to my dagger, and found myself facing Otter. There was a moon, though pale and mist-watered. In that light Otter had the beauty of a Sidhe-woman in a song: small, elfin, seeming to be only half-real, as though she would vanish away when the moon ceased to shine on her. Unconsciously I reached out to touch her, to make sure she was there and she came to me, pressed her body against mine, smelling of warm woman and woodsmoke and woodland, her face tilted to mine.

I stroked my fingers around the shape of her face and they delighted in the feeling of her skin. I bent my head and kissed her. She lifted against me and her lips opened to my searching tongue: I felt the warm pressure of her small breasts against me and the way her hands held me and the beat of blood that went through me and through her. I bore her to the ground, and my fingers found the fastenings of her kilt and jerkin as though they were familiar territory, and we made love, Otter and I, and I knew her hunger and satisfied it . . .

But even as we came together, there was a small voice at the back of my skull gabbling some truth I didn't want to hear. It was never drowned completely that night.

I woke up next morning, tired and sad and sick, and cold in the dawn, with my cloak put round me to warm me a little. But I was alone. She had slipped away while I was asleep, and I was relieved, glad she was gone. I knew then what the inner voice had been saying. Otter loved me, but I did not, could not love her: I knew it and she knew it, and so she had gone. I thought of her and the way she had made love, a little clumsily, but eager for me, welcoming me. I hoped I hadn't hurt her too badly. My thoughts of her were detached: I had taken what she gave, but what had I given her? She had saved me from the Queen, her brother had died for me and what had I given her? A child, perhaps?

And then I understood why she had come to me and made love that particular night and not before. I got up quickly and went down to the stream: there I washed until I was rid of the feeling of love-making, of her smell. And when I had finished I realized with a wry smile that there was still a warmth for her in me, and a strange sadness.

## IX

Across the stream as I finished, I could see the Queen's encampment and between a trampled torn-up area with bodies littered here and there. There were two heads on poles about halfway: I wondered idly whose heads they were and who had put them up, but I did not go and look. Instead I walked slowly back to camp.

The Sedantii who had been in the attack were sitting around eating tiredly, and some seeing to each other's wounds. A scream and a smell of scorched flesh told me that the cauterizing iron was being used in the small group by the fire. I felt uneasy because, after all, they had fought and I had spent the night making love, but none of them said anything: when I sat by the fire they made room for me and when I dipped my fingers in the stewpot, no one protested. I felt rather like a flea: I took from people and gave nothing in return, not even songs because I had no harp. Most of them went to sleep when they had finished eating.

Cuchulain got to his feet and left the little group by the fire. His hands and arms were splashed with blood and his face tired: the men he had left were wrapping something up in a cloak, ready to be carried away. There was a bowl of water near the stewpot, where the warriors had been washing their wounds: it had a scum on it by now, but Cuchulain dipped his arms in, washed most of the dirt off and dried his hands on his tunic. Then he sat down cross-legged by the stewpot and started to eat hungrily.

'Who was it?' I asked, to have something to say.

303

'Cett,' said Cuchulain shortly. 'We lost five men from my clan alone. He was the fifth, though if I'd got to him sooner with the iron he might have lived. He took a spear through his thigh which cut the big blood-vessel – someone tied it up, but still I was too late. There was no more in him.'

One of the crows on the field cawed out. Cuchulain stopped eating and looked up at me, but I knew he wasn't really thinking of me.

'He was married two months ago. He was one of my foster-father Sualtim's bastards – we used to go hunting together once, before I became the Sedanta. He was very good, a very swift runner: but I could outlast him and so he called me Dog – instead of Hound. He called me Dog again before he died.' He grinned at me. 'Do you remember the race we ran in Emain last Samhain, Lugh?'

I said nothing for a moment. It was unlike Cuchulain to make a mistake like that, but I knew he was thinking about Cett, not me. When I was sure I could speak naturally, as though it were no very important question, I answered, 'Yes.'

Then he looked at me properly, and flushed. He bent his head and ate quickly, gulped down a lump of gristle and licked his fingers. His odd, deep eyes, under their straight black brows – not Sidhe-eyes, but with a shadow there for all that – looked directly into mine.

'Forgive me, Lugh,' he said quietly. 'I should have thought.'

I shrugged. 'I must get used to it, I suppose,' I said. 'It's not likely to go away.'

He nodded: then he jumped to his feet with his usual suddenness.

'I think the Queen will be sending Mac Roth to me again,' he said.

'Why?' I came to my feet too.

Cuchulain picked a string of meat out from between his teeth with a fingernail.

'Well,' he said, around the finger, 'she'll want to know whether the single-combat agreement is still in force.'

'And what will you say?'

'I'll say that as long as she doesn't break it, I won't.'

'But Cuchulain!' I burst out, 'don't you know why Conor hasn't come yet? Don't you understand?'

His face darkened.

'I know very well why the King hasn't come yet. So does all Ulster. Either way: if I live or die, King Conor will lose in the end and he knows it now.'

'What do you mean?'

'Besides,' said Cuchulain, ignoring my question, 'I'm the Champion of Ulster.'

Mac Roth did come across to speak to Cuchulain later that day. He stood on one bank of the stream, while Cuchulain stood, arms akimbo, on the other. To look at him no one would have guessed he had spent all the previous night fighting, which was how he wanted to look.

They exchanged greetings and then Mac Roth gave the message Cuchulain had thought he would give.

'The Queen of Connaught wishes to know if the Sedanta still considers himself bound by the agreement to single-combat?'

'Tell the Queen of Connaught,' said Cuchulain, 'that the Sedanta will do so as long as she does.'

Mac Roth bowed, but he didn't go away at once.

'The Queen also wishes to know if you have a certain harper with you in camp?'

Mac Roth could see me perfectly well, where I stood leaning against one of the group of willows nearby, but he was too much the Herald to admit it.

'And if I have?' said Cuchulain, his voice cooling noticeably.

'The Queen might consider some reward if the harper were to be allowed to go back to his Queen.'

Cuchulain said nothing, though the Sedantii muttered angrily among themselves. I saw Cuchulain was not angry: he was laughing, silently as he always did, and Mac Roth looked exceedingly uncomfortable. Mac Roth had not forgotten the last time he had spoken with Cuchulain.

'Why not ask the harper if he wants to go back?' Cuchulain suggested.

I limped forward to the riverbank, unwillingly. Mac Roth knew perfectly well that he had lost the exchange completely – it had been a forlorn hope from the beginning as I was sure he had also known perfectly well.

I watched him without rancour. It was his job after all.

'Well, Mac Roth,' I said. 'What do you think I'll say?'

'I cannot put the words in your mouth,' Mac Roth answered carefully.

'Umm,' I said. 'In other words you want me to attack the Queen so she can have some good excuse other than the one you know, for putting a curse on me. And she can't put a curse on me for that – again, you know the reason why. Well, Mac Roth, tell the Queen of Connaught that Lugh Son of the Roman will come to her when he pleases and will not be bartered and exchanged like a slave. Tell her that, Mac Roth – and stand well back.'

His eyes flickered and he turned to Cuchulain.

'What does the Sedanta say to that?'

Cuchulain shrugged and smiled benignly on him.

'What can the Sedanta say to it? It's none of his business, being between the Queen of Connaught and her foster-son, Lugh the Harper.'

Mac Roth bowed. 'There will be a warrior of Connaught at the ford tomorrow.'

Cuchulain bowed slightly in return.

'I shall look forward to it.'

Mac Roth said something to me quietly in the language of the Tuatha de Danaan and then rode back to the Queen's camp, between the two poles with heads on. The crows rose and settled down again, like black leaves scuffed up.

'What did he say to you?' Cuchulain asked as we went back to camp.

'He said I should look at the two poles – the Queen gave me leave.'

'Oh? Do you know who are on them?'

'No,' I said, feeling a little sick, 'but I think I can guess.'

306

Conn and Facen insisted on going with me to see who the heads had belonged to, in case, they said, the Queen should try to recapture me while I was halfway across. We were watched all the time, but no one came from the Connaught camp.

I didn't need to go right up to the heads – besides, they were rotten and stinking. I knew them.

'Who were they?' Conn asked as we went back.

'The two men who guarded me in the Connaught camp,' I said, 'Brocc and Brod.'

That day too a hunting party came back with a wild boar slung between them on an ash-pole. Cuchulain decided to have a feast: he had captured a wagon of provisions coming from the south to the Queen, and there was mead in large quantities – very bad stuff, but still mead.

They built up the bonfire and carved the boar and roasted it and passed the meadskins round and had themselves a feast. I drank steadily all evening, determined to get drunk. At one stage I sang the dirty songs Brocc and Brod had taught me, which amused the Sedantii mightily; after that the mead worked on me to make me very sad and sorry for myself and I remember dimly, weeping on Conn's shoulder while he patted me and said between his hiccups that it wasn't that bad and no doubt I'd feel better . . . hic! . . . shoon. After that I was vilely sick and the ground came up to meet me. The last thing I remember before I passed out, was Cuchulain throwing bones at someone and someone else tripping over me as he got up to piss.

The next morning was quite as bad as it always is after that kind of feast: with mouth gummed up and throat dry and stomach tied in knots and fighting devils in your head and the certainty that you have made a fool of yourself. I had been woken by the preparations for Cuchulain to go and fight the latest warrior the Queen had sent. In the middle of it all I felt my way to the waterpot and put my head in, after which the world seemed slightly less deadly. I went with the Sedantii to a vantage point a little way above the stream, to watch the fight.

Standing at the ford, beside his chariot, with his hands on his hips, was none other than Ferghus Mac Roich. I heard Conn's muttered cursing beside me, but I took no notice: I was listening to what Cuchulain and Ferghus said to each other. The Queen was already breaking camp.

Cuchulain was silent for a moment, looking closely at Ferghus, with his head on one side like a blackbird at a worm.

'Well, Ferghus,' he said, 'if I were you, I wouldn't have come against me with only a wooden sword.'

Ferghus smiled shortly.

'Sure now, Little Hound, why should I use any kind of weapon on you?'

'Why not?'

'Think what a waste it would be – when I trained you myself? All those sword-exercises and beatings, gone for nothing.'

Cuchulain smiled and relaxed somewhat.

'What do you want me to do?' he asked.

'Now, wouldn't it be a lot more sensible if we . . . well, if we fought for a bit . . .'

'With swords?' enquired Cuchulain.

'With spears,' said Ferghus with dignity. 'I know you know how I came by a wooden sword. There's no need to remind me.' Ailell had realized Ferghus was sleeping with the Queen. His charioteer, Ferloga, had gone into the wood where the two were making love, stolen Ferghus's own sword, the Caladcholg, replaced it with a sword of wood as a comment, and given the Caladcholg to Ailell. Ailell had refused to give it back until the final battle with Ulster – and the situation was a great embarrassment to Ferghus.

'So we exchange a few blows,' Ferghus went on, 'and then you, Cuchulain, run away from me.'

'Now let me get this straight,' said Cuchulain. 'We exchange a few blows and then you run away from me.'

Ferghus shook his head.

'You run away from me,' he corrected.

'Pardon me, Ferghus,' said Cuchulain with elaborate

politeness, 'but could you explain just why I should run away from you, or anybody else for that matter. I've never done it before, remember, so I might not know how.'

'If you run away from me now,' said Ferghus, 'so I don't have to kill my own pupil, which would cause me regret, then I'll do the same for you in the final battle, when Conor comes down from the north at last, and you are too weak from wounds to do much against me. And if I turn and run then, the whole of Erin will follow me.'

Cuchulain talked quickly with Laegh and then said, 'Done, Ferghus!'

So, before the eyes of the Queen's watchers, who had heard nothing of what went before, Cuchulain and Ferghus fought a short battle, being very careful not to hurt each other in any way. After a while, Cuchulain turned and ran full pelt away from Ferghus. Laegh scooped him up in the chariot and brought him back to camp as though the Wild Hunt were on his tail. Ferghus swaggered undeservingly back to the Queen and Cuchulain and Laegh roared with laughter, holding each other up and wiping away the tears.

The Queen had shifted further north during the short fight, and we moved camp to stay with her. The next day there was a new man at the fighting place – Ferghus had refused point-blank to fight Cuchulain again until every man in the army had done it before him – and Cuchulain killed the warrior with not much more difficulty than usual. He seemed to have caught his second wind. He no longer bothered to take the heads of the men he had killed: he had lost count long ago anyway.


# X


I remembered the time not long after I had finished the first part of my training to be a bard, which I started when I was ten, though I stayed in the Boys' Troop of Cruachan until I was a man. It lasted eight years, and four of those years

309

were spent in a special school learning how to make my own songs, as well as the normal training. Afterwards I often went travelling round the nobles of Connaught with one of the bards of Connaught, a man called Iliach Mac Conaire. Even then Iollan Hen was too old to travel any more and he could no longer play the more difficult harp-music because of the stiffness of his fingers. Iliach and I stayed in many duns in Connaught, where I learnt songs and epics from the harpers kept by the greater nobles. We spent two years doing that and at the end of it I found I knew Iliach little better than I had to begin with: he was a very vague, dreamy man, who seemed scarcely to notice any happening that wasn't in verse, any speech that wasn't put to harp-music. His mind was littered with scraps of verse and riddling allusions and sometimes I was hard put to it to understand what he was saying. His harping was reasonably good, but at verse-making he was unequalled. But he was far harder to like than Iollan because he was so distant, and sometimes I found myself lonely.

At the end of one journey we came, in the rocks and hills of western Connaught, to the large dun of the clan-chief who ruled most of Domnand. As we rode up the rocky path to the gate of the dun Iliach turned to me and said,

'Well, Lugh, since you have the makings of an Amergin and Amergin had to stand somewhere to say his first englyn, and I feel a little like the Dagda after he ate his porridge ... You'll be singing in hall tonight.'

My heart thudded and I gripped the reins more tightly. It was autumn, but I began to sweat alternately – any harper will know the feeling: it is three parts fear of making a fool of yourself and one part pleasure at being the centre of attention.

'The epic?'

'Yes. Oghma should do, or Lugh Sunspear against Beli – I'll do the praise-song since you're no better at it than the Hard Ghillie or this wreck of a chariot I'm riding.'

'Who ... who will I be singing for?'

'*Whom* . . . ah . . . I forget. It can't be Daire – I heard he died. His son most likely, Ferdin, or Ferban or some such. Anyway, sing your best and you'll put on them the same spell as the Dagda put on the magic turtle – "Silence in your hollow head." Umm.'

We came to the gates and I announced who we were to the gate-guard. Iliach was well-known in those parts and we were let in immediately, given food, and baths were heated for us to wash in. The chieftain gave orders for a feast that night to honour us and I spent the afternoon worrying about it and practising all the songs and epics I knew.

That evening in the hall of seven pillars, smaller than the Queen's Hall at Cruachan, I could not eat. Too soon Iliach nudged me and I knew it was time to go into the middle of the hall and play. It was a long way to walk, I remember, and the stone was hard and I noticed that the skin was a newly cured one which still smelt of the tanning vats. I announced the epic – I had fixed on the story of Lugh Killing the One-Eyed Giant, Bcli, with his slingstone – in a voice which began rather reedy and unsure and ended stronger as I heard my own voice in the hall and realized it wasn't as bad as all that. At the last moment I turned to face the young chieftain: Ferdia Mac Daire was his name, and in the small moment between settling my harp, checking the tuning and beginning to sing, I noticed everything about him. He was big-built, with corn-coloured curly hair, almost but not quite red. He had a moustache and green eyes and the whole impression given by the fineness of the bones of his face and the way he smiled and talked and sat listening, his tunic of blue-green linen embroidered with black, the gold brooch holding the folds at his throat and the ram's-headed torc around his neck, was of someone out of the common, someone more gentle, more intelligent, different from the usual run of chieftains. Someone who was certainly as brave and honourable as any of them, but who would know the reasons behind his actions.

Then I began to sing and forgot the chieftain and the

company and sang and chanted and played harp to a silenced hall. When I finished and heard the clapping and drumming of knife-hilts on the pillars, I realized that Ferdia had been watching me intently throughout. I played some descriptions and pieces of a lament after that to quiet their shouts for more. When I finished and stood up to go back to my place beside Iliach, Ferdia beckoned me over. I went and bowed to him, but did not kneel down because I was not his clansman or his client. But he told me to sit beside him and we talked for a long time, liking each other instantly. He asked me many questions and when I had answered them he said, 'Do you need a place as a harper?'

'No,' I said, very much surprised, 'not yet at any rate. I haven't finished my full training yet and the Druids have yet to test me.'

He smiled. 'I wouldn't worry about that.'

'It's not an easy test. And I . . .'

'Yes, there were a few rough parts. The comic part where Beli is threatening Lugh Sunspear could have been funnier, but the song the Slingstone sang was the best I have ever heard it played.'

'Can you play harp?' I asked, confused.

He laughed. 'No. I can't sing – Cuchulain used to say he'd rather hear a lament by a dying crow than listen to my efforts at singing. But I've always liked to listen to those who could sing.'

'Cuchulain?' I asked. I had heard the name, but no more than that. It always seemed natural to me that everyone should love music: men like Munremar Mac Gergind who cannot hear anything beautiful in music were completely alien to my mind.

'Cuchulain Mac Sualtim – he's the Sedanta now, in Ulster. When I went to learn battle-skills with Scatha the woman-warrior on the Island of Skye, he came some time after and he was my spear-bearer and driver for a while. Then we became spear-brothers, Cuchulain and I, and we fought together in the raiding on Queen Aoife's people. He fought a single combat with her to decide the matter, as Scatha's champion, and he took her prisoner and made her his woman. She gave him the Gae Bulg and taught him how to use it.'

'Is he a good fighter?' I asked.

'A good fighter?' Ferdia laughed again. 'He beat me in sword-fighting several times, though I'm accounted the best in Erin. I'm still better than him in technique, but he has the magic touch, the fighting-genius – a harper would say, the Hero-light. There's no denying that. When he's in his fighting-madness I'd think twice myself about going against him, even if he weren't my spear-brother. He's a killer, is Cuchulain, the kind of man who likes to kill.'

'Do you hate him?'

'No! He's more than a year younger than me, but by the time we left Scatha, he led and I followed.'

I was staring at him.

'Strange, isn't it?' he said pleasantly. 'I'd say that about no other man. If I could make music as well as listen to it, I'd make a great epic of Cuchulain – only there will be no need, I think. Now tell me, what do you think of the Story of Edain . . .?'

We talked of other matters: when Iliach had sung, Ferdia gave him a silver enamelled bracelet. To me, next morning as we prepared to leave, he gave a big thick woollen cloak, dyed black and white; the kind that usually only noblemen and the very best harpers can afford to wear, and he gave me a gold brooch to go with it.

As we left the dun, Iliach said to me kindly,

'There! Didn't I say to you that you had the makings of an Amergin? Ferdia's generous as ever Nuadha Silverhand was, but he's never that generous without cause . . . Now who or what is the Great Sow, and what is the significance of her?'

'The Great Sow was a spell put on the land by the Tuatha de Danaan, and the Sons of Mi saw her on every hill when they came to Erin from over the sea. Its significance is the Land of Erin . . . ' I answered automatically, still thinking of Ferdia and what he had said.

Time passed and the incident slipped into the background of my mind, though I was sometimes reminded of it by mention or sight of Ferdia, and I kept the cloak until the crash. But after the business with Ferghus the Queen sent to Ferdia Mac Daire, chief of the men of Domnand and ordered him to come to her on pain of cursing and satires and dishonour: so, much against his will, he came. He knew very well what she wanted him for, but could not go against the threat of cursing which would harm his land as well as himself. And the Queen offered him bribes of horses and men and lands, cloth and gold and chariots, even Findabhair, who had been promised to so many men before, but he refused them all because he would not fight against his friend and spear-brother. But the Queen knew that if anyone could kill Cuchulain, Ferdia could, and so she persisted. After several days of getting nowhere, while Cuchulain continued to kill her men and her army melted with disease and hunger and desertion while Conor did not come, she held a feast for Ferdia. And at the feast she gave him drugs in his food and the spiced stew, and her Drink in his mead. So at last, drugged and half-drunk and taunted by the Queen, Ferdia agreed to fight Cuchulain the next morning.

The same evening Ferghus quietly left the Queen's camp, crossed the stream Cuchulain was camped behind, which was near Dun Delgan, and came to Cuchulain.

Cuchulain welcomed him and offered him what food he had, which wasn't very much, since full winter was upon us, though the weather still had a brittle fineness to it. And Ferghus stood awkwardly by the fire and told Cuchulain who was coming against him that morning.

The first thing Cuchulain said when Ferghus stopped speaking, was,

'But how did she get him to come?'

'Ferbaeth,' I reminded him.

He heard me, but I don't think he knew who had spoken. He reached for the sheaf of his spears which he had been

314

sharpening on a whetstone when Ferghus arrived, and took out the Gae Bulg. It was an outlandish spear which came from further east than Aoife of the Picts. It had a crossed four-edged head and long spines of whalebone round the neck, instead of heron- or kingfisher-feathers. This made it impossible to pull out of a wound without cutting away the nearby flesh as well. Cuchulain scarcely ever used it, but it was the deadliest weapon I have ever seen.

Cuchulain balanced the Gae Bulg seemingly casually on his hand and said slowly to Ferghus, 'You know, if any man had killed Ferdia, I would not have rested until I had got satisfaction and revenge a hundredfold for his death. But now I must kill him, Ferghus, or be killed myself, because once he's given his word there is no way of making him go back on it. So what can I do, Ferghus, what can I do?'

'You must kill him,' said Ferghus promptly. 'You know why. Will you promise me you'll have the victory over him, not let your life be taken. Will you promise me that?'

Cuchulain looked up at him. 'I can't promise that, Ferghus,' he said. 'I can only fight my best. Perhaps the Queen is right: maybe I won't be able to kill him.'

'You must,' said Ferghus simply and left.

None of the Sedantii went near Cuchulain that night, but I had to know something and so I went up to where he sat morosely looking into the fire, and sharpening his spears and sword.

'Cuchulain,' I said cautiously, 'may I speak to you?'

He nodded.

'I spoke to Ferdia Mac Daire once,' I began with care, 'when I sang for him. He said, in the course of conversation, that, speaking in terms of technique, he's better than you are.'

Cuchulain looked at me.

'Well?' he asked coldly.

'Is it true?'

For a moment I thought he would be angry, but he wasn't angry. Only, for the first time since he came back from the sidhe, the way he talked, the way he moved and sat, showed

315

how tired he was.

'Yes, it's true,' he said.

'And in other things than technique?'

'I don't know.'

Ferdia was already waiting at the ford in his chariot when dawn came. Cuchulain waited until the sun was above the trees and hills before he even admitted he was awake. Then he washed and dressed with slow care and finally told Laegh to get the chariot ready.

'It is ready,' retorted Laegh, 'and no one's stopping you from getting into it.' He was bad-tempered because he had been up since sunrise, because he was afraid for Cuchulain.

Cuchulain said nothing, but got into the chariot, and they rode down to the ford. I watched him as he went: Cuchulain was playing tricks with his short throwing-spears and shouting as the horses galloped across the rough sloping ground. It was difficult to believe that he was already wounded and tired out from long fighting: he had a magnificent belief in his own splendour and strength that truly made him stronger than other men. Also he was crazy, which always helps in the doing of impossible things.

The two men talked for a long time, while their charioteers made cautious acquaintance with each other. I, who am a bard, have made of that speech between the two beautiful poetry from my own imagination. I have no idea what they truly said to each other that time, but perhaps it is just as well. Such things are for the two concerned only.

They threw spears at each other for most of the morning, but it was only half-hearted: at noon they changed to stabbing spears and blood was drawn on both sides. When I saw that, knowing that Ferdia was fresh while Cuchulain was already tired and wounded, I left the fight. The camp was almost empty because Facen had gathered most of the Sedantii together and taken them north to harry the Queen's army. She had not yet reached the Nith, which was at high water, but we all knew that if Conor didn't come soon, he would be fighting outside the gates of Emain Macha.

316

I went a little way into the forest, in the direction of the
Sidhe of Muirthemne and whistled long and carefully in the
way Wolfling had taught me. I kept at it at intervals until at
last a small kilted man with feathers stuck in his hair rose
out of the brown thorns directly under my nose. When he
saw the way I was dressed he pointed his flint-tipped spear
at me and I said hastily in the language of the Tuatha de
Danaan, 'I am Lugh Mac Romain, who was once unknow-
ingly King of Connaught. I wish for the aid of the Mother of
the Sidhe of Muirthemne.'

His dark dreamy eyes hooded, in a way which reminded
me of Cuchulain when he was tired.

'What message shall I take to her?'

'Tell her this: the Hound is fighting a fight to the death
with his spear-brother Ferdia Mac Daire who is fresh and
whole while the Hound is weary and wounded. If the
Mother pleases, Lugh Mac Romain asks her to come with
women skilled in healing and see to the Hound's wounds, so
that he might win this fight.'

The little man nodded and repeated the message word-
perfectly. He turned and disappeared into the forest.

At the end of the day, as the sun lay bloody on the hills,
Cuchulain and Ferdia called a halt to the fighting. Both had
drawn blood, but that was all. They embraced and parted:
Laegh, and Ferdia's charioteers, made beds of rushes, with
cushions from the chariots for the fighters' heads on the north
and south banks of the Nith. I walked to where Laegh was
penning the Black Sainglenn and the Grey of Macha in the
same pen with Ferdia's two bays and told him what I had
done. He seemed more hopeful after that and even whistled
as he went to share the campfire with Ferdia's charioteer,
whose name was Ercol and a distant relation of his.

A little later the Mother stepped out of the dusk with a
woman by her side and two men carrying the bags of herbs
and bandages behind her. I led her to where Cuchulain sat,
washing his wound.

The Mother simply came forward, took the wet rag out of
Cuchulain's hand and threw it away. Then she started to

317

clean the scratch herself. Cuchulain looked up at me.
'This is your doing, Lugh,' he said.
'Yes.'
'Then you must go with the Old Mother across to Ferdia
and look at his injury too. Otherwise I can't let the Mother
come near me.'
The Mother smiled a sad hidden smile. I sighed. I suppose
I should have expected it, considering the way Cuchulain
thought of his honour.
And so, when the Mother had finished with Cuchulain, I
took her across the stream to Ferdia's campfire, where he sat,
oiling his shield-strap, though that was properly his charioteer's job.
He was exactly as I remembered him and characteristic-
ally he remembered me when I stepped into the light of the
fire.
'What do you want . . . Lugh Mac Romain, isn't it?'
'Yes. I have brought the Mother of the Sidhe of Muirthemne to see to the wound you gave Cuchulain, but he said
the Mother should also come across and see to your cut. And
so I'm here.'
Ferdia smiled. 'I could have told you that about Cuchulain.'
It never entered his head that the Mother might have come
to enchant him – because he knew Cuchulain. When the
Mother had finished dealing with his cut, he insisted on my
taking across half the supplies he had received from the men
of Erin, best pork and beef, mead and fresh oat-cakes, even
some dried beans, though the army was starving.
I turned to go, but he said, 'Lugh, do you have your harp
here?'
'No,' I answered, 'it's in Emain.'
He sighed. 'A pity. I should have liked to hear harp-music
again.'
As the Mother left me and I crossed the stream, wincing
again at the coldness of the water and carrying the bag of
provisions, I was cursing the gods who set two such men to
fight each other and made them such that they could not

come to some truce; cursing Conor and his cold-blooded plan, cursing the Goddess for her greed and for what she was. But that night, as I slept near Cuchulain's fire, before I took my watch, I dreamt of the Queen again and was woken screaming by Cuchulain. I passed it off by saying that I had eaten too much of the boar-meat. I could see Cuchulain didn't believe me.

Two days they fought on, seemingly suspended in time, while Facen snapped at the Queen's heels and killed the raiding-parties dispatched in the direction of Dun Delgan. As Cuchulain laid him down to sleep on the night of the third day of the combat, Laegh put his cloak of sealskins over him with a tenderness he would never have shown at any other time.

The Mother came up to me gravely and said, 'I can do nothing more for him, Lugh. If he wins tomorrow, then he does it with the help of the Morrigan.'

'Once men said,' I commented bitterly, 'that Cuchulain was the Morrigan's lover and that she came to him in a red chariot with a red spear in her hand and asked him to sleep with her and he did so. Where is the Morrigan now?'

'Need she always be the Red Battler?' the Mother asked gravely. 'Has she not many shapes, she, the Shape-shifter? Pray to her.'

'I have nothing to sacrifice to her,' I said, 'and I cannot pray to her.'

'Then you must hope,' she said, 'as I must.'

She turned and walked away, with the grace and power of the Queen: I was not afraid of her and not afraid when she spoke of the Morrigan, the Crow of Battles. I had become accustomed to looking behind the tattooed mask of the Sidhe-folk and I thought that the Mother of the Sidhe of Muir-themne cared more for Cuchulain than she admitted.

So the morning of the last day dawned and both sides knew it was the last day and the wonder of it was that the Morrigan herself was not there to witness it. There were fewer of the Queen's watchers: she was pressing north, trying to find a way round the ambushes of the Sedantii and the tribes of the Gap of the North and Cooley and the trickle of warriors coming now from the rest of Ulster, though not from Emain, where the army of Ulster was gathered still.

As Laegh readied the chariot, I went up to him and helped, because I felt so useless. He seemed more glad of my company than my help: I saw him put the Gae Bulg among the other spears in the sheaf and it was newly sharpened and polished. There were great blue circles under his eyes and he had aged enormously, as though each day of the fight had been ten years.

Cuchulain was washing himself carefully in the stream, ignoring Ferdia doing the same on the other side. He came back, many of the smaller cuts in him oozing still. For some strange reason he insisted that Laegh shave him and so, when the messy process was finished, I saw him cleanshaven as he had been when I last saw him at Emain. Shorn of his beard his face was shocking in its thinness and the deepness of the lines of fatigue and pain engraved on it. He was a grey colour. It seemed impossible that he should go on fighting that day, and so futile that he should have to.

Laegh helped him into his clothes for fighting in, whose rents Laegh had spent half the night mending. It was all red, even the boiled leather jerkin: Cuchulain's favourite colour was red, which was logical when you thought of it.

At last they were ready and Cuchulain came walking up to me. I wondered if he foreknew his death and was going to say goodbye.

'Lugh,' he said, his voice hoarse, 'will you watch this fight?'

'Of course. Why?'

'I want you to make a song of it,' he said, and all across his cloud-coloured face I saw his great joyous grin shine like a sunburst.

'Harp of the Dagda, Cuchulain!' I said, 'you're the most conceited man I have ever met.'

'Ah,' he said, 'but I have reason to be. Come on.'

At the ford, Ferdia was waiting, wearing his protective metal-ringed coat for the first time, wounded and exhausted too. He had shaved that morning as well. I swear that those two could have conquered the world if they'd had a mind to: they were like two halves of a nut.

The two stood on the platforms of their chariots while the horses shifted and snorted and the charioteers checked them without thought. For a long moment they stared at each other, wordless.

Cuchulain turned to Laegh and said softly, 'You know what to do if I'm losing.'

Laegh nodded.

'How shall we fight?' shouted Ferdia.

'At the ford,' answered Cuchulain in a voice which reminded me of Deirdre's after the death of Naisi: not because there was grief in it, but because there was no feeling of any kind in it.

Ferdia bit his lip under his moustache and turned and jumped from his chariot.

'Lugh,' someone said behind me as they started to fight. I knew the voice well and I turned slowly, almost unwillingly. The thud and clash of stabbing spears and shields sounded from the ford.

Otter was standing there, small and thin in her leather jerkin and short kilt, that I had pulled from her warm eager body . . . Her long hair was whipping free in the cold east wind and the bones of her face seemed more prominent than usual, her eyes darker.

'Otter, I . . .'

She put her hand gently across my mouth.

'I am a woman of the Tuatha de Danaan,' she said softly, 'and . . . and I have no need for one man.'

They were proud words, but I knew she was lying. I knew what she was feeling, but I could not love her. Angus Og help me, I simply could not love her. And she knew it and she had come back to me because the Mother must have told her I would have need of her. She had come to me, she, one of the People of the Goddess.

We watched the fight, from a little knoll near the ford. The waters were muddy with winter and higher than usual, knee-high, and it was a vicious battle.

At last Cuchulain seemed to gain a small advantage. He leaped up and tried to stab Ferdia over his shield with a spear, but the rings sewn on Ferdia's coat turned the blade. Ferdia threw him off the shield as though he were a child and he landed on his back in the churned mud of the shallows.

Laegh leaned forward and shouted, 'What are you playing at, Cuchulain? You look like a tired sow in a midden! Get up! get *up*! you pitiful excuse for a fairy-fighter . . .'

Cuchulain was already up and charging, but Ferdia knocked him to one knee and battered on Cuchulain's upraised shield with his sword.

'Fight, damn you, fight!' shrieked Laegh. 'You cowardly whelp of a whore's pet bitch . . . Oh, Morrigan! FIGHT!'

Somehow Cuchulain climbed to his feet again. His face was white, he was gasping for breath, but he charged screaming at Ferdia and they hacked at each other with swords, waist-deep in the deeper water.

Then, so suddenly it was difficult to see how it happened, Ferdia's sword flashed in like a red and silver fish and cut deep into Cuchulain's flesh. Blood spurted out and Cuchulain staggered back a pace.

Laegh groaned.

'Gae Bulg, Laegh!' gasped Cuchulain as Ferdia bore down on him, foam on his lips. Laegh leapt for the sheaf of spears, snatched out the deadly weapon and threw it to Cuchulain, who dropped his riven shield and caught it in both hands.

Ferdia lowered his shield, ready for the belly thrust. Cuchulain leapt high over the rim and stabbed the barbed head deep into Ferdia's chest under his ribs. They fell together, but in an instant, Cuchulain was up again, and tugging and pulling Ferdia to the northern side of the stream, helped by the buoyancy of the water. There, red from head to foot, soaked in mud and cold water, he looked at the fallen Champion of Connaught.

Very quietly he straightened Ferdia's limbs and held his head in his hands. Laegh came running over, shouting with pleasure and relief.

Cuchulain looked up at Laegh and Laegh stopped. Ferdia's face was grey and he made a tearing sound when he tried to breathe. Cuchulain wiped the bloody spittle from Ferdia's mouth and tried to push away the wet gold hair. Ferdia twitched his lips in what might have been a smile.

'Good battle,' he whispered.

Cuchulain bent closer on his knees to listen. But Ferdia breathed out a small dark trickle and there was no more from his throat but the death-rattle.

Cuchulain went on kneeling there with Ferdia's head in his hands, tears streaming down his cheeks.

'In the name of the gods,' said Laegh softly, 'it's a victory. You've won.'

'I wish . . . I wish I'd lost,' said Cuchulain, crumpling up quietly and falling across the body of his dead friend.

## XI

It was before noon of that day when Ferdia Mac Daire, Chieftain of the Men of Domnand, died. While Laegh and a few of the Sedantii who were there fashioned a litter to carry Cuchulain to Dun Delgan, while the Queen's watchers hot-footed to report to the Queen the outcome of the battle, I went to the paddock of ponies. Otter went with me.

I found a riding blanket and bridle and the small pony I had been lent before. While I caught it and put the bridle on, Otter watched me.

'Where are you going?' she asked.

'To Conor.'

'And after?'

'Out of Erin. I don't care where. Just away from here.' I don't know when I first made that decision, but I could no longer stay in Erin.

'Out of Erin,' she repeated in a strange voice.

'As soon as I can find a ship. Probably with Goll in the spring.'

I mounted carefully and rode through the gate, which Otter opened and shut for me.

'Where will you go?' I asked gently, knowing what the look in her eyes meant, but unable to say or do anything to ease it.

'Back to the sidhe,' she answered, turning and walking away, towards the forest.

I wanted to call after her, call her back and ask her to go with me, but I knew it would be a lie and the shout stuck in my throat. It was still in my throat when I turned the pony's head north and kicked savagely with my heels.

I rode hard for Emain between the bulk of the hills. I concentrated on staying on the horse and the thud of the hooves seemed to pattern my thoughts in their rhythm and Cuchulain and Ferdia and Otter mingled in my mind.

At last, after the quick evening had come on and the effort of gripping was sending a thrill of ache up my right leg, I saw Emain Macha gleaming ahead, the land around spangled with campfires and blotched and coloured by the tents and wagons and herded animals of the army of Ulster.

I was challenged at the thorn-hedge of the army, found the gate and was challenged again. I said I was from Cuchulain with news of the Queen, to save explanations, and they let me through without further argument.

I passed through the familiar sights of an army: men practising, women talking, children running under everyone's feet, herds of cattle and pens of horses and oxen lying down to sleep still yoked, piles of dung everywhere and the smell of peat-smoke.

I hurried through the camp and up the muddy road to the gate of Emain. There was more argument there when I demanded to be let through, but even so the name of the Sedanta carried weight and I was allowed in. I wouldn't let the man show me to the King's Hall, saying I knew it well enough and had no weapons to leave in the Speckled House. He was surprised since he didn't recognize me: I knew him, but didn't say so.

I walked to the King's Hall, seeping light in all directions, pushed aside the door-keeper and opened the door myself. I went straight in, followed protestingly by the door-keeper and looked round.

King Conor was sitting eating his evening meal in the crowded hall, surrounded by hostile faces in a little pool of silence all his own, seemingly uncaring. He looked older than when I had seen him last in the raid on Rath Ini at Maine's wedding. His beard and hair were no longer greying, but completely iron grey.

He looked at me in surprise and didn't recognize me. Seeing those curious, unrealizing faces, I understood for the first time just how much I had changed. I was wearing shabby, ill-fitting clothes; I had only trimmed my hair and beard, not shaved, and I was lamed in one leg. Furthermore, I was supposed to have died months ago and become crow-fodder long since.

'Who are you?' asked Conor in a tired voice. I had eaten and shown I was ready to answer questions by standing up.

'Lugh Mac Romain, King,' I said.

That got reaction. I knew they all believed me dead. It gave me an odd kind of pleasure to see Conor and most of the others lift their hands in the Sign against ill-luck in case I was my own ghost.

Truly, I felt they had the right of it.

'No,' I said, hearing my voice as tired as Conor, 'no, I'm not a ghost.' My leg was aching badly now and I leaned my shoulder against a house-pillar. 'I have come to bring you news of Cuchulain.'

Conor's eyes hooded themselves and his hand went to his beard in the old remembered gesture. There was a low growl and muttering from most of the warriors in the hall.

I looked round at them, lifting an eyebrow.

'You have maybe heard of him?' I enquired of the King. 'He was one of your warriors once, if you remember. In fact, I believe he once had some minor capacity as your champion, as the Champion of Ulster.'

I looked round again. Conor was watching closely. I stared straight into his eyes and listened to the quiet. My

325

blood thrilled in me as though I were holding a harp to my shoulder and playing a great story to them. I felt as though they were the harp; the hall the soundbox and the people in it the strings. I had only to flick my little finger and they would be prisoners to the golden chain of my voice. I had them.

'Poor fool!' I said. 'The Champion of Ulster.' I waited.

'Is he dead?' asked Conor at last.

'No,' I answered, 'but scant thanks to you, King, if he isn't. Since long before Samhain now he has been holding the border for you; keeping back the Queen of Connaught; waiting each day for the sound of your chariots in the north, for the shout of your men and the thunder of your horses and the dart of your spears in the battle.'

A pause through which the silence thrust.

'Poor fool. For how could he know what you are, King Conor, King of Ulster, his lord – how could he know your plan? Or, knowing it and being what he is, Cuchulain the Champion of Ulster, how could he pull back from his part in it, often enough though he was tempted to do so by the Queen?'

'What do you mean?' demanded Conor, knowing exactly what I meant. 'My plan?'

'Yes, Conor, your plan. The plan to rid yourself of Cuchulain's annoyance and the flower of the Queen's strength.' I made a little bow to him. 'A fine plan it is, and well it has worked, although you have not quite rid yourself of Cuchulain. The Queen is weakened though, and her army rotten with fever and hunger and the depressing effect Cuchulain has on men who fight against him. Cuchulain is in his dun with holes that birds could fly through in his body and if he was not dead when I left him, that doesn't mean he isn't dead now.'

'So?' asked Conor.

I felt the blood rush like wine to my head. I leaned forward.

'So! King Conor, bestir yourself and your men and come and fight the Queen and if you don't get the victory it won't be Cuchulain's fault, nor the fault of your plan, which, as I have said, is fine for its ingenuity! It will be the fault of your own sloth!'

There was a roar of agreement, shouts and applause, but Conor and I were unaffected by it, islands in the noise.

His eyes flicked here and there.

'So,' he said at last, 'I agree with you, Lugh Mac Romain. The time is ripe.' He stood up and raised his arms like a Druid. 'I, Conor Mac Nessa, King of Ulster, hereby recall my curse, the Curse of Macha, and lift it from Emain and the people of Ulster, and free all from the death-threat. And I will give three mares to Edain Echraidhe, Lady of the Horses, and thirty heads to the Morrigan, Queen of the Battlefield. So witness Earth-Mother and all the gods, the Earth, the Sea and the Sky.' He lowered his arms. 'We move tomorrow.'

He walked out of the hall, brushing by me. I stayed by the pillar and watched him go, wondering how it was he always managed to rob me of my pleasure. Then I told myself not to be a fool: at least he was moving. That was the important thing.

Men whom I had known began coming up to me and asking me how I had escaped death in Conor's attack on Rath Ini. I said merely that the chariot had crashed and I had been taken in and cared for by certain people. They soon saw I was in no mood to talk and left me alone. They went to see about their equipment, as if they hadn't all sharpened every blade and point a thousand times already.

Then Gennan Bright-face came up to me.

'You can sleep in my cubicle tonight, Lugh,' he said, 'since my father's away.'

I thanked him and followed him to the cubicle where I had first seen Cavath, Chief Druid, a year ago. Gennan ordered more food brought to me and as I ate, he watched me with eyes so like his father's that I thought he could almost have been Cavath as a young man.

'It was the Tuatha de Danaan who brought you in and looked after you, wasn't it?' he said abruptly.

I wondered how he knew, but the Druids have much connection with the Tuatha de Danaan – they were once their priests – although they now worship younger gods. Besides, it is not good to ask them how or why.

'Yes,' I answered.

'Who brought you there?'

'Ailell.'

'You were his friend once, weren't you?'

'I was – once. Yes.'

'When you were in the Connaught camp did you speak to him at all?'

'No. I think he avoided me most of the time.'

'Do you know why?'

There must be a reason for this questioning.

'You are a Druid: you must know. I would have been Ailell myself, and not him, if the previous Ailell had not burned the Queen's token before I received it and if I had not been lamed in that chariot crash.' Odd. Although I was gradually getting used to the idea of being lame, every time I mentioned it myself, it gave me an odd twinge of pain, as though refusing to admit it might make it go away.

Gennan's smooth clever face gave nothing away. It was harder to read than the faces of the Sidhe-folk.

'I know,' he said. 'Have you any influence with him still?'

'I don't think so.' Then I heard myself asking the question you do not ask of Druids. 'Why?'

Even more surprising, he answered me.

'We want to make a peace with Ailell which he will keep, so that the Queen doesn't attack Ulster again.'

I smiled.

'Don't try to make it until the Queen has been beaten. And even then it will only last for another six years, until this Ailell's time has run out.'

Gennan said nothing to that, but he had a very shrewd look somewhere in his expression. I picked the last bits of meat off the bone, threw it among the dogs for them to fight over and wiped my hands on the hay.

He understood what I was waiting for. He smiled and

reached into the corner of the cubicle, under a pile of cloaks and deerskins. He brought out a curved triangular shape in an otterskin bag, a bag embroidered richly with many colours, the fur glossy and brown.

'Here's your harp,' he said. 'I got Culain the Smith to make you a complete set of new white-bronze strings when he came here to see to the metal-work in the new House of the Red Branch. I've kept her in tune, but I haven't played her.'

I smiled at him and took the harp. I undid the drawstrings and pulled the bag off her and there she stood, warm-shaped as a woman, with the metal-work and the amber and garnets decorating her like the woman dressed to meet her man home from the fighting. The fire shone off the strings in the way I remembered and the shadow of the forepillar fell across the soundbox with the strings between it.

I settled her against my shoulder, listened to the chord I plucked and the way the notes fell sweetly together without any need for adjustments, and at last I felt complete. For so long there had been a part of me missing, and although I sometimes nearly forgot to feel the dull ache where the gap was, I had been yearning for her all the while.

I began to play her, letting my fingers find their own way at first and then slipping into an old song, the oldest song of the Celts: the Song of Amergin as he stepped on to the Land of Erin and invoked it to himself. He was a poet, which perhaps accounts for much else.

'I am the wind which breathes on the sea;
I am the wave of the ocean;
I am the murmur of billows;
I am the ox of seven combats . . .'

That is how I remember Emain Macha: a high hall of carven pillars and red yew screens, of shingled roof and doubled walls; filled with men whom I had known, but who now seemed like ghosts to me. I sat on a deerskin and played the harp for my own joy and took no notice of the listening silence of the others; a purely selfish pleasure as I sang the old Song of Amergin, which every poet sings differently. It is the song of any poet.

'I am the hawk on the rock;
I am a beam of the sun;
I am the fairest of plants;
I am a wild boar in valour;
I am a salmon in the water;
I am a lake in the plain;
I am a word of power;
I am a point of the lance of battle;
I am the god who creates in the head, the fire.
　Who throws light into the meeting on the mountain?
　Who announces the ages of the moon?
　Who teaches the place where crouches the sun?
　Who but I?'

When I had finished singing and playing, I reluctantly put away my harp, rolled over wrapped in my cloak, and slept like a child.

# XII

Before dawn the next day, the army of Ulster was breaking camp, each tribe and fighting troop upping their tents, packing their wagons, collecting their animals and arguing over who owned which. In the dun Conor's household was mounting up or checking the yokes of their chariots. I climbed up to the rampart and looked over from the gate-guard's look-out: where the campfires had speckled the home-pasture there was confusion and running about like a stirred ant-heap, and yet out of it formed uneven troops of men and horse, with the odd chariot here and there; where before there had been a small town, was now an army ready to move. Behind them they left the piles of rubbish and over-flowing rubbish-ditches. From the rampart I could see clearly the size of them, and I knew that it was still a smaller army

330

than the Queen's.

It was mid-morning before the army was ready to leave: even so they had broken camp with amazing speed. Conor mounted his chariot when all was ready, the gate was opened, Ibar shook the reins and the King clattered out of Emain Macha with all his household following in a bunch. They were fine and colourful in the watery sun: a moving meadow of reds and blues and greens, cloaks fluttering and helmets of all shapes glittering, the gleam of Wicklow gold at arm and throat and ear, hair flying, the ponies groomed and clinking with enamelled horse-bronzes on their oiled harness.

They moved south along the road and the army trailed after them. I mounted the pony I had ridden the day before, and rode out of the gates to find Conall and attach myself to his tribe as they went south. As I left I looked round at Emain and the debris left by the army, at the skeleton force manning the walls and the women moving sadly around, left behind. I wondered how many of them would shortly be keening dead husbands or sweethearts, brothers or sons.

Conall's tribe moved off: I dug in my heels and went with them. Gennan had gone on with Conor's household. When I had woken up that morning he had found me a slave-girl to heat me a bath and when I was clean, with my beard trimmed and my hair deloused, he gave me a gift of a full set of new clothes – something I needed sorely. The tunic was black with patterns woven into the hems in white and blue and red, which is more costly than dyed patterns or embroidery since it takes more skill to weave patterns into cloth. The cloak was dim and speckled green and brown, a fine, large, thick, close-woven nobleman's cloak, with a gold brooch to fasten it with, and a leather belt for my dagger. I had no other weapons since I was not going to fight.

As I rode along with the army, my harp jouncing on my back like a shield, feeling clean and not so itchy, my heart was very light. Not even the thought of the coming battle could dampen me at first, and I resolutely thought of other things.

331

We sighted the Queen's army just after we had forded the River Nith, which runs past Dun Delgan. It was already darkening and the sun had gone down, so Mac Roth and Conor's Herald conferred and it was decided that we would fight the next day. We made camp on a hillside, where there had been a small farm growing wheat and oats, though the farm was burned some time ago by a raiding-party of the Queen's.

Although I slept the night at Conall Cernach's campfire and watched the constellations of the Queen's campfires along with himself and his tribesmen, I felt a barrier between myself and them. They felt it too. I noticed Conall's birth-marked face turned towards me and looking at me queerly, as though he were not quite sure what to make of me. The scars twisting my leg were hidden by the riding breeches I was wearing, but I felt them to stand out through the brown cloth almost as if there was a light behind them. I told my-self not to be so self-conscious. It was not my lameness which made the barrier between myself and men like Conall Cer-nach, but what I was inside. It was the fact that I could see the things that would happen tomorrow inside my head, and so know them far more clearly than he ever would – that was what made the difference. That was what I had to hide, not the scars in my leg which made it ache a little when rain was coming or when I over-strained it.

I dreamed of the Queen that night, because she was so near me. I could almost feel her across the night.

The next morning the whole camp was buzzing by dawn: the charioteers putting on their leather jerkins and the richer of them their helmets as well, and sharpening the knives at their belts with which they could cut the traces if one of their chariot-ponies was injured. The warriors of the clans sat in circles painting each other with war-paint and shout-ing and trying out complicated thrusts and making boasts and bets as to how many heads they would take that day. The younger ones kept having to relieve themselves, much to the amusement of the experienced warriors, and the more stupid of them were half-drunk: no sane man goes drunk into battle since it slows his arm.

I felt out of place and obvious in the flurry of purposeful activity, so I borrowed a spear from Conall and went and found the pony I was using. I rode out of the camp to a piece of high ground with a stand of oak and ash trees on it, to watch the battle. I knew where it would be fought, since there was only one area broad enough and clear enough to manoeuvre on. To the north was the river and higher ground to the north-west. The field sloped south-east to the lush plain of Muirthemne, where they grew the best wheat and oats in the north, though the ground was heavy and difficult to plough and heavily wooded. This field had been cleared from the oak-forests and used to grow grain by the people who had lived in the burned farmstead. They had been Sedantii: two miles away eastwards through the trees was Dun Delgan, where Cuchulain lay wounded. South, where some more trees had been cleared for new fields, lay the Queen's army. There had been a night-attack by the combined Sedantii and tribes of Cooley and none of the army of Erin had had a full night's sleep. They were far fewer than they had been and I could tell that the Queen had lost more men through desertion of whole clans back to their home-duns even than through disease. But she was still stronger than Conor, despite the King's scheme.

As I watched, a small fat grey rabbit sat bolt upright and sniffed the air, ears pricked and tense. Then its white tail was flashing as it thumped the ground and dashed for the warren on the far side. Two others followed it and three more, in scattered directions, white tails bobbing like marsh-cotton in a wind. They disappeared as though the earth had swallowed them. A jay screeched warning and the birds which had been looking for worms flew up to the trees on the far side. I did not dismount, in case I had to escape from a pursuit or take part in the fighting.

I saw what had alarmed the rabbits: the Queen's army was coming on to the field and forming a gathered block, all her chariots at the front and herself in a red chariot at the centre of the line. A little later Conor's army came into sight and

333

arranged itself, but from where I was, it looked strange: Conor had not arranged it the way armies were always arranged, in a block. He had horse and the foot-warriors in a mass in the centre, but the chariots were lumped on either side. This made the army look much bigger than it in fact was, and there was a tremor as the Queen's army saw it.

I heard the dragon-shaped cornyxes blowing back and forth from both sides, back and forth, shouting their defiance. And then the two sides lumbered together: slowly, faster, then slamming together at a charge, shield meeting shield with a rumble like thunder, and the shouting and clashing of battle went up, while the Connaught charioteers let their warriors jump down and took their chariots out of the battle.

On the Ulster side the chariots on the two wings had crashed into the weaker sides of the Queen's army, curling them back, and the Ulster charioteers left the battle, but they came back separately to collect their warriors and charge elsewhere, sometimes singly, sometimes in groups of friends or tribes. The mass heaved and moved like something alive of itself, but in it I could hear the screams of men and horses as they fought and died messily. Watching from the shade of leaf-dropped oak-trees, with acorns underfoot still, it seemed separate, like a battle in a song. But as I thought that, I remembered as clearly as if it were truly happening to me and not simply painted across my mind, what a battle is. Like the mounds of dead horses and wounded men and bits of shattered, splintered wood and metal which were once chariots, rivalling the sun-chariot in finery (Oh gods, I knew, I knew!); the obscenity of a foot lying in the mud and nothing to show who it came from . . .

I shook my head and thought wryly that it would be better if I were fighting. It was only before and after that my mind vomited up these images: during the battle I knew I could be as wild as any man of them. That was strange, really: all past now.

The side of the Ulster army closest to me was wavering, giving way, falling back under the press. Some men on horseback broke away, and although Conor had seen and was coming across with his household in support, I knew that if the side gave way completely, then Ulster was lost.

Without intending to, I rode the pony forward, down the hill from the stand of trees, to where the scattered riders were coming. I had no sure purpose in mind, but as I came closer I saw that the man leading the Connaught attack from his chariot had a tuft of bushy grey hair on his head, encouraged with lime-wash: Ferghus!

('And if I turn and run then,' he had said, 'the whole of Erin will follow me.')

The doubt was spreading along the Ulster line: they were beginning to waver, they were giving back. There was a flurry around Ferghus and I could see him fighting with Conor, marked out by his golden tunic, until the press swept them apart again.

Cuchulain! Where was Cuchulain?

I turned the pony's head, leaned forward and shouted in its ear: it reared, nearly throwing me, and then started galloping westwards. I lay along its neck, slapping and shouting and cursing it, while its long coarse mane whipped at my face, making my eyes water, and I held on to its neck like bindweed. Muscles pounded against me, the pony's ears were flattened back. We careered westwards through the woods, never slowing to less than a trot, at a full-out gallop for as much of the ride as I could. There was no question of riding: the pony avoided the trees in the wood more by its instinct than my judgement, and I drove the willing beast unmercifully, galloping like the Wild Hunt and Cernunnos Lord of the Wild, its chieftain, racing for Dun Delgan, using Cuchulain's hunting tracks and the river to guide me, ignoring branches of the trees which swooped to knock me off the saddle and somehow missed. Foam flew from the pony's mouth and lather made my hands slippery on the reins.

At last we broke from the woods and on to Cuchulain's home-pasture, where the Nith flowed past and the smell of the sea blew. I forced the panting pony up the path to the

335

closed gate and bellowed up at the guard,

'Conor fights with the Queen. Ulster has need of Cuchulain!'

The shout was passed back into the dun and the gates opened. I slid from the pony's lathered back, giving it a quick pat as I hurried in. It was standing head down, foam dripping from its mouth, heaving. I hoped vaguely I hadn't foundered it.

The bustle of Dun Delgan was unclear to me. I hurried to the main hall, but even as I came to the door, it was opened and Cuchulain strode out, pulling on his jerkin, while Laegh followed after with his sword belt, sword and stabbing spear in his hands. They headed for the chariot-sheds, while his household raced for the armoury and horse-pasture.

Cuchulain was obviously a sick man: he was white and bandaged, and Laegh was keeping up a steady stream of protests, which Cuchulain ignored.

'Where?' he demanded of me, as I wiped the sweat and mud from my face and tried to collect my thoughts.

'The farmstead . . . two miles west . . . south of the Gap of the North.'

'Ferghus?'

'He was pushing back Conor's wing, last I saw.'

The chariot was brought out. Cuchulain took his shield and spear, while Laegh buckled on his sword belt, with a look at me which should have killed.

He climbed on to the chariot, and stood there unsteadily, while Laegh jumped on after him and took the reins in his hands. Someone brought me a piebald horse and I climbed slowly on its back, realizing I had to ride back. I had left my spear behind when I raced to fetch Cuchulain and someone passed me another, but I would not fight. Useless to explain why.

Cuchulain's household was gathered round him. He shouted his battle-cry: 'Macha, *Macha*!' and the Sedantii answered him: 'MACHA!' Then Laegh goaded the horses and the chariot rattled out of the gate eastwards. I followed on the outskirts of the band, my mind battered by the drum of horses' hooves and the shouts and pleasure of the men: they rode at a man's running pace, which seemed terribly slow, and I wondered if we would only be in time to avenge Conor's death, Conall's death, the death of Ulster. Then Cuchulain's chariot forged on ahead, as we came closer and could hear the battle, and I stayed by him, wondering at my own foolishness, wondering if I would have to fight after all, not very clear in the head, but knowing I wanted to stay by the wounded man in the chariot.

The sound of battle grew and we came out of the woodland. Laegh slowed the chariot almost to a walk while the rest caught up, and in that split second, we saw the doubtful wing of Ulster break properly and stream away, and Ferghus driving on through it.

Cuchulain yelled wordlessly and the Black Sainglenn and the Grey of Macha leapt forward. He bore down on the battle like a slingstone, a small dark man, hair flying, body wounded, face distorted with battle-madness and the joy of killing, down on the fighting groups of men, driving for Ferghus Mac Roich.

So they met, master and pupil, in the midst of battle. Ferghus threw a spear at Cuchulain, but Cuchulain ducked and Laegh swung the chariot in the path of Ferghus's. The grey warrior's eyes cleared, and he stared at Cuchulain, and there was a little space of quiet around them.

'Go back, Ferghus!' shouted Cuchulain. 'Go back!'

'Back?' Ferghus roared. 'Why should I? We're winning!'

'Go back! You swore to me at the ford you would go back before me in the last battle. You bound yourself to that when I went back before you and you had no sword. Go back!'

Ferghus stopped and lowered his sword. He spoke to his charioteer. The chariot-ponies were dragged round and their bleeding haunches goaded and they galloped away southwards. After him streamed the other chariots and horses, and after them the Sedantii on foot, following their chieftain and his household, and the men who had been running away when Cuchulain arrived shouted and surged forwards.

Ferghus burst out of the battle southwards and Cuchulain

337

raced after him, killing on both sides and screaming short, high-pitched screams. The fighters of Connaught, seeing Ferghus in full flight, broke and turned and careered in all directions and the whole battle reversed its movement as the army of Erin ran away after Ferghus, their leader, in full retreat. Ulster roared and thrust forward and the men who had been giving way a moment before, charged after their foes who were mysteriously running from them, and the whole battle-mass broke up and became a river of men and horses, rushing south through the forests.

The Queen, with Ailell at her side, gathered her household and they covered the retreat, holding the triumphant Conor from the backs of their men: the retreat overran the tents and the wagons were overturned, and the army soaked through the forest and, like the silver trail of a snail, they left behind a littering of bodies and wounded men and broken chariots. Last came the Queen: she was going back before Conor, but screaming like the crow on her shoulder and killing like a man. And for all my sudden chill of fear at the far sight of her, as I reined in the piebald horse and left the pursuit, I found myself admiring her again. She was magnificent as a storm was magnificent: she could have been the storm herself in her chariot, and the blood that spurted up from her darting spear, only the rain from a cloud rent by a bolt of the Dagda.

The pursuit dashed on through the woods. I turned westwards to Dun Delgan once more, thinking confusedly of Emer, the Queen, and Otter. The joy that had gripped me when Connaught broke, died and left me. Cuchulain would chase them until his strength gave out, or someone persuaded him to leave off so that Erin could go home to its duns and cattle and hills. The Druids would make a peace between the Queen and King Conor: until such time as Dalaigh, as Ailell died, Ulster would be safe from the Queen.

The matter was ended. I rode slowly back to Dun Delgan, across the field of slaughter, where only that morning there had been rabbits feeding. It was torn and stinking and muddy now, littered with corpses and cast-away weapons and

338

crashed chariots. The crows were already settling down with greedy cawings, in the lessening light of afternoon. Some time I would make a lament for those who died that day, but as I rode back to Dun Delgan and the sun set and the dusk deepened around me, I felt wrung out. There was nothing left to spare in grief for the bits and pieces of people strewn around me along with their weapons.

As the last of light faded from the sky, I came to Dun Delgan and was let in. Emer was waiting in front of the gate, still against the light from the torches. I rode closer, but did not dismount, for I was not going to stay there if I could help it. But then I looked down at Emer and saw her pallor and quiet, rich attraction. Her chestnut hair was drawn back from her face in a plait with little golden apples on the end, but her skin was white and taut.

'Cuchulain?' she asked.

'He won the battle,' I said.

'Is he . . . dead?'

'I don't know.'

She sighed and her shoulders drooped. I swung my left leg over the horse's neck and slid to the ground, put my arm round her, because my heart bled for her. She leaned against me a little. I felt a gush of desire for her again, from the sweet warmth of her body, but I knew that her soul was far from mine, riding with Cuchulain's in the chariot.

'There was no way we could hold him back,' she said softly.

'No. Not for him.'

'Once he told me he had known since the day he took arms that he would not live to count one grey hair on his head, that he would die in battle. How could I hold him back?'

'You could not.'

'Lugh, will he die?'

One day. Yes, even a man like Cuchulain must die, and yet it is often in their dying that they are immortal.

'Listen, Emer,' I said clumsily, 'this thing he has done, holding off the Queen and then coming into the battle to make Ferghus turn back, they are things that will be remembered for all time. Harpers will sing of the Hound – I am a harper, I know. This is the pinnacle. I don't believe he will die now. It will take more than just the army of Erin to kill Cuchulain.'

'Yes. That's what Laegh said when he fetched Cuchulain's clothes. I don't think he believed it.'

'But Cuchulain believes it, and if anything will keep him alive, that will.'

'Yes.'

She stood up straighter and gently disengaged my arm from around her shoulders.

'You are welcome to this dun,' she said to me, like a queen.

I followed her into Cuchulain's hall.


# XIII


They brought Cuchulain back much later that night. Laegh was weeping: he thought his chieftain dead, but Emer went to where he lay on the platform of the chariot and told them that Cuchulain still lived. They brought him into his hall and laid him on soft bracken and skins, and Emer tended his wounds.

For days she fought for Cuchulain's life, with Gennan Bright-face, who left Conor as the King returned to Emain Macha after the victory, and came to Dun Delgan. For days Cuchulain's life rose and sank, rose and sank, guttered, flickered and brightened again, like a candle in the wind.

Although it was winter, the wind veered round, carrying wet, milder weather from the south-west. And on that wind, not many days after the battle, came Goll the Trader in his sailing ship. He had been delayed by the winds in the far south of Erin, where he had been with Curoi. He put in at Baile's Strand and anchored his ship, and came up to the dun from the sea-strand: he had heard of the war between Ulster and Connaught and as soon as the winds would let him he had come north to find out about it, through seas which would have destroyed any ship of the Romans.

I remember his squat, funny shape now, standing in front of Cuchulain's unconscious body, the salt white in his hair, cursing all of Erin. His face seemed even more grotesque than it had been before, slapped together carelessly by a god with no talent for sculpture. He cursed in fine fluent Irish, and two foreign languages which I supposed were Latin and Greek. But it was Emer who sheltered Cuchulain's life, until at last his fever abated, his wounds began to heal and his death-like sleep became lighter. One night, in the dark before dawn, he came to consciousness and looked up with understanding at Emer, myself and Goll who were watching. He blinked in the light from the oil-lamp.

'Emer,' he said, very softly. She smiled back and touched his face with her hand. His eyes closed contentedly and his breathing deepened again.

I stood up quietly and went outside, followed by Goll. He looked at the greying sky and held his finger up to the wind. I raised my eyebrows in question.

'The wind will hold,' he explained. 'Surprisingly, since I've finished revictualling and stocking up with water. I'll sail for Prydein today – though whether I arrive there, sailing at this time of year, is another matter.'

'How much for my passage, Goll?' I asked.

He grinned.

'You can come for free.'

'I can't work my passage,' I warned.

'I know. I'm not blind, after all – I've only mislaid one eye so far. You can't limp up the rigging and you'd be useless there anyway. But you don't play the harp with your toes, do you?'

I smiled and said I didn't.

And so, with Cuchulain beginning to recover from his wounds and exhaustion in Dun Delgan and Conor eating the ashy fruits of his cunning victory in Emain Macha, with the Queen behind me – and still with me, though I didn't know that then – I walked down with Goll the Trader to Baile's

Strand. I took my leave of Emer at the gate of the dun, and there was only a small pain at the parting.

The tide was beginning to turn outwards as we crossed the beach to where the ship was. That was the first time I saw the sea close to and it took my breath away. It is so much wider and greater than you can expect; there is no comparison with it, though you use it to compare with everything from battle to making love. The sea is the sea. There is nothing like it, angry or calm, or merely present: the tresses of Manannan's wife; the fields of Lir; the waves charging the beach like chariots and men dwarfed before it as they are before the stars. I stared out across the green-grey and wanted to laugh and weep at the same time. My blood quickened, my stomach felt light as with wine and my hands itched for the strings of my harp. Oh, I would make a fine song of it, a fine song.

The sailors had rigged the ship and it was ready to leave: it was a ship that Caesar, the first of the Caesars, would have recognized perhaps, since it was made by the Veneti who settled in Prydein after Caesar defeated them. It was flat-bottomed and high-sided, of thick strong oak, the prow and the stern were as high as each other and the leather sail still furled on the mast. There was a peculiar beauty to it, ugly as a Roman accustomed to the gull-slender galleys would think it, something performing the purpose for which it is perfectly suited.

I followed Goll into the shallow water, Goll swearing at its coldness and got into the waiting coracle. We paddled over to the high sides of the ship and rope-ladders were dropped for us to climb up. It was very difficult, and the sailors hauled me up with little dignity, grinning and cracking jokes in a strange language.

But at last I was on the gently swaying deck, staggering with the unexpected movement. Goll cursed the sailors into pulling up the anchor. The sails were loosed and filled with wind, the man at the steering oar tightened his grip and the ship moved from the coast, from Baile's Strand and the yew growing there, dark as a full forest. Slowly the land and the beach and the places where Cuchulain's salt pans would be during the summer slipped away. It seemed as though it was the land that was leaving me, not I the land.

For a second I felt desolate, bereaved, sniffing the unaccustomed smell of salt and the seaweed caulking the planks. Then two shadows passed over me. I looked up and there were two white gulls flying overhead. They swept away my sadness with their loneliness. It was a proud and fierce loneliness I felt in them, a freedom. I smiled a little and half-raised my arm in salute to them. I turned away to the east and did not look back.

That was the first time I left Erin.

# List of Proper Names

N.B. 'gh' and 'ch' are pronounced like the soft 'ch' in Scottish 'loch'.
'bh' and 'mh' are pronounced 'v'.
\* indicates that the character appears in some version of the legends.

\*AILELL – (pr. Ayl*el*). The title of the King of Connaught
\*AINNLE – one of Naisi Mac Usnach's two brothers
\*AMERGIN – (pr. *A*mergin). See Glossary
\*AOIFE – (pr. *Ee*fa). Pictish warrior queen
\*ARDAN – brother to Naisi and Ainnle Mac Usnach
\*ATHAIRNE MAC ETERSCEL – (pr. Ath*i*rni). Chief poet of Ulster
\*BRICRU – (original sp. *Bricriu*). Trouble-making Ulster nobleman
BROCC & BROD MAC MAGACH – twin brothers, warriors of Connaught
\*BUINNE – a son of Conor's
\*BURACH – Ulster nobleman
\*CAIRBRE NAIFER – (pr. C*air*bri N*ay*fa). High King of Ireland, at Tara
\*CATHRACH CATUCHENN – woman-warrior at Emain Macha
\*CAVATH – (original sp. *Cathbhadh*). Chief Druid of Erin. Uncle to Conor and great-uncle to Cuchulain
\*CELTHAIR MAC UTHECAR – Ulster nobleman, one of the twelve Warriors of the Red Branch
\*CETHERN MAC FINTAN – (original sp. *Ceithern Mac Findtain*). Ulster nobleman, one of the twelve Warriors of the Red Branch
\*CONALL CERNACH – Ulster nobleman, Warrior of the Red Branch, Cuchulain's friend and spear-brother
CONIN – Lugh's horse
CONN MAC GEGE – warrior of the Sedantii, Cuchulain's tribe
\*CONOR MAC NESSA – (original sp. *Conchubhar*). King of Ulster
\*CORMAC CONNLONGES – Conor's son and first choice for succession, a friend of Cuchulain's
\*CUCHULAIN MAC SUALTIM – (pr. Cooch*u*lin, or Cooch*oo*lin. There are several different spellings of this name.) Chief of the

Sedantii tribe and so called 'the Sedanta'. Champion of Ulster, one of the twelve Warriors of the Red Branch, powerful Ulster nobleman. He is the main hero of the Ulster cycle of legends.

CURMAC DALTACH – Connaught Warrior

*CUROI – King of Kerry

DALAIGH – (pr. Dayli). Lugh's friend. Later Ailell, King of Connaught and Maeve's consort

*DEIRDRE – daughter of the poet Fedlimid. Supposed to become King Conor's wife, but eloped with Naisi Mac Usnach

DEVORGILL – Lugh's mother, sister to Maeve, a priestess

*DIARMENT – poet

DONALL – Connaught warrior, gate-guard of Cruachan

*DUVTHACH – (original sp. Dubhthach). Ulster nobleman, one of the Warriors of the Red Branch

*EMER – daughter of Druid Forgall the Wily. Cuchulain's wife

ERCOL – Ferdia's charioteer

*ETARCOMAL – Connaught nobleman whose lands border with Cuchulain's

FACEN MAC MORNAI – Sedanti warrior, one of Cuchulain's lieutenants

*FEDELM – seeress of the Tuatha de Danaan, from the Sidhe of Cruachan

*FEDLIMID – (pr. Fethlimith. original sp. Fedhlimidh). Poet, father of Deirdre

FERADACH MAC CONOR – a son of Conor's

*FERB – daughter of Gerg of Rath Ini and Maine Morgor's wife-to-be

*FERDIA MAC DAIRE – (also sp. Ferdiadh). The Chief of the men of Domnand, powerful nobleman of Connaught. Cuchulain's friend and spear-brother

*FERGHUS MAC ROICH – once King of Ulster but defeated in election by Conor Mac Nessa. Warrior of the Red Branch, powerful nobleman, later leader of the army of Erin and Queen Maeve's paramour

FIALL – woman at Emain Macha, Lugh's mistress

*FINDABHAIR – (pr. Finnavair). Queen Maeve's daughter

FINN MAC ROSS – warrior

*FOLLAMON – Conor's youngest son, still a boy

*FORGALL – Druid, Emer's father

GAIAR MAC RIANGABRA – Laegh's youngest brother, Lugh's charioteer

*GENNAN BRIGHT-FACE – Cavath's youngest son, a Druid
*GERG – Chief of Rath Ini, on border of Ulster and Connaught
*IBAR MAC RIANGABRA – Laegh's brother, Conor's charioteer
ILIACH MAC CONAIRE – a bard, one of Lugh's teachers
IOLLAN HEN – a bard, Lugh's main teacher and mentor
*LAEGH MAC RIANGABRA – (pr. Laygh Mac Ree*angabra). Cuchulain's charioteer and friend
*LAERE THE VICTORIOUS – (original sp. *Laeghaire*). Ulster nobleman, Warrior of the Red Branch, Cuchulain's friend
LUCUS – Roman, father of Lugh
LUGH MAC ROMAIN – (pr. Loogh). Son of Devorgill and Lucus the Roman. Maeve's nephew. Trained bard and warrior
*LUGAID MAC NOIS – (pr. *Loo*ghai. Original sp. *Lughaidh*). Ulster warrior and friend of Naisi Mac Usnach
*MAC ROTH – Queen Maeve's Herald
MAELCHON – name of Old King before he became Ailell
*MAEVE – (original sp. *Medhbh*). Queen of Connaught, matriarchal Mother-Goddess-on-Earth. Enemy to Ulster, Cuchulain and Lugh
*MAINE ANDOE – one of the Queen's sons, a friend of Lugh's
*MAINE MORGOR – one of the Queen's sons, came to marry Ferb
*MUNREMAR MAC GERGIND – (original sp. *Muinremar*). Ulster nobleman, Warrior of the Red Branch
MURGAEL MAC GELBAN – Connaught warrior
NIALL MAC CONOR – one of Conor's sons
NAIMAN OF THE SLAUGHTER – warrior of Connaught before Lugh was born, hunted his father, Lucus
*NAISI MAC USNACH – Ulster nobleman, Warrior of the Red Branch, Deirdre's lover, friend of Cuchulain's
*NATCHRANTAL – warrior of Connaught, one of the Queen's champions
*OWEN OF FERMANAGH – (original sp. *Eoghan*). Ulster nobleman, Warrior of the Red Branch
*RAEN AND RAE – two sons of Iollan Hen, harpers to the Queen
RINN – Connaught warrior, old friend of Lugh's
ROCHAD MAC FINGAL – Cuchulain's steward
*SCATHA – woman-warrior of Skye, trained Cuchulain, Ferdia and Naisi in fighting
SUIBHNE – (pr. S*uv*ni), See Glossary
TUACHEL MAC BUAN – Connaught warrior, Queen's lieutenant

# Glossary

| | |
|---|---|
| Albiu | earliest recorded name for Britain and Scotland |
| Amergin | legendary poet of the Men of Mi, the Celtic invaders of Ireland |
| amphora | Roman pottery jar for transporting and storing wine |
| Angus Mac ind Og | (the Young Lad) Celtic god of Love |
| Beltain | 1st May; the Spring Feast |
| Brehon Laws | an originally unwritten code of Celtic law, orally transmitted through the Druids, and not written down until medieval times |
| Britain | here taken to mean only the part occupied by the Romans |
| Bron Trograin | 1st August; Harvest Feast |
| Brugh na Boyne | Newgrange; cult-centre associated with Angus Og |
| caman | stick with flattened end, similar to hockey stick, for playing hurley |
| clientship | a pseudo-feudal system of protection and patronage in return for service in war |
| Dagda, the | Celtic Father-god, roughly equivalent to Zeus |
| Dian Cecht | Celtic gods' physician, roughly equivalent to Aesculepius |
| Druid | highest of three orders of learned men: priests, law-makers and judges |
| dun | a fortress, generally with one or more turf banks and ditches, usually dwelling-place of a chieftain |
| englyn | short, epigrammatical poem |
| Erin | anglicized form of Eriu, the earliest recorded name for Ireland |
| Fair Play | (Fir Fer) Primitive code of chivalry |
| Fianna | see Gailiana |
| fidchell | a hunting-game resembling chess, played on chequered board |

| | |
|---|---|
| Fir Bolg | here taken to mean an enslaved group of Tuatha de Danaan |
| Fomor | legendary early inhabitants of Ireland |
| fosterage | children would be sent to be educated away from home; very important bond |
| geasa | similar to a taboo: it could *not* be broken |
| Gailiana | group of special warriors, possibly akin to Caesar's 'Gaesatae' |
| House of Donn | equivalent to the Underworld or Hell |
| hurley | very fast ball-game, slightly similar to hockey, still played in Ireland, but with different rules |
| Ioruath | legendary hero |
| Lugh Longspear, etc. | Celtic sun-god and god of Arts and Music, etc. Similar to Apollo or Hermes |
| Magh Tuireadh, First Battle of | between the Tuatha de Danaan and Fomor, won by Tuatha de Danaan. Second Battle between Tuatha de Danaan and Men of Mi, won by Men of Mi (Celts) |
| Morrigan, the | Celtic goddess of Battle |
| Ogham | secret system of Runic lettering, used by Druids |
| Oghma | Celtic god of strength and words |
| Oimell | 1st February |
| protection | see surety |
| Prydein | here used to mean Scotland, not conquered by the Romans |
| rath | smaller fort or homestead, with single turf bank |
| Samhain | 1st November; Feast of the Dead |
| sidhe | faery-hill; taken to mean a dwelling place of the Tuatha de Dannan, (pr. Shee) |
| Sign of Horns | supposedly invoking Cernunnos, the Horned God, against bad luck. Formed by making a fist and sticking up forefinger and little finger |
| Suibhne | a warrior supposed to have gone mad in battle and lived wild for a time |
| surety | a strong warrior would guarantee another's safety and bind himself to avenge the other's death |

| | |
|---|---|
| Tir-na-nOg | Land of the Young, legendary islands in the West, possibly equivalent with Valhalla |
| troop | taken to mean a group of 150 men, probably equivalent of a clan's fighting force |
| Tuatha de Danaan | People of the Goddess. In legend equated with the gods, but probably the Bronze Age inhabitants of Ireland, before the invasion of the Iron Age Celts |
| Winter's Lap | winter solstice; 21st December |